Praise for the Novels of

Susan Holloway Scott

The King's Favorite

An *Historical Novels Review* Editor's Choice

"This is a wild joyride through Restoration England, with Nell firmly gripping the reins. Susan Holloway Scott is so intuitive with period language and so involved in the psyches of her characters, that you are at all times *there* with them, seeing what they're seeing, feeling what they're feeling—and always, *always* rooting for the petite whirlwind of a heroine." —Robin Maxwell, author of *Mademoiselle Boleyn*

"This is an entertaining . . . fictionalized memoir that brings alive from an 'insider's' perspective a transformation period in English history as Cromwell is out and the Stuarts are back in. Nell comes across as intelligent and witty as she uses double entendres to get the better of hypocrites who claim to know what is morally best for others (sounds so contemporarily familiar). Genre fans will appreciate the life and times of *The King's Favorite*, as the 'Duchess' of biographical fiction Susan Holloway Scott provides an insightful seventeenth-century tale." —*Midwest Book Review*

"Witty and fascinating, this fast-paced tale brilliantly conjures the bawdy, glorious court of Charles II as well as the gritty reality of seventeenth-century London. Natural storyteller Susan Holloway Scott handles her subject with thrilling expertise—her Nell Gwyn is at once outrageous, tender, and unforgettable. *The King's Favorite* is a luscious read." —Susan Fraser King, author of *Lady Macbeth*

continued . . .

Praise for

Royal Harlot

An *Historical Novels Review* Editor's Choice

"Having previously provided a fictional memoir of Sarah, first Duchess of Marlborough, Scott brings to vivid life another of the seventeenth century's most notorious, brazen, and powerful females. If anything, *Royal Harlot* is an even more assured, nuanced, and colorful portrait of a woman and her age.... In her intriguing portrayal, Scott tempers Barbara's rapacious sexuality while presenting a Charles who seems far less frustrated with her tempestuousness than the historical record indicates. And although the real Barbara was better known for her ambition and avarice than her maternal devotion, the novelist incorporates her motherhood to good effect. Among this novel's many strengths are Scott's impressive depiction of time and place, her evocation of the Restoration-era mind-set, the exuberance of the period, and her sure, succinct presentation of complex historical events. The reader can well believe that this is a memoir penned by a woman who—in reality—was clearly too busy living to ever write one!"

—Margaret Barr, *The Historical Novels Review* (Editor's Choice Pick)

"As in her popular *Duchess*, Scott captures in her latest historical novel the brilliance and hard beauty of Barbara Palmer (Lady Castlemaine), the Merry Monarch's most famous and enduring mistress.... Scott finds a careful balance in Barbara, not salvaging her as a sinner, but giving her something of a heart under all that reputation."

—*Publishers Weekly*

"The Countess of Castlemaine, labeled the Great Harlot of Charles II, never denies or regrets her nature in this fascinating rendering of an outrageous love affair that defies convention and public outrage in Restoration England.... Relating the details of Barbara's fictionalized life, the author takes into account the historical events and unusual influence of a powerful woman in the Restoration court, fleshing out the countess's adventures with gusto, her flaws all the more glaring in the waning years of her power. All in all, this is a thorough and imaginative re-creation of Palmer's long career and her extraordinary talent for manipulating circumstances to her own advantage, an informative and plausible treatment of the controversial life of a successful woman in a man's world."   —Curled Up with a Good Book

Praise for

Duchess

Named a Booksense Notable Book
by the American Booksellers Association

"Wonderful . . . whisks the reader into a period rife with intrigue, love, sex, war, and religious strife."
                    —*The Historical Novels Review* (Editor's Choice Pick)

"All the trappings of supermarket tabloids: intrigue, treachery, deceit, and sexual scandals."   —*Publishers Weekly*

"Susan Holloway Scott has brought to life the racy world of post-Restoration England in her richly researched and beautifully written *Duchess*."   —Karen Harper, author of *The First Princess of Wales*

"No dry dust of history here, but a vivid portrait of an intriguing woman with all her flaws and strengths. Rich in period detail, the novel also has all the ingredients necessary for a compelling read: conflict, suspense, intrigue, and the romance between Sarah and John Churchill, one of history's great love stories."   —Susan Carroll, author of *The Huntress*

"Compelling; it grips the reader from the very first sentence and never lets go. Scott does a wonderful job of bringing Lady Sarah and her world to life."   —Jeanne Kalogridis, author of *I, Mona Lisa*

"As wickedly entertaining as Sarah Churchill herself. . . . Scott brings Sarah blazingly alive in all her sharp-edged beauty and determination. Not to be missed!"   —Mary Jo Putney, author of *A Distant Magic*

The French Mistress

A NOVEL OF
THE DUCHESS OF PORTSMOUTH AND KING CHARLES II

SUSAN HOLLOWAY SCOTT

NEW AMERICAN LIBRARY

New American Library
Published by New American Library,
a division of Penguin Group (USA) Inc.,
375 Hudson Street,
New York, New York 10014, USA
Penguin Group (Canada), 90 Eglinton Avenue East, Suite 700, Toronto,
Ontario M4P 2Y3, Canada (a division of Pearson Penguin Canada Inc.)
Penguin Books Ltd., 80 Strand, London WC2R 0RL, England
Penguin Ireland, 25 St. Stephen's Green, Dublin 2,
Ireland (a division of Penguin Books Ltd.)
Penguin Group (Australia), 250 Camberwell Road, Camberwell,
Victoria 3124, Australia (a division of Pearson Australia Group Pty. Ltd.)
Penguin Books India Pvt. Ltd., 11 Community Centre,
Panchsheel Park, New Delhi - 110 017, India
Penguin Group (NZ), 67 Apollo Drive, Rosedale, North Shore 0632,
New Zealand (a division of Pearson New Zealand Ltd.)
Penguin Books (South Africa) (Pty.) Ltd., 24 Sturdee Avenue,
Rosebank, Johannesburg 2196, South Africa

Penguin Books Ltd., Registered Offices:
80 Strand, London WC2R 0RL, England

First published by New American Library,
a division of Penguin Group (USA) Inc.

First Printing, July 2009
1   3   5   7   9   10   8   6   4   2

 REGISTERED TRADEMARK—MARCA REGISTRADA

LIBRARY OF CONGRESS CATALOGING-IN-PUBLICATION DATA:

Scott, Susan Holloway.
The French Mistress: a novel of the Duchess of Portsmouth &
King Charles II/ by Susan Holloway Scott.
p. cm.
ISBN 978-0-451-22694-5
1. Kéroualle, Louise-Renée de, Duchess of Portsmouth and Aubigny, 1649–1734—Fiction. 2. Charles
II, King of England, 1630–1685—Fiction. 3. Great Britain—Kings and rulers—Paramours—Fiction.
4. Mistresses—Great Britain—Fiction. 5. Great Britain—History—Charles II, 1660–1685—Fiction.
6. France—History—Louis XIV, 1643–1715—Fiction. I. Title.
PS3560.A549F74 2009
813'.54—dc22   2009006122

Set in Minion
Designed by Elke Sigal

Printed in the United States of America

For L.C., the other nerdy history girl.

The French Mistress

Prologue

You have heard much wickedness spoken of me, haven't you?

Don't pretend otherwise, I beg you, for long ago I learned to see dissemblers for what they are. I know the truth, just as I know every word and breath of the hateful slanders that have been hurled at me. It is what comes of being a loyal daughter of France, here in this foreign land. I cannot change who I am, or what I have done. The English will always despise me, and that cannot be changed, either.

It was not always so, of course. Once, before I'd gone to Versailles and the great court of King Louis XIV, I was a girl like any other, shy and trembling, innocent of the power of my nascent beauty. But how then could I have guessed my future, or how my fate, my fortune, my very heart, would carry me across the cold gray water and into the land of my enemies? How could I have foreseen that I would come to love one king so that I might please another?

Fate, fortune, and games of the heart. None of it means anything now. All I can offer to you is the truth. The truth, as I swear to it by every star in Our Lady's heaven.

Whether you will choose to believe my telling, or lap up the lies of others—ah, that will fall on your conscience alone. Mine, you see, is clear.

And so I will begin.

Chapter One

I leaned a little farther from the window of my chamber, over the curling red ivy and the stone sill warmed by the late-autumn sun. All around me lay my family's lands, the fields cropped close and brown after harvest, and beyond that, in the distance, the slip of silvery sea. For eighteen years, this had been the length and breadth of my world, but now, today, that would change.

I pushed the window more widely open to look down at the hired carriage that was to bear me away. A groom held the heads of the leading horses while two footmen hoisted the well-worn traveling trunks (once my mother's, and now mine) with my belongings and lashed them onto the back. I could hear Papa in the hall, loudly delivering directions to the carriage's driver while my father's dogs yipped and yapped with excitement over so much commotion.

I laughed softly, unable to contain my delight. I had just passed my eighteenth birthday, and finally I'd have what I'd always wanted: within the hour, I would begin my journey to Paris, and take my place at the royal Court of Louis XIV.

"Louise, please, away from that window," Maman said as she entered my chamber, clapping her hands briskly together to garner my attention. "If your father sees you displaying yourself like some ill-bred harlot, he'll change his mind, and keep you here, as you'd deserve."

"Yes, Maman," I said, swiftly drawing myself back into the room and adding a small curtsy of contrition for good measure. I'd not risk anything to vex my parents now, not with my dream so near to my grasp. "As you say, Maman."

Maman frowned, and traced a small circle in the air before me. "Turn about, turn about," she ordered. "Let me see you."

Dutifully I turned for her, letting her judge me this final time. In my opinion, there'd be little for her to fault. The petticoat and jacket for my journey had been newly made to Maman's own exacting taste, a soft yet sturdy blue trimmed with burgundy velvet ribbons, and cut to show me as she wished me to be, modest and well-bred. Around my throat were the only jewels I owned, a strand of coral beads with a small gold crucifix, less for ornament than as protection against the wickedness and sin Maman was sure I'd encounter at Court. My thick dark hair was drawn back so tightly from my face that not a single wayward curl betrayed itself, the thick plaits pinned into a knot and hidden beneath a starched linen coif edged with a narrow band of lace.

I was proud of my appearance, and why shouldn't I be? Everything proclaimed me to be exactly what I was, the elder daughter of the Comte de Keroualle and the granddaughter of the Marquis de Timeur. I was a sweet-faced virgin from Brittany, fresh as dew from my education under the holy sisters of the Convent of St. Ursula Lesneven, and as achingly innocent as I could be of the great world beyond my father's lands.

Yet Maman's face showed no pleasure in me, nor approval. It was often that way. Upon first meeting, most people remarked on my mother's piety and saintly resignation long before they noticed her beauty, a most rare thing in a woman, and I seldom met her exacting standards.

"Where are your gloves, Louise?" she asked. "No lady would be without them."

"They're here, Maman," I said, retrieving them from the top of the chest. "I haven't put them on yet because the day is so warm."

"The day's warmth should be as nothing to your modesty, Louise." She sighed, as if my uncovered hands were the most grievous disappointment imaginable. Perhaps they were. She dressed herself with sober elegance, and if the dark colors and plain linen collars and full sleeves that she favored were no longer stylish, they were always immaculate, with never so much as a smudge, much like Maman herself.

"Is it any wonder," she continued, "that I pray so much for the Blessed Mother to guide you where I have failed?"

"You've not failed, Maman." At once I felt the familiar, dampening guilt that always plagued me where Maman was concerned. She was endlessly *good*, and I would never be good enough, and that truth was a sorry burden for any daughter to bear. "My sins come from my own weakness, not yours."

She shook her head and sighed wearily at the trials of having such a daughter. "You must make the most of this opportunity, Louise. You have great beauty, a gift from the heavens. In Paris the gentlemen will gather to you like bees to the sweetest blossom. You must take care, and not be misled by idle gallantry or a handsome, laughing face. A sober gentleman of rank and honor, Louise. That is what you must choose for your husband. If only your father—"

"I know, Maman," I said quickly, hoping to avoid once again hearing the misfortunes of our family. During the civil wars known as the Fronde, my father had supported the royal family and fought for the young King Louis, as was just and right, but with great sacrifices to his personal estate.

Once the king was restored to power, Papa had been too proud to join the other nobles in Paris clamoring for restitution in return for loyalty, and thus no lucrative appointments or gifts of gold had found their way to our distant château. To Papa's endless regret, there had been barely enough money to provide my older brother, Sebastien, with an officer's commission once he'd finished his schooling, and none left now to offer suitable dowries for me or my sister, nor even to admit us to a suitable convent as brides of Christ.

Instead I'd been made to understand that my future must be of my own construction. Though I would be paid one hundred and fifty livres a year for being a maid of honor—an amazing sum to me at that time!—that was as nothing for my future, and besides, it would soon be consumed by the staggering costs of living in Paris. Now I must not only beguile a wealthy, honorable gentleman into wedding me for my own sake alone, but also persuade him to share his gold with my parents and support them in their dotage, as any dutiful son would: a weighty responsibility indeed for my youthful shoulders.

"I know what is expected of me, Maman," I said. "I know what—"

"You know, you know, you know," Maman repeated in a dolorous singsong. "Oh, Louise, if only you were truly as wise as you claim! Do you know the burden these fine new clothes of yours have placed upon your poor father? Do you know how we will be forced to dine on mutton and turnips so that you might shine before the gallants at the Louvre?"

"But I do know, Maman," I said earnestly, though with the blind optimism of youth I doubted very much that our château's cook would be expected to prepare turnips and mutton. "And I will be ever grateful to you and Papa for—"

"Not only to us, Louise," Maman said, "but to His Grace the Duc de Beaufort as well. Without his beneficence toward you, there would be no journey for you today."

"I have shown His Grace every gratitude, Maman," I protested. The duc was an old friend of my father, a former comrade in arms from the Fronde. Because the duc was now the Grand Admiral of the Navy, he was often with the fleet in Brest, not far from our château, and thus a familiar guest in our home. "His Grace has told me so himself, and praised me for my pretty airs."

"Please, Louise, more modesty, I beg you." Maman clucked her tongue with dismay. "Recall that His Grace has shown you the rarest favor by recommending you for a place in Madame's household."

I nodded eagerly. Madame was the familiar name of Henriette-Anne, the duchesse d'Orleans, wed to Monsieur, the brother of King Louis himself. She was also sister to the English King Charles, with royal blood in her very veins. But what mattered to me, of course, was that this august lady was to become my mistress, and I her newest maid of honor.

"His Grace could see how much I wished to serve at Court," I said, again with more pride in myself than was wise before my mother. "He told me my beauty would be a welcome ornament to the Court, and that I'd be happy with Madame."

"Oh, my foolish, foolish daughter!" exclaimed Maman sorrowfully. "His Grace has been kind to you, yes, but he is also a man known for his shrewdness, and his understanding of politics. He is offering to bring you forward to Court not to please you, Louise, but to please others. If you find favor with those in power, then he means for you to remember him, and make sure he receives his share of that favor. It's the way of Court, how it has always been. As you serve Madame, His Grace expects you to serve him, too."

In my giddy enthusiasm, I'd realized none of this, nor had anyone bothered to explain it to me before now. Yet rather than turning me fearful or wary, the duc's expectation of my success and his confidence in me made me bolder still.

"I'll bring honor to him, Maman, and to you and Papa, too," I declared. "You'll see. Before long, everyone at Court will know me, even His Majesty himself."

"Louise, it's time." My father had come for me himself, his weathered face impassive. "You can't keep the horses waiting any longer."

"Oh, Louise." My mother's eyes were bright with unexpected tears as she embraced me one last time, her lips cool as they brushed across my cheek. "Never forget your faith, daughter, and always place your soul in God's hands. In time you will be charged with keeping your husband's soul for the True Faith as well. To be a good wife, you must not falter."

She marked me with the sign of the cross, and kissed me once again on my forehead. "May God in all His Glory guide you, Louise, and may the Holy Mother watch over you while I cannot."

After waiting so long, it seemed the rest of my leave-taking was done too quickly, a jumble of fond wishes and promises, weeping servants and barking dogs. Before I'd quite realized it, I was on my way, my family and home gone from my sight.

I wrapped my cloak tightly around myself and closed my eyes, determined not to cry myself. I must be brave, I told myself fiercely. I must be serene in my thoughts and charming in my demeanor, and smile as if I'd no cares in the world. I was bound to make my fortune, just as my brother, Sebastien, had done. Just as he had taken an officer's commission with the army to serve God, glory, and France, so now would I go to Court to claim glory of my own. I'd please the Duc de Beaufort with the influence he sought, and win the rich, solemn, titled husband my parents wished for me, and perhaps one for my younger sister as well.

And what did I wish for myself in that lonely, rocking carriage? What prize did I desire so dearly that I would trade the security of my home for its possession? I'd no thought then for titles or jewels or great houses. That came much later.

Ah, it almost shames me to speak of it now, my wish sounds such a simple, unformed longing, unworthy of the ripe opportunity presented to me.

I went to Court to find love, and be happy.

And by all the saints in heaven, how I wished I had.

Chapter Two

When my carriage finally reached the city, the driver took care to take me by way of the rue Frementeau so that he might play the proper guide, and point his whip toward the king's own palace, the Louvre. Though one wing was covered with a web of scaffolding—for even then, the king had a madness for building and refurbishing, never leaving any property in his possession to go untouched—I still stared with my country eyes wide at the sheer enormity of the Louvre, with row upon well-ordered row of gabled windows and towering brick chimneys.

While I would spend most of my days and evenings at the Louvre, as every good courtier did, my lodgings would be elsewhere. Slowly the driver inched the carriage along the crowded rue Saint-Honoré to the Place du Palais-Royal, and the residence of the duc d'Orleans, the king's brother. Here was where I'd serve as a maid of honor to the duchesse d'Orleans, and I eagerly gazed out the window at my new residence.

The Palais-Royal was smaller than the Louvre, less imposing, and yet more elegant, even to my untutored eyes. While the front of the Louvre seemed straight and severe as a soldier at his post, as was to be expected from its beginnings as a fortress, the Palais-Royal seemed full of curves and swells and flourishes, as beguiling as any lady of fashion.

Later I was to learn how correct my first impressions were, and how true these two palaces were to the nature of the two royal brothers. But on that autumn afternoon, for me even the Palais-Royal seemed very large and daunting, and I felt woefully unprepared to conquer it on my own.

Now most young ladies in my circumstances would have had another to accompany them, a parent or other relative or friend to make their introductions and ease their path into this new world. But my parents were too poor (and, truth be told, too shy of the Court and its manners) to have joined me on such a costly journey. Likewise my sponsor, the Duc de Beaufort, was far away from Paris in the Mediterranean with the French fleet. Thus I was forced to make this first venture on my own, friendless and with no other support than that which I could muster within myself: a tiny comfort, indeed.

But I would persevere. I took a deep breath to calm myself and whispered a hasty prayer as I unlatched the carriage door. I was already climbing down to the paving stones when a young footman in beautiful pale blue livery hurried forward to help me, clearly scandalized that I'd dare do such a thing without assistance.

"Good day," I said, keeping my chin high to mask my uncertainty. "I am here at the bidding of Her Highness the duchess."

"You and everyone else," he said with a bold-faced flippancy that shocked me. "Why else come at all, eh?"

I raised my chin a little higher. I'd no wish for him to see my discomfort, even as I felt my cheeks flush to betray me. "I have letters of introduction to Her Highness. She will be expecting me."

With further impudence, he pointedly looked from my hired carriage to my battered and worn trunks, and finally to my dress, clearly finding every article wanting.

"Please tell Her Highness that I have come," I said, fumbling in my pocket for my precious letters. "My name is Mademoiselle de Keroualle."

"Oh, aye, I'm certain Her Highness is waiting for *you*," he said with a sly rascal's wink. "Go on to the porter, there at the door, and if he believes you, he'll send you to Her Highness's quarters."

I gasped, horrified that I might yet be rejected after my journey. It was unthinkable that I should return home having failed before I'd begun, and impossible, too, for I'd not nearly enough money to continue the hire of the carriage. I blinked back my tears and clutched my bundled letters before my breast like a talisman of truth.

"I am who I say," I whispered miserably. "Truly. My letters will—"

"Hush, mademoiselle. I meant only to tease," he said, turning kind. "Her Highness won't send you back, not yet. But take care, pretty lamb. There are plenty of wolves waiting in Paris with far sharper teeth than mine."

I dashed away my tears with the heel of my glove and hurried inside the tall doors. I felt shamed that I'd let a servant unsettle me so. He was right, too: there would be plenty of others who'd be less kind to me, and I resolved not to be so tender again.

But oh, how insignificant I felt as I presented myself to the stern-faced porter in his blue-laced coat and curled wig, and then again as I hurried to keep pace with yet another footman as he led me through the palace. I'd never been in any house so large, nor so fine, and by comparison my family's ancient château with its rough stone walls and faded tapestries seemed shabby indeed. Paintings as big as life hung on the walls, the images so vivid I expected them to address me as we passed. There were looking glasses to magnify the light that filtered through the leaded windows, and narrow long tables with marble tops, and bouquets of marvelous flowers in porcelain vases.

Breathlessly I followed the silent footman through one hall, turned, then passed through a long gallery, up one staircase and then down another, twisting and turning until my head fair spun. I despaired of ever learning to find my way or, worse, of falling behind my guide and being doomed to wander this grand house forever like some unshriven soul.

But at last he stopped before a set of double doors, carved and gilded to herald their importance, and guarded by two tall soldiers with plumed hats, swords, and fearsome pikes against their shoulders. My footman's knock was answered at once by a man who could have been his twin, and as soon as my name was murmured between them, I was passed through the opening, and the doors closed behind me. Beyond a tall lacquered screen I could hear ladies' voices and laughter, and I'd only time to whisper the swiftest prayer before I was announced and introduced, and abruptly cast into their midst.

At once the voices stilled, and every face turned to face me. There were a dozen or so young women in the room, maids of honor and ladies-in-waiting, some at cards around a small table, others sitting on low cushioned stools to gossip and pretending to labor at the handwork in their laps. I was too stunned to distinguish one from another, gathering only the most general impression of glorious beauty and jewels and dresses richer and more elegant than I'd ever before seen, or even imagined. If I'd been heaved over the side of a boat into the deepest ocean, I couldn't have felt more adrift, nor more overwhelmed in my panic, than I did in that chamber.

Then the woman at the center of the blur smiled at me, and my fears fell away.

"Mademoiselle de Keroualle," Madame said with the easy assurance of one who knows all others will stop to listen to her words. "Welcome to Paris."

Surrounded by her beautiful attendants, Madame was herself not a conventional beauty in the fashion of the time. Dressed in green silk with pearls around her throat and more hanging from her ears, she was small and delicately thin with sleepy blue eyes, a wide forehead, dark hair, and a nose no poet would find lovely. But she was also blessed with an exquisite complexion, always (as I soon learned) referred to as "jasmine and roses," and a sweetness to her expression that gave her a kind of beauty all her own. Further, from that first moment in her presence, I sensed both the warmth of her nature and the rare charm of her person that made it impossible not to love her, and believe her to be far prettier and more beguiling than in truth she was.

"Thank you, Madame," I said, gaping and grinning so widely with relief that I must have looked a fool. "I am most pleased to be here."

In her kindness, Madame only smiled in return, stroking her

hand along the long silky ears of the small spaniel asleep in her lap. I stood before her another long moment until, to my mortification, I realized she was waiting for me to curtsy. At once I sank low, heels together, head bowed, and skirts spread as I'd been taught by both my mother and the good sisters. If I could have, I would have stayed like that, and hidden my shame from the others.

"You may stand," Madame said, unaware of my distress. "You come from Brittany, yes?"

"Yes, Your Grace," I said, struggling to keep my voice even. I *would* be brave. For the sake of those who were depending upon me, I would not falter. "My father's château is not far from the port of Brest."

"Oh, yes, now I do recall the particulars of your situation, mademoiselle," Madame said eagerly. "Your parents offered comfort and succor to my brother's supporters when they were forced into exile here in France."

"Yes, Madame," I said promptly, eager to seize upon any topic that did not include me. As a child I'd heard the sad-eyed Englishmen speaking to Papa about the grievous civil war in their country, and how wicked Protestants had seized the government and murdered King Charles I. This martyred king was the father of Madame and her brother, Charles II, who sat on the throne of England now.

"My mother took the most tender care of the English gentlemen visiting us," I continued, prattling on far longer than I should have. "Maman was especially mindful of the state of their eternal souls. She would read sermons to them, and stood as sponsor to any who would agree to be baptized in the True Church, and renounce their Protestant follies."

"Indeed." Madame's brows arched with surprise, doubtless marveling at my mother's piety, as everyone did. "I'd not heard of that, ah, aspect of your family's hospitality."

"It is true, Madame," I said blithely. Although Madame was English by birth, she was the only member of the royal family who had been raised a Catholic, instead of a Protestant; if she hadn't, I doubt Maman would have consented to my joining her. "My mother said it didn't matter to her if a soul had been born in France or England or

Rome itself, so long as it rose straight to heaven when its mortal life was done."

"Souls are perilously frail, mademoiselle," Madame noted gravely. "I fear at the time of my brother's exile, he was more concerned with the mortal bodies of his followers than their souls."

"He still is," whispered one of the other ladies, a sly whisper loud enough that all around her heard and laughed behind their hands or fans. "Or rather, those luscious mortal bodies he follows as well as those who follow him."

Such audacity shocked me. Not only was this man the King of England, but he was also Madame's brother, and wedded to the queen. If he did what this lady said, then he would surely be damned for the sin of adultery, and to venture such disrespectful scandal about him in Madame's hearing struck me as both unwise and ill-mannered. Ah, how much I had to learn of Court, and of men!

And Madame, it seemed, agreed. "My brother may be a king, Mademoiselle de Fiennes, but he is only a man, with a man's weaknesses," she said, her smile still upon her face, but the tension in her words offered an unspoken warning. "For all their strength, men lack a woman's constancy in love."

"They are all alike, Madame, faithless as mongrel dogs who sniff at every stray bitch," said the other lady, unperturbed, as she idly wrapped one lock of her golden hair around her finger. She was undeniably the most beautiful of the maids of honor, with blue eyes of a color to send gentlemen to sighing. But her beauty was kept from perfection by a certain sullenness about her mouth and in her general expression, marking her as the sort of lady who expected admiration and indulgence as her due.

"The truth cannot be denied," she continued in a languid drawl. "Whether highborn noblemen or low scoundrels, it makes no difference."

I saw how the other ladies shared glances of concern among themselves, as if this exchange was ominously familiar. The spaniel in the duchess's lap roused with a low grumbling growl, as if he, too, had been displeased.

"How unfortunate that you must speak from your own experience, mademoiselle," Madame said, her hand sleeking along the length of the little dog to calm it, or perhaps herself. "Why, I wonder, should you wish to share such sordid recollections with us? What is your reason for offending me in this manner?"

"I regret the offense I have given you, Madame," Mademoiselle de Fiennes said, at last slipping from her seat to curtsy in contrition. "I beg you to forgive me."

Yet as abject as the lady's apology might appear, even I could see that it was false, and not well meant.

"I should much rather you consider your words before you speak them, mademoiselle," she said, "than pardon them after."

"Yes, Madame," murmured Mademoiselle de Fiennes, still bent low, as she must until she was granted permission to rise.

"How much better it would be for your own soul," Madame continued, "as well as for these wayward gentlemen if you should pray for their enlightenment, rather than find fault for things they cannot change themselves. Is that not so, Mademoiselle de Keroualle?"

"Yes, Madame," I swiftly agreed, startled to be drawn into their quarrel.

"You see, Mademoiselle de Fiennes, how even my newest lady understands what you willfully refuse to see." Madame sighed wearily, more pale than before. "Rise, then, and pray be civil."

Purposefully she looked away from Mademoiselle de Fiennes, and back to me.

"The Duc de Beaufort claimed that you speak English," she said, employing that language to test me. "Is that true, mademoiselle?"

"Yes, Madame, I do speak it a little," I said, answering in kind as proof. "I learned from those same exiled English gentlemen who supported His Majesty your brother."

"Then perhaps one day my brother will be able to thank you himself in the language of our birth," she said. "He has chided me in the past for not having any ladies about me who spoke our father's tongue, and could give me that small comfort. But he would, I believe, approve of you most heartily."

"Thank you, Madame," I murmured, awed even to think that my

presence would be noted by the English King Charles. "I shall do my best to serve you however I can."

"I am certain you will." She smiled warmly, and glanced toward the other ladies around her. "Has Madame du Frayne prepared a place for Mademoiselle de Keroualle in your quarters?"

"She has, Madame," replied a young lady with coppery curls whose expression seemed to reflect and embrace Madame's kindness. "Everything is ready to welcome Mademoiselle de Keroualle. Her bed's to be next to mine."

She placed her hand over her heart with graceful humility. "I am Mademoiselle Gabrielle Marie-Anne de la Touraine, and I am pleased to welcome you among us."

Gratefully I smiled in return, eager for a kindness, perhaps even a friend. I'd need one in this place.

"Yes, Madame, we are all delighted to welcome the new mademoiselle among us," Mademoiselle de Fiennes said now, studying me in a manner that reminded me uncomfortably of a stable yard cat intent upon a wayward mouse. "But I wonder if she is in turn prepared for us. She seems so . . . *young* to be here, away from her mama. I worry for one so tender, Madame."

Concern flickered across Madame's face. "That is true," she said. "I should not want my own daughter thrust into this world before her time."

"But I am not so young, Madame!" I exclaimed, fearing my glorious new post would be taken from me before I'd so much as removed my cloak.

"No?" Madame regarded me carefully. "What is your age, Mademoiselle de Keroualle?"

"I am eighteen, Madame," I said, the truth, and my heart sank as I saw the fresh doubt flood her face. I was sure I was older than several of the other maids of honor gathered here, yet to my sorrow, I understood Madame's confusion. I did not look my years. My face had never lost the plumpness of a young child's, my cheeks being round and rosy and my lips full with a natural pout. Further, my mother had forbidden me paint, saying its use was the brand of a strumpet, not a lady. Despite her words, when I looked at the ladies' faces around me, all had lips reddened with carmine and eyes exotically rimmed with lampblack. I felt as scrubbed clean as last night's pots, and as unattractive, too.

"Eighteen!" repeated Mademoiselle de Fiennes, her eyes wide with incredulity as she appealed to the others. "If she is eighteen, why, then so am I!"

But this time, none of the other ladies were so rash as to laugh with her.

"Mademoiselle de Keroualle has no reason for dissembling," Madame said. "I do recall now that the Duc de Beaufort also gave her age as eighteen, and it's unlikely they would both misremember."

Mindful of her earlier misstep, Mademoiselle de Fiennes said nothing, though the tiny shrug she gave her shoulders expressed her skepticism without a word spoken.

"If Mademoiselle de Keroualle appears too young," Madame said sharply, "then it is not a fault of her innocence, but only a sorry judgment of the worldliness of other ladies at this Court."

"Forgive me, Madame, I did not intend to—"

"I have no interest in your intentions, mademoiselle," Madame said. She looked back at me, and her expression softened. "It will be refreshing to have such a measure of innocence beside me, Mademoiselle de Keroualle. I believe you to be of age for my service, and I'll hear no more of it. Come, you must be weary after your journey. Mademoiselle de la Touraine, will you please show her to the quarters of the maids of honor?"

I followed Mademoiselle de la Touraine's lead and curtsied, then remained facing Madame as we backed from the room as was proper with royalty. We passed between the guards at the door, taking no more notice of them than they did of us.

"It's not far," Mademoiselle de la Touraine said once we were beyond the hearing of the guards. She took short, swift steps, her slippers making almost no sound as her silken skirts rippled gracefully around her ankles: a skill I resolved at once to practice and acquire for myself. "Madame likes her ladies to be close to her, to keep from being lonely. You may call me Gabrielle if I may call you Louise. Our fathers are of the same rank, so there's no harm to it."

"Oh, yes, please, call me Louise." I smiled eagerly, wanting her to like me. "But how do you know of my father? He never leaves Brittany. He despises Paris, and refuses to come here."

"We know because he is your father, and you are here, as one of us now." Gabrielle made a dismissive little wave with her hand. "Everyone knows everything at Court, Louise, from the king himself down to the lowest maidservant in the scullery or groom in the stable. There are no secrets here."

"None?" I asked, skeptical of such certainty.

"None," she repeated with relish, the coral beads of her earrings bobbing against her cheeks. "One never knows what advantage might come from a certain scrap of knowledge. You saw how it was with Françoise—that is, Mademoiselle de Fiennes. She wouldn't have dared make such a fuss about your age unless she already knew your family possessed little influence with the king, or anyone else of note at Court. She knew there'd be no consequences if she teased you."

"But *why* did she do it?" I asked.

"For sport." Gabrielle paused at one of the tall arched windows that lit the hallway, gently pushing aside the heavy brocade curtains with her fingertips to glance at the street below to see who might be new arrived, and thus be the first who knew: a passion, I learned later, that she shared with nearly every courtier. "For amusement. Françoise is like that, you see. All of us maids have felt the prick of her cruelty at one time or another. She finds pleasure in the torment of others."

"That's wicked," I declared solemnly. "Why doesn't Her Highness make her stop?"

"Because of who she is," Gabrielle said, letting the curtain fall from her fingers as she turned. "Who she is, and who she lies with."

I stopped, determined to sort this out. "But she is unwed," I said, my voice falling into a whisper. "And she's also a maid of honor, which means she must be a—a virgin."

"Truly you *are* an innocent, Louise, if you believe that," Gabrielle said, her tone pitying. "There are as few true maids among the maids of honor as there are constant wives among the ladies-in-waiting, and the gentlemen are even more profligate. Françoise intrigues with the Chevalier de Lorraine, who in turn is the favorite lover of Monsieur, Madame's husband."

I shook my head. "That is not possible. How can two gentlemen be lovers?"

"They can if they are sodomites," she said, with as little concern for decency than if she were discoursing upon the weather. "There are a number of Court gentlemen who prefer to find pleasure with other men rather than with women, while there are also others, like Monsieur, who are true libertines, and amuse themselves with both sexes."

I shook my head in denial, unwilling (or perhaps truly unable) to comprehend such behavior. And here I'd believed adultery to be the greatest sin of Louis's court!

Yet Gabrielle understood my confusion. "I didn't believe it myself, when I first came to Court, but I swear by all that's holy that it's the truth," she said. "These rogues follow the Italian manner for their spending, and take each other in their mouths, or in their bottoms. You'll learn soon enough which gentlemen are so inclined. Not only do they paint and patch their faces like courtesans, but they will also make a show of sitting daintily on down-stuffed cushions, all the while boasting about the size of what they've recently accommodated within their nether regions."

"But that—that is an abomination, a perversion!" I stammered, sickened at the very notion of such acts. Surely my mother and father had not known of these activities, else they'd never have permitted me to come to Paris. "An act so debauched is a disgrace to God."

"It's also a capital crime against the Crown that can cost the participants their heads on the block," Gabrielle said wryly. "But though His Majesty loathes the practice, he can say nothing to stop it, not when his brother is the most grievous offender of them all."

She held her hand up before her, using her fingers as markers to tick off the steps to her argument. "Thus the king pretends he does not see, and Madame, though she knows that Françoise intrigues with the chevalier, also pretends ignorance for the sake of keeping the peace with Monsieur, while Monsieur himself looks away to avoid risking the loss of his own favorite love. Round and round and round we all must go, yes? There may be no secrets at Court, but there is much willful blindness."

She laughed, and there was something to that laughter that made me uneasy. Was my unwitting ignorance the true source of her amusement?

"What secrets do you have, Louise?" she asked, her manner merry despite the sordid nature of her revelations. "I can tell already that you're one of those determined to be virtuous, rather than a favorite. At least you will at first. That's the way it always is with country virgins."

"Not with me," I said, wishing I didn't sound so priggish. "I'll not give myself to any gentleman save the one I wed before God."

"I wish you well of that, if that is what you wish." She laughed again and winked, I suppose, to show she believed in neither virtue nor wishes. "But if you do preserve your innocence and remain a true *maid* of honor to Her Highness, then you'll find Madame will love you all the more. Here are our quarters."

Relieved to put aside our scandalous conversation, I followed Gabrielle past more guards, and into the quarters for Her Highness's youngest attendants.

"There are six of us maids of honor," Gabrielle explained, "as is proper for a royal princess. Madame du Frayne is the lady who is supposed to advise us, and keep us from mischief, and a dragon she is, too. You won't want to cross her. Of course there are servants to tend to our hair and others to look after our clothes and help us dress. You'll meet them all soon enough. This small parlor is for the maids to share in common."

The parlor *was* small, scarce more than a closet with a table and several straight-backed chairs. In one corner was a tiny shrine to the Virgin Mother for us to say our rosary, or other prayers. The single window opened onto a courtyard and faced the gray stone wall of another wing of the palace, with only a single slanting ray of watery Paris sunlight making its way into the room. I couldn't help but recall the window in my bedchamber at home and the sweet breezes and endless view of the countryside that I'd had there, and with that memory came a sharp, sudden pang of longing for everything I'd so blithely left behind.

"That door there leads directly to Madame's quarters," Gabrielle continued. "We're only to use it when she summons us to her. I know it all likely seems mean and low to you—I know it did to me, when I first arrived—but lodgings are at such a premium here at Court that they say there are marquises living beneath the garrets of the Louvre, and grateful for that. Here's the chamber you'll share with me."

I would have called it an alcove, not a room, and one without any windows or a door for privacy. For all that we were within a palace, it was not so very different from the pupils' quarters at the nunnery in Lesneven. Two narrow beds—mere cots, really, without proper bedsteads or hangings—were set against the walls, with two chamber pots, two washstands, two chairs, and a single looking glass on the wall between. Of more importance were the pair of tall wardrobe chests that held our clothes. A maidservant had already unpacked my trunks and hung my gowns on the pegs within, leaving the doors open for my approval.

I unfastened my cloak and hung it inside. I knew I was supposed to wait for the maidservant to appear again, that no real lady would tend to her own clothes, but a lifetime's habit was difficult to break, and besides, the simple act was one I could perform without fearing I'd misstep.

"Ooh, let's see your gowns," Gabrielle said, opening the wardrobe's doors more widely. "I'm so weary of the same ones here among us. This blue wool is rather fine, isn't it? But then, if my skin were as clear and white as yours, I'd wear blue, too."

She held out the skirts of each of my new gowns in turn, considering them one by one while I stood by anxiously awaiting her judgment.

I was mindful of the expenditure my new clothes had represented to my father, and how the rest of my family had been obliged to do without in some area so that I'd be able to represent them well here at Court. Maman herself had chosen every length of cloth with frugal care, and had cut away old lace from her own gowns to be washed and stitched freshly onto mine.

Yet even before Gabrielle gave her verdict, I knew what she'd say. I'd eyes to see for myself. The moment I'd entered Madame's rooms earlier I'd understood. How could I have missed the dress of the other ladies attending the princess this afternoon? For gossip and handwork, every one of them had dressed with more elegance, more artistry, and vastly more expense than the gown I'd intended for the most formal of Court occasions. Gabrielle need not speak a word aloud; her garb alone told me more of my lackings than any mere words ever could.

Her gown was fashioned of peach-colored silk satin of such a weave that it seemed to change from rose to pale gold as she moved, just as did that summer fruit. Her billowing skirts were cunningly gathered in neat cartridge pleats, while the bodice was the work of a master mantua maker, boned and curved behind a long, straight busk to accentuate Gabrielle's waist. Intricate rosettes of green silk ribbon blossomed from her cuffs, and a collar of finely wrought lace nearly half a foot wide circled her shoulders and was caught at her breasts with a brooch of pearls and carved coral, with more coral beads around her throat and hanging from her ears.

Beside such opulence, my new gowns—mostly wool or linen, with only one of silk, and no gay rosettes or wide lavish bands of imported lace or cuffs that fell open like a flower's petals around the elbow—seemed humble indeed, and a woefully inadequate match to my family's grand aspirations.

"The cut of these sleeves is rather amusing," Gabrielle was saying, though now I heard her words as condescending, not kind, and meant more likely to mock the poor country seamstress than to praise her ingenuity.

"Thank you," I said, keeping my misery to myself as I prayed that would be sufficient answer. My parents and all the other de Keroualles behind me deserved that much.

Gabrielle had come to the last of my gowns, lifting the skirts of the final one to glance beneath it, as if to find more hidden beneath.

"I wonder where that lazy porter must be with your other trunks?" she asked, though I was sure she knew perfectly well that there'd be no more. "We're all to go to the Louvre tonight with Madame for an entertainment, you know. Likely she'll present you to His Majesty then, and you'll want to dress to please him."

"I dress to please only myself," I said. "Not the king, or anyone else."

She gasped with surprise: likely the first honest reaction I'd had from her. "But, Louise, everyone dresses to please His Majesty! To catch his favor is the most fervent desire of every lady at Court."

"I would wish to please His Majesty, yes," I said carefully, "but as his loyal subject, not as an adulterous favorite."

"But it's not that way, not with the king," Gabrielle insisted. "Because he is His Most Christian Majesty and the most powerful monarch of God's will on earth, even His Holiness in Rome pardons him his indulgences. Besides His Majesty's reputation as a most pleasing lover, as every woman who has enjoyed the royal person will attest, he is a generous one, too. Jewels, benefices, titles, honors, estates! It is the surest course to success for any lady and her family at Court."

Jewels, benefices, titles, honors, estates. Surely such gifts would ease my parents' situation as they grew older. My younger sister would have a dowry to attract a husband. Royal influence would further my brother's military career, too, and please my sponsor, the Duc de Beaufort.

But was it equal to the dreams I'd had of a husband and children of my own? Would jewels and titles be worth the devil's bargain of my own soul and virtue?

Could the rules of heaven and earth truly be so different for those here at Court?

"When you have the honor of His Majesty's presence tonight, you'll understand," Gabrielle promised, excitement quivering in every word. "He is the very model of a king, and surely the first gentleman of the kingdom, not yet thirty years of age, tall and handsome and virile beyond reason. When he smiles in your direction, la! You'll melt and glow with the delicious honor of it, Louise, even you."

"Perhaps," I said warily, all the commitment I'd dare make. Though I was eighteen, I'd yet to feel the sweet sting of Cupid's dart. To be sure, I'd danced with young gentlemen from other Breton families and granted a kiss or two to be stolen in the garden, but I'd never experienced this melting glow that Gabrielle was describing, nor was I certain I wished to.

"This is no invention," Gabrielle assured me earnestly. "It has happened twice before, and likely will happen again. Both Madame la duchesse de la Vallière and Madame du Montespan began as young ladies in Madame's household before they became His Majesty's mistresses. When the king drops his lace-trimmed handkerchief before a lady, then the world becomes hers."

"His handkerchief?" I repeated, mystified.

"Oh, yes." Gabrielle nodded vigorously. "That is how he signals his desires. Everyone recognizes it as a perfect ritual. From respect, His Majesty will raise his hat to every female he meets, even if she is only a laundress—he has the most exquisite manners imaginable!—but he only drops his handkerchief before the fortunate lady whose beauty has captured his heart."

I listened, and silently resolved that I would never be so fortunate.

"You may believe me, or not," Gabrielle said, and swept her hand through the air briskly, as if to dismiss my foolish objections. "But after tonight, after you have seen *him*, then you will understand. And pray recall that they say even Madame was once half in love with His Majesty."

"Madame!" I exclaimed, for what must surely have been the hundredth time that day. "Our Madame? She loved her husband's brother?"

"The same. Now they claim to be no more than excellent friends, for whatever value there may be in that for a lady. But then, such is the power and majesty of our monarch." Gabrielle smiled, more to herself than to me. Most likely she was dreaming blissfully of the king, as it would seem every woman (save me) in France must do. "In time I expect you'll be as admiring as the rest of us, Louise, and as quick to put yourself in the way of his notice."

She glanced back at my wardrobe and wrinkled her nose with pointed disdain. "Though not, perhaps, until you've had some more . . . acceptable gowns sewn here in Paris."

"Mademoiselle de la Touraine!"

In the doorway stood a lady with a face so stern and severe I would have guessed her a Mother Superior, except that she wore a rich gown of dark purple and yellow instead of a somber habit.

At once Gabrielle curtsied before this fearsome woman, and I did as well, without pausing to question.

"Is this the new maid of honor, mademoiselle?" the lady asked, looking down her hawk's beak of a nose at me.

"Yes, madame," Gabrielle said quickly. "May I present Mademoiselle Louise de Penancoet de Keroualle? Mademoiselle de Keroualle, Madame du Frayne, our—"

"Later, if you please." The older lady clapped her hands together, as cracking sharp a sound as any musket's shot. "Her Highness requests Mademoiselle de Keroualle at once in her bedchamber. Go, girl, at once, at once! Never keep Her Highness waiting!"

"Yes, madame," I said quickly, and headed through the door that Gabrielle had pointed out to me earlier. "Should I use the direct passage?"

Madame du Frayne nodded with curt approval. "Go now, mademoiselle."

"You're quick to learn, Louise, aren't you?" Gabrielle whispered grudgingly behind me.

I didn't answer, but hurried to join my mistress. But Gabrielle was right. I *was* quick to learn, and already I'd learned the most important lesson of any court, and one I'd never forget or ignore: trust no one but yourself.

Chapter Three

The back passage to Madame's bedchamber was much shorter and more direct than the hall that Gabrielle had taken me through earlier. I'd no need of a guide here: the plain plastered passage led in only one direction.

The narrow arched door at the end stood ajar for me to enter, and I paused for a moment to smooth my skirts before I presented myself to Her Highness. I could hear her voice within, likely addressing a servant. I stepped forward, my hand on the latch to open the door fully. The princess stood with her back to me, her carefully arranged curls, threaded with blue silk ribbons and falling over her shoulders, and the sapphires hanging from her ears winked in the light from the fire.

Then the gentleman with her moved into my line of sight behind the half-open door, and I stopped with uncertainty.

He was the same height as Madame, but where she was slender, he appeared inclined to a plump softness, his doublet and sleeves pulling too snugly around his body. Yet it wasn't only his form that had a womanliness: his dress was the most extravagant I had ever seen on a man, fair erupting with hundreds of pale green and pink ribbon *galants* at the hem of his short doublet, at his elbows, and around the knees of his breeches. His stockings were embroidered with golden lilies, and topped by flopping cuffs of rose point lace. More lace formed his collar, stiffened and starched so high that his chin seemed propped up on a froth of white.

His black wig curled in ringlets to his waist, with more ribbons tied into lovelocks, and heavy rings glittered on half his fingers. But it was his face that made me gasp, an exclamation I barely smothered behind my hand. Gabrielle had not exaggerated. The gentleman was painted as garishly as an actress, his skin whitened to gleam like the shell of a goose's egg, his cheeks and lips reddened with cerise, his eyelids languidly darkened and lined with lampblack, with more to mark his brows into ink black arches. Yet despite so much womanly artifice, his features remained those of a man's, with a long nose and a firm, if pointed, jaw, and hard black eyes that would miss nothing.

Monsieur. I realized his identity with a start, remembering Gabrielle's description. The brother of the king, the husband of my lady mistress. Philippe, duc d'Orleans.

Though I knew it was wrong of me to remain and spy on them like this, however unintended it might be, I also realized that if I tried to leave I might be discovered by Monsieur and that would be infinitely worse. My only recourse would lie in remaining as still as I could until he left Madame alone and I could join her as I'd been bidden, and thus I waited.

"So it is true, Henriette?" Monsieur asked. "You have been plotting again with my brother without either my knowledge or my consent?"

Though I could not see Madame's face from where I stood, there was no mistaking how her shoulders tightened and narrowed, or how she clasped her hands together before her, as if to gird herself for his attacks.

"There are no plots, Philippe," she said, her words brittle, and without any of the lighthearted charm I'd heard earlier. "There never are, save the ones of your own invention."

"I do not invent, my dear, only perceive," he answered. "And what I perceive is a plot to undermine my authority, contrived by the two people that heaven orders I must trust the most."

Pointedly not looking in his wife's direction, he held his hands out before the fire. Most men would do so for the warmth of the flames, but from the way that Monsieur turned his hands, snowy-white as two doves, he seemed more intent on admiring how the flicker of the fire lit the jewels in his rings.

"How can a wish for peace between France and England serve to undermine you, Philippe?" Madame asked. "If your brother trusts me sufficiently to meet with my brother on his behalf, then why can't you do the same?"

"Diplomacy should never be put into the hands of a woman," he said, unaware of the irony of his words as he continued to admire his own unblemished fingers: or perhaps he understood perfectly, being Monsieur, and more a lover of men than of women. "My brother cannot possibly trust you with such a grave negotiation. He may tell you so, to flatter you and to amuse himself with your pathetic rejoicing, but he would never believe it."

"It is you who are pathetic, Philippe," Madame answered contemptuously. "Louis is secure in his manhood. He can trust women because he has no reason to fear them."

"Insults will not soften me toward your request, Henriette." His voice now carried a most masculine edge to it, and a menace that oddly seemed all the more dangerous on account of his decorative appearance. "You know I expect obedience in all things of you as my wife."

"But this is for the good of the country, Philippe, and for the benefit of the French people," she pleaded, her hands twisting together as her earlier defiance seemed to shrink away. "If I can but speak to Charles, in person and in confidence, then—"

"You will not go to England," he said, his voice as chill and unrelenting as ice itself. "You will not speak to your brother without my permission. You will remain here with me in France."

"Please, Philippe, please," she cried plaintively. "I beg you, for the love of God and France!"

"For the incestuous love you bear your brother, you mean," he said. "I'll not condone such unnatural affection between you Stuarts."

"Lies!" she gasped, and shook her head with such vehemence that her tightly arranged curls began to loosen and come unpinned. "The love I bear for Charles is pure and honorable, a just love between brother and sister. For you to speak of unnatural love, you for whom every unspeakable perversion is—"

"Silence," Monsieur said sharply, swinging around to confront her. "God has given you to me as my wife. Not your brother, not my brother, but God Himself. If I say you are to remain at my side, then you will."

She made a harsh gulping sob of despair and held her clasped hands out to him. "Please, Philippe. It has been nearly ten years since I've stood on English soil, ten years since I've seen my brother."

"It will be another ten years and more if you continue to grovel like this," he said with disgust. "You are the daughter of a king, yet you carry yourself with all the dignity of a common slattern."

"What do you want of me, Philippe?" I still could not see her face, but I knew she was weeping. "What must I do to please you, and earn the favor of a husband for his wife?"

"How dare you ask me such a ridiculous question?" he demanded. "Are you a simpleton, a half-wit? You know full well your duty to me, just as you know how you willfully withhold from me the one thing I most desire."

Madame's hands dropped back to her sides, her shoulders sagging. "Oh, Philippe, not that," she whimpered. "I beg you, not again!"

"It is your duty as my wife, Henriette." He took a step toward her, and she shrank away. "Your mother knew her role as a devoted wife, and as a true daughter of France. She gave your father three strong sons, while you refuse to grant me the only reason I have for tolerating you."

"Children are God's will, His blessing on a marriage," she said, her words tumbling over one another as she continued to inch away from him. "I cannot be faulted if He has not yet granted us the miracle of a son!"

"But God will punish a sinful wife through her husband," Monsieur said sharply. "An unnatural wife who prefers to abandon her husband's bed and country to dabble in men's affairs."

"That is not true, Philippe, none of it!" She twisted to one side, trying to slip past him.

He grabbed her arm to stop her, his grasp so tight upon her that she yelped with pain, or perhaps frustration. He pushed her backward onto the bed, and climbed atop her, pinning her flaying legs beneath his knees. She fought him still, reaching up to try to claw at his face and chest, and with a loathsome oath he struck his palm hard across her cheek. She cried out with pain and anguish and resignation, too, and covered her eyes and her tears with her hands so she could not see what he did.

In my inexperience, I remained still in the hall, unsure of what else to do, and the awful image of what came next was soon seared forever in my consciousness. With a shocking swiftness, Monsieur unfastened the front of his breeches and pulled his shirt to one side. At once his member sprang forth, already furiously engorged and as unappealing as the rest of him. Breathing hard, he tore aside Madame's skirts, heedless of how his impetuosity ripped the fine linen and lace hemmings. He pushed apart her pale thighs and fell between them, shoving hard without any preamble or pretense of lovemaking. Sparing not a single endearment to ease his wife, he grunted and found his own rhythm. She caught her breath, but that was all, and soon the only sounds were Monsieur's animal-like groans and the creaking of the bed's springs as he worked her hard, and without mercy or kindness.

I had never witnessed such a sight, either for its intimacy or its cruelty, and yet I could not make myself look away, even as hot tears of horror and sympathy for Madame's plight slipped down my cheeks.

Though it seemed to last forever, in truth Monsieur was quickly finished. His face was blotched and florid beneath its cracking white paint, the tendrils of his black wig sticking to his temples and the back of his neck. He withdrew his staff, inspected it briefly as if it were his most treasured belonging (and perhaps it was), and at last tucked it away. He slipped from the bed and the silent form of his wife. With disgust, not tenderness, he pulled her skirts back over her violated nakedness. Her eyes still covered, she moaned softly and rolled to one side, away from him, curling her knees up tightly against her chest.

And for Monsieur, there was no further reason to linger in his wife's bedchamber.

"I'll expect you to attend my brother with me this night, Henriette," he said as he gathered up his hat and cloak. "Do not disappoint me."

In my inexperience, I'd no idea what to say or do to comfort my new mistress. Perhaps this hateful treatment was common between husbands and wives of long standing. Perhaps the sweet love and poetry of courtship for which I so longed was destined to fade after marriage, and deteriorate into the wretched treatment I'd just witnessed.

Gabrielle had told me that everyone at Court was accustomed to looking away and pretending things were other than they were for the sake of ease. If I were wiser, or more worldly, perhaps I, too, would have followed that course, and returned to my new lodgings. But by nature I was too tenderhearted to slink away like that, and too honest to pretend ignorance. Madame had been kind to me when I'd been in need, and now I'd not leave her to suffer alone.

I waited until the latch of the door clicked shut and the sound of his heeled footsteps faded down the hall. Then I threw open the door and ran to Madame's side, kneeling before the bed so my face would be even with hers.

"Oh, Madame, my poor lady," I cried softly, "are you hurt? Are you ill? Should I send for a physician, or your lady's maid?"

She jerked her head from the bed, struggling to compose herself and sit upright once again.

"What could be wrong, my dear?" she asked, trying to smile though the mark of her husband's blow still stained her cheek.

"I—I do not know, Madame," I stammered with bewilderment, rising to curtsy beside the bed. "That is, forgive me, Madame."

She might have been able to be brave, but I could not. Suddenly my earlier tears returned, spilling from my eyes, and betraying all I'd seen. Her face crumpled as her misery swept over her, and to my surprise she took me into her arms and drew me close. Without a thought,

I slipped my arms around her narrow back, holding her tightly with my head on her shoulder and hers pressed into mine. Twined together that way, we rocked from side to side and wept shamelessly, taking as much comfort from each other as we gave.

Finally she pulled back and placed her hands on either side of my teary cheeks. She cradled my face between her palms with rare gentleness, yet also to keep me from looking away as she spoke.

"What you have seen, mademoiselle," she whispered urgently, her voice ravaged with emotion. "What you now know of my shame and my suffering: remember it well, I beg you, and if ever I come to grief, swear to tell all to my brother in England. Swear to it, mademoiselle!"

I swallowed, and nodded, even though I quaked before the awful burden of such an oath.

"I swear, Madame," I said fervently. "You have my word."

I gave it without thinking, too, for she was my mistress, my princess, and because one did not refuse anyone of royal blood. But the consequences of my oath that would come later— Ah, it would be greater than either of us could ever guess.

Though the Louvre, His Majesty's palace, was within sight of the Palais-Royal, Madame and her attendants did not walk between the two, but instead rode the distance in great lumbering carriages. I was among the most noble folk now, and walking, it seemed, was beneath us, an ignominious resort of common people. But noble or not, there was still much petty bickering among us ladies as we climbed into the carriages, with endless concern over who sat beside the window to be admired by the world, and who was made to sit hidden inside, and whose skirts were being crushed and rumpled by another's clumsiness.

Being so new, I didn't care, and gladly squeezed into the space I was given. I was to see His Majesty for the first time, and I'd ride in an oxcart if I must. Besides, after what I'd witnessed in Madame's bedchamber, the foolish chatter around me was a relief, soothing in its lack of consequence.

I was thankful, too, to be with so many others as we made our way through the halls and staircases of the Louvre. If I'd been impressed by the elegance of the Palais-Royal, then I was overwhelmed by the formal grandeur of the Louvre. His Majesty was famous for his insistence on perfection, both here and at his grand palace in the country at Versailles (likewise in a constant state of improvement). From the marble statues to the gilded frames on the life-sized pictures to the porcelain vases filled with flowers grown beyond their season in the royal hothouses: everything was exactly as it should be, and all of it designed to glorify the king.

I soon saw that this magnificent display extended not just to the furnishing of the palace, but to the courtiers themselves. The halls were as crowded with folk as if for market day, and every gentleman and lady seemed to be determined to outdo their neighbor in regards to their dress, with more extravagant shows of lace and ribbons and costly silk embroidery than I'd ever imagined.

However snide Gabrielle's dismissal of my new wardrobe might have been, there had also been a large measure of truth to her criticism. The gowns that had seemed so fashionable in Keroualle *were* far too plain in this company, and hardly suitable for my new rank. I'd no money for replacing them, of course, nor could I conceive of the cost of so much splendor here in the shops of Paris. I would simply have to hold my head high and rely upon the beauty that God had given me, not the labors of some mere seamstress. In a world that was ruled by pretense, I'd simply pretend that I didn't care that my gowns and jewels were so inferior, and plan for the day when my fortunes would rise, and I'd be the most gloriously attired of them all.

For now I wore my blue silk, with my grandmother's small gold crucifix around my throat. The lady's maid who served all the maids of honor had arranged my hair in the same style as the others, with elaborate curls bunched high on either side of my forehead and trailing down to my shoulders. Thin wires were cunningly threaded through the bases of the curls to hold them aloft, and though the unfamiliar weight felt strangely unbalanced on my head, I found the effect most elegant, and I was sure my hair had never looked so fine, nor so fashionable.

There was no momentous event at Court that night, no ball or play to be debuted. Instead the entertainment was a troupe of traveling Florentines, acrobats and low comedians. According to the other ladies in the carriage, this was one of His Majesty's favorite sorts of amusement on account of his grandmother having been an Italian princess, Marie de'Medici. There were others who'd spoken less kindly, who'd said that this Italian blood was also responsible for both the king's ruthlessness and his swarthy complexion; but already I'd learned to be suspicious of gossip, and not to believe whatever I was told.

Like a flock of gaudy chicks around their hen, we followed Madame into a large gallery with a row of four chairs and additional stools arranged at one end, before a makeshift space for the performers. Already the room was largely filled with courtiers and guests, all chattering with anticipation, and a small orchestra was playing light-hearted music, suitable to the coming players.

With others bowing and curtsying in deference, Madame made her way to one of the chairs in the front of the room. To me, knowing what I did, she seemed quiet and subdued, her smile a forced imitation of merriment. She was beautifully dressed, as was to be expected, and any pallor or lingering mark from her husband's blow had been expertly covered by powder and cerise. It grieved me to think that she could likewise hide her suffering, for it made me fear she'd had practice doing so. Monsieur had not joined her in her carriage from the Palais-Royal, and thus far he'd not joined her here, either. For her sake, I prayed he wouldn't.

"We stand back here, Louise," Gabrielle whispered, prodding me into place behind the chairs and stools. "I hope your slippers don't pinch, for we're not to sit the entire night."

"Who gets the stools?" I asked, looking at them with perhaps more longing than was proper. The gilded stools were low and cushioned with tapestry-covered seats tipped by fat, dangling tassels.

"You mean the taborets," she whispered in return. "They're only for the duchesses, just as the straight chairs are for those with royal blood—Madame and Monsieur—and the armchairs are for the king and queen. Everyone else must stand in His Majesty's presence, unless he expressly gives his permission. Not that he will. He is a formal gentleman, and he likes everything ordered just so."

"Even to having us ladies stand like soldiers?"

"Oh, His Majesty expects far more than that of us," she said, holding her painted ivory fan before her face so others wouldn't overhear. "I've been told that when he invites various ladies to join him in his carriage, he expects them to contain themselves entirely. He'll not permit the horses stopped for anyone to use the privy or find other relief, and if a lady fails to oblige, or faints from the strain, why, then he falls into a powerful rage, and the poor lady is forever in disgrace."

"That has happened?" I asked, more curious than shocked. "A lady disgraced for requiring the privy?"

"Oh, yes," Gabrielle said solemnly. "I told you. His Majesty is king, and he expects to be obeyed in everything. Even the privy."

But my attention had been drawn elsewhere. "Who is that lady?"

Gabrielle leaned to one side, the better to follow my glance. "The one with the gold-colored hair and the pearls in her hair? Merciful saints, what I'd do for pearls such as those!"

I nodded, watching the lady take her place on one of the taborets. She had the golden hair and wide blue eyes that I was coming to realize were the height of beauty at court. But she was also blessed with a voluptuous form and an indolent, knowing expression to her heavy-lidded eyes, and the way she moved through the crowded room, more a sensuous dance than a walk, drew the lustful gaze of most every gentleman present.

"She beguiled His Majesty, and no wonder," Gabrielle continued. "To think that she was one of Madame's maids of honor, the same as we are now, and next she'll bear the king's child."

"She's known to you, then?" So potent were this lady's charms, even to me, that at first I'd not noticed the swell of her belly beneath the silk brocade of her gown, richer than any other in the gallery. Most women I'd known had turned sickly and peevish when they were with child, and retired from society. This lady seemed to flaunt her belly like a prize, sitting with her fingers spread over it like a ruler with his hand upon his golden orb, the symbol of his power.

"She's known to everyone," Gabrielle replied. "I marvel that you don't recognize her yourself. Why, Louise, that is Madame la Marquise du Montespan."

"A marquise." I frowned, trying to recollect where I'd heard the lady's name before, and in what context. "Yet she sits on a taboret reserved for a duchess."

"That's because while she is a marquise, she is also the king's mistress," Gabrielle said, her voice full of hushed awe. "She has lodgings here in the Louvre near his, and he has lavished every manner of gift upon her. Others flock to her, knowing she has the ear of the king, and influence to match. What is a taboret beside that? Those close to His Majesty swear she has bewitched him as much with her wit as with her body. Ah, she has such power here at Court!"

Such power at Court. I tried to imagine what that would be like, to take my place in a magnificent room and know that every eye was upon me. This, then, was what all my peers among the maids of honor wished most ardently for themselves. Was the love of a king that different from the regard of ordinary men?

"Her child," I asked, feeling bold indeed to speak of such matters. "Is His Majesty the father?"

Gabrielle laughed wickedly behind her fan. "His Majesty believes he is, which makes it so, even if it is not. I doubt the marquise knows for certain herself. But consider the good fortune of her bastard child, to be owned by the king, granted a title and an income at birth!"

I considered the two empty armchairs near the marquise's taboret. "What of the queen? How does she bear to have her husband's mistress so near?"

Gabrielle shrugged. "It is not her right to object to His Majesty's wishes. After Montespan left Madame's household, His Majesty made her a lady-in-waiting to the queen. If Her Majesty accepted her husband's mistress as one of her attendants, then she will hardy object to having the marquise here tonight. Besides, what would the queen earn for herself by protesting? The king would not alter his wishes, and displeasing him is always unwise, even for the queen."

Just then, Madame turned in her chair, beckoning to me to join her. "Madame de Keroualle?"

"Yes, Madame." I shared a final glance with Gabrielle, who in that wordless instant made it clear that she was both surprised and chagrined by the duchess's favor toward me. I slipped my way among the other attendants to curtsy beside Madame's chair.

"There you are." Her smile was both welcoming and weary as she looked up to me. "Stay by me, mademoiselle. Your company pleases me."

As I began to murmur my thanks, I saw her gaze slide past me, and distress flicker through her eyes. Only a moment, and then it was gone, swallowed once again within her, but I saw it still. Instinctively I turned to discover what had affected her.

Monsieur had entered the gallery and was making his way to the front of the room, moving slowly among the others as he paused to greet friends and laugh with them. He was even more sumptuously dressed than when I'd seen him earlier, and he'd exchanged his wig, too, for one that had multicolored bows tied to ends of every lovelock. In the crook of one arm he carried a tiny white dog with matching ribbons tied into the fur of his trailing ears, while his other hand was tucked familiarly in that of another gentleman: Philippe de Lorraine-Armagnac, the infamous Chevalier de Lorraine. This man was as beautiful as an angel in face and form, and would have merited the sighs of a thousand ladies, save that he was painted and garbed with the same decorative luxury as Monsieur himself.

I'd never seen such a couple, nor one so open regarding their tastes and perversions. Yet knowing what I did about Monsieur and how he'd treated Madame, I watched him with his favorite and saw not his frivolity, but his menace. When he chose to sit on the farthest chair on the other side of the room instead of his place beside his wife, I shared Madame's obvious relief to have him safely at a distance.

"How pretty your hair looks dressed that way, mademoiselle," Madame said to me, her smile at once more relaxed. "The fashion becomes you."

I began to thank her, but before I could, a servant announced the arrival of the king. At once the entire company rose with a rustle of silk and a murmur of voices. Eager for my first glimpse of His Majesty, I rose up on my toes and craned my neck, striving to peek over the heads of the others. Though I couldn't yet see the king, I knew when he entered the gallery, for as soon as those near the door spied him, every gentleman bowed and every lady sank into her deepest curtsy, the motion spreading through the gallery with the rolling inevitability of an ocean wave.

Even Madame rose from her chair to curtsy, for though she was the king's first cousin with the blood of two countries' royalty in her veins, she was still his inferior. Of course I curtsied, too, and stayed low, waiting to be guided by Madame's actions. My heart raced with excitement as I heard the footsteps coming closer. At last, at last, I was to be in the presence of His Most Christian Majesty!

Even with my head bowed low, I could roll my gaze forward to look before me. First I saw before me a pair of the most elegant gentleman's shoes imaginable: golden leather with a squared toe, the high red heels that only the nobility were entitled to wear, tiny buckles sparkling with brilliants on the tongue, and then scarlet stockings embroidered with gold clocks at the ankles. The feet in the golden leather were large, the calves in the red silk muscular, the legs of a rider. Beside them was the ferrule of an ebony walking stick, clearly employed for effect, not for support, and perhaps even as a substitute for a scepter.

"Good evening, Madame," the king said, his voice solemn and polite. I was surprised he greeted her with such formality, considering they were family through both blood and marriage. But then he was the King of France, and she was only the duchesse d'Orleans, and I—I was so humbly born in comparison that I'd no right to judge either. "We are pleased you have joined us."

"Thank you, Your Majesty," Madame said softly, and I could hear the smile and the warmth in her voice for him. She stood upright beside me, her skirts slipping from her hands, and when all the other ladies around me began to rise, I rose, too.

"Who is this lady?" he asked, and with a start I realized he meant me. "Your new maid of honor?"

Quickly Madame introduced me as I curtsied again. "Mademoiselle's father has always been most loyal to Your Majesty, and served in your army. Further, her family offered comfort to the English refugees who supported my father and brother, with special tenderness for those who espoused the True Faith."

"We are grateful they have shared her with us," he said, and smiled. "Welcome, mademoiselle."

"I—I am honored, Your Majesty," I stammered. "Most honored."

I shouldn't have been startled to find His Majesty regarding me with interest. I was young and knew I was considered beautiful enough that even my country-fashion gown would not completely disguise me. I was a member of Madame's household, and I knew that had been the nursery bed for at least two of his mistresses. Also, and perhaps of most importance to the king, I was new to the palace, and it was widely understood that His Majesty distrusted strangers.

In turn I studied him, too. I'd heard so much of him—of his comeliness, his grace and manners, his absolute manly perfection—that I doubt I could have refrained from considering him even if I'd been ordered not to. I was eighteen, and he was my king.

And what did I see? A gentleman slightly over moderate height in the full glory of his manhood (he was then only just thirty years of age), dressed with splendor like the monarch he was, from the toes of those golden shoes to the top of his cocked black beaver hat, trimmed with a veritable crown of scarlet plumes. His wig was lush and long and very black, though I guessed that was likewise the color of the hair nature had granted him, matching his brows and slender mustache. His nose was long and narrow, his chin dimpled and full, and his mouth was poised in a half smile of constant pleasantry.

Yet as much as I was prepared to be impressed by the king's personal glory and magnificence, I was . . . disappointed. His expression was too careful, too reserved, without the emotion or passion that would bring his face to life. His elegantly almond-shaped eyes were shrewd rather than intelligent, and bright with ambition, but they shone with very little kindness.

I did not judge him handsome at all.

"You always choose the fairest flowers for your own, don't you, Madame?" he said, tapping his walking stick lightly on the floor as she smiled at me. "Please Her Highness, mademoiselle, and thus you will please us."

"Yes, Your Majesty," I said, but he was already turning away to join Monsieur and Madame du Montespan, and the empty chair that would, it seemed, be left unoccupied by the queen. Already I knew there would never be a handkerchief dropped before me, and the secret relief that came with that knowledge was boundless.

Beside me Madame watched him, her face as carefully composed as his had been toward her, the face of royalty at Court. Yet in her eyes, I saw the truth.

She loved him. Not as the brother of her husband, not as her king, but as the man she could never have. My poor English princess! I understood much now, and in my inexperience, I thought I understood everything.

I was wrong. Sadly, sadly wrong.

Chapter Four

The first snow of the season had fallen in the night, just enough to cover Paris with the most delicate veiling of white, like a confection feathered with sugar. It was hardly enough to keep Madame from her morning walk, and as soon as she was sufficiently fortified against the cold—fortifications that included layers of woolen petticoats and kerchiefs, a cloak and gloves lined in fur and a muff as well, for the princess, being so thin, felt any chill most grievously—we stepped out into the palace's gardens, and the bright morning sun.

"A beautiful day, Louise, isn't it?" Madame said, breathing deeply of the icy air. "I cannot fathom why anyone would wish to lie abed by choice on a morning such as this."

"Nor can I, Madame," I said, glad to be outside and away from the too-close quarters of my shared lodgings as well. The gardens behind the Palais-Royal were the princess's favorite place in Paris, and she lavished much time on her gardeners planning the beds and bushes. She claimed that this interest came from her English blood, that all people from Great Britain loved their gardens, though I doubted that so rough and wild a country ever produced a garden as precise and formal and overwhelmingly *French* as one belonging to the Palais-Royal.

"Mark this, Louise: the air's so cold, it shows my breath." To prove it, she puffed up her cheeks and slowly blew out, making a small cloud before her face like one of the four winds cartographers draw on the corners of maps.

I laughed, pleased to see how my breath, too, showed before me. I was the only maid of honor who chose to rise early with our mistress (who, with her usual kindness, did not make these walks a requirement for her ladies), and I'd left them all still noisily asleep, snuffling and mumbling with their hair tied in rags to curl and their faces slick with various potions designed to enhance their beauty. Being country-bred near the sea, I believed my skin benefited far more from walking out-of-doors than from any foul-smelling unguents, the most popular one at that time being distilled from the piss of small dogs.

For all the suffering Madame had endured in her life, she was still but twenty-five, and liked to set a brisk pace. Her other two constant ladies-in-waiting were older, and perfectly content to let me be the one who squired Madame between the clipped hedges and parterres.

But there was more than rosy cheeks to these walks with Madame. As we walked side by side, the princess began to confide in me as a trusted companion, and spoke to me of whatever filled her head. Part of her love for her gardens was because of their vast size, and the certainty that this was the one place she'd not be overheard by her husband's spies, and thus I was told many things of a most private nature. I heard more of Monsieur's infidelities and barbarous treatment of her, of how she'd wept when Louis had wed not her, but a Spanish princess; and how wounded she'd been when not once, but twice, he'd taken her maids of honor for new lovers.

I won't claim that I contrived this familiarity. I was only eighteen, and I hadn't yet curried my cleverness to that extent, or my ambition, either. I was lonely, and Madame was kind to me. In the beginning, it was as simple, and as complicated, as that.

But her tales saddened me no end, for I had come to love her not just as a mistress, but for her own sweet self. To see her treated so ill, with no recourse, was a sorry thing indeed. Who would have guessed that the life of a royal princess could be so unhappy?

There were but two topics that served to raise her spirits. The first (albeit the less interesting to me) was her daughter, Marie-Louise, six years of age and the only one of several infants to have survived. The second was far more fascinating: her oldest brother, Charles Stuart, the English king.

To hear Madame describe him, Charles was everything in both a king and a man that Louis was not: generous, charming, witty, and impulsive. Both cousins had suffered as impressionable boys at the hands of their subjects, surviving civil wars and injustices that had threatened their thrones. The uncertainty of the Fronde had made Louis innately suspicious of Paris and determined to rule implacably and at a distance from his people, while the far greater sufferings of Charles—the beheading of his father, King Charles I, the scattering of his mother and brothers and sisters while he likewise was in exile, a wandering decade in poverty unbecoming to any prince—seemed to have done the opposite.

In Madame's telling, her brother walked through the streets and parks of London with an astonishing ease, speaking to any man as he pleased. He attended the public playhouses, drank beside sailors in taverns, rode his own horses in races, and swam naked in the Thames River for all the world to see. With a sister's pride, she claimed him to be as tall as a giant and as handsome as Adonis, though with a nonchalance in his attire that made her despair. I longed to meet such a royal paragon, and when at last I confessed my desire to the duchess, she'd winked merrily, and vowed she'd do her best to make my wish come true.

Bereft of her husband's love in her life, she had turned her passion to making an alliance between France and England, and between Louis and her brother. If those two and their armies could join together against the Dutch, then there'd be a real chance of negotiating a lasting peace among them, and an end to the costly small wars that had been waged for twenty years and more.

There were many more fine points and subtleties of diplomacy to this plan, of course, many concessions back and forth that were not shared with me. But the one feature dearest to Madame's heart was also the one most likely both to infuriate and terrify the English, and that was for Charles to renounce his Protestant beliefs and embrace instead the Catholic faith of their mother. She wished for an alliance between England and France based not just on shared politics, but on faith, joined together against the hated Protestant Dutch. If the King of England could be drawn back to the True Church, then surely his nation would follow. To sweeten the prospect, Louis was offering a substantial amount of gold to Charles as well, a gift that Charles, who was perpetually impoverished (a curious situation for a king, but then English kings were forced to rely upon the largesse of their Parliament), could scarce afford to ignore.

Could there be a more glorious, more noble, more worthy design? Madame longed for this, prayed for it every day. I understood, and prayed with her. The final success would come down to the two kings, the two cousins, with this single young lady as a bridge between them.

This, too, Madame confessed to me in the garden, with such giddy pride and excitement that I came to believe in her powers, too. Monsieur might mock her ambition, but Louis trusted Madame far more than he did his waspish brother. Declining a secretary for such delicate correspondence, she sat at her desk each day and herself wrote feverishly long letters to both kings, letters that were sent only by the most trusted of couriers. Sometimes Louis himself visited her in her rooms, the two of them locked away to plot and plan (and whatever else they wished, too, I suppose), exactly as Monsieur most dreaded.

I could only guess at the contents of these letters—she did keep that to herself—but I knew that her dearest hope was to be a part of the final negotiations in person, in England. Not even Monsieur would be able to keep her back. She hadn't seen her brother since before her marriage, and a reunion on English soil was now her fondest dream.

And yes: by the time she finally would make that journey, I planned to be so indispensable to her that I'd be sure to be brought along, too. I'd ambition enough for that.

I ran my hand along the edge of a low wall, gathering up a mitten full of snow. Though it was too dry and light to pack into a ball to toss, I still could throw it up into the air to make my own private snowfall, and I laughed with cheery delight as the tiny crystals sparkled in the sunlight around me.

"Here, Madame, here," I called, scooping up more snow into my hands. "I'll do the same for you, if you wish."

Madame laughed, but held her oversized beaver muff up before her face to shield it. "No, Louise, I beg you, don't!"

She caught up her petticoats with one hand and began to run down the next path and away from me, her hood flopping back over her shoulders and her dark curls bobbing. This I took as invitation enough to chase her, laughing still with my hands filled with the snow.

"Wait, Madame, you've forgotten something," I called gaily, laughing so hard my words could scarce be understood. "Here, Madame, here, a most luscious favor for you!"

Yet just as I came within reach, she stopped abruptly, pressing one hand to her side. Her eyes were squeezed shut, her mouth open as if in pain.

"Madame, what is wrong?" I let the snow drop from my hands and swiftly went to take her by the arm and guide her to the nearest bench, sweeping the snow away now with a purpose beyond frivolous play. "Are you unwell? Sit, if you please, and I'll go fetch—"

"No, Louise, stay with me." Her voice wavered unsteadily, and she sucked in a deep breath, then another, before she finally opened her eyes again. "I didn't mean to frighten you. I—I was laced too tightly, that was all, and my busk felt as if it were pressing the very air from me."

"Then let me go—"

"Stay," she said, taking my hand and linking her fingers into mine to make sure I didn't leave. "That is, please stay with me. Please. I'll be better in a moment."

We sat together, and I watched her anxiously, wishing the color would return to her cheeks. I'd seen for myself that Madame's health was fragile at best. Because she was as delicate as a songbird, her bones were apparent through her flesh, her translucent skin stretched so tautly over them that it was possible to see her lifeblood beat within her veins. I was convinced that only her determinedly bright spirit kept her from failing, as any other woman would.

To see Madame falter like this made me recall the grim whispered portents I'd heard, predicting an early death for her. Four older sisters of hers had already died young, claimed well before their time. She was the last of the Stuart princesses, and I prayed Madame would not be soon to join them.

"Are you certain you are well, Madame?" I asked again. "You are sure?"

"I am." Her fingers tightened around mine, though from gratitude or pain, I could not say. "Besides, I can't be ill today. I've finally agreed to receive that wretched Duke of Buckingham, and if I don't, he'll go back to Charles with all manner of tales about how ill I am."

She forced herself to smile, more a grimace. "And I won't have that, Louise. Buckingham has always been a charming dissembler on his own without me supplying him with any further falsehoods."

"He's the ginger-haired Englishman, isn't he?" I asked, deciding to follow her lead to other subjects, and let my concern for her health pass. I'd seen the Duke of Buckingham both at the Palais-Royal and at the Louvre, one of many highborn Englishmen who presented themselves to Louis while visiting Paris. I'd remembered him because he reminded me of a fox. It wasn't just the color of his hair or the small pointed beard he affected. He'd a sly, glib air of superiority, as if he believed himself to be a thousand times more clever than these dullard French, and it was not pleasant. "The one who thinks so highly of himself?"

"The same," she said, her expression showing both her disdain and dislike. "That gentleman has plagued me all my life, Louise. Even now his sister is a lady-in-waiting to my mother, and the pair of them cannot be avoided here in Paris. Our fathers were friends, and he was as good as raised as another brother with my own. Surely Charles treats him so. But, fa, what a cuckoo he's been in our family's nest! Over and over again, Buckingham behaves with no regard to the laws of men or God, and again and again my brother will forgive him."

"I do not believe the duke finds much favor at our Court," I ventured with care. It was one thing to listen to her opinions of these royal folk, for to her, they were no more than any other vexing family members. But for me to speak with the same familiarity of these kings and dukes would be presumptuous, even treasonous. "His Majesty receives him, but not with any warmth."

"Nor should he!" she exclaimed, her vehemence finally restoring the color to her cheeks. "Would you believe that he once professed a violent passion for me, all for the sake of furthering himself? He was a member of the English party that accompanied me to France for my wedding to Monsieur, and he returned the honor by attempting to seduce me, and claim me as his own. His foolishness not only dishonored me and my brother, but Monsieur, too, until Louis finally packed him back to England. You can imagine the scandal, Louise. But that is how it's always been with Buckingham. He's a low, conniving rascal, and he never will change."

She clicked her tongue with disgust, and leaned back against the back of the bench. "The last time he was here in Paris, the winter before you came to Court, Louise, he'd had to flee England yet again on account of murdering another peer."

"Murder?" I gasped, for even among jaded courtiers, murder was still regarded as a mortal sin.

"Exactly," Madame said, her eyes widening with indignation. "He had abandoned his own wife to conduct a most despicable intrigue with the Countess of Shrewsbury, and when at last her poor husband challenged Buckingham to a duel, Buckingham murdered him."

"But it's not murder in a duel, is it?"

"It is when the cuckolded earl is known to be a bumbler with a sword, and when the duke is as good as a master," she said. "A low, shameful affair all around, made worse by my brother's pardon."

This surprised me even more than the crime itself. Madame seldom admitted any faults in her older brother, yet this was a large one indeed. For a king to be so loyal to so undeserving a friend: that was a revelation.

"And now this—this *rogue* of a duke dares come to me pretending friendship and compliments, as if I were still a callow girl of fifteen," continued Madame. "I am certain he wishes to usurp the confidence Louis places in me, and claim it as his own to my brother."

"You must not let him, Madame," I said, sharing her outrage. "You must not! You must hold firm. You've toiled too hard to do otherwise."

"But how?" she asked, throwing up her gloved hands with despair. "Buckingham is a wickedly clever man, able to insinuate himself into another's good favor at will. How can I stop such a man who always has my brother's ear?"

"Because you have his heart, Madame, and his blood," I said, my enthusiasm giving me the courage to speak boldly. "His Majesty may forgive this friend of his, but he trusts you as no other. Admit His Grace, receive him, and play the cordial lady that you are. Let him prattle on about himself, as gentlemen always do, and let him believe you share his own lofty opinions of his merit and designs. Let him fill the room with his puffery, but offer no words of value in return. Not a one."

"But when he asks me of the alliance—"

"Then you say nothing, Madame," I said firmly. "If he tries to beguile you with empty flattery, then turn his words about, and ask him his views as if they were the grandest things under heaven. If he's as vainglorious as you say, then that should be enough to divert him."

She did not answer at first, making me worry that I'd overspoken. She sighed, and looked down at the bench on which we sat, absently tracing circles in the dust of snow with her fingertip.

"You are right, Louise," she said finally. "There is nothing Buckingham prefers to the sound of his own voice."

"Then let him hear it, Madame," I said gently. "You've labored far too hard to let him or anyone else take this from you."

She smiled at me, her eyes squinting a bit against the brightness of the snowy morning. "You've become a wise lady, Louise. You've learned much since you've joined our household."

"Thank you, Madame," I said, pleased beyond measure by her praise. "But it is you who should take the credit, as my generous teacher."

"Oh, it's not to my credit," she said. "It's the Court that's changed you, not I."

It was true. I had changed in the six weeks since I'd come to Court, because I'd no choice left to me to do otherwise. I'd learned much since I'd traded my parents' château for the Palais-Royal, and most of those lessons had not been easy.

I'd learned that the role of a virtuous lady is perhaps the most lonely one of all at Court. When I refused to be led by gentlemen into darkened hallways or gardens to be kissed and fondled and worse, they ceased asking me to dance as well. Without either a fat dowry or a taste for flirtation, I'd become as good as invisible among the scores of other well-bred young ladies at Court. I'd no gift for singing or playing a guitar or harp to set me apart, or wit enough to make my jests repeated, the way Madame du Montespan's were. I was too shy for the elegant conversations of Madame de Sevigne, and too unschooled to discourse on books or plays, the way that Madame's good friend, the Comtesse de La Fayette, did with such seeming ease. Among the galleries of the Louvre, I wasn't even considered beautiful, not when His Majesty's tastes for ladies with golden hair and wide blue eyes had made my own too-contrary appearance woefully out of fashion.

What talents I discovered I did possess were not as apparent, but perhaps even more valuable. Because I was so often unnoticed, I found I could watch and listen to others undisturbed. In this way, I acquired the graceful skills of a lady of the French Court, from how to eat with the daintiest of bites, employing the table forks that were newly imported from Italy, to gliding down a staircase without looking at my feet. Because my convent education had been that of most well-bred girls in the country—to say my prayers demurely, and little more—I now sought to improve myself by reading the books Madame suggested from her library. In silent awe, I listened to the gifted and educated people who gathered about her at the Palais-Royal—playwrights like Racine and Molière, the poet La Fontaine, the soldier and writer the duc de La Rochefoucauld—and came to appreciate their words and thoughts.

But far more importantly, I learned to discern which people at

Court were of influence and why, and which could be ignored as pow-
erless. I learned all I could of the politics of the day, not only to understand Madame's conversation, but also that I might one day further
my own ambitions. For that was the single greatest thing I'd learned
at Court: that my success here would not depend on my securing a
wealthy husband, but rather on how well I twined myself into the life
of this slender English princess sitting on the bench beside me.

"I have every faith in you, Madame," I said gently, "and so does
your brother. I would not worry overmuch about the Duke of Buckingham. He may be your brother's friend, but you are and always will
be his sister."

"That is true," she said, but there was something wistful and sad
about how she gazed not at me, but out at her dormant garden, the
flower beds empty and the roses cut back and shrouded for the winter.

"Yes, Madame," I said, striving to cheer her. "And consider how
joyful a reunion you'll have with your brother next summer, and what
a glorious celebration he'll have waiting for you in London."

"London," she repeated, making the word sound hollow and
bleak. She drew her cloak more closely about her arms and hunched
her shoulders. "I'll tell you my small secret now, Louise, since in this
place it will not be a secret much longer. There will be no visit to my
brother next summer."

"How is that, Madame?" I asked with surprise. "His Majesty himself has sworn to you that—"

"This is no affair of His Majesty's." Her smile held all the bleak-
ness of a broken heart behind it. "Monsieur will have his way, exactly
as he wished it. What say does a wife have in such matters?"

I shook my head. "Forgive me, Madame, but I don't understand."

"Oh, Louise," she said softly. "I'm two months with Monsieur's
child, and pray to the Holy Mother that it's a son."

The news of Madame's pregnancy was greeted with much interest at
the Court. Despite the fact that Louis and his queen, Therese, had
been wed ten years, she'd given him only a single surviving son, the

dauphin. Monsieur remained second in line for his brother's throne, and if the child that Madame now carried proved a son, then he would become third, a significant inheritance waiting for an unborn infant.

Madame's mother, the frail Dowager Queen of England, who now devoted her fading life to holy reflection at her château at Colombes, immediately promised to have more prayers said to vouchsafe her good health and safe delivery. Blessed with a pious mother myself, I wept with Madame when she learned of her mother's good wishes, and together we sent up prayers for that aged lady's swift recovery from her own ills.

Monsieur appeared more disgusted than joyful, and with his usual callousness, expressed the hope that Madame would not die in childbirth—always a risk—and cause him to lose this important link to her brother. Louis in turn understood entirely that this child had been begotten not from love, but malice, and if he'd any doubt of his brother's intentions, Monsieur made it clear, cackling gleefully about the Court like a painted bantam rooster, and boasting of how he had stopped the intriguing of two kings and his wife, through the skill of his lovemaking alone.

In private his treatment of Madame became far worse. He gloried in her humiliation, alternating between spiteful gloating and the vilest of oaths to swear he would keep her perpetually pregnant rather than let her go to Charles. He taunted her with the Chevalier du Lorraine, kissing his favorite's fingertips and slipping sweetmeats into the other man's mouth while we were all together at table. He mocked Madame's thickening body as repulsive to him, and we berated her until she wept. In his cruel arrogance, Monsieur didn't bother to dismiss Madame's attendants before he attacked her, and we huddled together with shared misery, forced to sit by as silent witnesses. Yet because he was Madame's husband, he was by law free to treat her however he pleased, and no one, not even His Majesty, could come to her rescue.

The only one who showed true sympathy for Madame's plight was, as always, her brother Charles. In an outpouring of solicitude, he sent rare delicacies to tempt her appetite and cordials to build her strength, and even a beautifully extravagant barge for the river, lined in blue velvet and embroidered with gold, to keep her from walking overmuch: so delicious a plaything that Louis's queen begged to borrow it for her own use. Every courier from England brought another letter from him urging her to be mindful of her welfare, for the sake of herself as well as her child.

"Oh, mark this part, Louise," she said gleefully to me one morning, reading Charles's latest missive whilst still in her bed. Our early-morning walks had ended for now on account of her pregnancy and her increasing weakness, and after a late night of the mandatory grand suppers, fetes, ballets, gaming, masquerades, balls, concerts, and other entertainments sponsored by the king, it was not uncommon for the princess to lie abed until noon the following day.

"My brother's bound to be my nursemaid," she continued, "as well as my midwife and my cook. He's written as much here: 'For God's sake have a care of your diet, and believe the plainer your diet is, the better health you will have.' Ha, he's ordering that because he does not approve of me having chocolate and biscuits for my breakfast."

Purposefully she sipped that same forbidden brew from the tiny porcelain cup in her fingers, widening her eyes to me through the fragrant steam like a naughty child who is willfully disobedient. With her hair in a single plait and no paint on her face, she looked much younger, or at least closer to her true age of twenty-five.

"His Majesty wishes you well, Madame," I said. "I would doubt he truly cares overmuch what you eat or drink, so long as it benefits you and the babe."

"Oh, he cares, Louise," she said, looking back again to the letter. "He cares because he fears that chocolate and biscuits are too French, and therefore somehow grossly inferior to whatever it is that sturdy English goodwives use to greet the day."

I frowned, unsure of exactly what an English goodwife fed her family. "What *do* they eat? All I have heard is that the English dine exclusively upon roasts of beef and suet puddings, but His Majesty cannot mean for you to have that, not for breakfast."

"Not the roasted beef part, no," she admitted. "But what does this say of his low regard for French food? 'Above all, my dear Minette, have a care of strong broths and gravy in the morning, and avoid them all.' Strong broths and gravy in the morning? Oh, my darling broody hen of a brother!"

She began to laugh, but almost at once shifted into tears and pressed the letter to her heart, too overwhelmed by his love to do more.

It was often this way when his letters arrived. They were filled with such brotherly devotion and concern for the well-being of his dear Minette (for that had always been his pet name for Madame) that she read them aloud to me, often sinking into a melancholy humor before she was done. Despite her tears, her brother's words gave her courage, and more resolve than ever to push forward with the alliance.

And what did I make of the English king's letters? I was, of course, an audience by reason of my place, and not one by choice. The letters had not been written to me, nor had I any direct acquaintance with their author. They were peppered with little endearments and jests that had meaning only between the two royal siblings. But the more I heard of them, the more I came to feel as if I knew Madame's brother myself. For a king, he wrote with surprising informality, his letters written as his thoughts came to him, without a secretary's polishing. There was frank immediacy to his correspondence, an easy charm devoid of empty gallantry, and a wry wit that he didn't mind turning shockingly in his own direction, especially on the infrequent occasions when his sister had gently chastised him over some slight fault or error of judgment.

"If you were as well acquainted with a little fantastical gentleman called Cupid as I am," he wrote when she'd dared to question his ever-varying taste in mistresses, "then you would neither wonder nor take ill any sudden changes which do happen in the affairs of his conducting."

A little fantastical gentleman called Cupid: how I liked that turn of phrase! If the letters to Madame reflected the man who'd written them (and I'd no reason to believe they didn't), then surely I was beguiled, without so much as a smile exchanged between us.

I was eighteen, and ripe for love as all girls that age are. At Court I was surrounded with love and intrigue of every kind, and each night I listened to the breathless, giggling whispers of my fellow maids as they recounted their amorous adventures. I'd yet to attract a suitor of my own, and it was impossible in that Court not to long for love. Was it any wonder, then, that my fancy was drawn to Madame's brother, at once infinitely desirable, yet so distant and unattainable that my girlish dreams could run safely free and without consequence?

I took to studying the many portraits of Charles Stuart that adorned Madame's rooms, searching for more of the man in the letters. I saw a dark, handsome man in his prime, tall and lean, with melancholy dark eyes and a sensual mouth, a man who, in nearly every picture, looked as if he'd much rather be off doing something more exciting than posing. I liked that, especially after the rigidity that Louis imposed upon his Court. Whether he was a king or not, I secretly concluded that Charles's company must be more deliciously enjoyable than that of any other gentleman I'd ever met.

Unwittingly Madame fed this fascination of mine each time she praised her brother, or recounted some small amusing anecdote about him. I even listened to the stories of his rampant infidelities, and the countless women, highborn and low, who were said to pass through his bed. I was undaunted, even if the stories painted Charles as an English libertine-sultan with a harem of lolling beauties.

Louis had mistresses, too. Truly, what monarch didn't? For Louis, love was another war to be waged and won, with his mistresses only more trophies to display at Versailles as beautiful tribute of his conquests. He was even more brutally unsentimental with the less celebrated women he claimed for easing himself; we'd all heard his oft-repeated judgment of one such hapless lady, how he'd used her like a post-horse, mounted once, ridden hard, and never seen again.

But Madame's brother sounded different. To judge from her stories, Charles relished and delighted in his women, and treated love as a dance meant to please both partners.

Like so many innocents (and other women who should have known better), I believed Charles simply had yet to find a lasting love, a love that was worthy of him. I didn't quite dare to believe I might be that one, but each time Madame spoke of her brother, I let my too-idle fancy imagine myself in his company. I listened, and remembered, and just as she did, I prayed for the day when my life might cross with that of the King of England.

I'd not yet found the rich husband who had been my main purpose in coming to Court, but by the end of the year, I did have two other successes to my credit. Louis took note of my devotion to Madame, and rewarded me accordingly. After the fashion of Court, the reward was not granted directly to me, but to those I'd wished to favor.

Thus my old patron, the Duc de Beaufort, was made leader of a French expedition to help defend the distant island of Candia, currently under siege by the Turks. Though seemingly of little use to France, the king held this campaign in high regard, both because he had been begged by the Doge of Venice for aid (for there were few things that Louis enjoyed more than having another king or leader indebted to him), and because, as a dutiful Catholic ruler, he wished to defend a Christian stronghold against the infidel Turks, much as his ancestors had done long ago during the crusades to the Holy Land.

The command was a plum post for the duc, and he was pleased to see his early belief in me so swiftly rewarded. But there was more. My brother, Sebastien, was likewise granted a place in the campaign on the duc's staff, a most desired position of honor for one so young. My parents were duly impressed by my influence, and though they still wished for me to produce a suitable husband, they were proud that I'd achieved so much in so little time.

So was I. It was my first taste of patronage, received and given, and it would not be the last.

Chapter Five

"So you, then, are Lord Rochester." Wrapped in furs against the midwinter cold, Madame was sitting close to the fire in her parlor, with the rest of us attendants gathered around her and as close to the fire's warmth as we, too, could be. She glanced from the newly opened letter of introduction in her hand to the gentleman standing before her.

Nearly every Englishman of rank visiting Paris came to call upon the English duchesse d'Orleans; it would be uncivil (and impolitic) not to. Madame in turn was famous for her hospitality, and for a company that was generally less restrained and more entertaining than that to be found at the Louvre or Versailles. On account of her kind nature (as well as her desire to please her brother), no Englishman was turned away, though there were doubtless ones to whom she wished she could bar her door. She adored her nephew James, Duke of Monmouth, an early by-blow of her brother's now grown to handsome, if somewhat foolish, maturity, and I'd heard that there had once been some sort of careless flirtation (for though only five years separated them, they were by blood aunt and nephew) between them that had raised Monsieur's ire at the time. But Madame did not trust Ralph Montagu, the English ambassador to France, any more than she did the Duke of Buckingham. Now that the Earl of Rochester stood at her door, we'd all soon see where he would rank in Madame's estimation.

"I welcome you to Paris, my lord," she said, holding out her small-boned hand for him to kiss, "both as a fellow Englishman and as a dear friend of my brother."

A friend of the king, I thought, and eagerly I leaned to one side to look past the stiffened curls of the lady-in-waiting who blocked my view.

The Earl of Rochester was younger than I'd expected, of an age with me, yet already he had that worldly confidence and ease that seemed to be a mark of Charles's courtiers. Unlike most of the other young English lords, however, he was much better dressed, in a long dark green coat, fawn-colored boots, and a striking red waistcoat that must have come from the needle of a Parisian tailor. He was tall and dashing in his figure as well, and I'd venture he'd be skilled with the elegant sword he wore slung from a yellow sash at his waist.

Yet though he was a handsome fellow, almost prettily so, there was a cloudiness to his eyes and cheeks that hinted at a surfeit of debauchery, and put me on my guard. The English Court was said to be a wild, licentious place, and surely this earl, however young, already bore the look of having participated too freely in its pleasures.

With a dancer's grace, he now bowed low over his leg, sweeping his wide-brimmed plumed hat to one side as he kissed the back of Madame's hand. "I am your most humble of servants, Madame. You honor me with your generosity and your kindness."

He spoke perfect French, without a hint of the thudding accent of most other Englishmen. I was impressed, and so was Madame.

"According to His Majesty my brother," she said, "we should be the ones honored by your presence, Lord Rochester."

With a sigh, she withdrew her hand from his, showing a reluctance that would have fanned Monsieur's omnipresent jealousy, if he'd been there to see it. Then she raised her brother's letter of introduction and began to read aloud from it.

" 'Lord Rochester has chosen to take a little journey to Paris,' " she began, " 'and would not kiss your hands without a letter from me.' Well, then, you had your letter, and you had your kiss, didn't you?"

"I did, Madame," he said with a bemused half-smile that surely charmed every lady in the room. "And a most rapturous experience it was, I can assure you."

"You're a rogue," Madame said, laughing, and without a hint of true reprobation as she returned to her reading. " 'Pray use him'— meaning you, my lord—'as one I have a very good opinion of. You will find him not to want wit, and know that he did behave himself, in all the Dutch war, as well as any body, as a volunteer.' It would seem we should congratulate you as a hero, my lord."

"For the glory of England, Madame," he said. "Less a hero than a survivor."

There was an unconscious melancholy to his words that made me realize that while he had survived to be called a hero, a good many others—including others dear to him—had not been so fortunate. A sobering realization, that, yet also one that won him even more indulgence from us ladies, for his heartfelt modesty.

"So how does my brother?" Madame asked softly, easing the awkwardness. "Did you leave him well?"

"Oh, most fantastically well, Madame," he replied, his good humor restored. "I confess that this little journey of mine was of His Majesty's invention and not my own, but he did wish me Godspeed with a few days at Newmarket for the races."

Later we'd learn that the king's "invention" for the earl to leave England had been proposed as a kind of pardon, an alternative to him being imprisoned in the Tower of London. The earl's crime had been a grievous one, a drunken brawl to blows at the Dutch ambassador's table and in the presence of the king, yet Charles had mercifully (if impulsively) forgiven him: a tale that showed the peril of judging a gentleman on first appearance, especially one so charming as the earl.

"Oh, Newmarket," Madame said, her gaze rising toward the heavens. "How my brother does love his races! Tell me, did his horses win?"

"They almost always do," the earl said, "especially the ones he rides himself."

She made an anxious little exclamation. "Don't tell me that, I beg you! I cannot fathom why, after all my brother has suffered and survived, he would risk his very neck by playing the jockey on the back of some wretched nag!"

"Forgive me, Madame, I never intended to cause you distress," the earl said swiftly. "You know His Majesty is an excellent rider, as sure and strong as any Arab upon his desert barb."

"You're forgiven, Lord Rochester." Impatiently she waved away the ladies who hovered about her, wishing her to be more calm. "It's not you who vex me, but the rash behavior of my brother."

"Then let me speak of something else, I beg you," he said earnestly, and for the first time he looked as young as he must be. He might be able to coax a pardon from the king, but even he knew there'd be little forgiveness for upsetting the pregnant duchesse d'Orleans. "Of how the rebuilding of the city progresses, or the new plays this season, or—"

"Thank you, Lord Rochester, but my brother writes to me of all that," she said, then smiled winningly. "Tell me something of his Court, if you please, some scandalous scrap that he'd not tell me himself."

He raised one brow, his smile bemused as he considered a score of possibilities, no doubt each less suitable for polite ladies' ears than the one before. Yet as his smile grew, each of us polite ladies waited with eager, breathless anticipation, for who among us could resist news of a new scandal?

He tossed his hat lightly in his hand, making us wait, then leaned toward Madame. "Have you heard of Lady Castlemaine's latest gambit for attention?"

"I've not." Madame tipped her head to one side, indicating she was surprised, but most interested. This *was* scandalous, and most daring of Lord Rochester to mention. A thoroughly notorious lady, the Countess of Castlemaine had long been His Majesty's mistress, and had borne him many bastard children. "What has the sly creature done now?"

"She is my cousin, you know, through the Villiers, so she's few secrets from me," he said, teasing out his gossip. "Or from anyone else, for that matter."

"Indeed not!" exclaimed Madame, and when she laughed, we

all laughed, too. The scandals of Louis's Court were far too near for Madame to find much amusement in them, but the mischief at her brother's Court was another matter. There'd been a time when such frank talk of wicked folk would have shocked me, but no longer.

The earl leaned forward, as if in confidence. "They say that as the lady's corporal charms fade, she has resorted instead to flaunting her eternal soul for attention. She's begun private instruction with a priest, with the goal of converting to the Romish Church."

"But that is old tattle, my lord!" Madame scoffed, and rapped her knuckles on the arm of her chair to signify her disappointment. "I've heard that long ago, from Lord de Croissy. I suppose I should rejoice at another soul returned to the True Church, but that lady has proved herself so faithless in everything else that I cannot entirely believe her conversion."

"You are not alone, Madame," he said, and sighed for dramatic effect. "The French ambassador is famously knowledgeable, and famously willing to pay his sources, too. If I must compete with Lord de Croissy for fresh news for you, Madame, then I know I must fail. Unless you've not heard of the latest scheme of His Grace the Duke of Buckingham?"

"Buckingham?" Madame repeated, and though she smiled still, I sensed her instant uneasiness at the mention of His Grace. "What of Buckingham?"

"Not so much *of* him, Madame, as *from* him," he said. "Having observed His Majesty's interest in Lord Roos's divorce, Lord Buckingham has seized the opportunity, and is once again strongly pressing for the king to separate himself from the barren queen, and remarry."

"My brother would never treat Her Majesty so unjustly." Whether she did so consciously or not, Madame's hand crept over the small mound of her belly as if to protect the babe within. "It is hardly the poor queen's fault if she's not been blessed."

The earl smiled with wry sympathy, for to him this was just more idle gossip and speculation, and no more. "Buckingham would say that the security of the succession must come first, Madame. Last year he'd believed he'd even found a suitably virgin beauty in Lady Frances

Stewart, before she confounded them all and eloped with the Duke of Richmond. Quite the merry scandal that was, and I don't know who was made more angry by it, His Majesty or His Grace."

But Madame didn't care to hear of the elopement of Lady Frances, not when compared to the sorry treatment Buckingham proposed for the queen.

"It will not happen, Lord Rochester," she said firmly, reminding me (and likely everyone else) that she'd been born a king's daughter. "For my brother to put Her Majesty aside simply because Lord Buckingham wishes it, and sees some path to personal gain for himself— that is against the laws of not only England, but of God."

"But as the head of both the Anglican faith and the country, His Majesty can arrange matters to suit himself," the earl countered, still blithely unaware of how very personal this conversation was to Madame. "If His Majesty comes around to Buckingham's view, then he has the power to make it so."

"Lord Buckingham forgets that Her Majesty is Catholic, not Anglican," Madame said, doubtless thinking of how she, too, was a Catholic wife who had failed to produce the son her husband desired. "The queen will never agree to such a divorce, were my brother so cruel as to attempt it."

"Lord Buckingham would say that it is His Majesty's solemn responsibility to England to sire an heir to his throne, Madame," the earl said. "He would claim that the English people would much prefer a fertile Protestant queen to a barren Catholic one. He would say it, because he does. Being Buckingham, he tells it to His Majesty whenever he has his ear."

"Then I would remind Lord Buckingham that even my brother must answer to God, not to England." Suddenly Madame rose, catching us all by surprise as we belatedly stood with her. "Forgive me, Lord Rochester, but I find I am weary, and wish to rest."

Without another word, she swept from the room, leaving the bewildered earl. Her ladies followed, fluttering with concern. They believed she was retreating to her bedchamber to rest, and murmured all manner of solicitous suggestions and advice.

But I guessed otherwise, and I was right. As soon as her chamber door was closed, Madame was at her desk, writing to Louis, and to Charles.

"You see how cleverly the letter is devised," Madame said. "Monsieur Colbert de Croissy warned me that the Dutch raiders grow more bold all the time, and that I must needs take more care when writing to my brother."

She held out the packet for me to see: several letters from her, folded and sealed as usual. But this time a length of silk thread had been stitched through the center of the three letters, binding them together. At the end of the thread was tied a lead plumb that now swung gently back and forth in Madame's grasp.

"If the boat is boarded, then the courier will have my orders to toss the packet over the side," she said, tapping the plumb with her fingertip. "The weight will act as an anchor, and send my letters directly to the bottom of the Channel, and a good thing, too."

I nodded in agreement. While I was not privy to every detail in her letters, I did know that her role as an intermediary between the two kings had only increased in these last months. At her request, Charles had even sent her a code, known only to the two of them, to be used when writing back and forth regarding the alliance. She was wise to be cautious. Not only would the Dutch have wished to intercept her letters, but she feared the Duke of Buckingham, too, and with excellent cause.

She had repeated Rochester's troubling report to both kings, and both had rejected them in their way: Charles by soothing her and promising he'd no intention of divorcing his queen, and Louis by denouncing Buckingham as a liar and an ass. Yet neither king had rejected the duke outright, and Madame could see for herself that Louis still welcomed him as an amusing and useful guest at his Court. She did not exactly consider Buckingham to be an out-and-out enemy, at least not yet, but he would always put his own cause first and, further, disparage and belittle whatever she did as the work of a piddling woman: as sorry a testimony to the other ladies of his acquaintance as it was to his own conceit.

Now I watched as she wrapped the weighted thread around the letters, and tucked them away into her desk for safekeeping.

"That is very clever, Madame," I said, "and very wise, too. Will you be sending them by the ambassador's courier tomorrow?"

She shook her head and smiled proudly. "I've made other arrangements. Do you recall the Abbé Prignani?"

"The Italian cleric," I said, and no more. There was no forgetting a monk such as the abbé, who had come highly recommended to the French Court by the Electress of Bavaria. He was a member of the Theatines of Abruzzi in Italy, an order whose express mission was to combat the moral laxity encouraged by Protestantism, which explained why he'd become such a favorite of Madame's. But he was also extremely worldly, and given to the dark practices of alchemy and astrology, with more of a taste for the intrigues of foreign courts than for monastic seclusion and reflection. He was even credited with being able to foretell the future by casting horoscopes and following the pattern of the stars and moon. Surely he was more wizard than monk.

My mother, the most pious lady I knew, would not have approved.

"Yes, yes, that's the abbé." Madame nodded eagerly. "He'll be the one carrying my letters tomorrow, among other things. Ah, I do believe he is here now."

I rose to withdraw and leave her alone with the abbé, as had been her preference whenever he visited her.

"Don't leave, Louise, please," she said, motioning for me to remain. "I would that you remain."

I bowed my head, and stayed before my chair, as she'd bidden. I understood her purpose without any explanation. Ever since my first day in her household, when I'd inadvertently watched that terrible scene between her and Monsieur, she had asked me to attend her in certain private matters, such as this one. Just as on that first day, she wanted me to act as a witness, and prepare myself to recall it later, if needed. I guessed that she feared herself in danger, whether from her husband or from others. Peril was often the partner of those who played their lives on so grand a stage, whether by choice or by fate. Because Madame asked this of me, I did it, though it troubled me mightily.

The abbé joined us, a small man with heavy-lidded eyes that missed nothing, including my presence.

"You've come from His Majesty?" Madame asked him at once, with no civilities. "You understand what you are to do while in England?"

He glanced so pointedly in my direction that I blushed, but Madame impatiently waved away his objection.

"Mademoiselle de Keroualle remains by my wish," she said. "Now tell me. His Majesty explained your role?"

"His agents did, Madame," the monk said. "I have already accepted the invitation of His Grace the Duke of Monmouth, and will be his guest in London. While there, I am to insinuate myself into the good graces of His Majesty the English king, using whatever methods I judge best for the circumstances."

"Speak to him of chemistry and mathematical calculations," she urged. "He keeps a private closet at Whitehall for his laboratory experiments and studies, like some fusty old don."

Prignani bowed his thanks. "I will, Madame. I am to speak to His Majesty however I can, to persuade him to smile with favor on the French as allies."

"Yes, yes," she said eagerly, pressing her hands together over her belly. "And the rest, too."

"Of course, Madame," he murmured. "I am to counsel His Majesty in private about the True Faith, and all he would gain for himself and his soul by renouncing the folly of Martin Luther. I am also to explain to him how, as a king, he is responsible for the divine welfare of his people, and the holy magnificence he could achieve by returning all England to the Church."

"Exactly so." She sighed happily, sitting back in her chair. "Exactly."

He raised his hand, a curious mixture of regard and beneficent blessing. "I cannot thank you enough for the honor of your trust, Madame."

She smiled, and blushed with pleasure. "The honor comes from His Most Christian Majesty for accepting my suggestion," she demurred, "and not from me."

With Madame, everything was complicated like this, twisted back and forth and into itself like a silken knot without end. This little plot of hers involving Prignani was devised to assist both the kingdoms of England and France, yes, but also to preserve the greater Kingdom of Heaven by bringing the Church back to her native country. While she wished to bring both success and comfort to her dearest older brother and prove herself worthy of his love, her old affections for Louis were at play as well, and she longed to show him the strength of her devotion and fealty. Finally, she always looked for any way to vex Monsieur (this by feeding his jealousy regarding her and his brother), and to display her own political wisdom and acuity as a Stuart princess.

All of which I would present to any man fool enough to believe that diplomacy is too taxing for a woman's intellect, or that we've not the fortitude to manage the complexities of politics. Others gazed at Madame and saw only a slight, fragile lady of surpassing sweetness. I saw beyond to the strength and intelligence, and learned more from her than she, poor lady, would ever know.

"I understand that there is one more way I might oblige you, Madame," the abbé continued. "His Majesty's agent made mention of a special errand."

"There is." She retrieved the little packet of weighted letters from her desk and handed them to the abbé. "These are for His Majesty my brother the King of England. No one else must ever see them, ever. If you are challenged on your crossing, if there is so much of a glimpse of an unfriendly vessel on the horizon, then you must at once toss this over the side. Better to commit my words to the waves than to have them read by the wrong eyes."

"Yes, Madame, I understand entirely." He bowed, and tucked the letters into the leather pouch he'd carried with him. "You may rely on me to deliver these to His Majesty, and no other."

"It won't be an easy journey for you, abbé," she warned. "You'll learn soon enough. I fear that, from ignorance, most common Englishmen will despise anyone of our faith."

"God will give me strength, Madame," he murmured, making the sign of the cross.

"May He guide you throughout your travels," she answered fervently. Ready to bid him farewell, she awkwardly pushed herself from her chair, and I was quick to take her arm to steady her. She was five months gone now, and she'd weakened as the child within her grew, the heaviness making her clumsy and unbalanced.

"If you'll permit me, Madame, I also addressed that other matter you'd requested of me." He presented a folded sheet to Madame. "For the young lady, Madame."

"Of course!" Madame exclaimed. "How could I have forgotten? Mademoiselle, this is for you. I asked the abbé to cast your horoscope. I thought you might be amused to learn what the starry portents say of your future."

She passed the sheet to me, and I opened it slowly, not certain that I wished to know my life's future, or that foretelling it in this manner was entirely proper, either.

"Come, Louise, don't keep it to yourself," Madame said with all the eagerness I lacked. "Tell me what predictions the stars make for you."

With no choice, I forced myself to read it, scanning quickly first for ill tidings, then more slowly again, yet neither time did I find much sense to it.

"Forgive me, Madame, but it would seem to be more riddle than fortune," I said, offering the most succinct portions of the horoscope. "I'm to inspire great love yet also great hatred. I'm to become a duchess and the mother of a duke, but without ever being a wedded wife, as well as a queen among kings, but without a crown of my own. I don't begin to know what to make of that."

"Nor do I," Madame said, clearly disappointed. "That's no fortune at all."

"Such astrological contradictions are not uncommon, Madame," the abbé said solemnly. "There are the occasional birth dates that present a seeming puzzle, only to reveal their truths over time."

"I'm very sorry that Mademoiselle de Keroualle's was one of those," Madame said. "I'd wanted you to assure her she'd soon find a worthy gentleman who'd give her love and contentment in a happy marriage, not this foolishness about kings and great hatred."

"It's of no importance, Madame," I said gently. "Good fortune or foolish, I wouldn't worry overmuch on what the moon will predict for me."

Yet I could not put aside the curious words myself, turning them over and over in my thoughts as I tried to find their meaning. Still they made no sense, and at last I ordered myself to dismiss the abbé's horoscope as a testimony to idleness, the work of a flattering charlatan and no more.

Only later, much later, did I come to realize the truth in his words, for they were revealed in time to mean exactly what they said.

We all gave much thought to babies that spring. As Madame's time grew closer, her mood grew more somber as she focused her dwindling energy upon the coming babe. She was often in pain, and came to rely especially on costly potions drawn from Chinese poppy flowers to ease her suffering. Never strong, she feared the ordeal of childbirth, and did more to prepare her soul than in arranging matters for the child.

Because we maids of honor were all unwed and innocent (by rule if not by practice), we were not party to Madame's conferences with the midwives and surgeons, nor would we be included as witnesses to the actual birth. But among ourselves we spoke endlessly about whether the child would be the son everyone desired, or only another disappointing daughter.

There were other babies to discuss as well. In March Madame du Montespan had given birth to her first child by the king, a beautiful and robust daughter. It was all supposed to be a secret, of course, to preserve the dignity of the marquise's cuckolded husband, but everyone at Court knew the truth, just as we all knew the lady had been installed in a small, elegant (and convenient) house on the rue de l'Echelle, not far from the Tuileries. Louis was delighted with his new daughter. It had been nearly ten years since his queen had presented him with the dauphin, and his open impatience with that poor lady's efforts seemed to grow with this latest proof of his Bourbon virility.

Only his English cousin fared worse. Charles had likewise been wed for many years, but while the number of royal bastards blossomed at a rate distressing to Madame, the English queen's womb remained barren and empty, and the king without an heir. From Lord Rochester we learned that Charles had recently taken a most unsuitable woman for his latest mistress, a tawdry low actress named Nell Gwyn. Though Rochester declared her to be the most amusing little creature alive, Madame was horrified by how willingly her brother debased himself with such amusements. What a sorry waste of the royal seed, especially if it resulted in another woeful bastard instead of a noble Stuart princeling!

There was one more baby arriving in our world, too, one of less place in the world, perhaps, but of consequence to our household, and Madame's peace. I learned of it early one morning, that same spring.

"Do you hear that, Louise?" Gabrielle whispered to me from her bed.

It must have been soon after dawn, for I could hear the servants beginning their day in the hall outside. Our rooms were still dark: no one expected maids of honor to rise so early, especially after dancing at the Louvre the night before.

"She's been retching like that for at least a quarter of an hour," Gabrielle continued. "Surely she must be empty by now."

My thoughts still thick with sleep, I lifted my head from the pillow to listen. As Gabrielle had said, someone was being ill. I could hear the distinctive sound of vomit splashing into an earthenware chamber pot.

"Too much wine, whoever it is," I muttered, yawning. "Go back to sleep."

"No, no," Gabrielle insisted. "It's Françoise, and it's not wine that's making her sick. It's the bastard in her belly."

At once I was awake. For the haughty, beautiful Mademoiselle de Fiennes to have been trapped in her intrigues like this would be news indeed. When I'd first arrived at Court, she had been the most desired, and therefore the most powerful, of our little circle of maids of honor. Now, if she truly were with child, she was ruined. "Françoise? You are certain?"

"She's been sick like that every morning for the last week," Gabrielle whispered eagerly. "She's pale and poorly, too, if you'd but notice, and weeps over nothing. I'm sure of it."

The maid who'd been ill crawled back into her bed, unable to smother a small groan of misery and despair. I heard it and understood everything it signified, as likely did all the rest of us lying there in the dark. There would be no discreet house in a fashionable neighborhood for her, as there'd been for Athenaise du Montespan, no handsome allowance settled on her and her child. Françoise was ruined, in every sense. We'd no need to speculate who the father of her child might be, or wonder how he'd acknowledge his paternity. Sadly we all knew that, too. Two days later, the rest of the Court would know as well.

We were gathered around Madame in the front hall near the door, waiting for Monsieur and the Chevalier de Lorraine to join us before we climbed into the coaches that would convey us to the other palace for the evening. Weak and fearful of falling down the palais's many staircases, Madame had been carried down in an armchair supported by a pair of footmen. She was still swathed with her furs, too, no matter that the first sweetness of spring was in the evening air, and though she tried to be gay for our sakes, there was no mistaking the shadows of weariness beneath her eyes, or how the rosy paint sat awkwardly atop the pallor of her cheeks.

I marveled that she still found the strength for these long nights, but because Louis, with his insensitivity to others' suffering, expected her to be there in his company, she would go, even if she needed to have her servants carry her the entire way.

"Is there any word from Monsieur, any reason for his delay?" she plaintively asked one of the footmen. "He knows I don't like to keep the horses waiting so long. They suffer, you know, standing idle on the paving stones in their traces like that. What reason could my husband have for that?"

"I do not know, Madame," the man answered. "His Highness has left word that he was not to be disturbed in his rooms. He is, ah, engaged with the chevalier."

"Ah." Madame sighed with resignation. She rubbed her fingertips across her temples, making the three dangling pearls in her earrings sway against her cheeks. "No matter. We shall wait, shan't we?"

As soon as she'd spoken, we heard a man scream from upstairs, followed by angry, shouted words and a slammed door. We all turned as one to look up the staircase, dreading to see what manner of foul mood had captured Monsieur this time. I saw Madame's mouth tighten, as she braced herself for however he'd vent his foul humor on her.

He charged down the hallway, stopping at the top of the white marble staircase, a furious figure in black-and-scarlet satin. Behind him, as always, was his smirking, languid follower, the Chevalier de Lorraine, followed by several gentlemen attendants and servants, all striving to calm Monsieur—who, clearly, had no intention of being calmed.

"*You!*" he shouted, flinging his arm to single out one of us clustered below. "Strumpet! Whore! What you have done—what you have done!"

We maids and ladies gasped and made small frightened cries of distress, unsure what to do or say. In our midst, Madame pushed herself up from her armchair to confront him, her fury now a match for his own.

"Do not speak to me that way, sir," she ordered. "Do you understand me?"

"I do not address you," Monsieur said, looking past his wife. "It's that one, there, that I mean. You, you vile little whore, you!"

With her hand pressed over her mouth in panic, Françoise de Fiennes stepped away from the rest of us, poised to flee.

Madame looked sharply from her husband to Françoise and back again. Though there was little love lost between Madame and this particular maid of honor, I expected her as our mistress to defend her maid. Of course she knew the truth; being who she was, Madame likely knew far more about the affair between her maid and Monsieur's lover than the rest of us could even imagine.

"What can this young lady have done to you to deserve such language?" she demanded now. "What, sir?"

"What has she done?" Monsieur repeated, his voice rising shrill with his anger. "What has she not done! She has seduced this gentleman like the whore that she is, lured him to sin, debased him with her filth, and now dares claim he sired her bastard!"

"My maid of honor seduced the chevalier?" Madame repeated, incredulous. "You would believe that to be true?"

The chevalier stepped close to Monsieur, resting his hand fondly on the smaller man's shoulder.

"It is, Madame," he said, smirking with unabashed pleasure. "The little bitch quite raped me."

"That is not true!" cried Françoise frantically. "My lord, my lord, tell them the truth! Tell them how you love me, and promised to wed me!"

Unmoved, the chevalier sniffed with contempt. "You delude yourself," he said. "I could never love a creature like you."

"No!" she wailed, tears now streaming down her cheeks as she sank to her knees. "You swore to me, my lord! Love, devotion, marriage! You promised you—"

"Silence!" roared Monsieur. "How dare you challenge the word of a gentleman? Insolent, lying whore!"

He stormed down the steps, the ribbon-tied curls of his wig flying out behind. Françoise scrambled to her feet to escape, but her heel tangled in the hem of her petticoat and she pitched forward to her knees. Monsieur was at her in an instant, slapping her face and boxing her about her neck and shoulders to drive her forward.

"Out, out, leave my house!" he screamed, his blows raining down upon her. "I won't have a whore like you here, defiling everything you touch! Not near this gentleman, not near my wife! Out, out!"

Sobbing for mercy, Françoise staggered across the hall. As the two came closer, a porter with a dutifully impassive face opened the door and held it for Monsieur's convenience.

"Madame, please!" wailed Françoise, her shoulders hunched and her hands over her head against Monsieur's driving fists. "Mercy, I beg of you, oh, mercy, for the love of my innocent child!"

I looked to Madame, that lady of boundless kindness, expecting her to speak and give the order that would save Françoise. To my shock, her expression was every bit as empty as the porter's at the door: no mercy, no reprieve, no redemption. In silence she watched Monsieur shove Françoise through the doorway and down the steps to the pavement, and in silence she let the porter close the door, and muffle the lady's racking cries on the palais's steps.

She turned to meet the gaze of the chevalier, who was standing just behind her, a strange, unspoken exchange I could not begin to comprehend. One had won, I guessed, and one had lost, but now I'd no notion of who was the victor, and who the vanquished, besides the poor creature who'd been cast away by them both.

"Worthless, impudent whore," Monsieur muttered, smoothing the gold-trimmed sleeves of his coat as he came to stand before Madame. "Offal like her is not to be tolerated."

"It's done." With a long sigh, Madame slowly lowered herself back into her armchair and folded her hands over her belly. "Come. We're late, and we've kept the horses waiting long enough."

Françoise's crying outside the door had stopped. I do not know what became of her. When we returned that night, her belongings were gone as if she'd never been among us. I never saw her again. It wouldn't have been right if I had.

Monsieur motioned for the footmen to carry Madame's chair, and then he joined the chevalier, the two of them walking together through the door. Madame came next, with us following in her wake, a shaken, silent procession in our costly silks and lace.

In the time since I'd joined this household, I'd believed that I'd come to know and love Madame, and to trust her as my dearest friend at Court. Now I realized how little I understood, and how foolish I'd been to think otherwise. As for my trust— Ah, Court was no place for trust, nor for love, either.

Chapter Six

The violent departure of Mademoiselle de Fiennes from our household did little to relieve the constant unease between Madame and Monsieur. In truth it seemed to make matters worse, not better, for soon afterward, Monsieur announced that we were all to shift from Paris to Saint-Cloud to await the birth of Madame's child. To the world, he proclaimed this as a benefit to his wife, removing her from the demands of Court and the city. To anyone who knew anything, the real circumstances were abundantly clear: that Monsieur was far too jealous of Madame's meetings with his brother and the political power that she appeared to wield, while he himself had none. By removing her from Paris, he did indeed end the visits made by Louis to the Palais-Royal, as well as the numerous calls from the English ambassadors and other prominent English gentlemen.

But if Monsieur believed that banishment (for in essence, so it was) would be sufficient to end Madame's interest in an English-French alliance, then he'd woefully underestimated the strength of Madame's will. He could have borne her off to the farthest reaches of Creation, and so long as she had a messenger bound for Paris and London, she still would have continued to write to the two kings.

In the beginning, I couldn't imagine a sweeter place to be banished than the Château de Saint-Cloud. The château was Monsieur's country estate, just as Versailles belonged to his brother the king.

While the house and its parks offered all the felicitous airs of rural living, the journey to reach it was not arduous, being only twelve miles
on good roads from Paris. The progress of our household from one
royal home to the other took but a day, and that with our usual unwieldy cavalcade of ladies' coaches, gentlemen on horseback, guards
on foot and on horse, and wagon after wagon bearing servants and all
the baggage and trunks we couldn't possibly survive without, even in
the country.

But no one would mistake Saint-Cloud for some humble retreat,
a peasant's cottage blown large by a nobleman's whim. Like all younger
brothers, Monsieur sought to rival his sibling in everything, including
the magnificence of their houses. Saint-Cloud was of a size to match
the Palais-Royal, and its interiors were even more gorgeously decorated with elaborate plasterwork and gilded *rinceaux* of the flowers
and fruits grown on the estate. Every salon was lit by tall windows and
glittering chandeliers, and every wall was hung with either a looking
glass, a painting, or a richly woven tapestry.

A year earlier, I would have been full of wonder to be admitted
to such a place. Now my eye had grown discerning and my taste more
critical, and I could see for myself which pictures were considered the
works of masters, and which were no more than gaudy daubs meant to
bring cheer to a dark hall. Guided by Madame, I'd learned to recognize
and appreciate the quality that surrounds royalty, whether in a gleam-
ing lacquered cabinet from China, a length of finely wrought Vene-
tian *point de neige* lace to edge a pair of linen cuffs, or even a perfectly
baked cherry pastry, the edges crimped with exquisite perfection.

Such knowledge was part of any French lady's education, and a
valuable one, too. His Majesty expected his courtiers to set the taste
for all other Christian countries. I listened, and observed, and learned,
and resolved one day to be like Madame, and surround myself only
with the very best.

I'd plenty of time for such education at Saint-Cloud. After the
liveliness of Paris, the château seemed quiet, indeed. Our company
had shrunk to Madame's immediate attendants, a score of us ladies
and no more. My first confidante, Gabrielle de la Touraine, left our

household to wed a widowed but wealthy vicomte of her parents' choosing, and her departure reminded me all the more of how I was failing in my purpose to secure a suitable husband.

With the memory of Mademoiselle de Fiennes's downfall still sharp, Madame worried over the souls of her remaining maids of honor, and arranged for assorted clerics to come address us. Left to ourselves, we turned to less spiritual resorts like telling one another's fortunes, acting charades, playing cards, and reading romantic novels, like Madame de Scudery's *Clelie*, which only fed our thwarted longings. Endless games of loo and lansquenet stretched far into the summer night with the wagers rising to include golden louis d'or and jeweled earrings. I'd sit through a hand only when the stakes were low, not having the resources or the inclination at that time for deep play.

We'd no gallants, no beaus, for admiration or flirtations, a sorry lack for ladies our age. The only gentlemen we saw were Monsieur and the chevalier and their catamite accomplices, which is to say no proper gentlemen at all. Like a swarm of wasps, they would descend on Saint-Cloud to plague and torment Madame, then flee back to Versailles when Monsieur's jealous rage was spent.

The heat affected poor Madame so that she could not even find ease in her bed, but preferred instead to lie on an arrangement of cushions near the open windows, where she could hear the cooling sound of falling water from the château's garden fountains. Lolling like some pagan odalisque, she would read the letters from her brother and from Louis, and continue to plot the alliance that was so dear to her.

The news was not fortuitous, either. In early summer, word came that Abbé Prignani's mission had failed, and ignominiously, too. With the Duke of Monmouth to support him, the abbé's cleverness and his gift for prognostication had soon made him a favorite at an English Court that prized amusement. Guided by his astrological charts (and doubtless information from others), he made several predictions regarding His Grace's petty loves that came to pass, and astounded the Court. Soon Charles himself declared the abbé to be excellent company, exactly as Madame and Louis had hoped.

But like many men before him, the abbé soon began to believe too much in his own quite mortal powers. Instead of concentrating on the alliance between France and England, and on convincing Charles to declare his faith, the abbé frivolously boasted that he could predict the winning horses in races. Perhaps he'd enjoyed too much wine among the hard-drinking English, or perhaps he'd let himself be lured into overconfidence by the charming king. The sorry result was the same. At once Charles seized this chance to test him, and carried the hapless abbé off at a trot to the races at the spring meeting at Newmarket.

There, of course, the abbé faltered, and the horses he'd chosen lost. His erroneous predictions cost his patron, the Duke of Monmouth, heavy losses from wagers. Even worse, Charles gleefully packed the abbé back to Louis, praising the monk as the most loyal servant of France, and worthy of some other assignment.

"I cannot believe my brother would treat the poor abbé with so little regard," Madame said mournfully over the latest letters from both her brother and Colbert de Croissy. "To take him to Newmarket like that, as if he were some common jockey or tout!"

"Perhaps His Majesty judged that to be a fitting test of the abbé's gifts," I suggested carefully. "Every sporting gentleman knows there is nothing more difficult to predict than a horse."

"Oh, I know that, just as I know my brother," she said crossly. "Surely he is the most cynical of gentleman, and the most vexing, too. Mark this, Louise: 'You may be sure I will keep the secret of your prophet, Minette. I give little credit to such kind of cattle, and the less you do it, the better, for even if they could tell anything, 'tis inconvenient to know one's fortune beforehand, whether good or bad.' Oh, how he will plague me!"

I nodded, not daring to venture an opinion that might wound the princess further. Yet I agreed completely with His Majesty's good-natured advice, and his estimation of the abbé as well.

I hadn't forgotten the foolish fortune he'd predicted for me. If the king had swallowed that manner of nonsense, then he would have sadly slipped in my esteem. But hearing that he hadn't made him only rise higher. I could imagine him listening with a skeptical half smile

to the abbé's charlatan performance, concealing his true feelings behind his handsome royal face. How I wished I'd been there at Newmarket to watch, where this clever king's wry test of the abbé must
have granted better entertainment than any sport to be found on the
racecourse!

"I vow he will make a jest of anything," she continued, pressing
her fingertips to her temples and closing her eyes. "Another glass of
the lemon water here, Louise. That's it, child, thank you. My brother
does it to tease me, I know, but there are others who will spin this into
a righteous tempest. Buckingham, for one."

"Lord Buckingham?" I asked, pouring the chilled lemon water
from the silver pitcher into Madame's tumbler. "Why would His Grace
make the abbé his affair?"

"Because Buckingham pokes his long nose into everything," she
said darkly, sipping at the water without opening her eyes. "He keeps
his own stable at Newmarket, and because his nags were among those
who lost, he took a viperish dislike to the poor abbé."

"But His Majesty didn't," I said. "That's of more import, isn't it?"

She sighed mightily, the swell of her belly rising high before her.
On account of the heat, she wore only the lightest of linen dressing
gowns, and beneath it I could see the gentle shift of the child kicking
within her womb.

"With any other than Buckingham, it would be," she said. "But the
rascal's told Charles that his sister here in Paris—the lady waits upon
my dear mother at Colombe—swears I sent the abbé to London with
the sole and hateful purpose of discrediting *him*. Him, Louise, as if I'd
squander so much thought upon a creature such as Buckingham!"

"If His Majesty did not believe the abbé's predictions, Madame,
then surely he would not listen to His Grace, either."

"No." She opened her eyes to glance again at the letter in her
hand. "Charles found the entire business vastly amusing, as he does
most everything in life. Ah, I only wish Louis would feel the same!"

I nodded. It was impossible to imagine Louis laughing with
amusement over something as important as this. "Does His Majesty
also know of Abbé Prignani's failures?"

"If I know, then so does he," she said, refolding the letter and pressing it flat along the creases between her fingertips. "His Majesty will of course pretend he'd nothing to do with any of it, and neatly pass the blame to another's shoulders. Then he will look to me to concoct a fresh plan to deliver my brother, as if my brother could ever be meekly led into anything."

Discouraged, she tossed the letter away from her, letting it drop to the floor. "My brother doesn't need Louis as much now. His Parliament has been more generous of late, and voted more to his taste, and thus he can afford to be more independent of French gifts. No, the only sure way to persuade him will be if I can journey to England, and speak to him directly. Yet so long as I'm a prisoner here, what can I do? What can I *do*?"

"Don't upset yourself, Madame, I beg you," I said, hurrying to plump the cushions behind her. "If you are delivered of a son, then surely—"

"Oh, Louise," she said, and groaned. "It could as well be another daughter, and my prayers go for nothing."

"Well, then, a daughter," I said, striving to cheer her. "Once your babe is born—"

"Once this babe is born, then my husband will try his best to fill my belly with another, and another, and another after that, to keep me here in France," she said bitterly. "We women are no more than slaves to men's desires, Louise. You'll learn that in time for yourself. Slaves, and no more."

I blushed, and looked away, for what could I say to such an argument? I'd no doubt at all that Monsieur would do exactly as she'd claimed. He enjoyed using her with cruel purpose, and if it were left to him, from purest spite, Madame would never again see either her homeland or her brother. The alliance meant nothing to Monsieur, especially not when compared to the countless slights and injustices that he believed both Madame and Louis had inflicted upon him.

Suddenly I realized that I was gazing at the largest painting on the wall of Madame's salon: an idealized picture by Jean Nocret of Monsieur as the victorious warrior-god Mars, surrounded by symbols of masculine combat and come home at last to celebrate his conquest in the waiting arms of Madame, painted as an adoring, voluptuous Venus. The distance between wedded truth and romantic allegory might have been droll if it weren't also so painfully sad.

"England is so lovely in the summer." Madame's voice was soft with poignant longing, and she gazed from the window as if she herself could see across the Channel from Saint-Cloud to London. "It was summer when I visited last, you know, the summer before I was wed to Monsieur. Everything was green and bright, and the flowers— Oh, Louise, you would not believe how flowers prosper and bloom in England. How I should like to show them to you!"

"You will see them again, Madame," I promised, more from wishing it were so than from any real conviction. "His Majesty your brother will make certain of that."

"I pray that you're right," she said. Without turning from the window, she reached blindly for my hand and slipped her fingers into mine. "You would like my brother, too, Louise, even more than the roses. Ha, the great impudent rogue! He's not at all like these chilly French gentlemen, you know, for all they claim to be such gallants. I vow he could even make you laugh, my solemn little Louise."

"Yes, Madame," I said, fervently agreeing to everything. I was sure I'd like her brother, and far more than mere roses, too, and I was just as certain he could make me laugh. I wasn't solemn by nature. It was the Court, and the unhappiness of Madame's household, that had made me appear that way. "I pray that you may visit him as you wish, and that in your kindness, you shall include me as a member of your party."

Though we'd spoken often of this before, it was still surpassing bold of me to ask such an enormous favor. She trusted me, and in her way loved me well, but likewise I knew my rank and birth were too humble for such a considerable honor. As a reflection of French glory, Louis would insist on sending only the most beautiful ladies (and the ones with the most opulent jewels and gowns) to England. Yet I still girlishly dreamed of Madame's handsome, jesting brother, and did indeed pray for even a glimpse of him.

Given my audacity, it was just as well that Madame was so lost in her own musings that she didn't seem to have heard me.

"I do so much want to see my brother again," she said softly, little more than a whisper of the most heartfelt longing, as her fingers toyed restlessly with my own. A single tear slipped from the corner of her eye to slide down the curve of her cheek, echoing the drop-shaped pearls she always wore in her ears. "Charles, and England. I wanted to see them one more time before I died."

"You won't die, Madame," I said quickly, shocked she'd speak such a thing aloud. "It's God's will when He takes us for His own to heaven, Madame, not ours. You won't die, not yet."

"Such faith, my little Louise." She smiled wistfully, another tear following the first along her pale cheek. "It is His decision when we die, yes, and not our own. But sometimes, in my heart, I believe it would be better if I did."

Madame did not die then, of course. Yet her melancholy was only part of the ill fortune and sorrow that seemed to overhang us all that summer, and beyond.

In early June, Charles wrote to Madame with guarded joy to inform her that, at last, his queen was pregnant with a royal child. Madame could scarce contain her delight for her brother, writing letter after letter to him and the queen with advice for her health and that of the babe. But before the month was done, the queen's pregnancy ended in another miscarriage. Charles was devastated, and Madame shared his grief for so unfortunate a loss.

Alas, more was to come. In early summer, word came from the Mediterranean that the lengthy siege of the island of Candia had collapsed, and with it the Christian hopes for that land. The Turks took full possession, a defeat that struck Louis particularly hard. The losses to the French troops who had helped defend the island were severe, and the French warship *La Thérèse*, the flagship of the fleet, exploded and sank. Among the many fallen was my first benefactor, the Duc de Beaufort. I'd never forgotten his kindness to me, or how I'd repaid it with the post that had now led to his grievous death. I wept bitter tears for him, and for the unkindness of fate, which had stolen away such a fine gentleman.

In August, Madame was brought to bed of her child. Her labors were long and hard, and made more perilous by her fragility. At last she was safely delivered, but the babe was another girl, not the desired son. In disgust, Monsieur departed Saint-Cloud at once with the chevalier, without waiting to see either his wife or his new daughter.

I felt a thousand pities for Madame, not only for her suffering, but for her disappointment as well. Baptized Anne-Marie d'Orleans, the tiny girl was strong and fair, with a lusty cry that delighted her nursemaid, yet she seemed to bring her own mother little joy. How could she, when her very presence reminded Madame of Monsieur's jealous, abusive demands upon her person, both in the past and, inevitably, once again in the future?

Only a few weeks later, Madame's mother, the Dowager Queen of England, died at Colombe. Still weak from childbed, a devastated Madame insisted on attending the funeral and leading the mourners. Of the seven Stuart children, Madame had been her mother's favorite and her namesake. Though admirably pious, the queen was also known to have a demanding and difficult nature, and Madame was the only one of her children who'd remained close to her throughout her tragic life. Madame felt the death keenly. The depth of her grieving was remarked with concern by all who saw her at the funeral, and many feared she'd soon follow her mother to the grave.

Monsieur was irritated by the inconvenience of the funeral, forcing him to interrupt a monthlong season of hunting at Chambord for the services in Paris. To no one's surprise, he denounced Madame for calling him away from the hunt for such a reason. Louis heard of his brother's ill-mannered selfishness, and chided him soundly for it. Yet in his perverse way, Monsieur convinced himself that His Majesty's displeasure was somehow Madame's doing, and that, too, became one more excuse for him to torment her further.

Torment: that would seem a strong word to be used in regard to a royal marriage. But I assure you that to those of us who were privy to that marriage, torment was perhaps too generous a word to describe Monsieur's treatment of Madame. Consider as well how Madame's body had been racked by a difficult birth, with little time to recover before her soul, too, had been grievously wounded by her mother's death. Reduced to a wraithlike figure in shrouded mourning, Madame was so distraught that Bishop Bousset, His Majesty's own spiritual adviser and confidant, judged it wise to begin to help her prepare for her own demise and final judgment.

Most husbands would have treated a wife suffering from such despair with tender understanding. But Monsieur was more monster than loving husband, and he seized upon Madame's weakness like a savage beast will sink its teeth into wounded prey. He used any excuse to challenge her, and instantly escalated their quarrels into shouted oaths and threats of violence. He let the chevalier come between them, and always took his favorite's side against his wife. He jeered and taunted her about her thwarted journey to England, and just as she'd confessed to me, he vowed to impregnate her again to keep her in France. One night at table he swore before us all that Madame had become so distasteful to him that he'd require the chevalier to join them in her bedchamber before he could perform his husbandly duty.

I am not certain whether Monsieur acted upon this disgraceful threat or not; as much as Madame would share with me, there were mercifully some matters she kept to herself. But I do know that when he finally wearied of cruelly debasing her body, he began to do the same to her soul. He complained to his confessor that Madame had ill treated the chevalier, contriving so many artful lies in his case that the misguided confessor chastised Madame, accusing her publicly of a lack of Christian charity toward her husband's lover. If Monsieur could have contrived it, he would have had Madame banned from their chapel and the comfort of prayer until she apologized to the chevalier for her imagined sins and slights.

My poor lady was always near to tears, of grief, pain, anger, and resignation. To the rest of the world and the Court, she tried her best to be serene and honor the mourning she wore for her mother. Only in her letters to her brother did she reveal the nightmare that her life had become. Helpless from afar, he in turn wrote to Louis, ominously demanding that something be done to ease his sister's plight. As the hope of the alliance became more and more tenuous, Louis ordered his brother to show more kindness to Madame. But once again Monsieur misinterpreted his brother's words, the king's concern spurring him into another rage of unfounded jealousy toward his wife. It was as if the gilded walls of the Palais-Royal had become a battlefield, rife with hostility and attacks and no peace for any of us.

And then, to my own grief, the true meaning of war became sharply, shockingly clear.

There was nothing outwardly different about my mother's letter, written in her familiar hand and sealed with the same shiny blob of green wax. Inside, she'd covered only a single sheet, each sentence short and without comfort.

My brother, Sebastien, had been serving with the French forces at the siege of Candia. He had been attached to the Duc de Beaufort's men. He had fought in the same battle in which the duc had been killed. Sebastien had been wounded, a long, deep splinter wound from a shattered mast, but survived. He had been among the last Christians the Turks permitted to leave the island. He had returned to France with the fleet. On the voyage, his wound had not healed, but festered. He had grown feverish and declined. Only his desire to see France again had kept him alive. He had finally died as he'd been carried ashore in Provence, the waters of France splashing on his cheeks.

My mother told me to pray for his soul, and to be confident that he had died a hero, secure in God's love and now among the saints in heaven.

All I knew was that if I'd not come to Court and garnered the post for my brother with the expedition to Candia, he would be alive now, and eager to celebrate his twenty-third birthday in November.

Heedless of the tears streaming from my eyes, I ran to Madame's rooms, and threw myself sobbing on the floor at her feet, too distraught to explain myself. A servant took my mother's crumpled letter from my hand and gave it to Madame. She read it swiftly, understanding all.

"My poor Louise!" she cried softly, lifting me up into her arms. She held me close and let me weep against her shoulder. My tears soaked the silk of her bodice, my grief mingled forever with the scent of her perfume. She stroked her hand over the back of my curls, over and over as she did with her little dogs, calming me as best she could.

"Such a blow, such a blow," she murmured. "Ah, ah, your poor parents, to lose their only son."

That made me weep all the harder. I had come to Court to help my family, and instead, I had destroyed its very future.

"Your mother is wise, you know," Madame said gently. "Your brother is safe among the angels, in a much better place than this mortal world. But I shall have a mass said for him to ease his soul's way, and more prayers read for him by the sisters at Chaillot. Will that please you?"

"Yes—yes, Madame," I said through my sobs. "Thank you, Madame. But I—I must return home, to Brittany. I—I must go to them now."

"Leave Court, Louise?" She stared at me, incredulous and, with her black-bordered handkerchief, dabbed at the wet blotch my tears had left on her bodice. "Leave me?"

"I beg you, Madame, only for a short time, only until I—"

"But I fear that's not possible, Louise," she said, sadly, as if it weren't really her decision to make. "You are too dear, too necessary, for me to do without you, even for a short time."

Bewildered, I stepped back. Even as the tears still filled my eyes, I remembered to curtsy and show my gratitude, and remembered, too, that she was the duchesse d'Orleans, born of kings and queens, while I—I was not.

"Thank you, Madame," I whispered through my misery. "I am honored."

And at Court, that was all that mattered.

On Christmas Day, our household was to attend holy mass in the King's Chapel at the Louvre, with Bishop Bousset presiding. As was usual, Madame and her attendants had gathered for the coaches in the front hall of the Palais-Royal. Madame's elder daughter, Marie-Louise, was joining us, having been judged sufficiently old enough at seven years to sit with the adults. Though the little girl was dressed exactly as her mother in miniature from her lace cap and arranged curls to her black velvet gloves and fur muff, she still could not contain her excitement, no matter how many times her governess chided her.

"Is Papa coming, Maman?" she asked Madame, bouncing lightly on her little heeled slippers as she looked up at her mother. "We can't leave without Papa."

"I'm sure he'll join us soon, my dear." Madame smiled for her daughter's benefit, but still she glanced anxiously up the stairs, looking for Monsieur. "He won't wish to be late on Christmas."

"Christmas!" echoed Marie-Louise with relish, for that word is magical to every child, even a royal princess. Later, after mass and dinner, I knew that she'd be given the lady doll she'd so longed for, and that her mother had ordered with such care. "Here comes Papa, Maman. I can hear him coming!"

But the footsteps she'd heard belonged not to Monsieur, but to one of his servants, who came to bow solemnly before Madame.

"Have you word from Monsieur?" she asked, though of course we all knew that he did. Monsieur was never prompt, and this humiliating ritual of a servant or one of his gentlemen appearing to bear his excuses was more often repeated than not. "I trust he will be with us soon?"

The servant bowed again. "I regret to tell you that His Highness says he is unable to attend Your Highness at present."

Madame sighed, as she too often did. "Did he say when he will be able to join me?"

The man hesitated, obviously aware of the unhappiness his message would bring Madame.

"His Highness regrets that he will be unable to attend or accompany Your Highness," he said slowly, taking care to recite the Monsieur's message exactly as it had been given, "not until you come to his rooms and apologize to His Lordship the Chevalier de Lorraine for the cruel scorn you have shown him."

"Thank you." Madame's voice, usually so mild, now crackled with anger. It was one thing for Monsieur to shame her, but another entirely for him to do so before their daughter.

She took the little girl's hand, and with visible effort, put aside her own frustrations and smiled warmly at the little girl.

"Come, my sweet," she said with forced gaiety. "If Papa won't come with us, then you shall have his cushion in the pew, and sit directly beside me."

They entered the Louvre's Royal Chapel together, the little lady taking her father's place in the ordered procession and in the royal pew. The tenderness shown between mother and daughter was much praised, with many noting how sweetly Marie-Louise held the prayer book open for her mother, and how Madame rewarded her daughter by clasping one of her own extravagant pearl cuffs around Marie-Louise's tiny wrist to wear as a treat.

Still, it was Monsieur's absence that was most remarked and discussed and wondered over. The first speculation was that he must be gravely ill, to have missed such an important occasion. But soon the scandalous truth was rippling through the crowded chapel, each courtier whispering to the next when they should have been attending to the service and the bishop's sermon.

It did not take long before the king himself had heard the reason for his brother's absence, and from the grim set of his features, his reaction was not an understanding one. Instead he kept glancing back to where Monsieur should have been sitting, the white ostrich plumes on his hat fluttering with each turn of his head, as if that alone would somehow belatedly produce his wayward brother. Most times the king would find a way to excuse or ignore Monsieur's behavior, no matter how outrageous or wicked it might be, and much to Madame's sorrow, too. But from Louis's stone-faced glance, it was clear that at last Monsieur had stepped too far beyond propriety, and the next round of eager whispers in the chapel were set to guessing how and when a royal chastisement might take place.

Madame must have realized she was at the center of this new Court scandal—she'd been there so many times before—and yet throughout the service and afterward, she concentrated on her daughter and no one else, laughing happily as if she'd no care in the world, or at least no furious, debauched husband with a male lover waiting for her at home. Hand in hand, she and Marie-Louise walked apart from the rest of us along the covered pathway from the chapel through the palace's gardens.

The day was brisk and cold, the gray sky low and threatening snow. With their heads bent and their hoods tied tightly against the stiffening breeze, the other ladies hurried to return to the warmth of the fireplaces within the palace, their heels clicking across the paving stones and their silk skirts snapping like flags around their ankles. Only Marie-Louise's governess remained at a respectful distance, ready to remove her charge the instant Madame tired of her.

I lingered behind as well, watching Madame and her daughter together. Perhaps because it was Christmas, perhaps because I still grieved for Sebastien, I was missing my own Maman sorely. Though they were too far ahead for their words to be clear to me, Marie-Louise was obviously telling some manner of fanciful story to Madame, flapping her arms like a bird's wings. She made a crowing sound, and flung one spindly arm high toward the sky. The gold of her mother's pearl cuff caught the watery sunlight, a bright glittering spot against the gray clouds. Then the cuff flew from the girl's wrist, over the stone wall and the empty flower beds and into a pile of dry leaves.

Neither Madame nor her daughter noticed, nor did the governess, the three of them continuing on their way. I knew the value of the bracelet, in history as well as in the cost of the pearls and gold. The cuff was one of a pair that were among Madame's most cherished possessions, having been crafted in Florence as a gift for her grandmother Marie de'Medici, nearly a hundred years before. In every sense they were irreplaceable, and further, I hated to think of the little princess being blamed for having caused such a loss.

Thus without a thought I bunched my skirts to one side and ran round the stone wall and down the steps into the garden, and to the dormant bed in which the bracelet lay buried. Swiftly I scooped away the dry, brittle leaves until I found the jewel, lying in the dirt like true buried treasure. With my prize in my hand, I hurried back to the covered walk, determined to return the bracelet to Madame before it was missed. I turned the corner to where they should have gone, and stopped in the shadow of a thick stone column.

Marie-Louise was gone, no doubt with her governess, who had also vanished. In the center of the walk, curiously framed by a pointed antique stone archway, stood Madame and, with her, the king. They stood very close to one another, with her gazing up to him, as lovers will. I remembered the whispers, how long ago there had been an intrigue between these two cousins, and to see how she swayed toward him now, her face full of longing, I would have believed it. My poor Madame! Was this the weightiest secret kept within her heart?

Unsure of what exactly I was witnessing, I remained where I was, not wishing to disturb them either by presenting myself or by retreating and catching their notice.

"What was it this time?" the king was asking, concern giving his voice an unexpected urgency. "What did Philippe demand of you?"

She shook her head, her dark curls brushing over her forehead. "He wanted me to apologize to the chevalier, and would not come down unless I did."

"Not that," Louis said. "What did he ask of you first?"

I saw her shoulders draw up beneath her cloak, and she bowed her head in shame. "He ordered me to welcome the chevalier to my bed, and take them each in turn in my mouth in the Italian fashion, and then embrace him as another husband."

The king drew in his breath at that, and swore some manner of dark oath that I couldn't hear.

"Forgive me," Madame said unhappily, as if she were to blame for her husband's perversions. "Oh, please, please, forgive me, I beg you."

"This will never happen again, Henriette." He rested his palm against her cheek. "You have our word."

She slipped her hand over his, holding him there for another moment longer in gratitude, in regard.

"Thank you," she whispered so softly that I saw her lips form the words rather than heard them. "Thank you."

The king nodded, and said no more. Then he turned quickly away from her, and before I could move he was striding toward me.

"Your Majesty," I said, sinking low in my curtsy, my bowed head hiding my guilty flush.

"Mademoiselle de Keroualle," he said, lifting his hat to me. "Happy Christmas."

"Happy Christmas to you as well, My Sire." I rose slowly, my knees wobbling with nervousness beneath me. "Madame dropped her bracelet, and I found it."

I held the pearl cuff out in my hand, and prayed that it would be proof enough that I'd reason for being there, and was not spying.

But the king was looking at me, not the bracelet. "How old are you, mademoiselle?"

"Nineteen, sir." He was studying me closely, as if seeing me for the first time instead of the thousandth in Madame's company.

"Nineteen?" he asked, doubtful.

"Yes, Your Majesty," I said. "I swear to it by all that's holy."

He nodded, finally accepting, I suppose. Beneath the wide brim of his hat, his dark-eyed gaze flicked over me, missing nothing of my face and person. Yet he looked at me not with desire, the way he did with the Madame du Montespan and countless other women beyond her, but with purpose, as if deciding whether I would serve in some other manner.

It worried me, that scrutiny. Louis was not frivolous by nature, and seldom did or said things without reason. Where, I wondered, did I fit in his scheming? In all the time I'd been in Madame's household, he'd never before regarded me like this. What plans could he possibly be making for me?

"You are changed, mademoiselle." He nodded, leaving me to decide if he judged me changed to my improvement, or the reverse. "Her Highness needs you. Go to her."

I curtsied again, and once he'd walked past me, I hurried to Madame, still standing where the king had left her.

"I found your bracelet, Madame," I said, holding it before me.

"Thank you," she murmured, slipping the cuff onto her wrist as if it had never been lost. She was looking past me to the departing figure of the king, and her pale face was wistful.

"Things will be different now, Louise," she said softly, still looking after the king. "You'll see. He gave me his word. Things will change."

Though I nodded, I did not share her confidence. I'd been at Court long enough to have seen how the pledges of kings, while solemnly given, were not the most secure of promises.

I was wrong to doubt. Within the week, the Chevalier de Lorraine had been arrested and imprisoned on Louis's orders. Enraged, Monsieur protested, and Louis answered by having the chevalier moved to solitary confinement in the grim Château d'If.

Monsieur retaliated by carrying Madame and her ladies away from Court to his most distant estate at Villers-Cotterets, as much an imprisonment for Madame in being so removed from the Court as the chevalier's new residence was. Peevishly he informed Louis that he'd not permit her to return until the chevalier was released. Louis was not pleased to be crossed like this, and soon sent his own coach of state to bring us back to Paris.

The chevalier remained in prison.

And in March, the king announced that he would visit Flanders, and that the Queen, Monsieur, Madame, and a large portion of the Court would be accompanying him. Monsieur had no choice but to agree, and bring Madame with him.

The chevalier was at last released, but sent far away from France to Italy, where it was presumed (wrongly, as it later was known) he'd be too far away to cause his usual mischief.

All that spring we were in a frenzy of preparation. The official reason given for the Court's journey was that His Majesty wished to view certain Flemish territories that had recently been acquired and added to his own. No one was fooled. This short journey was but a first step to another, one of far greater importance to all involved.

At last Madame was permitted to visit England, and I—I was going with her.

Chapter Seven

DUNKERQUE
May 1670

Driven by the wind from the sea, the rain drummed against the carriage windows so hard that it sounded like small stones hurled by an angry hand. Closed inside the stuffy coach, we could still hear the lash of the driver's whip as he tried to urge the horses to pull the wheels free of the sticky mud that held them fast, and the swearing soldiers striving to push us clear with pikes and their own shoulders. Finally the coach lurched forward, and the five other ladies and I were again jumbled and tossed against one another like coins in a pocket.

"Mother in heaven preserve us," Madame muttered, her face pale and drawn as she braced herself anew against the cushions. Beside her Madame de Beaulieu, one of her ladies-in-waiting, began to dab at her forehead with a lace handkerchief soaked with restorative cologne, but irritably Madame waved her away.

"No more of that, I beg you." She sighed restlessly, striving to find any position of comfort in the rocking coach. We'd already tied the shades over the windows to keep out even the dull daylight at her request, once she'd confessed that the brightness made her head ache.

We'd been happy enough to oblige, from concern for her. Madame had been ill since we'd left Paris three weeks ago, and before that, too, truth to tell. She'd have spells where she'd cough for an hour without end, bent double with distress, and the only thing I'd seen her eat or drink was milk and chicory water; she seemed unable to take any other food or wine without retching horribly. There were those who'd begun to whisper that Monsieur was somehow slowly poisoning her. We who were closest to her feared for her health, and begged her to send for a physician or surgeon. She'd steadfastly resisted, not wanting to provide even the slightest reason for her not to continue on this longed-for visit to England.

But even the weather seemed determined to conspire against her hopes. Instead of the bright spring to be expected in May, each morning greeted us with torrents of rain. The roads became nearly impassable with mud and water-filled ruts, and this despite the king having employed thousands of men for the three months beforehand to mend the roads along their route.

It didn't help that we were such an enormous procession, as was expected for His Most Christian Majesty. In addition to the royal family, the king had also brought his two mistresses, Madame de la Vallière and Madame du Montespan. There were artists and historians to document the journey and musicians to make it more entertaining. The rest of the party included favored friends, attendants, assorted courtiers and diplomats, servants, and guards, and the horses, coaches, luggage, and wagons to support them. Finally, because Louis also wished to make this a display of his military power, we were accompanied by large numbers of soldiers, on foot and horse. When everyone was tallied together, we were nearly thirty thousand souls, and what would take a single horseman riding over a dry road a matter of hours took us days. As can be imagined, we were like an entire army invading the countryside, and our lodgings each night were crude and crowded. Even the greatest of ladies was expected to lie on her side and share a bed with as many others as could be contrived to squeeze beneath the coverlet with her.

In each village and town that the royal procession had passed through, we'd been forced to stop so that the local nobles and merchants could honor His Majesty with lavish banquets and tributes. These lasted hours at a time, and we all were expected to remain standing during the entire proceedings. Madame had been too weak to obey, and had fainted dead away several times, much to the displeasure of both the king and Monsieur. At one such dinner, Monsieur had cruelly told all the company how a fortune-teller had predicted he'd soon become a widower, and finally be freed of his inconvenient wife. No one had laughed, but that had not concerned Monsieur. Instead he had continued his usual jealous rants the entire journey, showering poor Madame with his criticism and scorn as surely as the rain had drummed upon our heads.

Yet at last, at least, that torment was done. Earlier in the day in the town of Lille, Madame's party had separated from the king's and turned north toward the coast. At the parting, the king had embraced Madame in a fond farewell; her husband had not. While Monsieur had granted her leave from him for a fortnight's visit to her home-land, Louis had extended that to nearly a month, what surely must have stretched before Madame like a delicious eternity.

Her relief at having left Monsieur behind had been instantaneous. No matter how wretched the weather might be or how ill she might feel, everything was improved by having him gone from us. We were a much smaller party now, only two hundred or so, plus our armed es-cort and our servants, and we should have been able to make a swifter progress, if only the weather were more agreeable.

"Can you see where we are, Louise?" Madame asked of me, the youngest in our coach and therefore the one to perform such low tasks. "Any landmark to guide us?"

Crouching there between the seats, I hesitated with my hand on the leather shade. "If you please, Madame, I cannot do it without let-ting in the sunlight."

"The rain light, you mean." She turned toward me and smiled weakly. "You have my leave, my dear. I am feeling better, you see. To know that every moment brings me closer to England—how could I not improve?"

What I saw was the same drawn and pallid face that she had been showing us, and thus with great care I lifted only a corner of the leather shade to peek outside, and spare her the brightness.

After the murky shadows of the coach, I blinked myself as my eyes grew accustomed to the day.

"What do you see, Louise?" Madame asked. "Pray tell us all!"

"I see trees, bent and blown by the rain, Madame," I said slowly, wishing I'd something of greater cheer to report. "I see fields, and stone walls, and of course our guard riding before us, and the others behind."

"No church spires?" she asked with disappointment. "No inns or signposts or other landmarks?"

"No, Madame," I said. "I fear 'tis much the same as we've seen for days."

"Days and days and *days*," she said with unabashed discouragement. "I must say His Majesty's kingdom might be a rich and bountiful country, but it's also a richly tedious one for travelers."

"Yes, Madame," I agreed absently. The coach was following a long curve in the road, and we'd just cleared a small hill. "Hold now, what I see— Oh, Madame, it is! The ocean, Madame! I can see it now for certain. The ocean!"

I *was* certain, too, and doubly excited by the prospect. Not only did it mean that our long journey by coach was almost done and England within our sights, but also this was the first time I'd seen the water of the Channel since I'd left home nearly two years before. Each morning of my girlhood I'd spied the sea in the distance from the window of my bedchamber, and I hadn't realized until now exactly how sorely I'd missed that view.

"The sea?" Madame cried, and to my surprise she found the strength to sit upright and lean close to me at the window. "Open the shade, Louise, so I might see for myself!"

The nearest lady rested a gentle hand on Madame's arm. "Take care, Madame, and mind your strength. Pray do not exert yourself without reason."

"But this is a reason, and the most joyous one of all!" Madame exclaimed gaily. "If we are near the water, then we're near to Dunkerque and our boats, and that much more near to England as well. Open this shade, Louise. Open it at once."

"Very well," I said. I untied the lashings that held the shade in place, and rolled the leather upward, tied it high. "There, between those two hills. That silvery stripe's the sea."

Madame squinted and winced, shading her eyes but refusing to look away. Then at last she spied it, too, and her face broke into a smile of such pure joy that it could have brightened the entire gloomy landscape.

"There it is," she said, and laughed, giddy with delight. "The sea, *my* sea! Oh, now we'll be at Dunkerque by nightfall for certain, and then my brother will be waiting to come meet me!"

"I pray you won't be disappointed, Madame," cautioned Madame de Beaulieu. "Surely His Majesty has many affairs demanding his time and energies in London, and you must not be disappointed if he isn't waiting for you when you land."

"But he will be," Madame replied with perfect confidence. "My brother has been waiting for me in Dover this past week, so eager is he to welcome me himself. He wrote me so, again and again, and he would not lie. It's I who have kept him waiting as we've wallowed in this mud and muck. But soon we'll be together again. Soon, soon, soon!"

I grinned with her, pleased beyond measure to have her so happy—more happy, really, than I'd ever known her to be. This single glimpse of the sea had done more for her than a score of surgeons ever could, and I wondered at how her sorrows seemed to have vanished so completely, and her suffering with it. For the first time in our acquaintance, she appeared a young woman of twenty-six, a princess born of kings and queens.

"Soon, yes, Madame, but even Your Highness must heed the sailors," warned Madame de Beaulieu, seemingly determined to play the role of the cautionary. "Most shipmasters won't put to sea in such a driving rain as this. Then there are also tides to be considered, and the difficult process of embarkment itself."

"That's as nothing to me, Madame de Beaulieu," the princess said fiercely, her gaze still intent on the distant stripe of water. "Consider all I've endured these ten years, and then ask again whether I'll be stopped by a wave or a raindrop or even a tide?"

I listened, and marveled. Could the coming meeting with her brother truly inspire so great a change in her? She might have been taken for a different lady entirely, now that she'd left Monsieur behind. I'd heard that when she'd been younger, she'd been a girl of great spirit and fire as well as charm, and that was what I glimpsed now.

"Forgive me, Madame," said the hapless lady. "I never meant to challenge you."

Madame nodded, at last turning away from the window. "I'll have you know this is no ordinary journey, my lady, no simple visit for pleasure. Surely you must have guessed as much from the gentlemen, the diplomats, among our escort?"

"Yes, Madame, I did," Madame de Beaulieu admitted, persevering still. "But then if there is such importance attached to your journey, wouldn't it be wiser to be cautious rather than rash?"

Slowly Madame smiled, a smile not of joy, but of a rare determination that I'll never forget.

"Perhaps it would be more wise," she said. "But pray recall that I was born a Stuart, and as a family we Stuarts have never been known to be cautious. If I chose to be safe, then I'd turn back now, and return to Paris with the others. But if I wish to secure the prize that dangles like the ripest fruit before both England and France, then I must be brave and stretch to seize it, no matter the risk of falling."

I thought it the boldest and most stirring speech I'd ever heard spoken by a lady, and my heart beat faster from excitement just to listen. Perhaps because Madame had shared other confidences with me, I trusted her completely in whatever scheme she intended. Perhaps I believed with her that her brother could accomplish whatever he set to do, or perhaps even then I'd decided my own course in the world would be every bit as brave and bold as Madame's declaration was on that rainy day.

But the older ladies were not so pleased. I saw the worried glances they exchanged with one another, as if they believed that the princess had quite scattered her wits or, worse, that she should be forcibly returned to the keeping of her husband, who would put a swift end to such ravings.

"You are certain that this is proper for you to do, Madame?" Madame de Beaulieu asked tentatively. "A great lady in your position?"

"I am," Madame passionately declared. "And with God and my brother to guide me, I will succeed."

Thus, in the earliest hours of the sixteenth of May, I stood on the heaving deck of an English royal sloop, standing close to Madame's side. Overhead the two flags—the red-and-white crosses on a blue background for England, and a silk banner with the golden Bourbon lilies in honor of Madame's presence on board—danced and snapped in the stiff wind. The sloop was part of an English squadron that had been waiting for us at Dunkerque, and though the skies had finally cleared enough for the English captains to clear the harbor, our brief crossing to Dover had proved a rough and challenging one. We two ladies were as good as alone on the deck at this hour, with the crew so occupied with their tasks that they kept a respectful distance apart from us, though always ready to assist the princess if necessary.

Not that they'd be needed. Proudly Madame displayed her ease at sea by clambering sure-footed up and down the companionways and across the slippery decks. She claimed such prowess was a natural gift granted to all English, on account of their being an island people and surrounded by water. It was certainly not a gift shared by her French ladies and servants. Every other member of her party save me was quaking and puking below, laid low in the most foul of circumstances by the rocking waves. Madame had been almost uncharitable regarding their distress, too, declaring it as proof of English superiority, at least where seafaring was concerned.

Not having so much as a drop of English blood myself, I wondered aloud that I wasn't stricken as well, but Madame had an answer for that, too. She gaily proclaimed I'd either sailors or fishermen in the distant reaches of my family tree, or, gazing toward the future, she said I must be destined to wed an Englishman. I scoffed at that, and reminded her of the empty foolishness of the Abbé Prignani's fortune for me, which made her laugh.

But then, on this day, it seemed most everything would make Madame laugh. She was that happy, that joyful, that relieved to be free of Monsieur. Like an old salt, she squinted into the blowing mist and rain, her dark curls limp from the spray and her fur-lined cloak beaded with seawater. Resolutely she turned her bare face (for she'd chosen to do without paint, rather than have it stream and puddle down her cheeks) toward the west, desperate for her first glimpse of England.

"The sailors believe we'll make Dover by dawn, Louise," Madame said to me, though her gaze never shifted from the wet, gray horizon. "To think that I could dine with my brother this very night!"

"Yes, Madame," I said, shivering inside my plain woolen cloak. If Madame did not feel the cold, then I was not permitted to feel it, either. "Perhaps you should rest now, to be refreshed when you meet His Majesty."

She shook her head, her gloved hands tightening on the wooden taffrail as if she feared I'd try to pull her away by force. "My brother will find me worn and changed and will scold me for it, too, yet I also know he'll love me still, just as I love him."

"Then please let me fetch another cloak to warm you, Madame, or—"

"I'm well enough, Louise." She sighed restlessly, slipping one hand inside her cloak to press the pain in her belly. In her excitement, she'd suppressed her many illnesses, but she couldn't make them vanish entirely, as much as she might wish it. Her brother *would* find her much changed, and perhaps he could make her agree to see his own physicians.

"You're quiet, Louise." Madame reached out to take my hand. "And here I thought you were the bravest of the lot."

"I'm not afraid, Madame," I said, and I wasn't. "I was trying to imagine England, that is all."

"England." Her smile softened. "You will like it, I think. It's a sweet, dear place, and now in the spring, everything will be lush and green and full of flowers."

"It must be very beautiful, Madame." Green and lush would be a pleasing change from gray and chill. I had grown so cold, I doubted I'd ever feel my toes or fingers again. "You've spoken of England with such fondness that I can scarce wait to see it for myself."

She smiled absently, lost in her own musings. "And the gentle-men, Louise! The English gentlemen all follow the lead of my brother, which makes them the most charming gallants in the world. In turn they'll judge you to be the most enchanting young lady they've ever seen. One look at your sweet face, and they'll be lost—lost! Perhaps you'll even find that special sailor you're destined to wed. England is full of them."

I felt my face grow hot with miserable shame, the way it always did whenever anyone teased me about marriage. I was nearly twenty, monstrously old to be unwed, without so much as the breath of a suitor hovering about me. At a time when most young ladies were considered in their prime at sixteen, I was perilously close to becom-ing a spinster, and a disgraceful disappointment to my family.

I dared to have great hopes for England. For the most part, I'd liked the English gentlemen that had come to call on Madame in Paris: they were often clever and amusing and handsome, too, if brash by French standards.

But not a sailor. "If you please, Madame," I said, glancing point-edly at one of the less savory of the sloop's seamen, a greasy, grimy rascal with a long, tarred queue and a single eye who'd been bellowing orders to the men aloft. "Not a sailor."

She laughed merrily, the light from a nearby lantern slipping into her hood to wash across her face. "There are sailors, Louise, and then there are sailors. Recall that all my brothers have loved their boats and ships. Why, my brother James is the Lord High Admiral of the Navy, as fine a sailor as any to be found, and he fought with great bravery in the last Dutch war."

I nodded, thoughtful. I'd forgotten how these English gentlemen embraced their navy. In France, the army was the gentleman's ser-vice, but in England it seemed that even the king's brother, the Duke of York, went to sea by choice. Perhaps there was some merit in the abbé's fortune after all, at least when it was combined with Madame's prediction, and I'd find myself loved by a seafaring peer.

But Madame misread my thoughts. "A sailor, yes, but not James," she cautioned. "I'm certain he'll be taken with you, as he is with most pretty young girls. But he is well and duly married, Louise, though he amuses himself with mistresses as if he weren't. Your parents trust me to do better than that for you."

"No, Madame." I was thankful that the overcast night now hid my face as I blushed again, though this time with guilt, not regret. I'd never once imagined myself with Madame's second brother; by her telling, he sounded dull and stubborn, if brave, and I'd not been taken with his fair-haired, ruddy face in the portraits she kept. But her oldest brother, Charles—that was another matter entirely, and I prayed she'd not ask me questions outright regarding him.

"No, no, indeed," she said firmly. "I've not brought you with me to see you commit a folly like that."

"Oh, Madame," I exclaimed, "I'm so grateful that you've brought me with you at all!"

She smiled, pleased to be thanked, as all noble folk were. "I always told you I would, Louise. It's an honor you earned with your loyalty to me, and one you deserved."

"But it's also one that many other ladies coveted," I said, which was entirely true. When the names of those chosen to accompany Madame had been made known, there'd been a good many who'd been grievously disappointed, and who'd shown that disappointment by spitefully attacking me as unworthy. "And for you then to grant me an allowance for new gowns—why, Madame, I can never thank you enough."

Though I'd known Madame to be most generous, I'd never expected her to do that, a rare gift indeed. She'd never said anything to fault my dress, humble though it was in comparison to all her other attendants, and while she had on occasion made me small gifts of gloves or scarves or gilt drops for my ears, there'd never been any munificence on this scale. I'd been able to have a half dozen new gowns made in the latest fashion and of the costliest cloth, with slippers and stockings and ribbons to match. For the first time, I shone among the other ladies, and I proudly knew I'd be noticed.

"I'm glad the things made you happy," she said. "You deserved them, too."

"They do," I admitted shyly, and with my arms outstretched, I spun lightly on my toes on the deck to make the skirts of my new traveling gown flare out around my legs. Not so much that I'd draw undue attention from the sloop's crew, but enough to show Madame my pleasure in my new wardrobe, and my gratitude, too.

But instead of delighting along with me, as the giver usually is with a gift, she only sighed, her smile faint.

"Oh, Louise," she said, "I wasn't supposed to tell this to you, but because I believe in my heart that it's better you know than not, I am going to share a secret with you. The gold for your clothes did not come from me, but from His Majesty."

"His Majesty?" Abruptly I stopped my dancing steps. "Not you?"

"No." She smiled, but sadly, or perhaps it was only a trick of the lantern's shifting light. "His Majesty was pleased with how you've served me, and wished you to be rewarded."

"That is most kind of him," I said, the answer I was expected to give. But the awkward silence that now fell between Madame and me betrayed expectations of a different kind entirely. We'd spent too much time in each other's company not to know the difference, and likewise we were too familiar with His Majesty not to recognize this as atypical of him. Louis was not a man given to act on kind impulse alone. With him, every action and word had a purpose and a reason.

But what reason could Louis have had for giving rich clothes to a lowly maid of honor like me?

"Charles has always preferred fair women with dark hair, and thus has set the fashion for them. You'll be regarded as a great beauty." She wasn't teasing me about sailors as she had before, but offering a warning that she expected me to heed. "There are a good many rogues among my brother's Court who will regard you as a delicious sweetmeat, to be gobbled up in one bite."

I nodded, and she reached out to cradle my chin with her gloved hand. "I am as serious as I can be, Louise. I would never forgive myself if any harm befell you."

"Yes, Madame," I said, so touched by her concern that tears stung my eyes. "I thank you, Madame, for everything."

"Everything," she said wistfully. "Oh, my sweet Louise, you don't begin to know what that means."

Yet even as she spoke, a flash of white in the watery distance caught my eye, and I gasped with excitement just as the lookout in the crosstrees over our heads called out the landfall.

"Forgive me, Madame," I said, "but look there! Boats, Madame, a flock of little boats coming toward us!"

"And land!" She made a wordless cry of purest joy. "Oh, Louise, that's England, there, that dark shadow on the horizon. England, my England at last!"

With land sighted, it felt as if the very vessel beneath us jumped to fresh life. The crew bustled at their stations, while Madame's servants and attendants recovered sufficiently to join her on the deck so that they would be in evidence when we made Dover. This last bit of water seemed to take forever to cross, with the changing winds making us cross back and forth as the captain strived to reach our destination. Slowly the sun broke clear of the horizon, a fresh dawn and a new day that made Dover's famous chalky cliffs glow with promise.

I feared my poor frail lady would expire from anticipation before we could arrive, she was in such a fever of excitement, and as the smaller boats from the port drew close to us in welcome, tears streamed down her pale cheeks. I remained close at her side, supporting her as best I could and blotting her face with her lace-edged handkerchief so she wouldn't look forlorn, but not once would she look away, so intent was she on that first glimpse of her brother.

At last a barque, sleekly elegant and flying an English lion on its royal pennant, drew alongside us. This vessel's deck was likewise as crowded as our own, but even among so many, one man seemed to make all others around him disappear.

He was a head taller than the rest, dressed in rich but somber dark colors that made him appear taller still. His skin was dark, too, nearly as dark as the sailors who weathered their lives in the sun, his features strong and manly beneath his long black hair. Even across the water I could sense the intensity of his presence and the power that lay behind the easy way he stood the deck, as if he'd been born at sea and not in a palace.

Because this, I knew, I *knew*, was the English king, Charles Stuart, and never for a moment did I doubt it.

He didn't wait until we'd moored to come aboard, or even for the sailors to throw a gangplank between the two vessels. Instead he jumped over the gap without hesitation, and bounded across the deck to Madame. He seized her in his arms, brother and sister reunited after so long apart. They laughed and cried and spoke over one another's words, then laughed and cried again, and their happiness was so complete that all of us who witnessed it wept with them. Another man, not so tall nor so dark that I guessed he must be her other surviving brother, James, Duke of York, stepped forward to embrace her. He was followed by a rough-faced older gentleman, who was her cousin Prince Rupert, and finally the young Duke of Monmouth, and all of it making for as fine a reunion of a family, royal or otherwise, as can be imagined. It was such a pretty sight that I watched with tears of my own, not just for Madame's joy, but for my own lost brother, Sebastien, knowing our only reunion would now be in heaven.

But even in the English Channel, the protocol of Court ruled all. At last Madame began to present her people to the king, one by one, each bowing or curtsying before him on the wet deck in order of rank and importance, as was proper.

My place would come next, near the end. For luck I touched my grandmother's small gold crucifix at my throat, and whispered a quick prayer for guidance. I was determined to put aside my usual shyness and be brave. I would *not* falter. I pushed my hood back so my face would show, and licked my lips one last time. I stepped forward and sank into the most graceful curtsy I could manage on the unsteady deck, my head bowed so deeply that all the king could see were my glossy black curls and the white nape of my neck.

"Mademoiselle Louise de Keroualle," Madame was saying. "You must be kind to her, Charles. She is my favorite maid of honor."

"Mademoiselle." His voice far over my head was deep and rich, ripe with amusement. To my shock, he took my hand in his and raised me to my feet, a gesture of favor far beyond my station, and one that scattered all my bold resolutions into disarray. Though I now stood as tall as I ever would, he held my hand still, as if he'd no wish to let it go, as if he'd every right in the world to claim my hand and me as his prize.

"Mademoiselle," he said, addressing me in French, "if you are one of my sister's favorites, then I am sure you must be one of mine as well."

Daring greatly, I lifted my gaze to meet his. He was smiling, smiling at me.

And oh, may the Blessed Mother preserve me, my fate with him was cast.

Chapter Eight

*B*ecause Madame's visit to England was to be only a month long, Charles had decided not to squander any of their time together in traveling, and to remain in Dover. Our lodgings were in the royal keep of Dover Castle, on the heights overlooking the harbor. We were told the castle was so vastly old that parts of its walls and towers had been erected by the conquering Romans of ancient times, and when I saw the worn stone walls and bluff square towers, I could well believe it.

Madame's bedchamber was in the corner of one of these towers, with the room I'd share with her other ladies nearby. Though the rough stones had been whitewashed in advance of our visit, I'd still the feeling of being inside a cave, carved and clawed from the rocky cliffs outside, and every bit as damp, too, with the rain that had plagued us in France following us to Dover. The ceilings were low, a series of vaulted arches, and the windows narrow slits that had been designed for defending the fortress with bows and arrows, rather than for admitting sunlight to a lady's chamber.

There could, in short, be no place less like the lavish and modern palaces where I'd spent my last eighteen months. And yet, because everything about this journey was an adventure, the castle seemed exactly right, like the magical keep of some fairy princess awaiting the return of her knight—or, as I thought with giddy anticipation, perhaps her king.

"Let me see you properly, Louise," Madame said as I joined her while she was having her hair dressed. She shifted her gaze without moving her head as the coiffeur in his black satin apron pinned a looped bow of red ribbons and pearls in the curls over her ear. "Come, stand here, directly before me."

I did as she bid, eager to show my new gown. I'd resolved not to consider too closely why His Majesty had chosen to make a gift to Madame for my clothes. Most likely it was because he wanted our party to outrival his cousin's Court in beauty and grace, and he'd deemed my humble wardrobe to be a sooty spot on so much French magnificence and style. No matter; what I said or thought would never have an impact on His Majesty, and thus I might as well accept this unexpected largess with grace.

Besides, I'd never worn a gown of such quality before, one fashioned precisely to my form by the Court's favorite seamstress in Paris. Sewn of satin the exact color of new leaves in spring with trimming of rosy pink, the close-fitting gown had exuberant slashed poufs for sleeves and deep cuffs and a collar of *point de Venise* patterned with lilies. My stomacher glittered with silver embroidery, and was clasped with glistening glass pearls set in more lilies. In fact, as I'd stood before the glass with a maid to dress me, I'd thought I resembled a spring flower myself, my beauty enhanced to glow with a delicate vibrancy that was enticing, and yet suitable for a maid of honor. If Louis had in fact wished me to be an admirable reflection of France, then tonight even he would have been satisfied.

Madame, it seemed, would likewise agree.

"Oh, my dear Louise," she said, her eyes widening with amazement. "Look at you!"

I grinned, and curtsied grandly, delighting in the feel of the shimmering silk flowing around me as prettily as the water in the fountains at Saint-Cloud. "You approve, Madame?"

"What a foolish question," Madame said, raising her hands upward to appeal to the heavens. "If you are not aware of your beauty now, why, then I am quite through with you, and I shall order you tossed over the walls and back into the sea."

I laughed, and curtsied again. "If you please, Madame, I am ready to dance with the sailors."

"Sailors!" The coiffeur clucked his tongue with disapproval, not being party to our jest. "Take care with this one, Your Highness, if she means to squander herself on sailors in the port."

"Oh, I don't believe that's what she meant." She smiled warmly, taking nearly as much pleasure in my appearance as I did myself. "I cannot speak for the sailors, Louise, but I am certain you'll capture the eye of every gentleman tonight."

"Thank you, Madame," I murmured. There was only one gentleman whose eyes I wished to capture, only one that mattered to me. I was in a fever to go below and test my new confidence, and see how I measured against the beauties of the English Court.

The coiffeur stepped forward to give a critical tweak to the twin lovelocks trailing over my shoulder. "Forgive me, Your Highness, but I believe she'd be much improved with a jewel or two."

"I think not," Madame said, frowning a bit as she decided. "Innocence like hers is better left without ornament."

I nodded with relief, for I'd no jewels of my own beyond my small gold crucifix. Madame could make up for both of us: she was richly dressed, as befit a royal princess, and bedecked with pearls and jewels that I recognized as gifts from both Charles and Louis, and pointedly not so much as a ring from her husband.

"Yes, Your Highness," the coiffeur said. "Though likely the young lady will have gentlemen enough offering to fill that void."

"Wicked rascal," Madame said, laughing, while I, as was predictable, blushed furiously at his sly double meaning. "That's exactly what I fear."

Several other of Madame's attendants had joined us now, and she rose from her dressing table, taking her fan from one of her maids as she readied herself to lead us downstairs. I slipped back among the older ladies of higher rank, as was my place, but Madame called me back.

"Here, Louise, stay with me," she said, taking my arm. I was startled by how she seemed to need my support, and looked to her with concern. I'd been so absorbed by my own excitement that I hadn't noticed how pale she was, or how shadows ringed her eyes beneath her powder.

"Madame," I said softly, so the others wouldn't hear, "are you too weary for this night?"

Swiftly she smiled with determination that belied her pallor. "No worries, not tonight," she said, patting my arm. "It's been a long day, that is all, yet I would not miss my brother's first grand meal for anything."

Nor would I. I matched my pace to Madame's, but if it had been left to me, I would have fair flown downstairs, I was that eager and excited. We made our way through the castle's narrow arched passages and down a long, dark staircase, and already we could hear the sounds of fiddles playing and people laughing and being merry. I'll grant, too, that Charles had ordered his people to make the gloomy old place as cheerful as was possible. Bright tapestries and hangings masked gray stone and huge bowls and vases of spring flowers were everywhere, for both color and fragrance.

I was expecting the same ceremony that accompanied Madame's appearance at the French Court, for as monstrous as Monsieur was, he was still second in line for the throne after the young dauphin, and he and Madame were duly honored and announced as such with fanfares. The company was expected to rise and curtsy or bow. As I soon learned (the first of many such lessons), this was England, and matters here were arranged differently.

Madame had scarce appeared in the arched doorway of the great hall before her brother himself came up the steps to greet her. At once she left me to fling her arms round his shoulders, much as they'd embraced earlier on the sloop, and effortlessly he swept her from her feet and into his arms. She'd grown so thin that she likely felt light as swan's down to him, and I wondered how great a difference he saw in her since she had left for France.

"Minette, Minette," he exclaimed, using his pet name for her, "I was near to sending the dogs up to search you out. At least the time you spent before your glass was put to good purpose. How fine you look! I vow there's nothing like a French tailor for rigging out a lady to best effect."

She laughed, her head tipped back with girlish delight. "You're always full of pretty rubbish, Charles," she said, and as he set her back down, she gave his arm a playful swat. "That never changes, does it?"

"No," he said, his grin wicked beneath his narrow black mustache. "Why should it?"

"It won't, which is more to the point, brother, you being who you are," she teased in return. "I'll grant that you're looking so handsome yourself that likely all the ladies believe your palaver. But I've never thought you'd be one to follow the fashion, and take to wearing a wig like all the other dancing masters."

He made a long, doleful face. "It's good that you'll be here for my birthday, Minette, so you might be reminded of how many years your poor old brother's been on this earth. Then you'll not be surprised at how many gray hairs this wig masks."

"Oh, hush, age means nothing to a man," she scoffed. "You'll never be anyone's notion of a poor, old man, and you know it, too."

Silently I agreed with her. I knew from Madame that the king's fortieth birthday would fall during our stay at Dover, and though that would make him more than double my age, to me that seemed impossible. In his dark gray coat, he was still tall and straight and as lean as any man half his years. His face did carry more lines than that of a callow youth, but those same lines only made his visage more provocative to me for all the worldly experiences they represented. On the left breast of his coat, over his heart, was embroidered the badge of the Order of St. George and the Garter, the highest order to be had in England, and this badge was all the mark of royalty upon his person. Louis chose to proclaim his kingship by dressing richly, with diamonds on the buckles of his shoes and rubies on his fingers, but such was Charles's confidence in who he was that he could dress for comfort and ease rather than display, and still be recognized as the monarch in any group of men.

Or so at least he seemed to my dazzled eyes, standing so close that, if I'd dared, I could have reached out my hand and touched his, and the knowledge made me shiver with wonder.

"Come now, let me show you to the table," he was saying as he slipped his arm around Madame's narrow waist to lead her into the room. "There's nothing like sea air to give a man an appetite."

Madame nodded happily, then turned back toward me. "Mademoiselle de Keroualle will join me."

Suddenly I found myself once again with the king's attention full upon me. It was as if everything else in that vast room around him vanished, and all I saw was his smile and the bemused expression in his dark eyes.

"I would like nothing better," he said, smiling warmly at me. "This way, mademoiselle."

Thus I found myself in a place I'd never dreamed I'd be, sitting and dining and sipping wine (and French wine at that, to my surprise) with the grandest and most noble folk of this land. The great hall of the keep was thick with courtiers, those sitting to dine and many more standing to watch. I was acutely aware of the honor I'd been granted, and humbled by it, too. Though I was at the same table as Madame and the king, I was farther down and beyond their hearing, amongst well-bred strangers who showed little interest in me.

I'd thought I spoke English passably well, but to be here amongst so many true English gentlemen and ladies, all of them speaking at once and on top of one another, made me realize I'd sorely overestimated my skills. My ignorance, my inexperience, and my natural shyness combined to swallow up whatever confidence my gown had granted me, and fearful of blundering, I sat wide-eyed, and said not a word. I was assiduously cutting the beef on my plate into tiny pieces—not for convenience in eating it, but to occupy myself—when the gentleman beside me rose and shifted his seat with another, and when I looked up, I smiled with grateful relief.

"Your Grace," I said to the Duke of Monmouth, an old acquaintance from the Palais-Royal. "Good evening."

"Good evening to you, too, mademoiselle." He smiled warmly,

choosing to speak French instead of English for my sake; having spent considerable time in Paris in the care of his grandmother, the late Dowager Queen of England, he was as comfortable in that tongue as his own. "You seem as if you're still at sea."

I blushed, and sighed. "Is it so very obvious?"

"I fear so," he said. "But in an entirely charming way. Besides, there's nothing I like better than rescuing pretty ladies in distress."

"Do you mean that?" I asked. Though there was a strong resemblance between him and his father the king, the duke was near to my own age, and not nearly so daunting.

"I do, with all my heart." He motioned for the footman to fill his glass with more wine, then rested his elbow on the table and his cheek on his hand, the better to regard me and my amply displayed bosom. "Pray tell me how I might help you, mademoiselle, and I vow I'll do my best to oblige."

I leaned closer to him, lowering my voice to be sure that those around us might not overhear. "Then tell me of the people here at this Court. Tell me which will be kind to Madame, and which she should fear and be wary of crossing, so that I might help her."

"What, Henriette?" he asked, strangely mystified by my request.

I nodded eagerly. "Yes, Your Grace. She would hold your opinion in high regard."

That made him brighten and smile anew. "She does?"

"Well, yes." That wasn't entirely true, but enough so that it wasn't a complete lie, either. Madame did like Monmouth—all of us in her household did—and his gallantries toward her made her happy, but she liked him in the way that she liked her little spaniels. He was pleasant and attentive, and with his curling dark hair and velvet dark eyes, he was very pretty to gaze upon. But he was also too easily impressed and led by others who wished to use him for their own gain, and was not clever in the ways a gentleman at Court must be if they hoped to prosper. I'd only to recall how he'd swallowed the Abbé Prignani's foolishness in its entirety. None of us was surprised that his duchess, a dour Scots heiress, preferred to stay far away in her native land, and devote herself to their children. As it was, Madame (or I) would never confide anything to Lord Monmouth of a serious nature or importance, for fear he'd be unable to contain a secret within himself for more than a quarter hour at best. Yet I wasn't above employing his weakness myself, and I'd no doubt that before the meal was done, he'd freely tell me all he knew of the company.

"Surely, Your Grace, in your position here, you can advise me," I continued, smiling as winningly as I could. "I only wish to serve Her Highness."

"Ha, who doesn't?" He glanced down the table to where Madame sat, and sighed gallantly. "I would help you if I could, mademoiselle. Truly. But to be honest, I do not believe Madame has a single enemy in all the world. She is a most perfect angel among women, and rare even among princesses. Wouldn't you agree?"

Foolish fellow, I thought. Everyone at the French Court had enemies; poor Madame's greatest foe was her own husband. I could scarce believe the English Court was any different.

Yet I smiled again, determined to try another stratagem. "Then tell me whom I should know, Your Grace. I've only this short time here in England with Madame to learn my way. Which ladies are considered good and wise company? Which gentlemen are no gentlemen at all, and should be avoided by a young lady such as myself?"

"That I can do," he said so cheerfully that I felt the pinch of guilt. "Of course you already know my father."

"Who does not, Your Grace?" I asked, even as I thought of how different the father was from the son.

"He's difficult to overlook, that's true, though I suppose that's how it should be since it's his Court." He let his gaze wander idly around the room. "That stout gentleman there, with the frizzed hair and starched white lappets beneath his chins. That's the Dutch ambassador. He's beside himself with worry, asking questions and peering about and wondering if my aunt has come to make some sort of pact between France and England that will leave his country begging at the kitchen door, hat in hand. Who would conceive of such an empty-headed folly? Sweet Henriette as a diplomat? Only a Dutchman, I say, and one of those for you to avoid."

I nodded thoughtfully, as if taking his advice. I was, too, in a way. Doubtless the king was likewise pointing the ambassador out to Madame, though with a different message for her from that which Lord Monmouth had offered to me. Clearly the duke had not been trusted with the real purpose for Madame's visit, and a wise decision, too, by whoever had made it.

"I'll tell you what the Dutchman does believe, mademoiselle," he said, leaning closer as if in confidence. "He believes that my father is planning to put aside his wife the queen on account of her barrenness, and that Madame is to offer Louis's suggestions for her successor. *That* is what he believes, and fears, for if Louis were to suggest a new queen, she'd surely be Catholic, wouldn't she?"

"I wouldn't know, Your Grace," I said, and truly I didn't. I had heard this plan before, from the Earl of Rochester among others, and I shared Madame's view that so fine a gentleman as the king would never treat his queen with so little respect. She was his wife before God, a union that could not be blithely dissolved by mortal man, not even a royal mortal. And yet even to consider that His Majesty might miraculously be free to wed again, a single bachelor in search of a fecund wife, made my foolish young heart giddy with a hope that had no foundation in either reason or logic.

Foolish, yes, but not so foolish that I'd confess it to the duke.

"I'll heed your warnings, Your Grace," I said, and wisely said no more. "If you please, who else should I mark?"

"The gentleman with the black plaster across the bridge of his nose is Lord Arlington," he said. "He claims the plaster's to hide an old scar from the war, but I ask you, can any scar be uglier than that black stripe across his face?"

I laughed, as any young lady would, especially since I knew that this was the limit of the duke's wit, poor man.

"Arlington's secretary of state, one of the gentlemen on my father's privy council," he continued, swelling with pride because I'd laughed. "Father trusts him implicitly, for being so clever. The man's traveled all about the Continent, and they say he speaks a half dozen languages, and can deceive in every one of them. His wife's Dutch, yet he intrigues with your King Louis. So there you are."

"He must be very clever, to keep so much in balance," I said. The only other privy councilor I'd met was Lord Buckingham, and he was clever, too, but in ways that made no sense. At least he'd not be here. The only one of Monsieur's demands that had been accepted by Louis and Charles was that Buckingham not be in attendance here in Dover; though it had happened nearly a decade before, Monsieur had not forgotten Buckingham's foolish attempts to seduce Madame before their marriage. Despite Lord Arlington's stripe of black plaster, he looked far too intelligent to make the same blunders that Buckingham had, and though it seemed he shared Madame's interests, it sounded as if she would be wise to be wary around him.

"Arlington is very clever, if also very pleased with his own cleverness," Lord Monmouth was saying. "He doesn't like talking to me. Most likely he'll find things to say to you, though, you being French and all. But take care what you say in return to him, for everything goes back to my father. The fellow beside him, the one with a face like a pug: that's Sir Thomas Clifford, another of the privy councilors. He's the one giving the Dutchman fits, on account of being a Papist."

"That does not surprise me," I said solemnly. Of course I knew how England's Christians had been led astray by a former king and into the wrongful ignorance of Protestantism, but this was the first time I'd encountered the prejudice for myself. "The Dutch are sworn Protestants, and hate anything to do with the True Church."

"So do most Englishmen." He screwed his face up with concern as he stared pointedly at my little crucifix, recognizing it as a symbol of my faith. "Forgive me, Mademoiselle, but so long as you're on English soil, you won't find much kindness for talk of the 'True Church.' Though most will guess you to be Romish, on account of being French, you'll do better to keep your own counsel where your faith's concerned."

That was far more useful advice than I'd expected from Lord

Monmouth, and I was grateful for it. If Lord Arlington and Sir Thomas were trusted advisers to the king, then I wondered if they'd be party to the discussions Madame was here to conduct on behalf of Louis. I'd venture so, considering that they both seemed to be sympathetic to Rome and France.

I considered this a long while, giving only half an ear to Lord Monmouth as he prattled on about others in the company of less import, about whose horses had won which races at the last meets and whose wife was deep in an amorous affair with which of her husband's best friends. Then Lord Monmouth said something that caught my ear as swiftly as an angler's baited hook will catch a prime fish, and pulled my interest back to him.

"That tall lady, there, on the other side of my father," he was saying. "The one that outshines all the others. That's the Countess of Castlemaine."

At once I craned my neck to see this infamous lady. Even in Paris, her name was well-known as not only the most beautiful woman in the English Court, perhaps even in all of England, but also as the most notorious, a lady who kept her hold on the wandering king's heart (and, it was whispered, other, more private parts of his person as well) by her eagerness to try any act in the libertine's carnal repertoire. Even while she'd been the official royal mistress with her own suite of rooms in the palace, she'd taken other men as lovers as freely as the king in turn took other women, and somehow managed to make him laugh at her infidelities. Her behavior quite scandalized Madame, who denounced her as an avaricious Messalina, and begged her brother to cast her off. But now that I'd finally seen her for myself, I understood.

She was no longer in her prime, of course, being nearly thirty years in age, and half of that lived hard from chasing pleasure. She'd born a slew of bastards to the king, too, and childbearing will leave its mark on even the strongest of women. But it mattered not: the Countess of Castlemaine remained as voluptuous as any pagan goddess. She was as tall for a woman as the king was for a man, with thick dark hair, pale skin, and heavy-lidded blue eyes that betrayed her wanton's soul. Her dress was sumptuous, more fit for a queen than for a mistress, with a true ransom of jewels scattered over her hair and person. Yet even if she'd been garbed in penitent sackcloth, she would still have drawn the lustful gaze of every man in the room by the sheer potency of her beauty, and I doubted even Madame du Montespan could rival her.

"She's very beautiful, my lord," I said, unable to keep the wistfulness from my voice. A king as rare as this one would naturally have such a glorious woman as his mistress.

"She's also in a righteous stew," Monmouth said. "After worrying my father for a month, he'd finally granted her the honor to be among the party to go fetch my aunt from France. But my aunt didn't wait, and sailed on her own, and so deprived Lady Castlemaine of being the first to welcome her."

I frowned. "Forgive me, Your Grace, but I do not believe that would have pleased Madame."

"But it would have pleased Lady Castlemaine, and that's all that matters to her," he said. "And to those around her, too. When she's in one of her furies, she's as shrill as any harpy. No one dares cross her."

"Surely His Majesty does," I protested, thinking how no one challenged Louis's will.

"My father prefers peace to war, mademoiselle, particularly in his bed," he said wryly. "Mark that ring on her little finger. That's new. I heard it cost him over three hundred guineas to quell that particular tantrum last month."

With considerable interest I studied the ring in question, an enormous table diamond cut wide and flat to display its size. I remembered how Madame had said I'd no need of jewels, but I'd have been quite willing to accept a ring such as this one.

"He may dawdle with other women like Nelly Gwyn, but Lady Castlemaine always remains," he continued. "Yet who could fault my father? There's no other lady like her."

"Nelly Gwyn's the actress, isn't she?" I asked, recalling her name from Madame's mention. It was the first time I'd heard Mrs. Gwyn's name here in England, though unfortunately far from the last. "Is she here, too?"

"Nelly here?" He laughed, I suppose at the unwitting absurdity of what I'd asked. "Unlikely, mademoiselle. Nell Gwyn's a common, lowborn player, an amusing little creature who cheers my father with her antics, but she has no place among us here."

I smiled politely. I chose not to venture that, according to Madame, the duke's own mother had likewise been common and lowborn, a Welsh tavern wench named Lucy Walter, and that only the king's kindness had raised James Croft from bastardy to his present lofty peerage as the Duke of Monmouth: for I'd learned early that certain observations, however pertinent, are better kept to one's self.

I did not wonder that Lady Castlemaine was here, while Charles Stuart's wife, Her Majesty Queen Catherine of Braganza, a most neglected lady, was not. Nor was I surprised to learn that the king seemed to dip and dally with as many other women as he pleased, as free as a honeybee who visits every lovely flower in the garden. The modes and mores of the Court were not the same as for common folk, who must obey their consciences and make their confessions. I'd spent my last two years in a household where my mistress was wed to a man who pined for his male lover, while she in turn sighed after her husband's brother, even as both the brother and the male lover plundered her own circle of ladies as if it were their private brothel, and my mistress accepted the gallant attentions of her brother's baseborn son. How, indeed, could the mistresses of Charles Stuart compare to that nest of writhing, duplicitous serpents?

"Ah, at last we're to have the dancing," Lord Monmouth said, thumping his fist enthusiastically on the table along with the other gentlemen around us, a heathenish, drumming din. They drank deeply, these Englishmen, and without regard for how swiftly their manners deteriorated as the wine seized their wits.

The guests who'd been standing were shuffled farther to the sides of the hall to make space, and the fiddlers put aside the softer tunes they'd been playing during the meal and began to play their instruments in earnest with a more vigorous fare. The king led his sister to the floor to applause and cheers, and together they took their place at the head of a set that included the Duke and duchess of York,

Lord Arlington and Lady Castlemaine (an unholy alliance, as I soon learned), and several other couples whose names I did not know.

In Paris we always danced in the stately, graceful manner that Louis himself preferred: a *bourée*, a *sarabande*, a *loure grave*, where every step and gesture was rehearsed and refined to perfection. In England, however, such formality did not appear to be the fashion. This first dance was as shockingly wild and untrammeled as those to be found among French peasants at harvesttime, and so exuberant that I feared for my frail lady. How she kept pace with her long-legged brother, I cannot say, what with the pair of them laughing and ruddy and jubilant in each other's company.

But before I could consider this overmuch, the duke seized my hand without any preamble, and pulled me to my feet.

"We've sat here long enough, mademoiselle," he declared, his face mottled with too much cheer, "and *Jack Pudding*'s my favorite. Come dance with me, if you please."

Truly, there was no permission to be granted, for His Grace was already hauling me through the crowd toward the floor to join the next set.

"Please, Your Grace," I said breathlessly, "what is Jack Pudding?"

"Why, this tune, of course," he said, squaring himself opposite me with his chin raised high. "Named for the kind of rascals who swallow prodigious amounts of black puddings for wagers. Here now, ready yourself."

He took my hands in his and bent low as the music—his favorite tune—signaled the proper beginning of the dance.

"But, Your Grace," I protested, "I do not know this dance!"

"You'll learn," he said. "Follow me."

I followed as he bid with the most miserable results, stumbling this way and lurching that, and trying to mimic the steps of the other dancers as best I could. This, then, was destined to be the first unfortunate sight the English Court would have of me, jerked about like a puppet on strings, and I would have wept if I hadn't been laboring so desperately to show some scrap of grace.

At last the dance ended and my suffering with it, and as I bowed my head and made my final curtsy before the duke, my only thought was of how quickly I could retreat back to my chair and shamefaced obscurity. Yet I was shocked to find Lord Monmouth had vanished, and in his place stood His Majesty himself.

"Mademoiselle," he said, offering his hand as elegantly as his son had not, "would you dance?"

"Oh, yes," I said, as breathless from the honor as from my recent exertion. I rose, and as if this scene was all by some greater design, the musicians now began to play a dance I knew, and knew well, a French piece with less of this English huffing and galloping and more opportunity for light conversation between partners. The first few bars we danced in silence, which gave me a chance to recover my senses and my wind so that I could concentrate on making a pretty show of my limbs for His Majesty's appreciation. Likewise, I was all too aware that every eye in the hall had turned toward us to watch. Kings were like that: every motion they made or word they spoke was studied, discussed, remembered, and recalled, and so, too, were any others honored by their notice.

So it now was with me. By the end of this dance, everyone in Dover would know my face and my name, and how I'd come to be here in Madame's party. I was grateful that His Majesty danced well, too, and made my own performance the easier. He moved with a manly grace and confidence, deftly marking his steps in perfect time and using his tall, well-made body to reflect my own, as the best partners will: doubtless a result of his French blood.

"You dance with exquisite grace, mademoiselle, as is only to be expected," he said as we came together in the dance. "You possess much charm to match your beauty. I can understand entirely why you are such a favorite of my sister's."

"Thank you, sir," I said, recalling how in England that was how the king was properly addressed, and I silently thanked Madame for teaching me that nicety. "I am honored by your notice."

"The honor, my dear, is mine." He smiled, ever ready to charm. To my surprise, he shifted to speaking French, both to make himself more agreeable to me and, I suspect, to render our conversation less easy to overhear. "I like a lady who's not so jaded that she's forgotten how to blush."

Needless to say, his notice only made my blush deepen, until to my misery I could feel the heat not only on my cheeks, but along my throat and across the pale expanse of my breasts revealed by my deeply cut bodice.

"Forgive me, sir, but I cannot help it," I said mournfully. "If I could forget, I would."

"Don't," he said, and as we turned to face each other again, I saw from the blatant interest in his dark eyes that he meant this not as flattery, but as truth. He did indeed like my blushes, though the reason was not quite so mystifying as I believed. In my innocence, I was as yet unaware that what to me was only a symbol of my embarrassment or shyness could also be perceived as a banner of amorous arousal, a banner that the worldly king was quick to read, and approve. "I wonder that my cousin Louis would part with you at all, even for so short a time."

I smiled ruefully. "I doubt that His Majesty has so much as noticed my absence, sir. I am not to his taste."

"Not to his taste?" he repeated. With his black brows raised with proper incredulity, he appraised me from my face to my toes and back again, and clearly found much to admire. "If that is so, mademoiselle, then I fear my cousin's taste is sadly misinformed."

I smiled as I turned away, as part of the dance. I saw that Lord Monmouth had left me for Madame, who seemed equally enchanted with the trade, so much so that I wondered if it had been arranged between them.

Nor would I find fault, either, and I was smiling still as I turned back toward the king. "His Majesty believes his taste—which is to say French taste—is without peer in the Christian world. I fear he would not agree with you, sir."

He chuckled. "My cousin and I often do not agree."

I drew my lips together in a moue of concern. "But I fear your cousin will not endure contradiction, sir. He expects to be obeyed in everything."

"So do I, mademoiselle," the king said easily. "But given the nature of my subjects and my country, I also understand the impossibility inherent in such complete obedience, and thus content myself with obedience in most things, rather than all."

I smiled, not believing a word of this amusing foolishness. He was a king, and without question he was obeyed. "You would prefer a concession, then, sir, to a conquest?"

"A conquest implies force, mademoiselle," he replied. "I prefer the possibilities to be found in a concession freely given."

I blushed again, and held my gaze steady with his. I was a virgin, yes, but I was also French, and from birth even virtuous French ladies understand the language of flirtation. I was well aware of the other meaning to our conversation, running like a dangerous undercurrent beneath the placid surface of a river, just as I understood the significance of such banter with the King of England.

The King of England.

This charming foolishness, with this man, excited and pleased me to a rare degree. How could it not? With his sister's encouragement, I'd let myself dream of him carelessly, for my own idle pleasure, for so long that I'd almost ceased to think of him as real. Yet here he was now before me, clearly made of very real flesh and blood and desire, too, and likewise I knew that if I ventured too far and risked too much, I'd be as irrevocably sucked beyond my depth as if in fact I'd plunged into that river hazard.

"You toy with your words, sir," I said, striving to keep my tone as light as any confection. "Do you prefer a concession freely given, or fairly won?"

The music brought us together, so close that our joined hands rose and my bare wrist did press against his where the ruffled cuff of his shirt fell back. I was startled by the unexpected intimacy of it, the warmth of his skin and the blood that beat at his pulse pressed so close against mine, and startled more that he purposefully held the pose longer than the dance required, so I'd not miss that he, too, had felt the sudden rush of heat between us.

"My sister warned me away from you, mademoiselle," he said

in a rough whisper as our faces drew closer, only inches apart. "She claimed you were too young and gently bred for me, and too near to the convent for my Court."

"Madame is kind to watch over me, sir."

"By your choice, mademoiselle, or hers?"

"Mine," I said, my whisper scarce more than a sigh. "Sir."

He released me then, letting me step backward as the dance required. Within my breast my heart raced like a frightened rabbit as I struggled to recall my wits. For nearly two years, I'd lived in a place that was overrun with lust and love, longing and desire, but this was the first time I'd felt any of it for myself, and like a novice tippler's first sip of wine, it had gone directly to my head.

Three steps to the left, slide, turn, three steps to the right. I ordered myself to concentrate on who I was, not what I felt. My cheeks might still be girlishly round, but I was a woman grown of twenty years, and it was time I presented myself like one.

" 'Such is our good pleasure that it be done,' " I said, bringing the conversation back to the safer topic of the French king when the dance returned me once again to the king. "That's what His Majesty your cousin says, and at once he is obeyed. 'Such is our good pleasure that it be done.' "

But the king was the king, and as such not so easily directed as I'd presumed.

"Good pleasure, ha," he said as the dance ended. "That may suit for my cousin, but for me, mademoiselle, my good pleasure will come from being with you."

Still holding both my hands firmly in his, he drew me closer and kissed me on each cheek, the whiskers of his mustache grazing over my skin. I started with surprise, my eyes wide and my mouth gaping, but he only smiled, and as he bowed, I realized that the other gentlemen on the floor were saluting their partners in the same fashion, and that the twin kisses were no more than the accepted conclusion of the dance. Belatedly I made him my own curtsy, and when I rose, the king was smiling still, though no longer at me.

"I've come to claim my dance, sir," Lady Castlemaine said, "and you with it."

Now I saw the flaws that age and sin had brought to her beauty, how the paint settled in the lines on her face and how her famous blue-violet eyes were at their core as hard as glass. She smiled wantonly at the king, and slipped her hand inside his coat to fondle him with shocking familiarity, while he only laughed.

"You've left me quite alone," she said, pouting slyly. "I've had no company at all."

"You're never alone, Barbara." The king pulled her roving hand from beneath his clothes and brought it briefly to his lips. As if to remind him of the price of her loneliness, she cocked her little finger, making the new diamond ring quicken and spark from the light of a score of candles.

"Pray, who is this pretty, sulky child?" she asked, sufficiently confident in his attentions that she could now deign to notice me. "I wonder that her mama lets her keep so late from her cot."

"This is Mademoiselle de Keroualle, Barbara," the King said, and this time his smile was for me, not her. "She is one of my Minette's attendants from France. Mademoiselle, the Countess of Castlemaine."

"My lady, I am honored," I murmured, showing her the respect her rank demanded, if not her history.

She studied me with rare frankness, the way one woman will to measure the worth of a potential rival. Then she smiled, slowly, as if to say she'd judged me no competition worth her bother.

"Sweet," she said, a single dismissive word. She looped her arm into the king's to lead him away, but also to make her possession clear. "Come, sir. Your rightful place is at the head of the set, not here."

She could not have been more obvious in her disdain for me had she spat at my feet. Yet the king did not notice, or leastwise pretended not to, and I recalled what Lord Monmouth had told me of His Majesty's preference for peace where Lady Castlemaine was concerned. Certainly he chose the easier (and more seductive) course now, curling his arm around her waist so that she might sway her full voluptuary's hip into his as they left me. Or perhaps he'd decided to honor his sister's request, and not toy with me further.

Nor was I left alone. I'd been noticed and admired by His Majesty, and my place here was secured. In ten minutes' time, my value had risen immeasurably. Now a flock of the same gentlemen who'd ignored my presence in their midst earlier was clustered about me, begging the honor of a dance.

Yet still I gazed after the king, and the long black curls that flowed over his broad velvet-covered shoulders. He was every bit the perfect gentleman I'd conceived him to be, and if I'd not been surrounded by so many others, I might well have sighed aloud, so deep was my pining for what I could not possess.

Though the wisest dons and philosophers will deny it, I believe that there are certain times when an unspoken wish can be made real by the sheer fervency of the wisher, and answered as if it had been said aloud. So it was now: for as I looked after the king with the most ardent longing in my heart, he suddenly turned back to meet my gaze over the unknowing countess's shoulder, as if I'd called his name and this was his reply. He smiled and winked at me, a small, delicious secret between us and no one else. Then he turned back to Lady Castlemaine, and the spell of the moment was broken.

That moment, yes. But what had begun between us that night would change our lives and many others, and even the fortunes of our mutual countries, for good, for ill, forever.

Chapter Nine

DOVER CASTLE, DOVER
May 1670

"Awaken, Mademoiselle de Keroualle, if you please," the maid-servant whispered, her hand on my shoulder. "Come, you must rouse yourself, mademoiselle."

Fuddled with sleep, I rolled over to face the voice that summoned me, squinting at the candlestick the maid shielded with her cupped hand. It was either very late or very early, with the single window in the stone wall still dark. All around me the other maids of honor slept, bundled and burrowed beneath their pillows and coverlets. Our chamber was cold and damp, and since none of us had left the dancing until well past midnight, I saw no useful reason for me to leave the snug and comforting warmth of my bed just yet.

"It's too early," I muttered, shaking her hand away. "Leave me."

"You must come, mademoiselle," the woman insisted. "Madame wishes you to join her in her lodgings as soon as you can dress."

That was different. Against my weary body's protest, I forced myself from my bed and, shivering, put a simple gown on. The maid-servant helped me dress my hair in the hall, where the candlelight wouldn't disturb the others.

"What is Madame's reason?" I asked as she brushed and pinned my heavy hair into some semblance of respectability. "Is she unwell? Has anything happened?"

"She did not confide in me, mademoiselle," the maidservant said, even more grumpy than I, for she'd been wakened even earlier. "All I know is that she asked me to fetch only you, and that you were to be dressed for day and brought to her."

It seemed odd to dress for day at this hour when night remained, but I did as I'd been bidden, and followed the maidservant to Madame's rooms. There were times when I believed that Madame had made some unholy pact against sleep, for truly she seemed to need only half the rest that others did. Her attendants soon learned this, much to their regret. We could be called to come to her at any hour of the night, and though we might struggle to keep our heavy-lidded eyes open, she would be as cheerful and alert as any morning robin, even daring to tease us as lay-abeds or laggards.

Thus it was when I joined Madame now. A dozen candlesticks and a large fire made her room bright, while she sat at a small table serving as a makeshift desk. She was already dressed as if it were midmorning, with a heavy woolen shawl wrapped over her silk gown and black knitted fingerless gloves. From the leavings on the tray at her side, it was clear she was likewise done with her breakfast save for the porcelain dish of tea in her hand.

"Good morning, Louise," she said briskly, looking up from the papers and letters before her. "I trust you slept well?"

"Yes, Madame," I said, even as I tried to swallow back another yawn.

"That was a deal of excitement last night, wasn't it?" she said, picking up her pen to make a note along the edge of one page. "There will be more. I can promise you that, so long as my brother's making the arrangements. I've never known another gentleman who so thrives on variety."

"Yes, Madame." I was glad I wasn't expected to say more. I'd wondered how much she'd seen of my dance with her brother last night, and further, if he'd spoken of me afterward. The two had spent much of the evening together (far more, in truth, than the king had spent with Lady Castlemaine, likely to that lady's peevish disappointment). But as much as I wished it, I'd no real reason to believe he would have raised my name or remarked me in any special way, especially if, as he'd told me, Madame had warned him away from me. I could hope, of course, even pray for his favor, but the unfortunate truth was that I was likely only one of the dozens of fair young women who crossed this king's path each day of his life. His amorous nature was widely known; for such a man, temptation must be everywhere.

"I was most happy to see you enjoy yourself, Louise," Madame said, as if reading my thoughts. "What did you make of the company?"

"The company?" I hesitated, wondering if she was using that vague phrase to inquire about my impressions of her brother. "To speak true, Madame, while I found the company most charming and delightsome, it was to me much like the French Court. There were many gallants, to be sure, but few bachelors, and fewer still of those were interested in securing a wife rather than engaging in another mere dalliance."

"Alas, that is the rule in most places," Madame said with a sigh. She slipped the papers into a leather folder, tied it closed, and tucked it under her arm as she rose from the table. "But at least I can promise you a fresh adventure this morning."

Mystified, I followed her to the door, and with two guards as an escort, we made our way through the sleeping castle. I'd still no notion of the hour, and the wind and rain that beat against the walls and windows masked any signs of a coming dawn. At last we reached one of the squared towers, and a suite of rooms so well-guarded with soldiers that I was sure they must belong to His Majesty. I followed Madame into the last chamber, a narrow room with an enormous fireplace and a roaring fire and a sideboard laid for a lavish breakfast. Down the center of the room was a long table, surrounded by heavy, dark armchairs with tall caned backs. The four gentlemen in these chairs rose as one when Madame joined them, their faces long and solemn, and not a hint of a yawn, despite the early hour.

At once I recognized them—the French ambassador, Charles Colbert, Marquis de Croissy; the two privy councilors I'd first seen last night, Henry Bennet, Lord Arlington, and Sir Thomas Clifford; and, of course, His Majesty the King—and at once, too, I recognized the solemn purpose to their gathering at this hour. The countless letters that Madame had written to Louis and Charles, the plans tortuously made and unmade and refined for a new alliance between England and France, would finally come to fruition in this room, far away from the frivolous celebrations in the rest of the castle. It was clear that these four gentlemen and one small lady were determined to alter the futures of their two countries at this table, and that they meant to do it in secret.

But why, I wondered, had I been included?

"Good day, Minette," the king said, coming forward to embrace his sister. "Did your feet keep dancing as you slept?"

She laughed, and reached up to tap her forefinger on the end of his long nose, a familiarity dared only by younger sisters to older brothers. "My poor feet could scarce climb the stairs, they were so weary, while yours, Charles—likely yours would be dancing still, if they weren't here."

"Ah, my dear sister, what you think of me!" He sighed, but his smile took away any hint of melancholy. "You are to sit here, at my side. You know these others, I believe?"

She nodded eagerly, her delicate head tipped to one side, and she smiled at the gentlemen in turn, winning each with a charm every bit equal to the king's. It was, I suppose, a gift to the Stuarts, that rare charm that won them so much with such ease: a small compensation for what they so grievously suffered and lost at the hands of that same charmed world.

But Sir Thomas was looking not at Madame, but at me, his expression decidedly disapproving. "Madame, might I ask who this young lady—"

"This is Mademoiselle de Keroualle," she said, linking her fingers lightly into mine as she drew me forward. "She is here by my invitation, Sir Thomas, and with my trust."

He shook his head, quick little bobs of disagreement. "The mademoiselle appears very young for such grave responsibility, Madame."

"Mademoiselle de Keroualle has the purity of youth to recommend her, Sir Thomas," Madame replied, the slightest edge of reproach in her voice. "She shall serve as my witness here, as she has served me before."

It was entirely true, yes, yet still I was honored and a bit awed that she'd chosen me from her vast number of attendants to be with her.

"The lady stays, Clifford," the king said. "It is my wish, as well as my sister's."

Swiftly I looked to him, surprised by his defense. He smiled, clearly delighted by my unguarded reaction. "You may take that seat by the window, mademoiselle."

"Thank you, sir," I said softly, and slipped into the chair he'd indicated. There I sat in silence, watching and listening and bearing witness to everything as Madame had wished.

It was not an easy process, this diplomacy, and vastly more tedious than I'd imagined. Though Madame fondly referred to the treaty as the "Grand Design," it was in fact far from grand, and there seemed precious little design to any of it. The French ambassador and the two counselors squabbled over every word and idea like mongrels with a mutton bone, raging back and forth to the very point of incivility. Only then would the king or Madame suddenly interject a new idea and calm the discussion.

Madame sat to the front of her chair, with her hands in their black woolen mitts clasped tightly before her on the table, and listening with care and eagerness, as was her custom. I could well understand her excitement. Few ladies of any rank were permitted to play such a bold part on the world's stage. Her determination was exhilarating, and her impassioned eloquence when addressing these gentlemen inspired me no end. She had persevered through much to reach this table, enduring the jealous rages of her husband and the near-constant illnesses that racked her slender frame. Not only would this alliance bring together her two countries, but it would also garner her the approval of the two gentlemen for whom she cared most in the world. I'd not forget her achievement, either, nor how hard she'd worked to gain it.

Her brother, however, demonstrated a far different style during the negotiations. Because he was both a man and a king, such talks must have long past lost their novelty to him. He sprawled in his chair, his long legs stretched before him under the table, where several of his spaniels lay sleeping. To disguise his true feelings (or so I guessed), he feigned uninterest with the discussion, even boredom, his thoughts inscrutable beneath his half-closed eyes.

Several times his restlessness drove him to rise from the table and go to the sideboard to forage for a slice of ham or bread with jam, for of course there were no servants in attendance, given the nature of these talks. Yet protocol continued to rule, and as soon as the king stood, the rest of us stood as well, from respect, though the others continued their discussion unabated. It was an astonishing thing to see, those serious lords popping up and down like jack-in-the-box, and a wonderfully foolish sight at that.

As the king returned from one of these little forays, his plate laden, he happened to glance my way, and caught me smiling with amusement. Chagrined, I blushed and ducked my head, which he likely interpreted as artful flirtation, rather than miserable fluster. He walked the long way around the table to his chair, purposely passing close to me. As he did, he took two Spanish oranges from his plate and placed them in my hands. He was turned so that none at the table could see his face, and knowing that, he raised his brows and pulled his mouth into a doleful grimace, I suppose to express his ennui, yet in the most comical and unexpected manner imaginable. Then he returned to his chair, his face once again solemnly composed, while watching me all the time as he waited to see my reaction.

To my horror, that reaction was both immediate and inappropriate. Laughter bubbled up within me, from both the silliness of the moment and my own discomfiture. Not wishing to disgrace myself, I did my best to swallow back my laugh, but only succeeded partway, making instead a dreadful snorting cough. Mortified, I bowed my head, and tried to think of the saddest and most tragic things possible. I heard nothing from the table that made me think they'd taken notice of my noisy misstep, though I suspect Sir Thomas must have rolled his gaze heavenward with this sorry proof of his misgivings.

Perhaps that emboldened me for what I did next, or perhaps I realized I'd not be reprimanded so long as the king himself was the cause of it. In any event, I swiftly peeled one of the oranges he'd given me, setting aside the peels neatly on the window's sill. When the sweet fruit was clean, I rose and took it to the king himself, curtsying prettily as I handed it to him. He smiled, both pleased and surprised, I think, and without a word I returned to my chair.

Figuring I had caused enough distraction, I occupied myself industriously by peeling the second orange, intending to eat it. Yet when I looked up, I saw the king was watching me. As soon as I raised a segment of the orange to my lips, he did the same, his gaze never leaving my own. The sweet juice filled my mouth, playing over my tongue, and I couldn't help but think of the other orange doing the same in his mouth, on his tongue, exactly as he'd intended. I ate each piece slowly, savoring it, and letting the tip of my tongue lick clean whatever droplets of juice dared escape my lips, and saw him do the same. Innocent though I was, I fully realized the suggestive nature of this little game between us, and what manner of lubricious acts he wanted me to envision with him. The blush that now stained my cheeks was a wicked one indeed, and knowingly so, too.

"Is that not so, Charles?" Madame asked, testy, as if she were repeating her question. "Would you not agree?"

He sighed, and turned back to the table. "I would agree that any English troops must be governed by English officers, and not French," he said, proving that he'd been minding the conversation no matter how else he'd been engaged with me. "I know it's the practice with other armies, but no English soldier will tolerate a foreign voice giving orders, nor should he."

After that, there was no further flirtation between the king and me. The discussions continued until the middle of the morning, and were adjourned for the day when the rest of the castle's guests were beginning to stir.

Not that either Madame or her brother retreated to their bedchambers to make good on the sleep they'd missed. Far from it. His Majesty appeared to share Madame's propensity for little sleep, made all the more incredible because he filled those extra hours awake with boundless activity. I suppose this must have been yet another quality inherent to the Stuarts, for in his past visits I'd noticed Lord Monmouth was likewise filled with this same rare and exhausting (to the rest of us) degree of enthusiasm and fortitude, and always eager to be off somewhere or another.

As soon as the meetings were done, the king proposed a sail around the harbor, the better to view the famous cliffs we'd only seen previously by the gray light of dawn. Madame immediately agreed, no matter that the weather remained dank and chill, with rain ever-threatening. With the effects of our crossing fresh in their memories, the majority of Madame's ladies declined this junket, but I'd no such qualms, and before long a small party of us was aboard the king's own yacht, sailing gaily across the choppy waves and through a misty fog.

Once we'd landed, the king declared he'd a need to stretch his legs, and off we trudged along the stony beach, with the same piebald spaniels who'd slept beneath the table now bounding on ahead to chase the gulls. Being young, and also desirous to remain in the royal company, I continued with them, and was rewarded with the king's happy delight that I could keep pace with his lengthy stride, the only lady besides Madame who could. With Lord Monmouth eager to support her if she stumbled on the stones, we were a merry, raucous crew, made more raucous still when the gentlemen began to sing sailors' songs that grew increasingly bawdy as we laughed and laughed. I'd never seen Madame as giddy as this, full of joy and without the heaviness that her life in France seemed to press upon her. But then, there was no amusement like this at the French Court, and while part of me was scandalized to see so little decorum among those of the highest ranks, I was young and could not help but enjoy such lighthearted jollities.

Likewise, too, I understood a second purpose to these entertainments. The king wished to present Madame's visit as entirely frivolous, a pleasurable reunion between siblings. The alliance that was being discussed in the hours before dawn was to be kept as much a secret from the other English courtiers as from the Dutch ambassador. What better way to hide so serious a purpose than behind a mask of idle amusement?

Finally Madame admitted she was in need of rest, and we retreated to our lodgings in the castle, while the king and Lord Monmouth went off for hawking in the fields nearby. Once inside, I realized how cold and damp I'd become, my hair hanging in tendrils and my face sticky from the salty sea spray. At Madame's doorway, I began to retreat to my own rooms to repair and recover, when she caught my arm to hold me back.

"A word, Louise, if you please," she said, drawing me into her bedchamber and closing the door after, so we'd not be overheard. Away from her brother's company, she'd wilted, her gaiety gone and the discomforts of her illness showing again on her face. She'd eaten little since we'd arrived, claiming it was excitement, not illness, that kept her from the rich foods being offered, but I doubted her words. She looked pale and weak, yet still determined.

I steeled myself, sure now I'd be scolded for my ill-smothered laughter during the treaty discussions earlier. But to my surprise, I'd guessed wrong.

"Louise," Madame began, her hands clasped tightly before her, exactly as they'd been at the table. "Louise, you know how I trust you, and love you best of my household."

"Yes, Madame," I said softly, more touched than I could say. "Thank you, Madame."

"I should thank you as well, my dear," she said, her smile bittersweet. "There are so few I can trust in my life, yet I have never once questioned my faith in you."

"I have been honored by your trust, Madame." I thought sadly of those who had in fact betrayed her, from the grand names like Louise de la Vallière and Athenais du Montespan to the more humble ones as well, footmen and maidservants and grooms who'd run directly to Monsieur or Louis himself to whisper their tattle about my poor mistress. There were too many who'd misused her this way, far, far more than she deserved. "My only wish is to continue to serve both you and France, and to be worthy of your faith in me."

"You are a loyal daughter of France, Louise." She smiled warmly. "Be sure that His Majesty is aware of it, too."

Again I nodded, and recalled the curious conversation I'd had with Louis in the gardens outside the Louvre, last Christmas Day. I wondered if he'd known then that I was to be here in Dover now. Perhaps he'd already determined that I'd have this role as a spectator to the negotiations—a role that I'd nearly spoiled with my foolish behavior. At once I could anticipate Louis's displeasure when he should learn of it—for though Madame would not mention it, the Marquis de Croissy would not be so reticent. I could find myself in disgrace at our Court or, worse, sent home to my parents, and my spirits plummeted.

Yet Madame seemed to sense the shift in my humor, and reached out to rest a reassuring hand on my arm.

"Don't doubt yourself, my dear," she said gently. "You've done well, very well, and no one here would say otherwise."

I wondered if that meant she'd defended me to the ambassador, or whether here in the less oppressive air of England, my misstep was not so dreadful as I'd feared.

But Madame's own fears, it seemed, had landed in another corner altogether.

"I have the greatest regard for you, Louise," she said, "but surely you must know that I love no one more on this earth than my brother."

"Yes, Madame," I said, and with equal care. "No one could deny the devotion you and His Majesty share."

"No one should," she said almost fiercely. "And yet because I love him as a brother, I am also aware of his flaws as a man. Louise, I beg you, have a care with him."

"You mean the oranges, and laughing as I did," I said contritely. "Please, Madame, forgive me, I beg you! I never intended to giggle and laugh like that, not when—"

"Do you believe I care about small mischief like that?" she exclaimed. "Oh, Louise, that is as nothing. As nothing!"

I searched her face, bewildered. "Then what is, Madame? What is it you fear?"

"That you'll believe what he tells you, and mistake desire and gallantry for love," she said, her eyes full of anguished tears. "Guard your heart, Louise. Kings have none to lose, you see. No matter what else may happen here, guard your heart."

The pattern of our days remained the same for the next week. The secret discussions for a new alliance continued each morning, and were followed by every manner of entertainment: balls, hunts, sailing parties, suppers, and amusements. We walked, we rode, and the king himself led the more daring of the gentlemen to bathe and swim in the sea. We made one long trip to Canterbury to see a ballet and a play performed by the Duke of York's company, followed by an elegant meal at St. Augustine's Abbey, and on another day, we clambered aboard the royal yacht and sailed up the coast to review the fleet stationed there, as pretty a sight as ever there could be.

The king sought my company as often as was possible, for dancing, conversation, and flirtation, blithely ignoring any wishes his sister may have made in my regard. To be desired and pursued by a king is a heady honor, and with it came a recognition and a power I'd never had at the French Court. Everyone in Dover knew me, and flattered me, and wished to be with me so that some of my golden burnish as a favorite might shift to them.

Yet I'd not needed Madame's warning to know the danger, as well as the honor, that came from the king's pursuit. He himself was temptation incarnate, and my body sorely desired to succumb. But I'd seen enough of the world to understand that if I gave myself to him in that flower-covered castle, his interest in me would soon fade. The moment I sailed back to France, I'd be forgotten, my maidenhead gone forever and, given the numbers of bastards he'd already sired, likely another of my own in my belly as a remembrance. I'd kept chaste too long to toss it away like that now, and besides, my virginity was the sum of my dower.

Did I already love the king? I cannot say now, nor could I have done so then, either. I was still of an age that finds it impossible to separate divine love from common lust, exactly as Madame had feared, and in truth, when one is but twenty, there's likely little difference between the two. I knew that when he smiled at me, I forgot all else around me save him. I knew that my name on his lips was the most enchanting sound I'd ever heard. I knew that when his fingers closed around my hand, my heart quickened and I felt a feverish desperation for more intimate caresses. I knew that each night I tossed with restless, wanton dreams of him that made me wake with my limbs a-tremble, my breathing short and my body soaked, and my thoughts tumbling with wicked imaginings of lying with him.

Thus for that month, I skipped along a line as perilous as any ropewalker's at a fair. While I relished the king's attentions, I took care not to make myself too eager, too ardent. I would not be alone with him, though often we would make a small party with Madame and her constant squire, the Duke of Monmouth. I smiled and I laughed, and I let the king kiss my cheek and my hands, but no more. It was at once extraordinarily difficult, and extraordinarily delicious.

But whether I loved him in Dover: ah, I do not know.

"Mademoiselle de Keroualle, here."

I stopped on the staircase to see who had spoken. Tables for cards had been set up after supper, and the gaming was fierce. The English, it seemed, were willing to risk most anything on the turn of a jack or queen, with wild shrieks and howls of excitement from both ladies and gentlemen alike. I did not play, of course, being in no position to risk a loss, and as a result Madame had sent me up to her rooms to fetch a box of the peppermint lozenges that gave her ease.

"Here, mademoiselle." The Marquis de Croissy stepped from the shadows near a window and bowed his head to me in greeting. He was striking rather than handsome, with ivory skin and a narrow, crooked nose, and the distinguished face of a gentleman long in the king's service. As usual, his manner was quiet and subdued, for he found it more useful in his profession as an ambassador to go unnoticed than otherwise; I'd certainly not seen him as I'd passed by, and I wondered uneasily if he'd been waiting there for me.

Not that he would ever confess it. "You catch me stargazing, mademoiselle," he said instead, gesturing toward the long window beside him. "For the first time since we left Paris, the clouds have parted, and the stars have revealed themselves."

I glanced past him as if studying the sky, too. "If we're fortunate, my lord, we'll have sun tomorrow. Pray excuse me. I am on an errand for Madame, and she expects me—"

"Her Highness will excuse you for another minute or two." His smile was bland, without showing his teeth. "More likely she's so interested in whatever Lord Monmouth is whispering in her ear that she's forgotten she sent you away in the first place."

"Madame is happy, my lord," I said, defending my mistress. She was openly enjoying the attentions of the young duke, delighting in having such a handsome, young squire at her beckoning, and without the jealous rages of Monsieur to tarnish her enjoyment. "Her Highness is *happy*."

"She is, she is," he said, soothingly. "And so is her brother. You have done well, mademoiselle."

At once I was on my guard. "Forgive me, my lord, but I've done nothing."

"You are modest, mademoiselle," he said. "His Majesty is a restless gentleman. Your presence during our little talks has calmed him greatly. It pleases him to gaze upon your beauty."

"I am there at Madame's wish," I said warily. "If the choice were left to His Majesty, I doubt I'd be included."

He shrugged, his hands open, as if to say there was no telling what this English king would do.

"This king is ruled by his cock, mademoiselle," he said bluntly. "You need not blush on my account. It's common enough knowledge. You can be sure that our own Most Christian Majesty has taken note of his English cousin's proclivities, and how they can best be exploited for the benefit of France."

Since I'd been here, I'd learned that the ambassador had done much more than merely take note. Lady Castlemaine was openly receiving French gold and jewels from him in exchange for her supposed influence over the king. To my countryman's chagrin, however, that same lady was also receiving subsidies from the Dutch ambassador and likewise any others who offered.

"The English king is like other men in that regard," I said warily. "I am sure he enjoys the beauty of many women."

"But these other women are not French, mademoiselle," he said. "And he *is* the king. If an opportunity were to present itself—"

"There will be no such opportunity, monsieur," I said, recoiling, my cheeks hot with shame at what he was proposing. To dream idly of indulging the king was one thing, but to be pandered to him like this was another entirely, and I wanted no part of it.

"You're very proud, mademoiselle," he said, glancing pointedly at my gown, "especially for a lady who has already accepted royal generosity."

Too late I remembered the new clothes I'd been given before this journey—clothes that I now realized were meant to present me more favorably to the English king. I remembered Madame's hesitant explanation that had really explained nothing, and her warning about her brother, and felt like the greatest fool imaginable.

"I am not some common slattern, my lord," I insisted, "but a Christian lady, a Keroualle, and my father's daughter."

"You are also a daughter of France," he said, his voice suddenly harsh. "If the English king chooses to act upon his obvious desire for you, then you—"

"Good evening, my lord," I said curtly. I began to turn away, meaning to leave and continue on my errand before I rashly said something I'd later regret, but he caught my arm and stopped me.

"We all serve France, mademoiselle, and we all serve our king," he said softly. "You, Madame and I. We are here together in Dover for that purpose alone. We only differ in how we prove our loyalty. You would be wise to remember that, mademoiselle."

I pulled my arm free. "No one has ever questioned my loyalty to France."

"Take care no one does, mademoiselle," he warned, and raised his hand in dismissal. "His Most Christian Majesty expects nothing less."

. . .

On the twenty-second of May, the new treaty was signed and sealed in the keep's tower room. As I listened to the final details as they were agreed between the two countries, I could well understand why this alliance was to be kept secret, for there was much that was shameful about it.

Only two years before, Louis had signed the Peace of Aix-la-Chapelle with Spain, accepting the territories of Lille, Flanders, and certain other portions of the Spanish Netherlands in return for ceasing further hostilities, presumed claims based on his queen's inheritance. The agreement had been mediated by the supposedly impartial allies of the Triple Alliance: England, the Republic of the Seven United Provinces (the proper name, though seldom employed, for the Dutch and their territories), and Sweden. Now Louis had taken England as a more advantageous ally, and he intended to ignore the earlier Peace entirely, and aggressively strive to claim more of the Spanish territories for France, and Dutch ones, too, if it could be managed.

Charles was even more duplicitous. Forgotten was England's role in the Triple Alliance, and the goal of halting Louis's relentless expansion. Now France was made England's much more attractive ally, and Charles agreed to join with Louis in a fresh war against the Dutch. These were old dreams for both kings: Louis wished to rule as much of the Continent as he could beneath the flag of France, while Charles in turn wanted the English to reign unchallenged at sea, with English trade ruling the world.

There were many other carefully defined clauses within this document, deciding which country would supply certain troops and whose navy would engage in which waters, as if these two kings and the single princess were cheerfully dividing toy soldiers and boats instead of the lives of men. To secure Charles's good faith, Louis also agreed to pay his impecunious cousin three million livres Tournois, a great sum of gold pieces that would make the English king independent from the demands of his quarrelsome Parliament.

But the single clause of the treaty that would likely be most difficult for the English king involved his eventual conversion to our Church. In return for what Louis offered in gold and military strength, Charles was publicly to accept the teachings of the Church of Rome and announce his conversion, as soon as the welfare of his kingdom would permit. Madame was overjoyed that her brother had accepted this clause, as was the Marquis de Croissy. While I could rejoice in principle, in the harshest of reality, I now feared for the English king's life at the hands of his unruly Protestant people when they learned of what he'd promised.

In the handful of days that I'd been in Dover, I'd seen for myself that what Lord Monmouth had told me that first night was true: the English did hate Catholics. From the shopkeeps in the town who made unsavory jests about holy sisters to the toasts that mocked His Holiness the Bishop of Rome that were drunk each night by the noblemen in the great hall of the keep, there was only intolerance, suspicion, and black-hearted loathing. Catholicism and Catholics in general were regarded as anathema of the worst sort, and even I had soon begun tucking my grandmother's crucifix into my bodice, to avoid the crude jibes that it inevitably drew. For a country so firmly Protestant and scarcely ten years removed from the rule of that puritanical fanatic Oliver Cromwell, the king's promise to convert would be a troubling declaration indeed, and I didn't wonder that the only councilors admitted to this secret and signing this treaty were the two already sympathetic to Catholicism.

I understood, too, why the king had been so obliging to Monsieur about excluding the Duke of Buckingham. Lord Buckingham also sat on the privy council, and by rights he would have had to have been included in this treaty. But he was also a staunchly belligerent Protestant, wed to the daughter of one of the old Puritan grandees, and he would have spoken out sharply against an English king declaring for the Catholic faith.

Yet perhaps because I was young and this my first experience with diplomacy, I was likewise the only one who knew of the new treaty who seemed to have any misgivings about it. The rest happily celebrated with toasts and rejoicing as the papers were signed, and though the reason for their happiness was perforce left unspoken, their collective humor rose even higher.

To my endless relief, Lord de Croissy said nothing further to me about my supposed role in the negotiations. Instead he returned to how he'd been previously, scarce taking any notice of me at all. Perhaps he believed I had done what was necessary to secure the English king's signature on the treaty; perhaps he'd simply realized, as was true, that I'd not near the power over the king that he'd ascribed to me, and that I was no longer worth his trouble. Either way, I was relieved, and like all the others, I set myself to enjoying the next weeks without that particular care to burden me.

With her long-desired goal met, Madame in particular threw herself into the daily amusements with a feverish intensity, so much so that again I feared for her health. She ate nearly nothing, slept little, and danced late every night. It was an old tale, the pitiful moth drawn irresistibly to the brilliant, fascinating glow of the flame, yet when I saw Madame drive her own fragile body to wrest all the pleasure she could from these few days in England, I could think only of that delicate, determined moth and its disastrous fate. My poor lady, I thought, my poor, dear, tormented lady!

But, ah, the moth, and the flame, and the ruin that came from it: how much better if I'd only thought first of myself.

Chapter Ten

DOVER CASTLE, DOVER
June 1670

I greeted our last day in Dover with mixed feelings. I was sorry, very sorry, to see this magical time end. In an ancient, foreign castle, I'd been like a princess in the old romances, revered for my beauty and admired by a king.

But my own tale, I knew, would have no sweetly romantic ending. My fantasy king was already wed to another, and besides, even if he were not, he desired my body, not my hand in an honorable wedlock. Nor could I overlook Lady Castlemaine and his other mistresses (including the lowly actress who, I'd heard whispered, had this week given birth to another of his bastards in London).

In Paris, I wouldn't exactly return to the scullery in rags, but Monsieur was enough of a monster for any fairy tale, guarding his gates and ready to pounce the moment we returned. I would put aside my beautiful new clothes, tainted as they were; perhaps they'd even be taken from me, for not having been sufficiently earned. Before long I'd fall back into the same patterns as before, and once again at the French Court I'd stand to one side and watch while others danced. To be sure, it was not an unpleasant life in Madame's household, but it had none of the excitement or success I'd found here in Dover.

For one last time, I walked with Madame and a group of other courtiers along the rambling defenses and parapets of the castle overlooking the sea. Of course the king was with us. On account of his sister's imminent departure, he seemed more quiet than usual, even melancholy, and he left the customary singing and good-natured tom-foolery to his other gentlemen. To no one's surprise, the skies were again misty gray and threatening rain, as they had been for nearly all of our visit, something none of us would realize had been a sad portent until later.

As was usual with these walks, our party began to separate as some chose to dally on purpose, finding lovers' amusements among the stony crenellations once reserved for soldiers alone. Before long I found myself alone with the king, though whether by accident or his design, I could not say. Gentlemen (and ladies, too, to be fair) can be most ingenious when giving chase. This had happened with us before, and each time I'd contrived a way to rejoin the others before the king had found a chance to make much use of our solitude.

But now, given that it was our final day, and likely the last I'd ever see of him, I did not rush to escape. Of a sudden, I'd made a decision, a decision that I would now act upon. I slowed my pace and he did likewise, until at last we stopped altogether inside a little niche in the wall. He understood, I think, or so I judged by his smile.

"How it grieves me to know you're all to leave England tomor-row," he said softly. "I've never liked partings."

He looked down at me from beneath his wide-brimmed black beaver hat, pulled low on his brow to keep it from blowing away in the wind. His bark brown coat was trimmed with loops of black velvet, such as any country gentleman of rank would choose, except for the badge of the Order of St. George and the Garter sewn on the breast. The gold and silver threads gleamed dully in the gray afternoon light, a most muted reminder of his royal majesty.

"I will be sorry to leave, sir." With a wistful sigh, I wrapped my hands more tightly into my cloak, for it was chill for June. I leaned over the stone wall, the better to gaze out at the sea, and when my hood blew back over my shoulders, I left it, enjoying the feel of the breeze playing over my face and through my hair. "I am most grateful to Madame for bringing me here with her."

"I am as well." Under pretext of likewise admiring the view, he came to stand closer beside me.

"Pray the sea won't be as choppy tomorrow, to ease our crossing," I said. His arm brushed mine, and I shivered from his touch, or leastways the very thought of it. "Madame's household has few born sailors among them."

He chuckled, not because there was any humor to be found in what I'd said, but simply because I'd said it, a pleasing realization to me.

"But Minette tells me you're one of them, mademoiselle," he said. "She claims that you two were the only ladies who did not puke."

"We were." I grinned, and brushed away a mist-dampened tendril of my hair from my eyes. "She was so eager to see Dover that we spent near the entire night on the deck."

"Ah, Dover." He leaned a little farther over the wall, looking down at the unassuming small town huddled between the castle's walls and the harbor. "When I first returned to England, I landed at Dover. My two brothers and I ate a seaman's breakfast of salt pork and peas on board the ship, and then were rowed ashore. I'd never seen so many folk in one place as were gathered to welcome us, here on this same beach."

"It must have gladdened you no end, sir."

"Oh, it did, it did." He smiled, the deep lines on either side of his mouth curving upwards. "But likely that's all as ancient history to a young lass like you."

"Ten years ago, sir," I said. He must have guessed me younger from my round face, the way so many folk did, but I saw no reason to correct him. If he thought me younger, then so be it; most gentlemen preferred innocence in ladies, anyway. "Not so long past."

"No," he said, turning thoughtful. "Though some days it seems longer ago than others. I wonder how large the crowds would be to welcome me now."

"Larger than before, sir," I answered eagerly. "When they greeted you then, they'd only the promise of the future. Now that they know how you will do most anything for them, how could they not love you more?"

He turned away from the sea and toward me, his face with the bemused expression that I'd come to associate with him. By now I understood it was not because he had a wry or cynical nature. Rather, I believed he often employed that pleasant guise to hold the world at a distance, and to mask his true feelings and thoughts. It seemed a very French way of doing things (even for an English king), and made perfect sense to me. Yet it also made me long to earn the favor of his confidence, to see behind this genial defense to the man he was working so hard to protect.

"How could my people not love me more?" he asked, repeating my question with a practiced incredulity. "You've been trusted with certain knowledge of me, mademoiselle, that very few people in my kingdom possess. You know this, and the perils such knowledge entails, and yet you still would speak of how much my people would love me?"

"That knowledge, sir, tells me that you place the welfare of your people above all things," I said, and I believed it, too. "If they would look past their initial intolerance, they would see that this alliance has made England stronger than she was before. The two greatest countries in the world pledged to work together: how can that not be a fine achievement?"

"A wise speech for one so young, mademoiselle, and proof that you not only listened, but comprehended." He smiled, yet watched my face shrewdly for my reaction. "Is that what you believe for yourself, or what Louis has primed you to say?"

I blushed, yes, for when did I not with him? Yet in that instant, I also realized that he believed me to be Louis's pawn, which, to my sorrow, I suppose I was.

"Ah, sir," I said softly, my own smile tinged by sadness. "You would seem to have certain knowledge of me and my own perils as well."

He smiled wryly. "It would seem we have much in common, mademoiselle."

"Perhaps, sir." I sighed, and leaned my head back against the wall behind me with a show of weary resignation. If I also displayed the pale vulnerability of my throat and my plump, small chin for his delectation, then so be it. "Perhaps."

"You're an enigmatic beauty, mademoiselle." Lightly he ran his fingertips up the side of my now-exposed throat to stroke my cheek. "A rare creature, that."

I smiled, wondering if he could feel the excitement rising in my blood beneath his fingers. I'd imagined this so many times before, and now that I was faced with the luscious reality, I could scarce control my passions. I shifted against the wall, unable to keep still with him so close. I'd nowhere to retreat now, even if I'd wished it.

"Not rare, sir," I whispered. "French."

"That must be it," he murmured, his eyes nearly black beneath the brim of his hat. "My people would have difficulty understanding you, too."

"But, sir," I protested slyly, for being with him was making me feel sly indeed, "we've done nothing that needs explaining."

"Then I vow it's past time we did." He turned my face up to his to kiss me, and for the first time, I let him. It was no hardship, nor great sacrifice, for at that point my blood likely ran with the same heat as did his, or maybe even more. He kissed me slowly, richly, exactly as a king should. He tasted salty, from the sea, and the tiny bristles of his mustache tickled and prickled at my lips. He made me forget all the frantic, fumbling kisses that had been stolen from me by gallants my own age, and instead he kissed me for my pleasure as well as his own. He kissed me not as a king, but as a man in his glory, and with a sigh of joy I gave myself over to his embrace.

Sensing my imminent surrender, he slipped his hands inside my cloak and around my waist, pulling me close against his chest. I swayed into him with giddy delight, letting his mouth take possession of my own. The scores of tiny gilt buttons that edged his coat and the waistcoat beneath pressed into me as he held me more tightly, and further, I felt the length of his eager scepter hard against me, ready for employment as soon as his master chose.

Yet like every maid who wishes to avoid ruin, that was also a warning I knew well to heed. To be taken for the first time on the parapets of Dover Castle was not truly what I wished, nor what I deserved, either. I was not meant to be some casual conquest. I was meant for . . .

more. I wasn't precisely sure what that more would be, not yet, but I'd become convinced my future might lie here in England rather than in France. To this end, I'd wanted to be certain the king would remember me, but in a way that could be useful to me in the future, and not merely titillating to the rest of the Court for a single afternoon.

Before my will weakened, I slipped free, taking care to turn with grace as I did. "Forgive me, sir, but I must go. The others are waiting."

He frowned, surprised, but didn't try to press his advantage by force. "Then let them wait. They will, you know."

Such is the perfect confidence of kings! "I dare not linger, sir," I said, my regret genuine. "I do not trust my own passions in your company."

I'd hoped that would please him, and it did. He smiled warmly to coax me, taking my hand lightly in his own. "You've only to trust me instead, sweet."

"But I cannot, sir," I said sorrowfully, bowing my head. "I cannot. As much as I might wish such a confidence, it would not be right, not like this, on the eve of our departure."

"Then stay," he said, and it was to his great credit that he made it sound a natural appeal, one friend to another, and not a royal command. "You'd like London."

"If you were there, sir, I'm sure I would," I said, smiling sadly. "But forgive me. I cannot oblige."

"Why, if we both wish it?"

"Oh, sir," I said, "my place is with Madame."

"Minette." He sighed mightily, his handsome dark face full of love for his sister and melancholy that she was leaving. "That is true. My sister trusts you as few others."

"I'm honored to serve her however I can, sir," I said, in perfect truth and without calculation. I glanced back to where she could just be seen in the distance, with Lord Monmouth and several others. "She's been so kind to me, yet all I have to repay her with is my loyalty."

"You have, mademoiselle." He raised my hand to his lips, his gaze not leaving my face as he kissed my fingers. He looked at me as with hungry desire, true, but also with such admiration that I knew I'd won in the way I'd hoped. "I will not forget you, Louise."

"Nor I you, sir," I said softly. "Nor I you."

I expected this to be the end of the king's pursuit of me, leastways for this visit. With no real reason than that I wished it so, I believed that our paths would cross again, in some other fashion, and with a more lasting result as well. After that single kiss, our parting on the wall had been genial, and there'd been a sweet note of concession and farewell to it. But I'd underestimated the depth of the desire I'd inspired within him, and how much, like all men, he hated being denied a prize he wanted.

Later that evening, we gathered in the great hall for the final meal and the amusements that followed. The coming farewells weighed heavily on everyone's thoughts, and our gaiety had an empty, forced ring to it. Madame sat as close as she could to her brother, and throughout the meal, she would freely weep, leaving her tears to course unchecked down her cheeks.

As was usual among royal folk (excepting, of course, the heartless Monsieur, who never offered his wife any tokens or remembrances), there had already been many exchanges of costly gifts between them—pictures, jewels, and gold—as tangible proof of the enormous love shared between brother and sister. Most generous had been the king's special present of two thousand gold crowns for Madame to build a chapel to their mother's memory at Chaillot, the place where that pious lady's heart rested. As the meal continued, Madame began fondly to list all her brother's gifts yet again, and overwhelmed anew by his largesse, she announced that she needed to offer him another in return. She beckoned to me across the table, and at once I went to her side.

"Louise," she said, motioning for me to crouch down so I might hear her whisper, "you know where my jewels are kept. Go to my chamber as swiftly as you can and bring back the green casket."

I did as she bid, returning with the leather-covered box. All her most precious jewels were contained within, and I couldn't imagine the value of what I held tightly in my hands. By then everyone else had learned what Madame intended, and when I entered they all turned toward me with anticipation. There was interest in me as well as the jewels, for of course by then there was likely not a soul left in the castle unaware of how I'd been alone in the king's company that day.

I came forward between Madame and the king, sinking gracefully into a kind of half curtsy as I offered the leather-covered casket up in my hands. I knew I must have presented a pretty sight, the rose-colored silk of my gown falling around me on the stone floor as I made my obeisance, and the murmur of admiration that rippled through the room agreed.

"You must decide, Charles," Madame said. She didn't take the box from me, but left it in my hands as she unlatched the lid and pushed it open. "A small token, for remembrance's sake."

She held up each piece in turn for his choosing, displaying each to best advantage in the candlelight, almost as if she were the keeper's assistant in a goldsmith's shop instead of a princess. She showed him a hexagon brooch of black onyx surrounded by pearls, an oversized ring with a cluster of pearls set in a swirl of pale blue enamel like a swirling wave, a pair of clips with twinkling sapphires and diamonds in the shape of roses, a cunning golden cupid offering a bouquet of rubies and pearls. They were all beautiful, precious things of the rarest artistry, and around us people excitedly craned their necks to see. Even at Court, there were few privy to the contents of a royal princess's jewel box.

I was, and often, too, and so as I held the box, my thoughts were elsewhere. With my head still bowed, I dared to glance up at the king through my lashes. He wasn't looking at his sister or the jewels, or listening to her, either.

He was looking only at me.

"Whatever you wish is yours, Charles," Madame was saying. "Choose whatever will remind you of this time we've had together."

"Ah, that is an easy choice, Minette," he said, smiling. He leaned forward toward the casket in my hands as if to pluck one of the jewels his sister offered. But instead he reached out and with his long fingers cradled my chin, turning my face up toward his so I could see his smile.

"I've made my choice, Minette," he said, looking squarely at me so his meaning could not be in doubt. "This is the only jewel I wish to keep with me."

I was stunned, overwhelmed, shocked into speechless silence. Could this possibly be true, or only another of my fervent imaginings? He wanted me so much that he'd claim me here, with his sister and his Court to bear witness. He wanted me to stay in England, he wanted me with him, he wanted to rescue me from my hopeless future in France, he wanted—

"Oh, Charles, no," Madame said impatiently. "Don't be ridiculous. Mademoiselle de Keroualle is a young lady of a good French family, not some sort of heathen slave girl to be bartered on your whim."

"But you asked my wish, Minette, and I answered," he said, feigning ingenuousness. "She'll be safe enough here with me."

Madame's scolding scowl said more than any words, and gently but forcefully she removed his hand from beneath my chin.

I felt instantly bereft. It was not my place to beg, of course, or plead my own wishes before royalty, yet I prayed silently that Madame would somehow understand that this was a possibility I might wish for as much as did the king. Selfishly I forgot my loyalty to her, as well as my responsibilities. All I could remember was how the king had kissed me that afternoon, and how much I wanted him to repeat the experiment.

As, I suspect, did he.

"Sweet sister," he began anew, coaxing. "Sweet, dear Minette—"

"No, Charles," she said again, so firmly that all the others who'd been watching our little tableau with breathless delight now tittered to see their much-indulged king denied like a naughty puppy. "Her parents gave her over to my safekeeping, and I won't disappoint their trust. If you had offered Mademoiselle de Keroualle a respectable place at your Court as an attendant in the queen's household, then we might have discussed it, but not like this."

"Then I'll make her one of Catherine's maids," he said quickly, seizing the only possibility Madame offered. "She can have her own lodgings at Whitehall."

"Lodgings at Whitehall," Madame repeated skeptically, making it clear that she believed those lodgings in the royal English palace would be much closer to the king's quarters than the queen's. "No, Charles, I am resolved. Mademoiselle de Keroualle will be returning to France with me tomorrow, and that is an end to it."

But it wasn't, not for me. I didn't care that the English courtiers regarded me with fresh licentious interest, perceiving sin where there was none. They were courtiers, and it was their custom to assume their great king would never bother to claim me publicly like this if he hadn't already enjoyed my favors.

No, what grieved me most was the dreadful quandary that the king's rashly public declaration presented to me. With the optimism of youth, I'd already decided that the English Court offered me a more welcoming opportunity than the French one ever had. I believed that my beauty, my graces, my talents would receive more appreciation in London, and that the attentions paid to me in Dover would only continue as my due.

But if I were now to seize the English king's offer to join his wife's household, the only real position I would be accepting was one lying beneath him, as his mistress. All London would know it, too. There would be no other possibilities. With everything so predestined, the king's infatuation with me would likely soon fade and be done, and with little reward to me. I'd seen enough of the world to predict what my fate would be after that: to survive, I'd be forced to accept the advances of some other eager gentleman who desired to go where His Majesty once had been. I'd serve as his mistress until he, too, tired of me, and another lesser fellow would follow, over and over as I slid down the precipitous decline of fashion and rank to abject ruin and death.

In short, His Majesty's impulse had made me pause and consider. As much as I might wish otherwise, I was but a fledgling in these games of courts and kings. I'd still a great deal more to learn, and if I were to prosper, I must take care to suppress my own desires, and heed the warnings of my head, rather than the longings of my heart.

"I saved you, Louise," Madame said later that night, when we were at last alone. "I love my brother beyond all measure, but for him to ask for you like that was wickedly wrong of him, and wrong for you, too. You may not realize it now, but I did save you. I saved you both."

By every possible standard, Madame's journey to England would be judged a success. The next day she returned to Louis with the Secret Treaty, signed by her brother and safely in the Marquis de Croissy's keeping. She had triumphed where so many other experienced diplomats had failed, and she was assured of Louis's favor and endless gratitude for her achievement. She had won the fickle English Court anew with her boundless charm and spirit, and with it helped swing their favor toward France. She'd had a blessed respite from her intolerable marriage. Most of all, she'd had a month's holiday in the land of her birth and in the company of her family, led by her favorite brother—a month where she'd been feted and cherished and loved with a devotion she'd never have in France.

Thus it was little wonder that Madame's departure was miserably unhappy, and as washed with tears as any funeral cortege. No one wanted their darling, delicate princess to leave or, worse, to be given back to the French, who did not appreciate her. Countless vows were sworn that she must return to England again at the soonest possible convenience, while final kisses were given and embraces made, and so many bouquets of English flowers were tossed to us that the deck resembled a floating garden.

Madame was so overcome with sorrow that the king was forced nearly to carry her aboard the yacht, and the tenderness with which he held her on the deck made even the most jaded courtiers weep anew. When at last the captain could wait no longer or miss his tide, the king refused to disembark, and remained on board with us as the anchor was weighed. Still he stayed with us as our little vessel left the harbor and made its way into the open sea, and we were nearly out of sight of the land he ruled before, finally, he left us for one of the other boats that had accompanied us.

The other ladies tried to persuade Madame to come below with them to the cabin where she would be dry and warm, but she shook them off, and sent them away. Yet I understood. I kept to her side, just as I had on the first night of our arrival. Blindly she took my hand in hers, her teary gaze never wavering from the boat that carried the king.

He was likewise standing at the rail, the wide brim of his hat pulled low and his dark hair blowing back from his broad shoulders. His gentlemen, too, stood apart from him a respectful distance, and I was certain I'd never seen a more lonely figure of a man. Who would ever have dreamed a great, powerful ruler would feel such grave melancholy? I longed to ease his suffering, or somehow lighten the burden that bowed those manly shoulders, and as I stood with Madame, I could no more look away from him than she herself. My heart wept for Charles as surely as did my eyes, tears shed in perfect sympathy to both sister and brother.

"I will come back," Madame whispered, as if her brother could hear her still over the ever-widening breach of the sea between them. "I swear it, Louise, and mark my words for me, lest I ever dare forget. I *will* come back."

"So shall I, Madame," I said softly, still unable to look away from the distant dark figure that was the king. "So shall I."

Madame's little fingers tightened into mine in wordless response. Truly, what was left for us to say? Together we remained side by side in the gray mist, long after England and her brother had both slipped beyond our sight. King, princess, and me: our lives had become curiously twined, we three. Yet on that gloomy morning I could never have imagined how much more tightly my life would be bound in with those Stuart siblings, plaited together one over the other.

Our return to France was as anyone could have predicted. We were met at Dunkerque by a guard supplied by the king (ah, how hard it was to remember that that simple word referred once again to Louis, not Charles!), and they escorted us back to Paris. The weather was hot and sunny, and where on our earlier journey we'd fair drowned from the chilly rain, now we felt as if we were baking, our elegant coaches turned to rolling ovens. But at least the heat meant that the roads were dry and passable, and we were soon in Paris once again.

Madame's reunion with Monsieur was predictable, a heated battle before us that doubtless led to him enforcing his marital rights in the most hateful way possible once they were alone. Her meeting with Louis was far more pleasant, for he praised her accomplishments lavishly before the entire Court. That was beyond bearing for Monsieur's jealous nature, and within the week he took us away to Saint-Cloud, where he hectored Madame constantly for details of the treaty that had made her more important than he.

But Madame was changed. I could not say precisely how, or even when this had occurred, despite all the time I spent in her company. She was more restless than I'd ever before seen her, finding no peace at any task or amusement for longer than a few minutes before she rose with impatience, eager for something else. She did not sleep at all, instead wandering the château's vast gardens like a phantom wraith imprisoned by the moonlight. Her ethereal beauty and charm seemed of a sudden to have vanished, and her face had grown frighteningly plain. She who had never complained suddenly gave voice to an unending litany of pains that plagued her, concentrated in her stomach and her side.

Physicians were called and consulted, and duly proclaimed Madame to be suffering from the results of the impoverished English diet. They advised her against bathing and walking, and she ignored them. Yet clearly something was not as it should be with our dear princess, and those who loved her prayed for her deliverance, for it seemed far better to entrust her to God's hands than to those of mere mortal men.

On the last Sunday in June, she dressed early as was her custom and met with Monsieur, who was leaving for Paris. She visited her older daughter, Marie-Louise, who was sitting for her portrait, and dined with her ladies. Feeling unwell, as was sadly usual, she called for a cup of chicory water to ease her discomfort. No sooner had she emptied her cup than she began to gasp and clutch at her side.

"My God, what pain!" she cried out, sinking to her knees as two of her ladies hurried to support her. "Oh, preserve me, I've—I've been poisoned!"

"Poisoned, Madame?" exclaimed one of the ladies, her eyes round with a horror shared by us all in the room. In a Court so full of enemies and plots, poison was a constant fear, and there was not a one of us who did not think at once of Monsieur and the chevalier.

"Yes, yes, I am sure of it!" cried Madame, her face twisting with agony. "Oh, merciful Mother in Heaven, save me!"

At once she was undressed and carried to her bed, while the distraught waiting woman who'd prepared the chicory water was seized and questioned. Before several witnesses, some of the remaining water was given to a dog as a test with no ill effects. That should have been proof enough of innocence, but still no one believed it, and when the silver cup that Madame had used was found to be missing, there was no reason not to believe the worst. Monsieur's passionate hatred of her was too well-known to be ignored. Of course Madame had been poisoned: she'd said so herself. The only question was how it had been arranged.

Yet the physicians and surgeons who rushed to her bedside were reluctant to agree, and I cannot say I blamed them. Who would wish to be the one to tell the king that his brother was guilty of such a dreadful crime? The physicians first declared Madame was in no danger, and suffering from no worse than her usual digestive complaints. But as her obvious agony intensified throughout the evening, they could no longer ignore the obvious, and finally admitted her life might be in peril.

Amidst so much feverish activity, my only role was to stand by the wall of her bedchamber with Madame's other attendants. We were there to support her if she needed us, but our main purpose was to serve as witnesses, whatever the night's outcome might be. Some of the ladies prayed, a soft murmur of beseeching to match the beads slipping through their fingers, and some sobbed openly to see such suffering.

Overwhelmed by my own helplessness, I watched as the physicians tended my poor lady, one holding her leg steady while another used his knife to cut her for bleeding, the recommended location and course for pain of the abdomen. Her small foot was as white as alabaster in his hand, and almost as lifeless, as the physician squeezed the blood from her heel—livid red drops against the pallor of her skin—until the porcelain cup he held beneath her heel was filled.

When the bleeding brought no change, the physicians next forced Madame to swallow powder of Spanish vipers. This was a rare and costly decoction prepared from the skins of those snakes, and considered the very best antidote to most poisons. Alas, all it did now was induce a violent vomit, a terrible purge that made Madame writhe and weep in pain. Finally the physicians conceded there was nothing further to be done, and having failed to save her mortal body, gave her over to the priests, who would try to do better with her eternal soul. Reluctantly (or so it seemed to us), Monsieur sent word to his brother.

All too fast, Madame's bed was transformed from the spot where she'd sipped chocolate and played with her daughters and her spaniels into the solemn place where she must await her death. Any such unhappy farewell has its rituals, but for royalty, everything was magnified until it almost seemed a tragic play whose inevitable climax would be the heroine's death.

Soft-voiced priests replaced the physicians and their awful instruments. The heavy curtains of Madame's bedstead were looped back and candles placed to ring around it. The most elaborate armchair in the room was placed beside the bed in case His Majesty should appear. Madame's sheets were refreshed with ground herbs and myrrh, a too-sweet scent I'd ever after associate with death, and an elaborately embroidered cloth, rich with gold thread and intertwined crosses, was laid over the coverlet.

Even Madame herself was made ready. Though she'd never lost consciousness, she looked as if she were fashioned from wax, her once-bright eyes glazed and dull as the color of life drained from her famously beautiful complexion. Her sweat-soaked hair was smoothed back and hidden beneath a coif of fine white linen. Her face and hands were tenderly washed with cologne and her favorite rosary looped through her fingers. Though she still could not keep back the groans of her suffering, she did seem to take comfort from these ministrations. Everything was arranged to help her make peace with God, and prepare herself for death.

Her daughters were roused from their beds and brought to their mother, a heartbreaking sight. I doubted the two sleepy girls understood what was happening, and the baby most certainly didn't, only giving a wail of protest as she was held to Madame's lips to kiss. One by one, her household was likewise permitted to step close to the bed to bid farewell, and as my turn came, I tried to smile through my tears. Even in her considerable pain, she knew me, and whispered my name, as precious a blessing as I could ever wish. I knelt and kissed her hand one last time, her fingers chill with death, and too soon my time with her was done. I could not contain my grief after that, my tears spilling in sorrowful abandon as I staggered back to my place among the other ladies.

Soon after, the king himself appeared, so overwrought that he rushed to Madame's bedside without any of his usual decorum. With him came both Madame de la Vallière and Madame du Montespan, both of whom still held affection for their former mistress, and several others wishing a final glimpse of the princess. Another who rushed to pay his respects at the deathbed was Ralph Montagu, the English ambassador to France, and I could all too easily imagine the devastating report of Madame's death that he would immediately send to his king.

Last of all came Monsieur. We all watched him closely for any signs of remorse for what he'd done, yet his painted face betrayed nothing. He spoke not a syllable of love to his dying wife, and shamefully offered no comfort to her as a husband should. As had always been the case in this hideous marriage, poor Madame was left to forgive him his sins toward her—we all could hear her ragged whisper— yet Monsieur's eyes remained dry and his expression impassive. He was the only one among so many to remain unaffected, and not to his credit, either.

Soon after midnight, Bishop Bousset, the king's own consoler and preacher to the Court, administered the Last Sacrament and Extreme Unction to Madame, and then granted her the greatest gift of forgiveness. Just as the bishop had comforted Madame's mother, the English Dowager Queen, on her deathbed such a short time before, he now performed the same unhappy service for the daughter. He held his own crucifix to Madame's lips for her to kiss, and with that, her soul finally slipped free of her tormented body.

Less than a fortnight ago, Henriette-Anne had been laughing and dancing merrily with her brother at Dover. Now she lay dead before me. To be sure, I'd seen ample evidence of her fragile health and constitution, but I'd always believed the strength of her spirit would be enough to protect her. Yet what spirit can triumph against poison? What grace can survive in the face of such malevolent wickedness as Monsieur had displayed? Scarce a month before, Madame had enjoyed her twenty-sixth birthday. She had been only a handful of years older than I was myself, and her death was as harsh a reminder of the dangers of this Court and the capriciousness of fate as I could ever have.

My despairing heart could not believe Madame was gone. I'd lost my mistress, my patroness, my protector at Court, but most of all, I'd lost my one true, dear friend.

Whatever I did next, I must do myself.

Chapter Eleven

I missed Madame more than I'd imagined possible. Her warmth, her friendship, her courage, her protection, all had been stolen away from me in those few terrible hours, and in the days that followed I was so devastated by her loss that I feared that I, too, might follow her, perished from grief.

I was not alone. Madame's death shocked all Paris. It was not only the unexpected suddenness of having so young a lady snatched from our midst, but the suspicious circumstances that surrounded her demise as well. The whole city spoke of nothing else, yet still the facts remained uncertain, even to us who had witnessed the death. All that was known for sure was that Madame had declared herself to be poisoned, and that the physicians attending her had administered the proper antidote, but to no avail. Further, the silver cup from which she'd last drunk, considered to be the agent of the poison, had yet to be found, and was presumed to have been stolen away by whoever was guilty. Everything beyond that was rumor and speculation. But no matter which version was whispered, Monsieur was at the center of it.

The other constant, of course, was that no one dared speak of poison before the king. Surely he must have suspected his brother, too. How could he not? He'd known the misery of the Orleans marriage, and he'd seen for himself how badly Monsieur had treated Madame.

Nor could he have had any illusions about Monsieur's character or the wickedness that rotted his brother to the very heart.

Yet as was so often the case with Louis, the reality of what had happened was much more complicated. True, there were few things worse than having one's brother poison his wife. But because that same brother was also the heir to the greatest monarchy in the world, Louis would require absolutely unquestionable proof of guilt before he'd act. It was much easier and less disruptive to the Court to believe that Madame had in fact died a natural death. The official autopsy, attended by many witnesses both French and English, concluded the same: that the poor princess's liver and intestines had been insupportably decayed and gangrened by a boiling, impetuous bile that had caused her agonizing death.

But many at Court still speculated that Louis must have asked Monsieur to swear that he hadn't poisoned her. When Monsieur (a natural liar if ever there was one) vowed that he hadn't, then Louis had chosen to accept his brother's oath, and put all other possibilities from his mind.

Which is not to say the king was unmoved. Louis was visibly shaken by Madame's loss and wept with sorrow before us, a rare thing indeed for a man who usually kept himself so tightly reined. Madame had been his dear friend from childhood, a confidante, and perhaps even a lover. He missed her sorely. He ordered a state funeral for her to take place in August (a delay that was expected in royal deaths in order to accommodate the elaborate preparation) with the full complement of honors usually reserved for a Queen of France. Though by custom he could not attend himself, he did plan to send his wife the queen as his representative, another considerable show of respect, and Bishop Bousset was already composing a suitable eulogy.

While the king grieved, Monsieur did not. In the weeks following Madame's death, he was never once observed to weep or seem otherwise discomfited, as would be expected of a new widower. Instead he seemed obscenely happy, almost gleeful, as if he'd been the one freed from a monstrous spouse, and he showed no respect for his lamented wife. Publicly he declared that she must have been poisoned by the Dutch at Dunkerque as she traveled, a special potion designed to claim its victim much later to divert suspicions. It was an unlikely tale, and he the only believer.

To the outrage of those who truly mourned Madame, he picked and rummaged like a magpie through her most personal belongings, searching for anything that might feed his jealousy, even into death. He took all the gold her brother had given her in England and claimed it for himself. He refused to return the rare jewels Madame had inherited from her mother, Her Majesty the Dowager Queen of England, jewels that belonged by rights to the English royal family, and not to Monsieur. He read her private letters aloud, mocking them to his sordid friends. He interrogated those of us ladies who'd been closest to Madame, demanding what we knew of his wife's dealings with the English on Louis's behalf. One night, when there was gaming at the Louvre, he brought a beautifully embroidered gown that Madame had worn in Dover and tossed it carelessly onto the faro table, declaring the gown to be his stake.

More perverted still was his fanatical interest in the rituals of mourning. He demanded that the rest of the Court consult him in every detail of dress and etiquette and insisted that he be included in all arrangements for his wife's funeral. Every member of his household and staff was expected to wear deepest mourning. Despite the hot summer, he ordered his two young daughters by Madame dressed in dark purple velvet, the prescribed mourning for a princess. Both nine-year-old Marie-Louise and the infant Anne-Marie were forced to receive the long stream of courtiers and dignitaries who came to the Palais-Royal to offer their formal condolences on the death of their mother. Even if proper, this was a grotesque spectacle, and unnecessarily cruel to the little girls, who were still too young to comprehend fully their loss.

Monsieur's orders weren't limited to his daughters. Standing with the two French princesses was their cousin, the five-year-old Lady Anne of York, the younger daughter of the English king's brother, the Duke of York. She was a princess in her own right but a shy, unlovely, and unwanted child with watery eyes. Lady Anne had been sent to

Paris the year before, first to be raised by her grandmother, who had soon died, and then shifted to her aunt, Madame, who had also perished. Now, by Monsieur's whim, this forlorn little creature was also swathed in purple velvet and set up as one more prop in his elaborate tableau.

As sympathetic as I was to the plight of this English princess, I worried much more about the English king. Knowing how close Charles had been to his sister, I could scarce imagine what he must have felt when he'd learned of her death. Yet imagining was all I *could* do. With Madame gone, the procession of English visitors with the freshest English news and tattle had ceased to find its way to the Palais-Royal. I'd grown accustomed to knowing everything, but now I knew nothing, and that forced ignorance fair drove me to madness.

At last one evening at the Louvre, a fortnight after Madame's death, I glimpsed the English ambassador, Ralph Montagu, across the crowded reception room. As quickly as I could I made my way to him, and to my relief he remembered me at once.

"Mademoiselle de Keroualle!" he exclaimed, his thin-lipped mouth curving into a smile. *"La belle Bretonne!"*

I curtsied prettily, or as prettily as I could whilst dressed in mourning wool, without any ornament. "Good day, Mr. Montagu," I said in English. "I'm honored that you recall me, sir."

"Oh, I'd be a poor fellow if I forgot a face as pretty as yours, mam'selle," he said, then composed his expression more solemnly. He was a pleasant man, though his downturned eyes and long nose made him look more doleful than by nature he was. "A sad time for us all, isn't it? To think of how happy we all were at Dover, and now this. Poor princess, to die so young."

"She is with God and the angels now, sir," I said softly, and made the sign of the cross to honor my mistress. "But might I please ask after His Majesty? How has he borne the unhappy news?"

"Very badly, I am told." He sighed and shook his head and, taking me gently by the arm, led me to an alcove near a window, where we could speak with more privacy. "When Sir Thomas Armstrong arrived with the grievous news, the king refused at first to believe it. Yet when he read the letter from His Most Christian Majesty, the one accompanied by the princess's ring, he could no longer deny the dreadful truth. They say he collapsed from the shock of it, and withdrew to his darkened chamber to lie prostrate on his bed. For a week he remained alone within, refusing food and company in his sorrow."

"Oh, poor, poor sir!" I cried, wishing it were in my power to comfort him. "He loved her so, and to lose her so suddenly must have been nearly beyond bearing. I pray that he finds comfort in the other ladies about him. Her Majesty, or Lady Castlemaine."

"No, mam'selle," he said. "He could tolerate no company. I suspect any lady's voice or touch reminded him too painfully of what he'd lost in the princess. They say the only two admitted were his oldest manservant and Lord Rochester."

Tears of sympathy welled in my eyes. I could understand why he'd choose an old friend like Lord Rochester, a gentleman who, beneath the merry mask of his wit, carried the same air of melancholy as the king. But for His Majesty to refuse comfort from any softer voice made me suspect not the depth of his grief, but the shallowness of the ladies around him. How could they claim to love him and not be eager to ease his sorrow and pain? If I were in London, I wouldn't have left him to pine alone in the dark. I would have steadfastly remained at his side, ready to lessen the grief we both shared for the lost princess, and I would not have left.

"There now, I didn't intend to make you weep," the ambassador said, clearly one of those men made uneasy by ladies' tears. "We all grieve for Her Highness, eh?"

"I grieve for her, and I fear for His Majesty," I said, blotting at my eyes with my black-bordered handkerchief. "How can I not?"

"But my latest word is that the king is much improved," he said, wishing to cheer me. "They say now he is not so much distraught, but rather furious with his cousin for letting such a crime go unpunished."

Now it was my turn to be uneasy, and cautiously I glanced over my shoulder to make certain we were not overheard. "His Majesty believes Madame was poisoned?"

"He does," he answered firmly. "Who does not? There is nothing but outrage in London, and because of it all Frenchmen must be on their guard lest the rabble choose to make them accountable for the princess's death. Surely you have heard the question His Majesty put to Louis's emissary."

I shook my head.

"He asked when the Chevalier de Lorraine would be returning to the French Court," Montagu said with outraged relish. "That's what he said, bold as new brass, and who can fault him? You saw Madame die, mam'selle, as did I. How can you have any doubt after that?"

"It is not my place to ask such questions, sir," I said carefully. We all were distraught over Madame's death, but I did wish the ambassador would be less bold in expressing himself. I doubted I'd ever become accustomed to the blustering frankness with which these Englishmen spoke, even the most politic ones.

"It may not be your place, mam'selle, but it certainly is His Majesty's to ask after the circumstances of his sister's murder," he said bluntly. "He has, too, and he's yet to have answers from any Frenchman. Considering the barbarous manner with which our poor English princess was used by her husband while still alive, and then what I have heard of that vile catamite de Lorraine—"

"Please, sir, I beg you, guard your words," I whispered urgently. I'd heard this same story myself, of course, one of the many scandalous theories then rippling about the Court. Though still banished to exile in Italy, Monsieur's old favorite, the Chevalier de Lorraine, was being credited with having his pawns murder Madame. The chevalier was said to have purchased a specially lethal poison from Florence (the center for all such nefarious drugs), infused in a paper that was then wiped inside Madame's cup. Thus those who drank from the same pitcher of chicory water were unharmed, and only Madame perished. I could well believe that the chevalier would wish Madame harm, for he had always perceived her as a rival, and besides, she was the reason for his banishment.

But I was not so foolish as to discuss any plot involving the king's brother here at the Louvre, not with all the eager ears around me. I placed a cautionary hand on the ambassador's sleeve.

"Please, sir," I continued. "I do not know the custom in London, but in Paris there's a danger to speaking too freely."

Montagu cocked his brows, surprised that I'd show such caution. "You are wise to take care, mam'selle."

I tipped my head in graceful acknowledgment. "If one wishes to prosper at Court, then one does well to be wise."

"One better damn well be wise in this den of mincing rogues, else one will find oneself poisoned." He smiled, regarding me shrewdly. "Not many ladies are so reticent."

"But not many ladies are in my situation, sir," I demurred with a sigh. "I'm a lady without a fortune, you see. With Madame gone, I've no true friend left at Court."

"You were one of her ladies, weren't you?" he asked, though it was clear he already knew the answer. "A maid of honor. What shall you do now without a mistress? Have you another place here, or must you return to your father's house?"

"I cannot go home, sir," I said, and my shudder was genuine. My parents had sent me here to make my fortune or, more specifically, to wed it, and after nearly two years, I'd accomplished nothing in their eyes except failure. If I returned home now, my father would deem me a shameful inconvenience, and soon find an excuse to send me to a convent, where I could at least pray for the soul of my brother. "I fear a spinster daughter would not be welcomed."

"I'd wager you'd be welcome most anywhere, mam'selle," he said gallantly, his gaze flicking downward to appraise my bosom, shrouded though it was in black mourning. "A great beauty such as yours most usually is."

"You are too kind, sir." It was still curious to me how every Englishman I met delighted in my face and form and praised my beauty to the heavens, while my own countrymen seemed impervious to my charms: proving, I suppose, that even Venus is susceptible to fashions set by kings.

"That's honesty, not kindness," he said. "How long before Monsieur turns you out, eh?"

"Not before Madame's funeral." Our quarters at the Palais-Royal were a strange, haunted place now. Those of us who remained were too idle, with the uncomfortable air of those who'd overstayed a supper with the host waiting at the door. Yet it was still a place at Court, however sorrowful the circumstances, and I was loath to leave it without another as replacement.

Unless, of course, it was in the ambassador's power to offer me a new place with the English queen, the same position that his king himself had first suggested at Dover.

"We ladies will not be 'turned out,' as you call it," I continued, determined not to let my hopes run away with my senses. "His Majesty would not permit Monsieur to treat us ill."

Montagu snorted. "He's permitted a great deal more than that."

I didn't smile, not wishing to condone his flippancy. How brashly these English did speak, saying aloud whatever came to their heads!

"I should say I will remain at the Palais-Royal until September," I said, "unless another place is granted to me before then."

"September." He nodded, watching me closely. "I expect by then you'll have been given another position here?"

"I will have decisions before me by then, yes," I said, purposefully not answering one way or another. The truth was more definite, and harder, too. Most of Madame's remaining attendants had already moved to other households at Court, some shifting to Her Majesty while others had simply chosen to retire and return to their homes in the country. But I'd no well-connected sponsor to present me to the queen or a doting husband to welcome me home, and on account of my loyalty toward Madame, I could scarcely expect the vengeful Monsieur to act on my behalf and recommend me to another. Though poor Madame wasn't yet buried, there was already talk of him remarrying, and the new Madame would want attendants of her own choosing.

Thus I'd plenty of reason to lie awake at night, plagued by my sorry future. Desperation is never a soothing companion, and who could fault me for weeping into my pillow with frustration, and fear, too? In fact the only real offer I'd had was the one that Charles had made to me in Dover, when I'd been holding Madame's jewels. Of course I'd no wish to confess that now to the ambassador, though I suspected he might already have known about it.

"Surely your king will find you a good place, mam'selle," he said, shamelessly prodding for more information. "Considering how well you served Madame, I'd think there'd be some plum waiting for you."

"I'll know soon enough, sir," I said, and forced myself to smile. I wondered if he was entitled to repeat his king's offer, and I wondered, too, if I'd accept it if he did.

But all he did now was smile in return, pleasantness without any offer, and then set our conversation on a very different course. "Have you heard the Duke of Buckingham's on his way from London?"

"No, sir, I did not," I murmured, my expression unchanging to mask my disappointment. From Madame and my time in Dover, I knew Mr. Montagu was more an ally of Lord Arlington, and that they viewed Lord Buckingham as a dangerous inconvenience, even a rival, much as Madame herself had. But if the ambassador hoped to see me betray myself for one side or the other, then he'd be disappointed. I'd long ago mastered how to hide my true feelings behind the calmness of a well-bred French lady, and it would take far more than the arrival of the Duke of Buckingham to discomfit me.

"His Grace will be representing His Majesty at Her Highness's funeral," the ambassador continued. "But he's also here to complete the details of a new treaty between England and France. I'm sure you must have heard of it while you were in Dover."

Ah, so here was my true test. I knew, just as did he, that there were no further details to be completed regarding an alliance between England and France. The Secret Treaty had been signed, and I'd been a witness. But the Secret Treaty had been exactly that: a secret to be kept closely among those few of us who knew of its existence. Madame had made sure I'd understood, and I had, along with the reasons for the secrecy.

Yet without further explanation, I also understood why the Duke of Buckingham would be here now. Over and over he'd been referred to as the Protestant duke, the one royal councilor who would never understand the clause regarding His Majesty's conversion to the True Church. Any treaty that His Grace might now be ordered to negotiate must be false, designed to mask further the Secret Treaty that had come before. What better way to reassure a nation of uneasy Protestants than to have the unwitting Protestant duke act on their behalf? Surely this must be the final piece of Madame's grand design, and I couldn't help but think how much she must have enjoyed arranging for the arrogant Buckingham to play the dupe.

I understood it all, yes. But likewise I understood that the ambassador wished to gauge my trust with so precious a secret. I'd not disappoint him. Madame had trained me too well to do that.

Instead I smiled with bland and guileless sweetness, an expression that came easily to my youthful face. "Forgive me, sir, but why speak to me of politics and treaties and other such affairs of gentlemen? I fear they are beyond me entirely."

He smiled slowly. "Surely your mistress must have mentioned this treaty to you," he prompted. "Everyone knows how much it meant to her for France and England to come together as allies."

I shook my head, as if in confusion. "Her Highness spoke of many things to me, sir, but as my mistress, not as a foreign minister."

His smile widened. "But what of your master? Monsieur has shown great curiosity in this matter, demanding details of his brother's latest alliance. You accompanied Madame to Dover, and were privy to many of the affairs there. Surely Monsieur has spoken to you of his wife's doings in England, or what she discussed with her brother the king?"

"Oh, sir," I said, full of regret. "I am sorry, but you grant me too much credit, far beyond my knowledge and station. Monsieur did ask me, yes, but I told him no more than I tell you now. If you asked me which jewels Madame pinned into her hair, or which gown she'd worn when we attended the ballet with His Majesty her brother, why, that I could tell you. But not the other."

"Very good," he said, nodding with approval. "And what if His Grace the Duke of Buckingham were to ask these same sorts of questions of you? His Grace is a charming, handsome rogue, and far more beguiling than my rough old face could ever be. Would you give him the same answers, my dear? Or could he wheedle more from you?"

"Oh, no, sir," I said with conviction. "He couldn't, because I cannot offer what I do not possess. And your face is not so rough as all that, sir. Pray, don't fault yourself. A certain ruggedness is most agreeable in a gentleman's face, and a pleasing sign of virility to ladies."

"Virility!" He laughed aloud, patting the sides of his brocaded waistcoat with delight. "By God, mam'selle, you are a jewel, just as His Majesty claimed, and like the best jewels, there are a good many more facets to you than are first perceived."

"Thank you, sir," I said, and smiled, too. "If that was meant as a compliment, that is."

"Oh, it was, it was, as you know perfectly well, you little minx," he said, chuckling still. "No wonder His Majesty was so taken with you. You've discretion and modesty and cleverness to equal your beauty. Upon my word, I couldn't say that of any other lady that the king's fancied, or the parade of strumpets, either."

"Does His Majesty fancy me?" I asked breathlessly, my careful guile forgotten in one shameless, impulsive moment. "Oh, please, tell me! Does he remember me?"

"Oh, aye, he remembers you well enough," he said, and from the smug satisfaction in his voice, I realized at once I'd betrayed myself. "Dover was not so long ago, my dear, nor are you the kind of lady he'd soon forget."

My cheeks grew hot with dismay. Without a thought, I'd tipped my cards toward him, and given him the advantage over me. Now he knew I cared for His Majesty not as a king, but as a man, and that desire made me vulnerable. As much as I might wish it, I couldn't take back my incriminating words, but I still could recover if I could make him remember I was a French lady, and not another common English hussy.

"Indeed, sir," I murmured, clasping my hands before me exactly as my mother did when dealing with ill-behaved servants. "It is a great honor for any Frenchwoman to be remembered by His English Majesty."

He frowned, and to make sure he was properly discomfited, I touched my fingers lightly to my only ornament, the little crucifix about my neck. To a Protestant Englishman, that should be reminder enough that I was different.

I smiled, not smugly, but shyly. "Might I beg a great favor of you, Mr. Montagu?"

"Of course, mam'selle," he agreed, gallant, but uneasy, too, as if worried about what I might ask. Foolish gentleman!

"If, as you say, His Majesty does remember me, would you please convey to him my condolences for Her Highness's death?" There was no guile to the tears that now filled my eyes. My sorrow was genuine for Madame's memory and always would be. "Please tell him that though I cannot comprehend the severity of his loss, I do think often of the pain he must feel. Please tell him that despite what he may hear, there are those here in France who truly do mourn her, and feel her loss most grievously, and please tell him that—that I pray for him, sir, and for Madame as well."

"That's your favor, mam'selle?" the ambassador asked, incredulous. "That's all you want me to tell the king on your behalf?"

"Yes, sir," I said softly. "I would have the king know that he is much in my thoughts and my prayers. That's favor enough for me, sir, and all I ask."

Before Mr. Montagu could reply, I glanced swiftly back over my shoulder, as if hearing the summons of another in the room.

"Forgive me, if you please, but I'm wanted," I said. "Good day, sir, and thank you."

"You're a rare, kind lady, mam'selle," he said, his face full of admiration. "A gentle—"

"I'm sorry, sir, but I must go directly." I dipped him a hasty (but graceful) curtsy, then turned and slipped away. I hurried my steps through the crowded room as if I truly had been called on some urgent errand, twisting and turning so I knew I'd be lost from the ambassador's view.

As soon as I was certain he could no longer see my face, I smiled. I couldn't help it, and why should I? The ambassador believed me to be a rare, kind lady. I might have erred once, true, but I'd proved to myself that I'd still a few cards left to play.

And for the present, I'd won.

Chapter Twelve

Château de Versailles
August 1670

Restless as always, Louis shifted the Court from Paris to his château at Versailles soon after Madame's death, to reside there until the funeral in Paris at the end of August. Monsieur agreed that his household should follow the king's to the country, perhaps bowing to his brother's insistence, perhaps simply because he'd wearied of having us all under his exclusive care. Whatever the reason, I was glad to leave the city behind, and glad, too, not to return to Saint-Cloud, where I sadly sensed Madame's departed spirit in every corner of the house and gardens. By contrast, Versailles reflected only the king's magnificence and an impersonal one at that, and in a strange way it was easier for me to find peace for my own reflections and sorrows if I were only an insignificant one among a crowd of many, than in the too-empty rooms of Saint-Cloud or the Palais-Royal.

As Ralph Montagu had warned me, George Villiers, Duke of Buckingham, arrived to join us later that week. He'd often come to Paris before to visit his sister, who served at the Court, or to avoid his own king's disapproval over his latest mischief in London. But as Madame had often said with disgust, no matter what trouble His Grace contrived to find—and he found much—his king always forgave him.

Lord Buckingham's appearance now was proof enough of that. In London he was living the most scandalous life imaginable, having cast out his wedded wife in favor of his mistress, the Countess of Shrewsbury, whose husband the duke himself had murdered in a duel. Now this wicked, unremorseful lady was said to be lolling in the duke's house, great with his bastard child, yet still the king had sent Lord Buckingham to Paris as his official representative to Madame's funeral, and as the minister in charge of negotiating a new treaty.

If a man of such low character and habits had been sent to Versailles at any other time, I would have expected Louis to take offense. Offense, however, was not an indulgence even the king could afford at present. Montagu had told me that Charles and the rest of England believed the princess had been poisoned, and it was whispered that the letters the English king wrote to his French cousin were full of accusations and uncomfortable questions.

Why was Louis so quick to accept that Madame had died a natural death, when all the circumstances seemed to suggest otherwise? Why had Louis not protected the English princess more closely, and instead left her to founder and languish under the attacks of her husband? Why hadn't she been loved and treasured in France the way she had been in England, the way such a sweet and generous lady deserved?

Worse still, Madame had apparently confided the more sordid details of her wretched marriage to her brother at Dover, details she'd heretofore not trusted to letters. Charles was rightly appalled, and demanded answers that Louis did not possess. Charles's raw grief overcame his more usual politesse, to the point that he'd threatened to withdraw England from any further talks and alliances with France.

Thus Louis was faced with the challenge of not only soothing a grieving brother, but also preserving his long-desired alliance with England, and the first step Louis took was to welcome the odious Lord Buckingham (and by extension all Britain) with a considerable show of regard. Despite our Court's mourning, the duke was honored with receptions and fetes and suppers, and given a choice place at Louis's side, whether whilst hunting or dining. When Louis opened the negotiations for the new treaty, he was expansive and accommodating, agreeing to most everything that Lord Buckingham proposed.

Why shouldn't he, considering everything of note had been decided earlier in Dover and these negotiations were an empty sham? But in his ignorance, the duke believed that the ease of the negotiations was due entirely to his own facility, and puffed his chest out all the more on account of it.

To further the good feelings of the English, Louis even went so far as to grant Lord Buckingham's lover, that wayward harlot countess, a gift of ten thousand gold livres for their unborn child. Louis guessed that all of this would be reported back to Charles and, more, that the vainglorious duke would likely embellish the largesse even further in his telling.

Louis's judgment proved right. To anyone who'd listen, Lord Buckingham boasted of how well he was being treated, and how he was certain no other English peer had ever been received with so much pomp and awe: all of which, of course, he deserved.

I suppose that once he'd been a handsome gentleman, for in his aging, debauched face I could sometimes glimpse the remnants of a faded charm and comeliness, but despite his strutting pride, I found little left in his appearance to impress me. His vulpine face was often puffy and lined with the marks of the previous night's excess, several of his teeth were brown and broken, and there were streaks of gray in his wispy ginger-colored mustache and beard. He was careless in his dress, too, with the cuff of a costly shirt trailing lace and greasy spots from a long-ago supper scattered over the breast of his well-tailored coat.

Out of the duke's hearing, there was much amusement made at his expense, a sport that I did not share. I remembered too well how Madame had distrusted him for his cunning and cleverness as well as for always having her brother's favor. While others mocked the duke's dress, I watched how he rode to the hunt with great skill yet also a wild intensity, and considered, too, how he'd a reputation as a masterful duelist. Gentlemen with those skills are often reckless with their lives, and pursue everything they do with the same abandon, as if always with a blade in their hands. Reckless men make for dangerous men, and, like Madame, I resolved to avoid Lord Buckingham as long as I could.

It should have been an easy resolution to keep. Though I'd been introduced to him as one of Madame's attendants, I was relieved that he seemed to have no memory of me now. Even if he had, I doubted he'd pay me any court. I was far too insignificant a creature for him to bother with.

But though in France I'd no way of realizing it, my value had risen dramatically in England since His Majesty had taken so much notice of me in Dover. Because Monsieur had made his exclusion a condition of Madame's visit, the duke had not been there, but he'd heard much about our visit, and most specifically about me. And, like the excellent hunter that he was, it didn't take him long before he'd tracked me down.

It was late in the day, at the end of a long, tedious, and hot afternoon. As powerful as His Most Christian Majesty might be, not even Louis could control the weather, and ever since the Court had returned to Versailles, we'd been plagued by a relentless heat. As the sun had dropped lower in the sky, the day had grown more bearable, and I'd agreed to go walking with several other ladies and gentlemen beside the Grand Canal.

The canal was an enormous rectilinear pond, crossed by a second, lesser one, that the king had had created in the château's park. The canal served several purposes: not only did it contribute to a pleasing, glittering vista from the château's windows, but it also acted as a kind of reservoir, collecting and storing the water that was pumped to the many fountains throughout the gardens and park. In addition, it was a place of amusement, the setting for elaborate fireworks and mock sea battles, as well as a collection of gilded gondolas, much in demand for flirtations, that had been sent to the king as a gift from the Doge of Venice.

On this particular evening, the canal offered a pleasant retreat for a promenade. The wide, flat expanse of water made the air seem more agreeable, and the rustle of the evening breezes through the tops of the tall Italian poplars was more sweet than any choir. Sweet, too, was the freedom of this hour, a rare thing at Versailles, where most of the day's activities were minutely ordered for us courtiers. From six to nine thirty, His Majesty would be occupied with his private secretary, and none of us would be expected to attend him until ten o'clock, when we were all required by ritual to stand in the antechamber of the king's suite and watch him dine with the rest of the royal family. Until then, our time would be our own.

Our little party walked in the shade of the poplars, though we ladies still carried parasols and wore wide-brimmed lace hats against any errant sunbeam. The company was acquaintances, not true friends, and when I wearied of their chatter, I let my steps slow so that I lagged behind, yet no one took it amiss. I paused and closed my eyes, relishing how the breeze played over my face and ruffled my skirts around my ankles. Alas, I was not alone for long.

"Good day, Mademoiselle de Keroualle," a gentleman said behind me, an English gentleman, for all that he spoke French. "Here you are at last."

I was so startled, my eyes flew open, and I drew back. "Your Grace," I murmured. Swiftly I closed my parasol and curtsied. "You surprise me."

Sweeping his hat from his head, Lord Buckingham smiled warmly, and placed one hand over his heart. "You surprise me, too, mademoiselle. Descriptions of your beauty didn't begin to prepare me for the magnificence I find before me at this moment."

"You honor me, Your Grace." I did not smile, not wishing to encourage him. Instead I glanced toward the rest of my party, twenty paces away. "Pray forgive me, Your Grace, but I should rejoin my friends who—"

"They can wait." With forceful grace, he stepped close to me, blocking my way of escaping to the others. "I cannot."

I stood my ground, fighting my instant urge to bolt and race away. That would not do, of course, for ladies did not run like country hoydens. He was tall and thick, a formidable figure. I did not flinch before him, but slowly furled my parasol to hold square before me in my hands. I was not so foolish as to believe that I could overpower him with my humble weapon of ivory, silk, and bone, or that I'd even try to defend myself. Rather I wished to demonstrate my composure, and prove to him I'd not be flustered by his bullying. Besides, I wasn't in any real danger from him; the others of my party were increasingly distant, but still within hearing, and if I called out to them in distress, I was certain they'd come to my rescue.

"Then speak, Your Grace," I said evenly. "I wait for your every word."

That made him laugh. "You pleased my king, mademoiselle. He has spoken of you incessantly since Dover, of your beauty, your charm, and your wit, but most of all, of your innocence. You drove him quite mad, you know."

"Indeed," I said, determined not to betray my true feelings for the king again, as I had with Ralph Montagu. "I am sorry, for that was not my intention."

"No?" He raised his ginger brows in disbelief, but also amusement. "There's scarcely a young woman in England who doesn't wish to set the king to lusting for her."

I smiled ingenuously. "But I am different, Your Grace. I am French, and I am a lady."

"Oh, you are that," he said, studying me closely, like a connoisseur with a new acquisition. "You're that, and more."

I felt my cheeks flush beneath his scrutiny. "Are you disappointed, Your Grace? Did you wish me to be otherwise than I am?"

"You surpass all my wishes, and my expectations, too," he said, nodding with satisfaction. "You're as fine a French lady as I've ever seen. I'm thoroughly enchanted."

To my surprise, he held out his arm to me. "Will you walk, mademoiselle? I've found that conversations are often more agreeable when they're not planted square on the ground to take root."

I smiled, for I'd not expected him to make so light of his own restlessness. No wonder he'd such a reputation for charm when he wished to employ it. I was flattered that he thought me worth the effort. Perhaps, I thought, it would be better to have him as my ally than otherwise, particularly if I wished to see His Majesty again.

"Thank you, Your Grace, you are most kind." I slipped my hand into the crook of his arm, and let him set an ambling pace beneath the lengthening shadows of the poplars.

His conversation, however, moved much more swiftly.

"As beguiling as you are, mademoiselle, you are not the only woman claiming His Majesty's attentions," he said. "Little Nelly Gwyn has just last month presented him with his latest bastard son."

"She is the actress, yes?" I said. "Madame feared she was too much below the king. She said such a . . . connection was debasing to both the king and his crown."

"Ah, well, poor Nell can't help that she was born in a brothel, can she?" he said with such ripe condescension that I almost felt sorry for the woman. "But yes, she's the actress. A merry little soul, but she hasn't enough substance to occupy the king for long."

"I should have thought Lady Castlemaine did that." I glanced up at him from beneath the lacy brim of my hat. The duke was a large man, but not so tall as the king, which I suspected must vex His Grace mightily. "She is a most beautiful lady, Your Grace, and His Majesty appears most attached to her."

He grunted. "Barbara is a most beautiful, greedy, lascivious, old shrew, and I should know, since we're cousins."

"Cousins?" I repeated, letting his shocking judgment of the lady pass unremarked. "Lord Rochester told me once that he was her cousin as well. The lady has many connections."

"Yes, and most of them have traipsed through her bed," he said, waxing more philosophical than harsh. "But she's done well for herself by the king. A slew of his handsome brats, as much gold and property as she could grasp in her pretty hands, and now a duchy."

"She's been made a duchess?" I asked in awe. That was the highest prize for a royal mistress, and seldom granted; as a reward for her devotion, Louise de la Vallière had been made a duchess by Louis and given the estate at Vaujours to accompany it.

"duchess of Cleveland, Countess of Southampton, Baroness Nonsuch, all for her own self, and none for her poor old cuckold husband," he said cheerfully, as if we were discussing the heat of the day instead of the most wicked of scandals. "Which is only fair, since she's the one who earned them. What whore likes to share with her pimp?"

"I would not know, Your Grace." I blushed again to hear such frank language. Yet this was a path I was at least contemplating for myself. Would he speak of me with the same coarseness if I'd let the king have his way at Dover? Would the pleasure of being a royal favorite lessen the humiliation of being called a whore?

"No, that is true. You wouldn't know," he said, and laughed, clearly delighted with my response. "Forgive me, mademoiselle. I spend precious little time in the company of innocents. But as for Barbara—she should take care to enjoy her new titles, for I'd venture the king means them as a fond fare-thee-well."

"You mean that he has tired of her?" I asked with curious surprise. He'd certainly still seemed enthralled with the newly minted Lady Cleveland at Dover. While he'd kissed me on the last afternoon, it had been common enough knowledge that he'd spent all his previous nights in her bed. Yet this had been the way with Louise de la Vallière, too; she'd been made a duchess shortly after His Majesty had shifted his amorous attentions to Madame du Montespan.

"He's tired of her, and who can fault him?" the duke declared. "We're all weary of her harping. She's held sway over the royal cods for ten years, a righteous long time for any woman. But she's vulnerable now. You'll see. She'll fall by Christmas, and be swept away like any other old leavings. If the proper rival should appear before the king, a lady with sufficient support within the Court to match her beauty, then Barbara could be toppled even sooner."

He looked down at me in a most meaningful way. I understood, of course. I was an innocent, not an idiot. He thought I'd be that proper rival, with him there to guide me. But still I thought it better not to admit to recognizing his proposal just yet, and instead continued to play the lady who in fact I was.

"There's more to the tale, too, mademoiselle," he continued when I did not reply. "Our queen is barren as a stone. No one can deny it any longer."

"I pity Her Majesty," I said softly, and I did. Madame had said she was a good Catholic lady, faithful to a fault and woefully shy. How it must wound her to see her husband's seed sown so freely, and with so much bastard issue, while her own womb remained empty.

"Pity her all you wish, but pity won't change the facts," the duke said with surpassing arrogance, showing he'd no pity at all for the hapless queen. "For the sake of all Britain, the king must secure his throne with a proper heir. Though it pains His Majesty to act, it's apparent to everyone that he means to put this queen aside on grounds of her barrenness, and take another."

"Why do you tell me this, Your Grace?" I asked, my heart racing within my breast at so dizzying a possibility. "These are the grand affairs of royalty, not lowly maids of honor. Even if His Majesty were cruelly to divorce Her Majesty, then he would be bound to wed another lady of equally exalted blood, a princess or grand duchess in her own right."

"He might," he said, making a little fillip with his fingers through the air before us, "or he might not. Considering the ill luck he's had with a princess, there are those who believe he should look elsewhere for his breeding stock. Of course the lady must be of some rank, and with an unblemished past. We shouldn't want any questions about the issue, you know."

A virgin: that was what he meant by "an unblemished past," and likewise I knew he meant me. But surely there must be virgins in England, other young ladies with noble families and reputation?

"It would make perfect sense that a new queen be French," he continued, reading my thoughts as clearly as if I'd spoken aloud. "The king's always been inclined that way, for his mother was French. And what better way to seal this new alliance I've been negotiating with your country than with a fair new queen?"

I looked away from him, my thoughts in turmoil. It was one thing to be considered as a royal mistress, and quite another to be mentioned as a future queen.

Her Majesty the Queen of England, Scotland, and Ireland.

Ah, no wonder my head fair spun!

But though I knew the duke had the ear of the king, I could scarce believe he'd be trusted with this particular errand. Why should he wish to link himself to my lowly star, except for what he could selfishly gain for himself? I remembered how Madame had not trusted him, and how that should be warning enough for me to do the same. I reminded myself to recall the duke's reputation for bold and extravagant behavior, how he plunged in whole where more cautious gentlemen would dip but a toe. I thought of the more circumspect ministers I'd met in Dover, Lord Arlington and Sir Thomas Clifford, and how the king had trusted them with the enormity of the Secret Treaty, while Lord Buckingham was being made to be the unwitting puppet of this second, empty treaty. If I were to ally myself with one faction over another, I'd be far wiser to trust those gentlemen rather than this mercurial duke.

Yet despite what I'd learned at Court, I was still young, still impressionable, and to my misfortune, all too willing to be flattered when this grandest of prizes was dangled before me. With a willful abandon that matched Lord Buckingham's own, I eagerly swept aside every objection my cautious conscience raised and embraced this ridiculous scheme. There was no doubt that the king needed an heir, and a young wife with a fertile womb. Lord Arlington and Sir Thomas were more staid, true, but they were comparative newcomers to the king's confidence, while Lord Buckingham had been his closest friend from boyhood. It would be entirely natural that His Majesty would trust him now with so delicate an arrangement. I'd only to look at the French Court to see how a king would play his courtiers and ministers against one another by way of keeping power to himself.

What seduced me most of all was the idea of becoming Charles's wife and queen. It wasn't only the power and wealth that beckoned, though to be sure that was a glittering temptation. No, the true reward would be the man himself, and I'd joyfully become his wife, his consort, his guiding star.

I'd be his most precious jewel, just as he'd said. I would give him delight in his bed and bring cheer to his heart, and be the most loyal subject in his entire kingdom. I'd bring respectability and decorum to his Court (which did sorely need it), and I would help to guide him to the True Church, as he'd already sworn to do in the Secret Treaty. I would love him with boundless devotion, which he of course would return to me many times over. In my girlish enthusiasm, I never doubted that I could succeed where no other woman had, and win his exclusive fidelity. I'd only to recall the fondness with which he'd gazed at me on the wall at Dover Castle, and how our single kiss must have been a pledge for our joined futures.

In short, I dreamed, and I dreamed high and sweet. As I walked beside Lord Buckingham, I was like another of the ancient race of lotus eaters—a people who, having once tasted that rare flower, forgot every common care and responsibility in favor of unending bliss.

"You are quiet, mademoiselle," the duke said, rousing me at last from my delicious reverie. "I trust I haven't bored you with my talk."

"Oh, no, Your Grace, not at all!" I exclaimed, and belatedly I realized he was teasing me, his face smug and faintly mocking. "That is, you speak of many interesting things, and it is much for me to consider."

"Oh, yes, I'm sure it is," he said expansively, and gave a little pat to my fingers as they rested on his arm. "But you'll have time enough for considering. There are many steps to be taken before anything can be made widely known, and for the present it will be best to keep what I've told you to your heart alone. No tattling to your little friends, eh?"

"Of course not, Your Grace," I said quickly, eager to appear obliging. I'd been keeping secrets since my first day in Madame's household, and I wasn't about to begin spilling them now, especially one that might involve me. "You may trust my confidence entirely."

But despite my declaration, he was frowning, his thoughts elsewhere, and his hand over mine tightened painfully. "You've not heard from Arlington in this regard, have you?"

"Lord Arlington?" I repeated, surprised both by his question and the change in his manner. "No, Your Grace."

"What of Clifford?" I heard suspicion in his voice bubble up from nowhere, giving an unsavory edge to his words, and his grasp clenched clawlike over my poor fingers. "Has he written to you? Or that rascal Montagu. I know he's here. I've seen him sniffing about your skirts."

I trembled with uncertainty, trying to pull free.

"Answer me," he ordered sharply, jerking me back. "What does Montagu want from you? What has he told you of the king remarrying?"

"Not a word, Your Grace, I swear!" I cried. I was privy to many secrets with those other gentlemen, but not one involving a second wife for the king. "If you please, Your Grace, you are hurting my hand."

He mumbled an oath, but instantly released my hand, staring at his fingers as if they'd acted without his knowledge. He sighed, and lifted his hat long enough to smooth his wig beneath it. Then, finally, he looked back to me, his expression as cheerfully composed as if nothing untoward had happened at all.

"I'm sure you understand the reasons for delicacy in this matter, mademoiselle," he said softly. "Arlington, Clifford, Montagu: they all believe they know the king's mind, but they don't, not as I do. I ask you, who has been trusted with this treaty? Which of us has King Louis fawning and nibbling from his hand? Which minister's the master of them all, eh?"

I knew what he didn't, and that the real master of them all was, of course, His Majesty their king. But I also knew better than to acknowledge more than I should, and so once again I feigned a meek humility to hide my secrets.

"I am honored by your confidence, Lord Buckingham," I said, and curtsied for good measure. "I vow that I will keep your secret, no matter who may ask me."

"Do that," he said, and smiled. "The world is full of simple fools, mademoiselle, those who prefer to wait for what they are given. But then there are those who bravely seize whatever fate may offer, and claim it as their own."

Did he mean to advise me by that tidy little epigram, or was he only referring to himself? I'd no answer, but to my relief he did not seem to expect one. I'd yet to learn that this was often the case with the duke; he was so serenely confident of his own innate superiority that he went through his life without requiring the approval of others or even their comment.

Now that I had done what he desired, he seemed almost to have forgotten me. He swung away from me, humming a scrap of a song as he sauntered a few steps closer to the water, then stopped. With his hands at his waist and his legs angled apart, he resembled some sort of roguish buccaneer captain on the quarterdeck of his pirate vessel, surveying the wide-open sea instead of this royal conceit of canal.

"What is this body of water, mademoiselle?" he asked over his shoulder. "What river?"

"That's His Majesty's Grand Canal, Your Grace," I said, cautiously coming to stand beside him. The summer sun was low in the sky now, turning the water's surface a brilliant, shimmering red. "The gondolas and the miniature galleon as well as the boathouses at the head of the canal were gifts to His Most Christian Majesty from the Doge of Venice."

"All from the doge?" he said, gazing out over the water. "Hell."

That was hardly the proper reaction to so artfully constructed a vista, and His Majesty would have been most vexed to hear it, but by now I'd decided there was very little that was proper about the duke.

"Yes, Your Grace, the Doge of Venice." Like every other courtier, I felt a certain national pride in Versailles as representing the very best of French craft and art (which was to say the very best in all the world), and I was eager for the duke to appreciate it, too. "It is a masterpiece of engineering and design. Its surface covers over forty-four hectares, or over a hundred of your English acres, and its shore is more than four miles around."

"His Majesty has a canal, too," the duke said. "It lies in St. James's Park outside of Whitehall Palace, in London. I've never measured it myself, but I'd venture its breadth to be thirty feet and its length perhaps a hundred at best."

"I'm sure it is very pretty, Your Grace," I said.

"It has ducks," he said flatly. "And a single damned gondola, a gift from that same damned doge. What the devil is a doge, anyway?"

I wasn't sure if his question was asked for the sake of pure rhetoric or not. Yet because I didn't wish to appear rude, as if I'd not been attending his observations, I answered him as best I could.

"I believe that the doge is the chief magistrate and leader of the Republic of Venice, Your Grace," I said. "A most ancient and venerable office."

"If Charles saw this," he said, "it would break his heart."

"I'm sorry, Your Grace," I said softly, and I was. I'd not forgotten the melancholy that shadowed the English king's handsome face, and I'd no wish to see it sadder still for the sake of an oversized garden folly. "I'm sure that wasn't the intention of His Most Christian Majesty when he had it built."

"Of course it was," he said bitterly. "That's the whole purpose of every last looking glass and golden table fork in this place: to prove that you French are superior to everyone else, and to make sure the rest of us know it. And believe me, Charles does."

"I am sorry, Your Grace," I said again, for what else could I say? "I am sorry that everything French is so unpleasant to His Majesty."

"Not everything, mademoiselle." He turned his back on the Grand Canal, and looked at me with such purpose that I couldn't mistake his meaning. "There is one specific example of French beauty that will give him only the greatest joy, and by God, I mean to see he receives it. Are you ready, mademoiselle?"

"I am, Your Grace," I said, and raised my chin to prove my resolve. "I am."

He laughed with sly delight, and winked. "Come, then, let me return you to your friends."

I took his offered arm, and in truth by then I was trembling so with excitement that I'd need of his support. I'd listened, and there by the banks of the Canal, I'd made my decision. I was done with relying on others to decide my future. I meant to seize what fate was offering, and claim it as my own.

Madame's funeral was arranged for the twenty-first of August. Paris seemed filled with dignitaries from other countries who'd come to pay their final respects to the princess, and at the same time curry a bit of favor with the French king. Though the gatherings at the Louvre were somber at this time, as they should be, Louis expected us ladies to attend and be our most charming before the foreigners, at least as well as we could manage in our deep first mourning.

On one of these evenings, I had joined the others in the rooms set aside for gaming. I was not playing, of course—I'd still not the means to be able to toss away what little money I had—but I did take pleasure in watching, seeing another's cards and deciding how, if they'd been mine, I would play the hand. I was standing to one side of a table with several other ladies, languidly fanning myself, when one of the royal pages came to summon me away.

I excused myself and followed him, curious as to why I'd been called. Because I served no lady at present and it was doubtful I'd be requested by Monsieur, I could think of no reason for it.

"Where are we going, sirrah?" I asked the boy as soon as we were in the hallway. "Who has sent you for me?"

"It is not my place to say, mademoiselle," he said, taking obvious pleasure in refusing to share his knowledge. The pages were often like this, puffed full of their own importance as if the entire palace depended exclusively on them. "My task was only to fetch you, no more."

"Impudent little rascal," I said, and jabbed him in his brocade-covered arm with my closed fan. "It won't hurt you to tell me."

"You'll learn for yourself in time," he said with airy superiority, "because you won't learn from me."

But as I followed him through the palace and past the guards, I realized soon enough who had requested my presence. We went through two more sets of doors and another group of guards, and then I alone entered the small reception room, and found myself in the presence of His Most Christian Majesty.

He was sitting in a tall-backed chair before the window, his hands resting on the cushioned arms and one foot elegantly placed before the other, with the huge satin bow on each shoe presented as if a gaudy butterfly had landed on the royal foot. He was as usual beautifully, extravagantly dressed: his coat and breeches of black satin (black being the extent of his mourning for Madame) densely embroidered with gold thread and festooned with at least a hundred yards of ribbon, his hat crowned with scarlet plumes and jewels scattered on his fingers and person, even on his hat.

I realized full well that so much magnificence was not solely for my benefit, and that he was doubtless on his way to join the others for the evening's amusement. Still, as I sank into my deepest curtsy, I was both honored and awed to be alone with him. Although this solitary summons was unusual, even curious, the king would most likely tell me his intentions for my future, and grant me a new place elsewhere within the Court. It wouldn't matter now that I'd longed to go to England to try my luck at the English Court; unhappily, nothing had come of Mr. Montagu's hints, and Lord Buckingham's schemes still remained as insubstantial as the air. If I were to be offered a new position here in France, I would accept it at once, with gratitude and no hesitation, and as I curtsied, I had to swallow back both my excitement and my relief.

"Mademoiselle de Keroualle," the king said, solemnly lifting his hat to me, "good evening to you."

"Good evening, Your Majesty." I rose, my hands folded before me in proper respect. I'd not seen him in such close quarters since I'd met the English king, and I was struck by both the similarities and the differences between the two. They both were tall and handsome and dark, with black hair and a regal mien, which was understandable for cousins who'd shared a common grandfather.

But where the English king had laughed easily and found much in the world to please him, his power tempered with warm kindness and generosity, the French king was as severe as a graven image, his expression unchanging and his dark eyes as intent and unblinking as any hawk's as he regarded me. I thought of how most every woman in Paris was dazzled by Louis, and desired to be his mistress above all things, yet as I stood before him, I could not imagine sharing so much as a kiss with a man who seemed so remote.

Ah, but the English king, and what I dreamed of sharing with him . . .

"Mademoiselle," Louis began, jarring me back to his presence. "Mademoiselle, we have been most pleased with your loyalty to us and to France, and most especially to our lamented sister, Madame."

"Thank you, Your Majesty." Tears—my constant companion in the dark days following Madame's death—once again sprang unbidden to my eyes at the mention of her name. "Her Highness was most dear to me, and it was an honor to serve her as I did."

He nodded gravely, as much emotion as I expected he ever showed. "You served her well, mademoiselle. But that service is done, and we must now decide where you shall go next."

"Yes, Your Majesty," I said, breathless with eager anticipation. "I pray that I might continue to serve you and France, however you decide."

"A true daughter of France," he said with approval. "Before Madame died, she told me of how useful you were to her in Dover, and how much you pleased her brother the king. She praised both your discretion and your delicacy in diplomatic matters that required perfect trust, and she had every faith in you."

"Thank you, Your Highness," I said softly. My dear Madame! Even in death, she seemed to be looking after me, and I promised to light another candle to the Virgin Mother on behalf of her soul.

"You are aware of the devotion shared between Madame and her brother His Majesty the King of England," he continued. "Although Madame had become one of our family and represented our interests faithfully, her brother trusted her more than any minister or ambassador, and without her nothing would have been accomplished in Dover. You begin to understand, mademoiselle."

I nodded, not trusting my voice to reply. My being chosen to accompany Madame to Dover, the lavish new clothes that had been given me, the praise I'd not sought from Lord de Croissy, and the warnings from Madame I'd not wished to hear, even how I'd been permitted to linger at Court after her death without any other place being offered to me. I understood now. I understood everything.

"We cannot lose that sweet voice in his ear, whispering in favor of France." He smiled suddenly, the twin crescents of his tiny mustache curving upward. "We would have you be that voice, mademoiselle. The voice of France."

"I—I am honored to be chosen, Your Majesty," I stammered. I

tried to remind myself of my ambition, and that this was exactly what I wished, what I wanted, what I'd already agreed with Lord Buckingham. I tried to remember the magic I'd felt when the English king had smiled at me, and better still, when he'd kissed me.

I tried, and failed, for what was being proposed to me now sounded sordid instead of glorious. There was no mention of me becoming the new queen, and not a breath of love. My maidenhead, casually offered as a token from one king to another: where was the glory in that?

"It was no choice. There is no other lady who could do this, you see." He clasped his hands together, his eyes bright with enthusiasm. "His Grace the Duke of Buckingham has already asked for you to accompany him on his return to London to accept a place in the household of Her Majesty the Queen of England, but it is assumed that the king, not the queen, will be most pleased by your appearance in London. Our cousin is fascinated by you, mademoiselle, and again we must praise you on your success at Dover. You will find it easy to achieve a final seduction, but then, who knows more of such affairs than a beautiful young Frenchwoman?"

He laughed, pleased with his wit and his plan, but my head was full of questions—questions that, because of his exalted rank over me, I could not ask unless he gave me leave.

"You will be richly rewarded, of course," he continued, "both by us and by our cousin, who is by all accounts most indulgent with ladies. In return, there will be certain expectations of you. You must make sure that he confides in you as he did in Madame, and relay what he tells you to us. You must take every opportunity to support our cause to him, and dissuade him from returning his sympathies to the Dutch."

Again I nodded, overwhelmed. I was not merely to be a gift, a plaything. I was to be a spy in the bed of the King of England, coaxing him ever closer to France, and if I were ever to be discovered— Ah, even I recognized the infinite danger in that.

Yet still the king continued on. "Most of all, mademoiselle, you must keep your role a secret from the English. They can know none of this, especially not our cousin. No matter what affection you may come to feel for him, your loyalty and your duty to France must always come first."

"Yes, Your Majesty," I said softly, taking his reminder close to my heart. He was my king, and I'd no choice but to obey. I was a Keroualle, and for hundreds of years my family had prided itself on their complete loyalty to the throne. My dear brother had given his life for France. What the king now asked of me was as nothing compared to that.

"You may rely entirely on me, Your Majesty." I bowed my head, both in fealty and beneath the terrible burden of my new role. "Entirely."

Chapter Thirteen

Ten days after Madame's funeral, I found myself in the Duke of Buckingham's lavish traveling coach on my way to the port at Dieppe, where we would be met by a royal yacht, and carried thence to England. With me I'd a half dozen trunks with all my belongings, including the new gowns I'd acquired before Dover and several others, even more lavish, from the same seamstresses, which had been ordered without my knowledge.

I hadn't questioned the sudden appearance of this new finery, any more than I'd questioned how, for the first time in my life, I'd acquired my own lady's maid, a plain, quiet young woman named Bette. Since my private audience with the king, I'd learned to accept things like these without questioning them. It was all part of the same grand plan that was sending me to England. If what Madame had negotiated was called the Secret Treaty, then surely I'd become the most secret clause attached to it.

A secret I might be, yes, but I was no longer ignorant of the circumstances of my new situation. Though the king had given me only the most basic facts, others among his ministers had been more forthcoming. From them I learned that the king himself had suggested I be trusted with my new role, based largely on what Madame had confided to him. I was flattered, of course, but I also wondered what exactly Madame, who'd always been so protective of me, had told him, and now, sorrowfully, I'd never be able to ask her myself. The French ministers believed the English king to be a clever, crafty man, but entirely vulnerable where women were concerned. Over and over they congratulated themselves (but not me) on having found a Frenchwoman suitable for their purposes, until I wearily began to feel like the wooden horse of ancient Troy, being drawn to the gates of Whitehall Palace.

The English gentlemen were no better. The English ambassador, Mr. Montagu, fair crowed, convinced his reports regarding my grace and beauty had brought about my appointment, and would soon also result in an extra measure of royal favor cast his way. I'd letters from Lord Arlington and Sir Thomas Clifford, as well as from their ladies, remembering themselves to me with agreeable welcomes, and doubtless hoping I'd remember them to the king, too. As unfamiliar as I was with the English Court, I doubted that every new attendant there received this amount of attention from ministers of the privy council. In truth it seemed that everyone in London must consider me already at least a royal mistress, as if neither I nor the English king had anything to say in the matter.

It was, of course, that same royal gentleman whose letter I most desired, just as I realized full well I'd be disappointed. Even in the less formal English Court, His Majesty could scarce be expected to take time from ruling to write to me. For now I must content myself with my memories of Dover, and my heady dreams of the future.

Helping to tend and nourish those dreams with the greatest care had been His Grace the Duke of Buckingham. With the first version of the new (though false) treaty duly completed by the French and ready to be reviewed again by the English, he had devoted his last weeks in France to being my near-constant squire. I soon learned that while the duke's once-handsome features had faded, his gift for charming persuasion remained in full, seductive flower. I vow he could coax the fish from the seas and the birds from the sky, if he wished it or, more likely, if he thought he could turn it to his benefit.

He deftly perceived my loneliness, and how much I yearned to quit the sorrows of the Palais-Royal. He told amusing stories to make me laugh, something I'd nearly forgotten how to do in those melancholy times, and he was never above mimicking others to make his jests more amusing. I ignored Madame's warnings of how faithless the duke could be, and likewise ignored my own misgivings, not the least of which had been the way he'd grabbed my arm by the canal. Granted, I was young and foolish and more vulnerable than I realized, but he was also quick to see how ready I was to leave off my old world for a new one with more promise, and he fed my ambitions. Whenever he could contrive to be with me, he took care to fill my willing ears with whatever he calculated would please me best—a dubious companion for any lady, as later I would come sadly to understand.

But then I gladly listened as he praised my face, my form, my grace, and predicted that not just the king, but all England, would come to admire me. He painted himself as my champion, and took full claim for my new advancement. He swore he'd been the one to convince His Most Christian Majesty to part with me. He told me again of his scheme to use me to displace the duchess of Cleveland from favor, and also more of the confidential plans for a royal divorce. He spun wild fancies of banishing the present queen to a distant island for safekeeping, and of me, garbed in cloth of gold and strands of pearls, placed on the throne in her stead—such glorious, romantic fancies that I indulged in again and again until they began to take on the golden luster of reality. In his company, I could forget that I was meant to be a spy (a most perilous forgetfulness), and instead thought only of being loved by a king.

Three days alone in a coach with the duke, however, had stolen some of the glow from this new champion of mine. At his insistence, we'd traveled without stopping except for refreshment and to change horses, stealing sleep as best we could in the coach.

Or rather, the duke slept, and I did not. Newly fortified with wine at every stop we made, he sprawled with abandon across the seat opposite from mine in the carriage, perfectly unconscious of my presence. He rested his boots, dirty with the muck of the various inn yards, on the leather cushions, closed his eyes, and instantly snored away, the ends of his mustache blowing gently with each puffing, noisy breath.

I had never spent any time in such close and constant contact with a gentleman, and as my despairing exhaustion grew, I could not help but feel my own discomfort, and be more convinced than ever that I'd not the fortitude for Christian martyrdom. Weariness sharpened my critical faculties as well, and as the carriage rolled through the countryside, I took note not only of the duke's cease-less snoring, but the sourness of his breath, the flecks of tobacco on his waistcoat, and how his linen was not exactly as fresh as a great noble's should be.

By the time we finally reached our inn in Dieppe, I could have wept with joy. Politely declining his offer to share dinner, I fled up-stairs to my room, undressed and, after washing with Bette's assis-tance, fell into a deep sleep, blissful in my duke-free solitude.

I awoke the next morning greatly refreshed, my room filled with cheery sunlight and Bette drawing back the curtains to my bed to present me with my morning chocolate and biscuits. But along with my breakfast, she brought me disturbing news.

"The innkeeper wishes me to tell you, mademoiselle," she said as she handed me a porcelain cup, "that His Grace the Duke of Bucking-ham departed last night, and sailed for England with the tide."

I gasped with surprise. "That cannot be, Bette," I insisted. "The innkeeper must be mistaken. His Grace would never abandon me like that, and risk displeasing His Majesty."

"Forgive me, mademoiselle, but he has," Bette said sadly. "I did not believe it myself, and after he told me, I asked others to make certain. There was a letter here awaiting His Grace, a letter written ad-dressed in a lady's hand. His Grace read it as soon as it was presented to him, exclaimed loudly in English, and immediately made plans to find passage and sail."

"Then surely he left a letter of explanation for me," I said promptly. "Doubtless he'd no wish to disturb me last night when he was called away, and chose to explain his departure in a letter. He wouldn't leave without that courtesy."

But Bette only shook her head, the long lappets of her linen cap swaying gently back and forth against her cheeks.

"Forgive me, mademoiselle, but there is no letter," she said. "His Grace is gone, and without leaving word for anyone as to when he would return."

I dressed at once, determined to find the answer to this mystery for myself. The cold truth brought little comfort. His Grace had in fact received a letter from a lady, his mistress the wanton Countess of Shrewsbury. Waiting in Dover for him to return to England, she had felt that her time had come to be delivered of their bastard, and had written to beseech him to join her as soon as was possible.

I could now understand his haste on the road from Paris, and why, too, he'd felt such urgency to leave in the night. A woman giving birth is always in peril, no matter whether the child is legitimate or not. But I'd scant sympathy for his abandonment, and none at all for his having done so without so much as a hasty note of explanation or promise to return. He'd not only disappointed me, but his master His Majesty as well. I had been left behind with as little ceremony as a broken wheel, and with as little warning, either.

Having always been well cared for in my life, for myself or as part of a larger party, I'd no idea what to do next beyond waiting. I could only pray that His Grace would in time return for me, or at the very least send the royal yacht to collect me, as he'd promised. Not even a gentleman as blithe as the duke would dare risk the displeasure of two kings.

But the innkeeper and his wife viewed my situation in a different light. They considered first my youth and beauty together with my costly clothes, and then balanced that against the duke's much older and more worldly appearance and his hasty disappearance, and finally decided that I represented a seduction followed by a disappointed elopement. Delicately the innkeeper's wife inquired whether I would soon be expecting the arrival of my father, or perhaps an older brother, to retrieve me home. Loath to confess my true situation (and truly, who would believe it?), I could only sigh forlornly and shake my head.

But as the days stretched into a week and my letters to His Grace went unanswered, the innkeeper began to regard me with less charity. An unattached yet beautiful young lady residing in a public inn without a suitable escort or companion too often attracts unsavory mischief, and can quickly become a bane to those who wish to keep a respectable house. Further, my dwindling personal funds were casting me nearer each day to impecuniousness, and in desperation I finally wrote to the English ambassador, Ralph Montagu, in Paris to advise him of my plight, and beg for assistance.

At once Mr. Montagu wrote to reassure me and apologize for the duke's neglect, and soon after an escort drawn from his own household arrived in Dieppe to join me. More important, he wrote to Lord Arlington in London, describing how Lord Buckingham had seemingly forgotten me. Immediately that good gentleman sought to repair everything that the duke had put awry. He dispatched a royal yacht to collect me along with the ambassador's escort from Dieppe, and further, he and Lady Arlington invited me to come directly to their own lodgings in the royal palace (instead of the French embassy, as had been previously arranged) as their guest.

He also regretfully informed me of the depth of Lord Buckingham's neglect: for though the duke had left me for his mistress, that lady's distress had proved premature, as is often the case. But instead of returning to me in Dieppe, the duke had gone with his paramour to London, and thrown himself once again into the merry distraction of the town without a single thought to spare for my welfare.

I was by then thoroughly weary of Lord Buckingham and disgusted by his careless ways, and ready to confess that, in choosing my English allies, I'd erred mightily. Lord Arlington with his blackplaster'd nose might be less amusing than the duke, but he was also vastly more reliable, and with grateful relief I accepted his invitation.

In my lonely hours at Dieppe, I'd had much time to reflect on my situation. I'd resolved not to be led again, as I had been by Lord Buckingham, and to listen more closely to my own counsel than to that of others, who would wish to use me for their own purpose. In the final reckoning, only I would be accountable for my success or failure, and my misadventure with the duke had only served to hone my ambitions to a keener edge.

Thus on a brisk, brave afternoon in September, I finally arrived in London, and made ready to claim it as my own.

Just as Paris was to France, London was the greatest city in the country of England, and also like Paris and the river Seine, London straddles a river of its own, the Thames.

Beyond that, on that first day on the deck of the yacht, I could see no other similarities.

Paris is an ancient and elegant city, filled with fine houses, palaces, and churches handsomely made of stone, with gardens and parks, all carefully planned to please the senses. I had heard that London was an equally ancient city, first contrived by the conquering Romans of the mighty Caesars. But my first eager glimpse as I arrived by the river showed little to reflect so glorious a beginning. The most substantial edifice of stone to be seen was a walled, fortified castle called the Tower of London (or so I was told by one of the sailors, who also proudly pointed out the place's pet ravens—a macabre sort of pet, by my lights); here both the highest prisoners of the state as well as the crown jewels were secured.

The rest of the buildings we passed were a squat jumble of timber and plaster, with only a few wrought of stone and brick, and everything crowded to the very edge of the river's banks. Instead of inspiring towers of cathedrals rising high into the sky, there were only shingled roofs and a forest of dirty chimneys, each spewing a foul smoke that I later learned came from the Londoners' preference for sea coal in their fires.

Because London served as a port, I saw more symbols of trade than anything else, unappealing warehouses and goods stacked high. The river itself was so clogged with vessels that it made for an incommodious passage, and an unpleasant one, too, from the numbers of coarse watermen and sailors calling and shouting fierce oaths at one another. The fact that I was sailing in the king's own yacht made no difference, either, and I was shocked by the lack of respect shown to it.

"They know His Majesty's not aboard, mademoiselle," explained the Comte de Grammont, one of those carefully chosen and sent to escort me by Mr. Montagu. This agreeable French nobleman was a fond acquaintance of the English king and had lived for many years here at his Court, having been banished by Louis from France for some long-forgotten peccadillo. I could have no better guide upon my entry to London, or one more willing to speak freely by way of educating me.

"Sailors are clever enough to guide their ships by the stars and the moon," His Lordship now continued. "It's no wonder they can tell when their king is about, too. Otherwise they would be showing his yacht more regard."

"But how can they know for certain, my lord?" I asked, indignant on the king's behalf. "His Majesty could merely be below in the cabin, away from their view."

"They know he is not, because we do not fly his pennant from our staff," the comte explained kindly. "His Majesty is very popular with his subjects, mademoiselle, and because he often goes out among them, they are well tuned to recognize his presence."

Perplexed, I frowned, striving to make sense of this explanation. I couldn't fathom a king who would wish to go among his people. Louis seldom did. After the travails of his childhood during the Fronde, he disliked and mistrusted the common people of Paris almost as much as he did his nobles, and preferred to keep them all at a distance.

"If that is so, my lord, then they must also know His Majesty's program for each of his days," I said, remembering the rigorous, unvarying program of Louis's day, so punctual a routine that his courtiers claimed a pocket watch could be set by the king's movements. "I suppose in that fashion they must know that he would not be sailing at this hour."

"No, mademoiselle," the comte said with a polite small sigh. "They'd know no such thing, for the King of England keeps no program. He acts upon whim, and follows his fancy for each moment. He is a busy monarch, to be sure, and seldom at rest, but it is impossible for his courtiers to predict where he might be in the course of a day or evening."

"But how can they properly serve His Majesty if they've no knowledge of where he might be?" I asked, shocked. "How does his watch know when to guard his person?"

"That is only one of the challenges of the English Court, mademoiselle," His Lordship said. "Though to be fair, it is the same as any other royal Court. If one wishes to prosper, one learns the monarch's ways, and adjusts one's self to follow, and to please. As will you, mademoiselle."

I considered this in thoughtful silence. I remembered how, in Dover, the king's activities had often been impulsive and seldom predictable, but I'd judged that to be only on account of the circumstances. I was realizing I'd even more to learn than I'd first believed. Yet as His Lordship so wisely said, I would adjust.

Near the Tower, we were forced to leave the yacht behind, with our baggage unloaded and carried the remainder of the way by cart. The comte and I (and my maidservant, Bette), however, simply shifted to a smaller craft sent to meet us from the palace, a long, low boat with liveried oarsmen—an inconvenience made necessary because the yacht's sails were too large to pass beneath London Bridge. Deftly the oarsmen steered us through the narrow archways, skirting through the foaming currents with a speed that made me gasp and cling to my seat as the spray flew over my cloak. I'd only a glimpse of the bridge above me, a huge and wondrous affair, with shops and houses built on its crossing span, and the decayed heads of long-dead villains on pikes on one end.

The view beyond the bridge was far more sobering. Not long before, the city had suffered a malignant outbreak of the plague that had claimed nearly one hundred thousand lives, a quarter of the populace. Soon after that had come a horrific fire that had destroyed a quarter of its buildings and left thousands more Londoners homeless and many places of business ruined, a double measure of misfortune for any people to bear. Now, four years later, little had yet been done by way of rebuilding. I could still see the remnants of the fire, with weedy, rubble-filled plots where houses once had stood, the tilting remnants of brick chimneys, and blackened timbers that continued to loom o'er their neighbors like twisted skeletons of ebony.

After this grim sight, I could appreciate anew the melancholy I'd often seen on His Majesty's face. What prince could witness such terrible destruction cast down upon his people without being affected by their suffering?

"What caused the fire?" I drew my cloak more closely around my body. It was cold so near to the water, or perhaps the sight of the burned ruins chilled me. "Was it lightning? An untended cook fire or hearth?"

The comte shrugged elaborately. "No one knows for certain. The king ordered an inquiry, of course, but their only conclusion was that it had been an act of God. Ha, an act of God! Would that his people had been as credulous!"

"Why?" I asked curiously. "What did they believe was the cause?"

"What they believe is the reason behind every misfortune," he said. "The French. More specifically, the Romish French. Don't look so startled, mademoiselle. It's a fact of living in this place. We are blamed for everything, and nothing. The English are so jealous of us French, yes?"

He smiled archly, but his words did not seem a jest to me. I remembered instead what Lord Monmouth had once told me about the unreasonable suspicion and dislike the English bore toward Catholics, nor could I forget Ralph Montagu's certainty that most Englishmen believed that their English princess, our Madame, had been poisoned by her French husband and his lover. There was no sense to it, this blind English hatred for the French, but their sentiments certainly made for an unsettling (and more than a little frightening) welcome for me. Truly, the task of serving my king and my country's interests in so hostile a place was going to be challenging indeed.

"There's Whitehall Palace, mademoiselle," the comte said beside me. "That ramble of gray stone and red brick hanging over the river. Doubtless that is not what you expected either, is it?"

He was right, and he laughed to see the bewilderment that

must have shown on my face. When I thought of the French royal residences—Versailles, the Louvre, Saint-Cloud, Fontainebleau, the Palais-Royal—I pictured well-ordered and proportioned grandeur that reflected not only the glory of the inhabitants, but of all France as well. I should never have dignified what I saw before me now as a palace, certainly not a palace for one of the greatest kings of the Christian world. Oh, it was sufficiently large and the situation beside the river was agreeable, but it *was* a ramble, more a long string of disparate towers and roofs, windows and porches, seemingly tossed together by a score of different builders to suit a score of different patrons, and with all the regard of a child's play blocks, too.

How could Madame, who'd had the most exquisite taste, have pined for this unwieldy heap of stone and mortar? How, too, could so handsome and fine a gentleman as the King of England have this as a reflection of his grandeur? And how had such a dingy, piebald manor ever come to be called Whitehall, when there was nothing fair or white about it?

My wonder only increased as we disembarked at the palace's private landing and made our way up the long flight of stone steps. We were greeted by several royal guards and footmen, all of whom recognized His Lordship, and soon we were being led to the lodgings of Lord and Lady Arlington. I was very willing to follow, for if the exterior of Whitehall had appeared disordered, within it seemed ten times worse, with so many halls and staircases and galleries, often crowded with gentlemen and ladies and servants, that I soon lost any sense of my direction.

Also distracting was the amount of attention His Lordship and I drew as we walked past the others. Though no one greeted me by name, it was clear from what I overheard that most already knew who I was. Clearly they believed I knew no English, for they made little effort to speak discreetly as they offered their judgments on my appearance and how I'd please His Majesty. I held my head high, my expression serene, as if in fact I could hear none of these comments, yet some were so crude and common that I couldn't help but blush, and that, too, became grist for their vulgar wit. I tried as best I could to concentrate instead on my new surroundings, eager for any hints at His Majesty's preferences.

Now I vow I will be honest. In some of these halls and rooms, I did spy an occasional Italian picture or ancient statue of merit, a tapestry or looking glass of genuine quality—mind you, my eye had been well trained by Madame—but for the most part the pictures and other furnishings were drab and woeful. Far worse, however, was how there seemed to be dogs everywhere, wandering about among the crowds and relieving themselves wherever they chose. No one took any notice, nor did any of the servants hurry to do away with the leavings. It was an altogether foul practice, and one that helped give the palace more the air of a kennel than a home for a king.

By the time we finally reached the Arlingtons' lodgings, my head ached with all I'd seen and heard and (regretfully) smelled. Yet as soon as we were ushered inside, I felt as if I were once again in Paris. As a member of the privy council, Lord Arlington had been granted an entire suite of rooms overlooking a large green park, and surely everything within these apartments had come from France or Italy.

As soon as Lady Arlington was introduced, I understood, for it was instantly clear she was a lady of refinement, and a fitting match for His Lordship. Born Elisabeth van Beeverweerd in the Netherlands, she was the granddaughter of Maurice of Nassau, Prince of Orange, and I wondered how Lord Arlington, who had urged the English to make war on the Dutch, had come to choose a Dutch heiress as his wife: a love match, I supposed, being the only explanation for it. Yet perhaps because we were each of us foreigners among the English, I felt at once an affinity to this handsome, elegant lady. Perhaps, too, I sensed the slanders she'd survived, for later I heard terrible, malicious stories whispered of her, of how she and certain other wanton ladies would perform lewd naked dances for drunken gentlemen in the private rooms of taverns. What I saw then was only her generosity to me, and how, as we sat together, she fell into speaking French to me most naturally, with only the slightest Dutch accent coloring certain words. She seemed among the most welcoming and gracious ladies that I'd yet met, especially after the travails I'd endured these last weeks.

The Comte de Grammont soon left us, and Her Ladyship herself showed me to my bedchamber. We took tea together, talking of nothing and everything as women will, the late-afternoon sun slanting low through the windows until the curtains were drawn and the candles lit for evening. As we spoke, I learned among other things that these handsome rooms in the palace were only a minor pied-à-terre to them, to keep them close for the convenience of the king. The house they regarded as their true home was on the country side of the park near the Mulberry Garden, a large and extravagant establishment simultaneously called Goring House, after the lord who'd built it, and Arlington House, after the present owner, though it amused Her Ladyship to refer to it both ways. It also became clear that her husband had confided everything of my situation to her, and that she'd no false modesty or outrage over the possibility that I'd become the king's mistress. To her it seemed no more than another place at Court, and that went far to put me at my ease in her company.

As we finished our refreshment, she had her baby daughter brought to present to me, a beautiful infant named Isabella. This tiny girl was the only child of the Arlingtons' union and much doted upon by them. Surely this child was a rare blessing from God upon their marriage, considering how Her Ladyship must have been close to thirty-five years of age when she'd borne her and His Lordship at least fifty. I watched her hold her lovely daughter, laughing and kissing her sweet small face, and I thought wistfully of all that Lady Arlington possessed—rank, honors, fortune, an adoring husband and a lovesome child—and how charmingly agreeable her life must be.

My trunks and other belongings arrived, and as Bette began to unpack them, Lady Arlington insisted on coming to my bedchamber to watch and see what I had brought. She exclaimed over my gowns, inspecting each with delight over the style, the cloth, the lace, and the workmanship, and praising the Parisian seamstresses as surpassing all others.

"You'll draw His Majesty's eye in any of these, that's certain," she said with approval as she ran her fingers lightly over the sleeve of a saffron-colored satin gown. "He does like to see a well-dressed lady, and with your beauty, he'll be blind to all others. This would be an excellent choice for your first meeting."

"Forgive me, my lady, but I'd already decided on this one as most appropriate." I held out a plain gown of dull black wool, more mourning of the same I'd been wearing for Madame. I wished to honor my mistress—that was true—but this gown was not quite the sacrifice it might appear. Though somber, it was made of the softest wool imaginable, and cut to flatter my form with cunning perfection. Since Madame's death, I'd learned as well that the sad colors of mourning were unexpectedly becoming to me, making my alabaster skin the more striking by way of contrast, and that the narrow white bands that were the only permissible trimming served to brighten my smile further, my perfect teeth already being one of my best attributes.

I suppose that this might be perceived as a shocking vanity, turning the banners of loss and grief into worldly display. In England, perhaps it would be viewed in this shameful light, but in France, looking one's best was only another way to demonstrate respect and regard for the dead. Every French lady with the means kept at least one elegant mourning gown in her wardrobe in readiness against the vagaries of fate. I was no different. I'd come prepared with gowns for the three stages of mourning, from this unadorned black of the first three months to the less somber grays until by next spring I could once again wear the colorful gowns I'd also brought. At least that was the rule at the French Court; it could well be different here.

But Her Ladyship, I suppose, had no way of realizing this. "Lord Arlington told me you'd been given leave to lessen your mourning."

"I have, my lady," I said, for I'd been granted permission by Louis himself. The choice to continue in mourning, at least for now, was entirely mine, and one I instinctively believed was both respectful toward Madame and also best for my cause. It was a risk, of course. The king might prefer to be diverted from the memory of his sister, rather than reminded of it. But when I considered his devotion to Madame, I'd decided that the surest course to his affections would be to continue to link myself to her in his thoughts, and this seemed to be the easiest way to do so.

"There will be time enough for the bright gowns, my lady," I said softly. "I believe His Majesty would appreciate seeing how I still honor the memory of Her Highness."

She looked back at the gown, her pale eyes turning thoughtful.

"The king might indeed prefer that," she said slowly. "He grieves deeply for the princess."

"Then most likely he'll prefer it if I wait a little longer before I come to him like a gaudy canary bird." I smiled sadly, my thoughts returning to Madame as they so often did. "I don't wish to seem too eager, my lady, but when will I be presented to His Majesty again so that I might offer my condolences to him myself?"

Lady Arlington nodded, clearly pleased to look forward to my future at Court. "Later this week, once you have recovered yourself from your journey, you'll be presented to Her Majesty. After that, we can discuss when you will begin your duties in her household, and move to more suitable quarters among her other ladies. But as for being presented to His Majesty—no, I don't believe that will be necessary."

"Not necessary!" I exclaimed. "But that is why I have come here, my lady. How can it not be necessary?"

"Hush, mademoiselle. Calm yourself, pray," Her Ladyship said. "Of course you'll see him, and soon, too. I only meant that you needn't be presented to him again. He met you at Dover, and that is sufficient. He's not forgotten you, that is certain."

"Forgive me, my lady," I murmured contritely, now feeling foolish. "I misspoke."

"There's no harm in your enthusiasm," she said, patting my arm with gentle concern, her touch eerily like Madame's. "We are not so formal here as they are at Versailles. The king will stand on ceremony when it is necessary for matters of state, but in his own affairs, he prefers a less confining manner. He knows you are here now with us. I expect he will come to welcome you tomorrow morning."

"He'll come to me?" I asked, shocked, but pleasantly so. What rare favor, to have the king come to me, rather than the other way about.

"I should think so," she said, and smiled again. "You needn't worry about the propriety of such a call, my dear. I'll take care to attend you when he appears. You won't be left alone with him, not in the beginning. His Lordship has told me how you are a lady and gently bred, and how you were a treasured favorite of the princess. We must treat you with the respect that is due a lady of your station."

"Thank you, my lady," I said, and quickly brushed away the tears of gratitude that filled my eyes. Although I'd resolved to follow my own course—as I would with the mourning gown—it would be useful to have friends like this lady, whom it seemed I could trust. I'd not had such a one since Madame's death. I could only hope that now my lonely days might be done. "Thank you for your kindness."

"It is as nothing, my dear," she said with a warmth that again touched me deeply, "and I'm honored to have you here as our guest. But I've chattered enough, and you must be weary. You'll want to wake early, you know. His Majesty rises with the sun, and begins his day by walking through the park with his dogs and his gentlemen. I should expect him to call here after that, under pretext of seeing Lord Arlington. You should be ready to receive him."

"I will be ready, my lady," I said, smiling with anticipation. "You'll not have to rouse me. Madame kept early hours as well, and I'm accustomed to it. Sometimes we wondered if she ever slept at all."

"That is the way of the Stuarts," Lady Arlington said, laughing softly. "They're a busy lot, with not a moment to squander on anything as uninteresting as sleep."

She rose to leave my bedchamber, pausing for a moment before my dark mourning gown, hung on the door of the cabinet for wearing tomorrow. She reached to run her fingers over the soft wool, smoothing a scrap of lint away from the dark cloth.

"My husband was impressed by you in Dover, mademoiselle," she said, as if addressing the gown and not me. "The moment you appeared today, I saw for myself that his praise of your beauty was no exaggeration. But he'd also spoken highly of your wisdom and discretion, complements I questioned in a lady as young as you are. Even Lord Arlington is apt to credit more to a pretty face than perhaps he should."

She glanced over her shoulder and smiled at me, as if sharing a secret that women alone could understand. "Now I find I must apologize to him, a difficult task for any wife. His first judgment of you was well-deserved. You are wise and discreet beyond your years, and clever, too, I suspect. You are not above a few words of advice, are you?"

"Of course not, my lady," I murmured, for advice from this lady could be of considerable use.

"Yes, you are clever, my dear," she began, "but never forget that the king is infinitely more so. You must take considerable care in managing him. Never speak directly to him of political affairs, or show any aversion to those who are near him, no matter how taxing or trying some of those rogues may be. Loyalty is one of his greatest qualities, but only if you can garner it for yourself."

"I shall try my best, my lady," I said, and bowed my head in acknowledgment of her sagacity. What she'd said was true for all courtiers, whether ladies or gentlemen, and I would do well to heed every word.

"I believe you will, mademoiselle," Her Ladyship said with approval. "No wonder the king desires you. What an agreeable change you'll make from the bold and brazen slatterns he usually chooses!"

"Thank you, my lady," I said, realizing the significance of this compliment. She could make all manner of jests about her husband's judgment of me, but I suspected hers held equal weight, and if I'd failed to impress her favorably, I'd have had a much more difficult path for myself at Court. Thus I curtsied again, the better to convey my gratitude. "I am most honored."

"We'll all be honored if you succeed in pleasing the king, my dear. I am sure you won't forget us, and share the favors that His Majesty might drop your way." She gave the gown one final brush with her hand and turned back toward me, her hands folded at her waist. "You were right to choose this gown. You'll please the king by wearing it."

"That is my only wish, my lady," I said fervently, "to please His Majesty."

"You will." Gently she took my face in her hands and kissed me on the forehead. "Now sleep, mademoiselle. The morning, and His Majesty, will be here soon enough."

I smiled up at her, giddy with expectation, and who could fault me for it? In the morning, His Majesty would be here with me. With *me*.

And no, I did not sleep at all.

Chapter Fourteen

This was how I would always remember my first glimpse of the king in London.

Unable to sleep, I drew a chair close to the window and sat with my bare feet curled beneath me to watch the sun rise, the clouds turning gray, then pink, and finally breaking apart to reveal the new day. From Lord Arlington's lodgings, I could see the green swatch of the park stretching out behind the palace. The grass was crossed by numerous paths, empty now of visitors at so early an hour. The only notable witness was a large single bronze statue on a marble pedestal, a likeness of an ancient warrior, scaled beyond life, who in his full manly nakedness raised his clenched fist in salute toward the palace. Oblivious to this bronze combatant, white swans and brown ducks glided on a long rectangular pond—the English canal that Lord Buckingham had described to me—whose surface shone silvery bright in the early sunlight, and a score or so of wild deer grazed upon the lawns. The very tops of the great oak trees were beginning to shift their color for autumn, green leaves fading into gold.

As was common at this season of the year, a mist had risen from the ground during the night, and now only a few patches of it remained, softening the scene likes wisps of fairy gossamer. Through this mist, beneath the oaks, I saw the movement of a darker form: more deer, I thought, or perhaps some other creature in search of its breakfast.

I leaned forward, my elbows resting on the sill, and the shadowy form in the mist took a more human shape and became four gentlemen. The three who walked behind I did not notice, except to see that they were there. How could it be otherwise, when the tallest one striding boldly in the fore was the king?

He was dressed in dark colors, though whether in somber mourning for his sister or simply by his usual custom, I did not know. He walked briskly, his long legs making his stride so long that the other gentlemen labored to keep pace. I smiled, remembering that stride from Dover and how he never seemed to tire. His dark hair fell back over his shoulders and his coat was open from his exertions, the white linen of his shirt in stark contrast to the otherwise unrelieved black. Scurrying incongruously around him were a half dozen of his spaniels, their ears flopping and their tongues lolling as they, too, hurried not to be left behind.

At this distance, I couldn't make out his features beneath the shadow of his flat-brimmed hat, yet still I leaned closer to the glass, my fingertips pressed to the cool surface, as if that were enough to see more. He seemed everything a king should be: virile, strong, handsome, and masterful.

"Good day, Your Majesty," I whispered, and smiled fondly. "And what a fine day it is with you to grace it."

Abruptly he stopped his walking, and the other gentlemen stopped with him. He said something that made them all laugh (for the jests of kings are always amusing), and then, to my horror, he turned and pointed up toward my window, and looked directly at me.

I gasped and tumbled backward, my chair crashing to the floor in a most clumsy fashion. Given the sun, the distance, and the glass pane between us, I doubted he was able to see me spying on him, but I still felt the shock of his attention as surely as if we'd been only a few feet apart. More shocking still was the realization that he could be on his way to these quarters, and I was still in my nightclothes, with my hair frowzy and undone.

"Mademoiselle!" exclaimed Lady Arlington, drawn to the room by the thump of my chair. Unlike me in my night shift, she was fully garbed for the morning, complete to the pearls around her throat and in her ears. "What has happened? Why are you not dressed?"

Chagrined, I pointed to the window. "Nothing has happened, my lady. I was looking from the window, and saw His Majesty, and—"

"Yes, yes, and now he in turn shall see you in this sorry, slovenly state if you don't hurry." She clapped her hands briskly. "Now make haste. Call your maid, and dress yourself at once. At once!"

It was as well that I'd already settled on wearing the mourning gown without further ornament, and that in the same plain spirit I'd decided not to paint my face or eyes nor dress my hair in any elaborate fashion. Thus when the king did arrive and I heard his voice greeting Lord Arlington at the entry, I was ready to present myself exactly as I'd planned, sitting on a cane-backed chair as the epitome of well-bred, artless innocence.

Prepared as I was for this moment, I couldn't keep my heart from racing with excitement and more than a little anxiety, too. So many people in both England and France had contributed to launching my adventure and had worked together to bring me here, with an equal number of ambitions and hopes now resting on my plump white shoulders. Not the least of these ambitions were of course my own, for while my other sponsors would glide to another if I were to fail, I'd only myself to look to for my future and whatever fortune I could make.

But nothing was certain. However charming I remembered His Majesty to be, he remained no more than a man, and an inconstant one at that where the fair sex was concerned. In the time since I'd seen him last, he might have found another lady, more beautiful and more obliging. He could have lost interest in me for being French, or suspected the hand of his cousin Louis, or perhaps I'd ceased to interest him for being so readily offered. He might have returned his devotions to Lady Cleveland, or even to Her Majesty.

In those final moments before he entered the room, I thought of all these unhappy possibilities and a score of others, yet not once did I ever guess what really came to pass.

"You recall Mademoiselle de Keroualle, sir, I am sure," Lord Arlington said as he opened the door and ushered the king and Lady Arlington into the room. "Mademoiselle, His Majesty."

I had only the most fleeting impression of his dark-clad height looming over me and the face I remembered so well, before perforce I bowed my head and curtsied. I kept low, my downcast gaze fixed on the floorboards as I waited for him to speak, and give me leave to rise. I waited, and waited still, my heart racing within my breast and my palms damp with worry as I held my skirts and wondered miserably what I'd done wrong.

Then suddenly he seized my hands and drew me up himself, pulling me upright so unexpectedly that I gasped aloud, just as I'd done earlier at the window. Now unavoidably, inevitably, my gaze met his, and I could not have looked away even if I'd wished it.

His Majesty wept.

"When I see you, mademoiselle," he said, his voice full of torment, "I see my sister at your side."

"Oh, sir," I said softly in French, scarce more than a whisper as sympathetic tears of my own stung my eyes. My mourning had played its role, but now I almost wished it hadn't. I dared to weave my fingers more closely into his, squeezing them gently to offer what wordless comfort I could. "Oh, sir, I am sorry!"

"She was so happy at Dover," he said. "You know. You were there. And then—then it was done."

"You needn't say more," I urged, wishing to save him the pain. "Please, sir, do not do this to yourself."

He shook his head, more at the unfairness of Madame's fate than to refuse my comfort. "You loved her, mademoiselle, and she loved you and trusted you. She told me so herself."

"But she loved you above all others, sir." To see a gentleman let his tears fall so shamelessly was the most poignant sight I'd ever seen. "She spoke of you on her deathbed, and now even in heaven, I am sure she watches over you."

That made his dark eyes fill anew, yet at the same time I saw his jaw tighten with a determination that seemed at odds with his grief.

"Arlington," he said without turning toward His Lordship, "pray take your lady and leave me with Mademoiselle de Keroualle."

To be honest, I'd been so rapt in the king's emotions that I'd forgotten the Arlingtons remained in the room with us.

"Forgive me, sir," said Lady Arlington with her usual soft-spoken grace, "but for the sake of the lady's honor and modesty, I should prefer to remain."

"And I, madam, prefer that you should not," he said, more sharply than I'd expected. "I wish to speak to this lady alone."

As favored as the Arlingtons were, not even they could refuse a royal order like that.

"As you wish, sir," Lord Arlington said. He bowed deeply, and took his wife's arm so they might withdraw together. The door clicked shut after them, and I looked back to the king.

"Come, mademoiselle, sit with me," he said, and led me over to a nearby settle. This furnishing was long and commodiously wide, and fitted with numerous soft cushions of silk velvet in the Italian manner. With dismay I wondered if he intended to make use of its convenience to make his first assault upon my virtue. But sorrow ruled, and though we sat side by side, to my relief passion was the furthest thing from his thoughts.

"Mademoiselle," he said, still clasping my hand as he looked directly into my eyes. "Mademoiselle, I would ask that you be as truthful and loyal to me as you were to my dear sister."

I placed my free hand over my heart and bowed my head with sweet grace. "You have my pledge, sir."

He nodded, pleased. "You attended my sister when she died, yes?"

"Oh, yes," I said as another tear escaped my eye. "I was with her when she was first stricken, and remained until the end, and after."

"Then tell me all," he said firmly. "I've heard it from others, but none that I trust to tell me the truth. Tell me now, mademoiselle, and leave nothing out."

I took a deep breath and did as he bid, relaying every detail of those dreadful last hours of Madame's life. From the chicory water to the final consolations of Bishop Bousset, I omitted nothing, exactly as he wished.

Now was when I'd expected him to display the depth of his loss, but again I was wrong. As he listened, his eyes were entirely dry, his earlier anguish replaced by complete concentration on my words, and a steely determination to miss nothing. Several times he interrupted me to ask some detail I'd forgotten—what antidotes had been administered, and whether blades or leeches had been used for the bloodletting, and where Monsieur had been at this or that time—and when I answered, he nodded, and asked me to continue.

It wasn't until I'd finished that I realized I'd never spoken of Madame's death to anyone else before this: not because I'd wished to keep it close, but simply because no one else had asked it of me. In Paris, I'd been too insignificant to anyone other than Madame, and besides, everyone else I'd known who might have been curious had witnessed the death as well.

But now I felt as if an unhappy burden had been lifted from me, as if by telling Madame's story to her brother, I'd made my final peace with my dear friend and mistress. It was as if I'd been destined to do this last favor for her, almost as if she'd contrived it to be so. Perhaps in some strange way, she had.

"Thank you, mademoiselle," the king said, his voice heavy. He'd not wept again, but his expression remained inexpressibly sad, and I'd only to recall the more joyful times earlier this summer to understand. "Now I would ask one more question of you, and again I trust that you will answer me in perfect trust. Do you believe Minette was poisoned?"

He wished the truth. In these circumstances, what brother wouldn't? Sitting together as we were on the settle, the difference in our heights was lessened, our faces nearly even. Beneath the black brows and heavy lids, his dark eyes seemed capable of finding the truth in me even if I didn't venture to offer it.

Did I believe Madame had been poisoned? In my troubled heart, I did. From the first day I'd spent in her service, I'd seen too much of

Monsieur's loathsome cruelty toward his wife to believe otherwise. Her death might not have come from a deadly potion or herb, as most had suspected and the physicians denied, but there are other ways to poison the soul that are just as fatal to a tender constitution like Madame's, a thousand small abuses and hateful indignities that would kill over time. No magistrate in France would ever charge Monsieur with the crime of murdering his wife; there must be absolute proof to punish the brother of His Most Christian Majesty. But I believed one day Monsieur would face a higher, more awful judgment, and then he would not escape unscathed.

But was that what her brother now asked?

Montagu had warned me that the king not only believed Madame had been poisoned by her husband, but that he also believed that Louis was protecting his brother. Crimes like those could destroy the new alliances (both the secret one I'd witnessed and the false one that had been the work of Lord Buckingham), and could even lead instead to war between England and France. I'd been charged to keep this from happening, to soothe the English king's worrisome tempers and incline him back toward France, and to tell him whatever he needed to hear.

Madame had worked hard for the sake of this alliance, and now it was my turn to preserve it. This would be my first challenge as an agent for my country and my king, and if I were the true daughter of France I'd always claimed to be, then it shouldn't have caused me the slightest qualm or regret. To falter would be to betray my country.

But the English king knew none of this.

"You may speak freely here, mademoiselle," he said gently, misreading my hesitation. "This is England, not France, and the duc d'Orleans is no longer your master. You're safe here."

I still clasped his hand in mine, our fingers loosely twined together. Now he gently laid his other hand over mine, covering it by way of reassuring me.

"Tell me," he coaxed. "Tell me what you know."

I looked down at his hand over mine, his long, dark fingers, which were nearly as expressive as his face. He wore no rings to show his station, no bejeweled ornament of state, nor did he need them, such was his confidence.

"Please, mademoiselle," he said. "For Minette's sake, and mine."

"Her Highness had been unwell for many months, sir," I began, still looking down at his hand over mine instead of his face. "From the time of her confinement last summer with the Princess Anne-Marie, and even before. She was often in discomfort and restless, and often could find no position that would bring her sufficient ease for sleep. Some nights she did not sleep at all, but wandered like an unquiet spirit about the gardens of Saint-Cloud. More and more foods distressed her and made her ill and wretch, and she lost so much flesh that her gowns were all remade smaller, else they would have hung flapping loose about her person. She even had extra pleats and furbelows stitched in place to give her more presence."

I paused, remembering sadly how thin Madame had become in the last months before Dover. It had been shocking to see her as she was dressed, how the bones of her spine showed like knobs in a row through her too-white skin. When her maids had laced her stays each morning, there'd been nothing spare to draw in, the stitched bones of the stays sitting directly against her ribs.

"What did her physicians say?" the king demanded. "Surely they would not neglect their duty if she were so ill."

"After a certain point, sir, she refused to consult them," I said. "She forbid us to send for them."

"She told me none of this," he declared. "If she didn't trust the French physicians, then I could have sent her Englishmen."

"It wasn't so much a matter of trusting the physicians, sir, as her not wishing to hear what they told her," I said. "I believe she knew how ill she was, and feared the worst. If she let no doctors near her, then she could pretend her woes were only another passing complaint that would cure itself."

"But that is madness!" he exclaimed. "Why would she have done such a thing?"

"I can only guess, sir," I said, taking great care with my words. "But she did fear that if she showed any weakness before Monsieur, he would have forbidden her to come to Dover. And that—that she could not have borne."

He shook his head. "My poor Minette," he said, his voice bleak with despair. "How could I have not known at Dover?"

"She'd not wish to cause you worry, sir, or take your care from the affairs," I said. "She was so delighted to be here in England and in your company that I don't believe she felt any pain or suffering while she was here, until the day we left. I'd never seen her more gay, more filled with joy and happiness. That is how she'd wish to be remembered, sir. That, and for the great love she always carried for you."

He rose abruptly, going to stand before the window with his hands clasped tightly behind his back. He stared out at the park, at the gold-tipped oaks and the first visitors beginning to walk on the crossing paths. In the distance I could hear the drums of the changing guard on the Parade, dogs barking and the rumble of a carriage as it drew before the palace. I doubted the king perceived any of this. Instead I guessed his head was filled with visions of his youngest sister, laughing as she danced on the beach with her arms outstretched and her faced turned up to the sky.

I stood (for of course I'd risen when he did, as anyone did in a royal presence) in respectful silence before the settle, determined not to interrupt his reflections. Given the endless demands a king must have on his time and person, I was sure the best gift I could offer at such a time would be silence and whatever peace that came with it.

"Thus you do not believe Her Highness was poisoned?" he finally asked, to the window and not to me.

"I fear she died of many things, sir," I said gently. "But I do not believe malevolent poison given her on the day of her death was one of them. No, sir, I do not believe that was so."

"You would then absolve d'Orleans and the Chevalier de Lorraine?"

I addressed his back and broad shoulders. "I do not believe either is guilty of that particular sin, sir."

He made a low growl of scorn. "You would say that Louis is innocent as well?"

"I would, sir," I said with full conviction. "He was devoted to Madame, sir, and if you'd but seen his—"

"I've seen enough of Louis and his devotion," he said wearily. "More than enough."

"Yes, sir," I said softly, and sighed. I'd done as he'd asked, and I'd done what Louis had asked of me as well for the sake of France. No one could ever say otherwise. I'd told the truth, yes, or at least what I'd told was true. I could only pray that Madame's immortal soul would understand what I'd done, and forgive me for it, too.

At last the king turned, and came to stand before me. He'd changed there by the window, drawing upon some private strength deep within. His face was now composed, his emotions tidily buried again, and though I knew he'd not been ashamed to weep before me earlier, I doubted he'd do it again, leastways not today.

"I thank you, mademoiselle," he said, his more usual genial self. In this he was like his cousin: both kings had the most cordial manners. "For your honesty, your loyalty, and your love for my sister."

"I am honored, sir." I curtsied in acknowledgment, my black skirts spreading around me on the sanded pale floor.

"I rather think the honor is mine." For the first time that morning, he smiled. Not with joy, or merriment, or even amicable pleasantness, but with more of the same sorrow that seemed to lace everything he did. As much as I understood—how could I not?—I wished to do whatever was needed to ease that sorrow. I longed to make him happy, to smile with delight and to laugh with joy. That was what I thought when I gazed up into his deep-lined, handsome face, and further, it was what I resolved to do.

No wonder, then, that I smiled as warmly as I dared in return. "Surely Your Majesty's honor must be the most valued in all of England, sir. How could one such as I merit so great a prize?"

"Because of who you are, mademoiselle." He narrowed his eyes slightly, studying me as if for the first time. "I do not know how it's possible, but I vow you are even more beautiful than I recalled. Might I ask the privilege of calling on you again, mademoiselle?"

I opened my eyes widely with a pretty show of incredulity, for I understood well the game he'd begun.

"But you are the king, sir," I protested, "and these rooms lie within your palace, in your capital city, within your country. Why should you ask my permission?"

"Because while I am a king, mademoiselle," he said, his voice low, "I am first a gentleman, just as you are a lady, and deserving of my respect."

He was standing over me now, with little respectful about how he was looking down at me, and most especially down at the swell of my breasts. My gown was first mourning, yes, but the plain linen kerchief pinned over the front of my bodice was of the sheerest linen, more enticing than modest.

I let my smile fade, letting him dictate what came next. King or commoner, men were much alike in such circumstances. I was certain he wished to kiss me, and certain, too, that he'd act on the impulse. I'd already kissed him once in Dover, and I expected to kiss him again now. One kiss, I decided, and no more, yet still my heart raced with nervous anticipation. He bent lower, and I raised my face toward his, letting my lips part in unspoken invitation.

Yet as he slipped his arm around my waist, he glanced down and frowned. He shook his head and sighed, his gaze still fixed on my black gown.

"Minette warned me away from you in Dover," he said heavily, "and she was wise to do so. For us now, so close to her death, it would be wrong."

"Now you are the wise one, sir," I said, and though I thought my own weeping was done, the mention of Madame's concern for me was sufficient to send another tear slipping from my eye. Even in death, she would protect me. "What is wrong now may in time turn round to be right. One never knows what fate may bring, sir, or what tomorrow holds for us."

"Tomorrow," he repeated. "I will return to you tomorrow, Louise."

"Please do, sir." I smiled as he used my given name, and felt that single tear puddle in the dimple on my cheek. "I should like that above all things, and so, I believe, would Her Highness."

Quickly, before I thought better of it, I leaned up and kissed him on each of his cheeks in turn, the way we French do by way of salute. Surprised, he smiled crookedly, and touched his fingers to the place on his cheek where my lips last had been, fair disarming me with that alone.

"She would," he said. "She would. And so, I vow, will I."

I learned during that first fortnight that the king was a gentleman who kept his word, particularly when it pleased him to keep it. Early each morning he came to call on me, exactly as he'd promised, and some days he came in the afternoons as well. Although Lady Arlington had promised to be present, she never attempted it again after the king had sent her away during the first visit. Nothing was said of this arrangement; it simply happened. As soon as His Majesty arrived, the servants were dismissed and the door was closed and latched for exclusive privacy. I was happy enough to be left alone with the king, and he hardly objected to having my company to himself. Neither Lord nor Lady Arlington asked how we passed the time in their front room, though I suspect they were like the rest of the Court, and envisioned His Majesty and me engaged in every manner of lascivious play. I will grant that they'd excellent reason to expect such was the case. As astonishing as it seemed, the stories I'd heard from Madame of his many conquests were apparently underestimated rather than over-, and even the genteelly reticent Lady Arlington could name a score of former conquests without effort. The king's infatuation with me at Dover had become widely known, and, royal Courts being what they were, all in Whitehall (and beyond) assumed that I had capitulated as soon as he had pressed his desires, the way it had been with all the others.

The truth, however, was far less titillating, as truth so often is. Behind that latched door, the king and I would sit together on that same settle. I would offer him refreshment after his walk in the park, and whether it was tea, coffee, wine, or ale, I poured and served him myself with an artful grace that he much admired. What man does not like to have a beautiful woman dote and fuss over him in an obliging fashion, letting him imagine how that same eagerness to please him by way of a silver chocolate mill would likewise be the same in the bedchamber? While he sat with his cup or glass, he would tell me of his day, his dogs, and the weather, until before long we would inevitably be once again drawn to speak of Madame. As close as these two royal siblings had been, their lives had been so separated by the cruel vagaries of war and fate that in fact I had spent more time in Madame's company than had the king. However belatedly, the king now seized the opportunity to learn more of his sister's life in Paris, a life he'd unfortunately shared only by way of her letters, and he never tired of hearing me recount the most ordinary details concerning Her Highness.

I suppose I could have turned petulant at this, or been vexed by having the king so close to me, yet wishing to speak exclusively of another lady instead of directing his attentions toward me. I wasn't, not at all. Madame would always be far too dear to me, and in fact I took my own comfort from speaking of her, just as he did in listening. It was as if I were once again with Madame in the confidence of her bedchamber, though instead of hearing her speak of her brother, now I was speaking to him of her. If such a thing were possible, his devotion to his sister only made him glow more brightly in my esteem, for it is a rare man indeed who will be so open about those he loves.

Was it any wonder that I treasured the intimacy of our conversations, or that I valued this time alone with the king to experience his intelligence, his loyalty, and his wit without having to share him with others? I'd no doubt that he was in fact the first gentleman of his realm. No other could come close. I might have been sent to him as a sort of gift (and certainly an agent) by my king, yet it was as a woman I sat beside him on the settle, eager to be dazzled by his person and company.

Thus we conversed, and held each other's hands as good friends will, and when the hour came for him to take his leave, we would kiss in parting, again as friends, not lovers. The presence of Madame's spirit was too strong between us to permit anything more, nor at that time did we wish it. In his eyes, I'd become an extension of Madame herself, representing not only those last happy days at Dover, but also embodying many of the same qualities that had made her so dear to him.

I suppose the rest of the Court would have roared with laughter to see us so restrained, the great libertine prince and the virgin he'd brought clear from France to deflower. I'll grant, too, that shared grief and solemn mourning must seem a most curious foundation for the lasting love that grew between the king and me.

Yet so it was. For when those two weeks were done and the first stage of mourning with it, the king had come to know me not as a wanton or one more maidenhead that he'd victoriously claimed, but as a lady and a friend. Away from the public rooms of the Court, he had seen me at my best. He'd relished my beauty, yes, but he'd also been pleased by my loyalty to his sister and thus to his family. Alone together, where he'd not be judged by his intolerant English subjects, he'd delighted in my very foreignness, in the thousand small ways a French lady knows of making life more enjoyable.

I'd learned my lessons well at Madame's side, and already I was putting them to most excellent use here in London. To him I was now Louise, not mademoiselle, and while I still called him by his title and always would, in my thoughts he had become only Charles.

Too soon this time was done, and reluctantly the king decided I must be presented to the queen, and assume my duties as a maid of honor. With the end of September, the first stage of our mourning for Madame was officially done, and there could be no further excuses made for keeping me apart from the rest of the Court.

I was eager to join the others, too. In these weeks, I'd come to a significant decision regarding my future: not to yield to the king for as long as I could hold him at bay. Resistance and denial were difficult gambits to maintain, infinitely more complicated than the simple bliss of surrender. But I'd learned that saying no to a gentleman who always heard yes was a powerful lure, and the longer I could refuse him, the more secure my place would ultimately be.

I could tell His Majesty's desire for me had increased at least a hundredfold since I'd come to Whitehall, and maybe more. I was the same jewel he'd coveted in Dover, but because I remained beyond his possession, my value had only grown. I'd become the greater prize in his eyes, to be pursued no matter the cost or risk.

And as for me: what did I desire? Why, that was answered easily enough.

I wanted it all.

Chapter Fifteen

"Is there anything I might fetch for you, ma'am?" I asked, leaning down closer to the queen so I might hear her reply over the musicians. "More sherry, or another orange?"

"Thank you, no, mademoiselle, I am sated," she said, shyly patting my sleeve as if that would compensate for her heavy Portuguese accent. "What makes me best happy is you here."

"Thank you, ma'am," I said, and once again took my place behind her armchair. She twisted around to make sure that I was there, then smiled and fluttered her fingers, heavy with rubies and diamonds, to me before she turned back to watch the dancers.

Best happy, indeed, I thought. I'd only served in Her Majesty's household for three weeks, yet already I'd become one of her favorite ladies. I'd not planned it to happen, especially when I considered the growing attachment I bore toward her husband (and now my Charles). I'd merely treated her with the respect and deference that was due her rank and person, and performed whatever small tasks she'd required, the same as I'd done for Madame.

But Catherine of Braganza was nothing like my first mistress. Small, squat, and dark, she had the misfortune to be wed to a man who adored ladies who were tall, graceful, and fair, and if they were clever and amusing, all the better. The poor queen possessed none of these attributes, and though she'd been the Queen of England for nearly a decade, she still struggled with the English language and a lisp caused by her protruding front teeth. She suffered from severe headaches and a wealth of other ailments that limited her time abroad from her bed-chamber. Worst of all, she'd not done what as a royal princess she'd been born to do, which was to provide an heir to her king.

Though Charles did not appear to fault her for what was so obviously her shortcoming in this area and not his, the rest of the Court was not so kind. She reminded me of a certain girl who'd attended convent school with me: a plain, unlovesome girl who was tolerated only because her father was a wealthy wine merchant and she an heiress. Behind her back, however, she'd been the butt of all our cruelest jests and most mocking imitations, and so it was now with the pitiable queen.

In a rare moment of supreme unfeeling several years before, Charles had even insisted that Catherine accept the then Countess of Castlemaine as a lady-in-waiting, with the predictable results. Lady Castlemaine had done nothing in her post except to claim her income and scorn Her Majesty at every opportunity, while the poor queen had been thoroughly humiliated by that lady, and her own husband's lack of regard.

Yet I had liked Catherine as soon as I'd been presented to her, and pitied her, too. Though I was not so shy as she, I could sympathize with her, and since I'd also come from another Court much like her native Portugal where ritual and protocol were rigidly obeyed, we could commiserate with one another about the lack of manners and politesse at Whitehall. Our conversations could take peculiar turns, for I spoke no Portuguese and she no French, leaving us to muddle about in our differently accented English, but even that drew us closer, foreigners in a strange land. Further, we shared the same faith in the Roman Church, and she soon invited me to take mass with her in her private chapel, and make confession to her priests, a lovely, welcoming offer in that den of untrammeled Protestantism.

As a result of all this, she now claimed me as one of her dearest companions, and wished me always at her side for the Court's entertainments, such as this one tonight. Surely she must have known of Charles's interest in me and mine in him, however wrongful and adulterous it might be. He made no secret of it, and besides, she'd seen enough of his predilections to guess what would come next. But though she was queen, this poor lady was so desperate for trust and friendship that she overlooked this flaw in me, and embraced me as if I were her dearest friend from girlhood.

Now she beckoned to me, and obediently I stepped forward to listen.

"I am chill, Louise," she said, touching her shoulders to demonstrate. "Pray fetch my shawl to me. The red one of silk."

"Yes, ma'am, as you please," I said, though I could not fathom how she could be cold. The company around us was very close, with far more people squeezed into the palace's Banqueting Hall tonight than was comfortable for dancing. I liked this room above all others I'd thus far seen in Charles's palace: a large, double-cube room built fifty years before by his grandfather King James I, for the purposes of dining, masques, and other entertainments. It was elegantly proportioned and beautifully decorated, with artfully carved columns and volutes and much gold leaf on the carvings and a glorious painted ceiling overhead, and by my reckoning, it was the only chamber in the entire rambling warren of Whitehall that was worthy of any palace.

The tall arched windows that lined the walls beneath the galleries should have offered breezy relief, but because the queen was often cold like this, the king had ordered the windows to remain shut for her sake. To the rest of us, the room was now a-swelter, an unseasonably warm evening made warmer still by the heat from the scores of candles and the exertions of the dancers as well as the close-packed guests.

Still at the queen's side, I waited for the musicians to finish their tune and the dancers to leave the floor so I could cross to Her Majesty's quarters. Some of those in the great room before me I already recognized—Lord and Lady Arlington, Lord Monmouth, Lady Cleveland, the Duke of York, Prince Rupert, Sir Thomas Clifford, Lord Buckingham (that vile, neglectful rogue!), Lord and Lady de Croissy—but many more I did not, and in a way I was grateful that my duties placed me squarely at Her Majesty's side, and apart from the vigorous activity on the floor, well fueled as it was by wine.

At last the music stopped with a few raucous shouts to mark its conclusion, and I made my parting curtsy to Her Majesty.

"I'll be back directly, ma'am," I promised. But I had gone but a few yards when a firm hand closed round my arm.

"Mademoiselle de Keroualle," the king said, his smile warm and his swarthy face flushed darker still from dancing, "pray come dance this next with me."

"Oh, sir, please," I stammered, flushing with confusion. I'd not expected to be recognized in any special way by the king this night, and he'd startled me. I'd seen him from afar, of course—Charles was so much larger than other gentlemen that he always stood tall in any crowd—but he'd been as occupied with other courtiers as I'd been with the queen. Now I glanced back to that lady in her red plush-covered armchair, as guilty a glance as could be. "Forgive me, sir, but Her Majesty has only just sent me on an errand, and I—"

"You may be excused, mademoiselle," the queen interrupted. I was surprised she had overheard us and her expression showed her to be both wounded to be abandoned, yet sadly resigned, too. "Go to His Majesty, yes."

"Yes," he repeated, nodding cheerfully at her before he turned to beam at me. "You must dance now, mademoiselle. It's been doubly ordered by a king and a queen."

"But I do not know these English dances yet, sir," I protested, try-ing to pull away. "I've no wish to seem clumsy before the company. Another time, once I've—"

"I'll have them play a dance you know," he said, drawing me closer. "A sarabande. Every lady at my cousin's Court can dance a sarabande."

He stopped a passing footman, and sent the man off to give the music master his instructions. He slipped his arm around my waist so I'd not escape and drew me through the crowd toward the floor. Nor could I protest any longer in good faith, for he was right: every French lady *was* taught to dance a sarabande, and I was no exception.

But to make this complicated dance my first performance before so many with the king as my partner was surely tempting the worst of fates. With its triple steps, dragging measures, and elegant, practiced gestures, a sarabande was a dance with scores of traps for the unwitting or unwary—or, as in my case, for the very nervous. If I stumbled or tripped now, or turned one way while the king turned another, why, that would be all that anyone here would remember of me: that French maid who was so vastly dull and clumsy when she dared to dance with His Majesty.

"Come now, Louise, don't play timid," he teased as we took our places with the other couples on the floor. "Else everyone will believe I'm so poor a partner that you've no wish to dance with me."

"I fear it will be the other way around, sir," I said unhappily, "and that others will wonder why you bother with me."

"Oh, I doubt that," he scoffed, taking each of my hands to begin, yet pointedly studying me at the same time. My gown was still plain, but of a soft gray sacernet with a muted, dull finish that showed my own coloring to excellent advantage, and the lack of trimmings and ribbons displayed both the neatness of my waist and the ripe bounty of my breasts. "Any man here would take you for his partner, my dear. Lucky I am that I claimed you first."

I opened my mouth to remind him that luck had little to do with the choices of kings, but the music began first, and I'd no choice myself but to pay heed to it. I listened to the rhythm and matched my steps both to it and to the king mirroring me, and before long I'd fallen into the magic of the dance exactly as he'd predicted, even enjoying myself. I'd known from Dover that Charles was an accomplished dancer, full of energy and grace, and no doubt he regarded the sarabande as one more of his sports, like racing horses or tennis, to be mastered and won.

Yet as the dance progressed, however, I realized it wasn't the pursuit of a stuffed leather ball that Charles was considering, but me. There is a sinuous, suggestive quality to a well-danced sarabande that can make those watching blush. For this reason, we were forbidden to learn it at school, and it wasn't until I was at Louis's worldly Court that Madame's dancing master had taught me the steps and the elaborate gestures that went with it. Two partners can explore more interesting postures than in other dances, more unabashed display to each other, and more opportunities, too, for brief exchanges of flirtatious conversation, which of course Charles employed.

"Your dancing is superb, my dear," he said, shifting to French so others around us would have more difficulty in overhearing. "You're too modest, pretending otherwise."

"Dancing is important at the Court of His Most Christian Majesty, sir," I said, teasing him with a primness at odds with our movements. Now that I'd overcome my first uneasiness, I was enjoying myself thoroughly. Though there were several other couples on the floor with us, we were the only pairing that was being watched and, I guessed, admired, too. "Every lady knows her steps."

"And I'll wager every gentleman is grateful for it, too," he said with approval. "You're looking surpassing beautiful tonight, Louise."

"Thank you, sir," I said, turning artfully beneath his raised arm. "I venture that you are likewise a vision of manly grace to rival Apollo himself."

He laughed at the silliness, even as the compliment pleased him. I liked how his dark eyes sparked when he was happy, a twinkle (if that, too, were not so foolish a word to apply to the eyes of a king) that had a conspiratorial gleam that was most engaging. By that I knew he was happy now to be dancing with me, most happy, and the very male half smile confirmed it.

"If I'm to be Apollo," he said, "then you shall be my fair Diana."

"Ah," I said as I turned beside him. "The virgin goddess, yes?"

"The only one on Mount Olympus," he said, his voice so low and dark that I blushed prettily to hear it, as doubtless he'd intended. "A sorry fate for any goddess, that."

"I do not know if she'd agree, sir," I said archly. "She's also the goddess of the chase, from having never been caught."

He chuckled wryly. "And the moon," he said. "That's hers as well."

"A new crescent moon, beautiful and silvery pure," I said. "A most suitable emblem, I should say."

"There's such a moon in the sky tonight, you know," he said. "Step outside with me now, sweet, and I'll show it to you."

"Truly, sir?" I asked, and laughed. "Was all that other nonsense only to invite me into the moonlight?"

"It was meant to disarm you," he admitted freely. "If I'd asked you outright, you never would have agreed."

I turned on my toes, spinning my skirts against his legs. "Who's to say I've been sufficiently disarmed to agree now?"

"Come with me at the end of this dance," he said, "and we'll decide together."

I didn't answer as I turned away, letting him fear I'd decline. I might still; I wasn't sure. As much as I longed to bask in the moonlight with Charles and share whatever mischief he'd planned, I knew I'd do well to be cautious. He could be most persuasive, and like every king, he did not like to be denied.

"Name a favor," he said when we faced each other again, "and if I can oblige, then you must, too."

"Then dance next with Her Majesty, sir," I said, naming a favor that I was sure would cast his plans askew. It was a calculation, yes, but it was also a true favor, for I'd seen Catherine's disappointment when he'd asked me instead of her. "You danced with her to begin the evening, and not since."

He frowned, genuinely confused. "What manner of favor is this, Louise?" he asked. "Is that your wish, or hers?"

"It could be both, sir," I said, and smiled beguilingly up into his face. "Kindness given is often rewarded."

At that moment the dance ended and I curtsied.

"Very well, Louise," he said, his answering bow perfunctory. "You'll have your kindness."

He left me, heading directly to where Her Majesty sat and offering her his hand.

"What a peculiar sight," the gentleman beside me said. "Was that your doing, Mademoiselle de Keroualle?"

I turned, and recognized him at once. "My Lord Rochester! I am honored, my lord. I've not seen you since last year in Paris, in Madame's drawing room in the Palais-Royal."

"A veritable lifetime." He bowed, and winked slyly. "Much has changed since then."

"Indeed, my lord," I said, thinking sadly of Madame. The earl had changed, too, and not for the better. He was still handsome, still dressed to the very teeth of fashion, but the first hint of decay that I'd observed last year had blossomed and grown. He was now thinner, his cheeks more pale, and the brightness in his eyes seemed more feverish than wholesome. I remembered how these had been the first signs of Madame's final illness, and I prayed for the young earl's sake that I was mistaken.

"Indeed, yes," he said blithely. "You, for one. I recall you as a veritable mouse in Paris. A beautiful mouse, to be sure, but a mouse that hid quaking near the wainscoting. Of all the ladies about Madame, I never would have imagined you would be the one to leap so far. Now look at you!"

I raised my chin in defense. "Am I no longer beautiful, my lord?"

"Oh, beautiful, yes, yes, but no longer a mouse," he said, "unless you're a most clever one, with your eyes intent upon seizing the cheese."

I laughed to hear myself described as any sort of mouse, but like everyone else, the earl was too occupied in watching the king lead his queen to the floor. Charles was being kind to her, too, smiling warmly at her with genuine affection. Some men are faithless in their marriage from disliking their wives, but that could never be said of Charles. I remembered how Lord Buckingham had vowed the king would banish and divorce his queen for her barrenness, but to see him with her, I doubted he'd ever do anything so cruel, even for the sake of his succession. Faithless, yes, a hundred times over, but never cruel. It was a bitter realization for me, of course, because of all my giddy, girlish dreams of becoming queen myself, and a pox on Buckingham for feeding me such nonsense as fact.

I watched them dance, watched how Charles gallantly did his best to show Catherine off to advantage and mask her missteps. If I could but claim a measure of that devotion for myself, I thought wistfully, if I could have a share of his heart for my own!

"Don't be glum, fair mouse," Lord Rochester said, doubtless reading my face. "You're already to be congratulated, you know. If what I've heard is true, then you've managed to take hold of the royal cods without spreading your own legs. Quite the admirable accomplishment."

My cheeks grew hot at his bold vulgarity, and I did not answer it.

"Ah, you blush, mademoiselle," he said, amused. "Thus the scandal must be true. A French virgin! No wonder you've dazzled the king. Virgins at this Court are as rare as a snowflake in the Arabian desert, and as fragile, too. The only other one I recall to confound poor Charles was Frances Stewart, for all it brought her."

"Forgive me, my lord," I said, purposely chilly to show my disapproval. "But I do not know the lady."

"You wouldn't," he said, more entertained by my manner than chastised. "Her time at Court was done long before you appeared. At the time Frances Stewart was another fair flower nurtured in Louis's Court, with the most stubborn maidenhead in all Creation. The king laid siege to it for years with no relief, and in the end the lady ran off to wed the Duke of Richmond and gave away cheap what she could have sold high."

"For years?" I repeated thoughtfully. I'd no idea there was such precedence before me. To be a duchess would be a fine prize, true, but I'd other ambitions beyond that.

"Long enough to drive the king near mad with lust," he said. "He was in a righteous high dudgeon after that folly, I assure you."

I glanced at him sideways, unable to resist his scandal-mongering. "Was the lady ever able to return to Court?"

"In time, yes, after the fire in the king's prick had found another bush to burn," he said. "She returned a new-made duchess, but no one cared. She'd taken the smallpox soon after her marriage, you see, and her loveliness was thoroughly ravaged."

"How dreadful, my lord!"

"Oh, aye," he said carelessly. "They say poor Richmond was inconsolable. What is worse than being saddled with an ugly wife?"

I frowned again, deciding that whatever illness was plaguing the earl was poisoning his tongue as well as his body. "Are you always so cruel to ladies, my lord?"

"Not the ones I like," he drawled. "Go on, mademoiselle, try me. Ask my opinion of any lady you see here. I vow there's at least half a chance that I'll not slander her."

I glanced about the room, determined to test him. The dance was done, but before the king and queen had finished their courtesies, a tiny, copper-haired woman had sprinted onto the floor to claim it as her own. Her boldness was rewarded by cheers and laughter, and the king himself stopped to greet her. At once the musicians began to play a sprightly jig, and all alone this brazen little creature began to dance, prancing and hopping as if possessed by demons, her skirts spinning shamelessly as high as her garters.

"That one, my lord," I declared, pointing to the dancing woman. "I'll venture you cannot say anything good of her."

But to my surprise, his face softened. "What, of Nell? What could I say that she hasn't said herself? She was born a whore and a happy one at that, and so she'll die, unrepentant and merry."

"Nell, my lord?" I asked, looking at the infamous actress with new interest. I'd pictured someone with more presence, more beauty, a woman able to command the stage. I'd never imagined this vulgar little creature with her hair tumbling down, kicking her feet high in the air before her. It was one thing to see the king with the queen, and even with a famously extravagant beauty like the duchess of Cleveland, but another entirely to picture him with any woman so common as this. "That is Nell Gwyn?"

"Who else could it be?" the earl asked, smiling fondly as he watched her. "Aye, that's Nell, and you won't hear me say a cross word against her. So there's your proof of my rare geniality, mademoiselle, though I wager it's not what you'd expected."

None of it was what I'd expected, no. I watched as the king laughed and applauded Nell Gwyn's jig, and watched, too, with pleasurable relief as he turned away from her to escort the queen back to her seat. The actress was left alone on the floor with her cheek turned up for a kiss that didn't come, there with all the Court as witness. Then she cackled uproariously to cover her disappointment, and plunged off into a crowd of male courtiers to do who knew what.

"Prepare yourself for boarding, mademoiselle. The king's bound this way," the earl said. "You, Nell, and the queen, too. I vow he'll take to juggling at Bartholomew Fair with this many balls in the air."

I paid the insolent earl no further heed, but made my way at once to Charles's side. He'd executed the favor I'd asked, leaving me no choice but to fulfill mine in return. Not that I wished to refuse. Having seen him merry with other women chaffed sorely at my pride, and made me all the more eager to have him to myself in that moonlight, no matter the perils.

Without a word he claimed my hand, raising it briefly to his lips before he began to lead me through the crowd of bowing courtiers and from the room. I smiled with blushing triumph, even as I knew I'd be the centerpiece of tomorrow's tattle. Let them talk, I decided, full of bravery and bluster myself. I'd know the truth and so would the king, and that was all that mattered to me.

But as we neared the door, the impudent small actress popped up before us like a child's jumping jack. I suppose she felt she still merited more of Charles's attention for her vulgar dancing, yet this was astonishingly forward even in the English Court.

What came next, however, was far, far worse.

Tipping her head at a sharp angle, the actress cocked one hand over her head and the other at her waist, an exaggerated mockery of the sarabande's elegant postures, and, of course, of me.

"Parley-voo-hoo-hoo, mon'sir?" she asked in a low English parody of French. "Dance-say à la frog, mon'sir, o-wee, o-wee?"

Others around her laughed and sniggered at her foolishness, but the king did not.

For myself, I was simply too shocked to respond.

"There now, Nelly, enough," Charles warned with more mildness than I thought she deserved. "We've no need of that."

But she wasn't done. Still holding true to her mockery of the sarabande, she took several purposely clumsy steps, ending so she was facing me. Then she screwed up her face into a terrible grimace, making her eyes into the narrowest of slits.

I gasped as if I'd been struck a blow. In a way, I suppose I had. As with many people, my sight was weak at a distance, and without thinking, I sometimes would squint by way of compensation. Though I'd not been aware of it this evening, I must have done so when surveying the company, long enough for this dreadful woman to have seized upon it as a flaw, and turned it now against me.

It was wickedly done, and though I should have expected no more from such a slatternly snip, I did expect the king to defend me.

I expected, yet he did nothing or, rather, nothing by way of punishing the woman. Instead he merely frowned at her—a black scowl, to be sure, but not enough to affect one of her coarse sensibilities— and drew me past the others and from the hall.

I was too wounded to speak as he led me through the halls of the palace, too unhappy so much as to notice where we were amidst the many halls and staircases until, at last, we'd stepped into the privy garden. This was a large square garden enclosed on all sides by the palace walls and galleries, expressly for the use of the royal household. The garden itself was insignificant compared to what I'd been accustomed to in France—white stone paths that crossed in the center of the green beds, punctuated by a handful of white marble statues on pedestals. Yet by moonlight the garden's plainness was much improved, and given the unseasonable warmth of the evening and how Charles and I were alone together within it, I should have been most content.

"Here's your moonlight, my fair Diana," Charles said with a proud and sweeping gesture of his arm meant to encompass both the garden and the moon-swept night. His smile gleamed white in the shadows, the very picture to me of a romantic hero. "With you in it, there's no prettier sight to be found."

"Pretty words, too, sir," I said, and tried to smile. Yet to my sorrow the memory of Nell Gwyn's insult rose again like sudden bile in my throat, and I turned away quickly, hoping he'd not see my distress.

"Oh, sweet," he said gently, coming to stand behind me. He rested his hands on my shoulders, warm and comforting, and yet somehow so tender that I felt tears in my eyes. "You must not heed Nelly. I'll grant she went too far, but she cannot help herself. Like a drunkard craves his ale, she must make others laugh, and she never does consider the consequences."

"But she insulted you, too, sir," I protested. "For her to imitate—"

"It's done, Louise," he said firmly. "I don't know how such things were treated in my cousin's Court, but here it's not worth troubling over."

Indignantly I turned to face him, not hiding the tears on my cheeks any longer. "If such a person as Mrs. Gwyn were to mock a lady of the queen's household at the Louvre, let alone His Most Christian Majesty, why, sir, that person would be hauled away in chains."

"Truly?" he asked. "Then it's well for Nell she's never left England."

"Perhaps, sir, it would have been well for me if I'd never left Paris."

"But not for me." Gently he brushed away my tears. "I cannot begin to tell you how happy I am that you are here with me."

I heaved a small, shuddering sigh, wanting very much to believe him. "I've never so much as met her. Why would she do such a thing to me?"

"I told you, Louise," he said, "because she cannot help it. But also because she may fear that you are a lady, and more beautiful than she."

I sniffed again, resting my open palms on his chest as I gazed up at him. "Do you believe I am, sir?"

"I do," he said, and smiled. "When you danced with me, I judged you the most beautiful lady in the room."

"Thank you, sir," I murmured, slipping my hands along the front of his coat and looping them around his shoulders. "Thank you."

He eased his arm around my back, drawing me close into the crook of his arm, a warm and cheering place to be. Yet as he gazed down at me, his expression was more serious than seductive, and so was his voice.

"You cannot let such little things vex you, my dear," he said. "If Nelly's drolleries are the worst you have to bear, then your life here will be charmed indeed."

"I'll try, sir," I whispered, running my tongue lightly over my lips. I would most likely have agreed to anything then, with his arms linked about me and his body pressed close to mine. "That is, if you wish me to stay."

"Ah, my dear goddess," he said, his gaze intent upon my mouth, "I've never wished for anything more."

He kissed me and I welcomed him, my arms around the back of his neck to steady myself. I'd expected him to kiss me as he had in Dover, and after a fashion, I suppose he did. But perhaps because of how well we'd danced together, or the lover's spell of the moonlight, or because we'd spent so much time of late in frustrated flirtation, there was a heated urgency to this kiss that startled me. I kissed him in return, yes, for I doubt I'd the will not to. But soon his hand shifted away from my waist, and I felt him spread his fingers across the curve of my bottom to push our hips more intimately together. There was no mistaking his ardor, or the demanding need of his cock.

"Enough of this teasing, sweet," he urged in a gruff whisper, his breath harsh against my ear. "Come with me to my rooms, where I can fuck you properly in a bed, as you deserve."

"Oh, sir, please," I said, deftly disentangling myself from his embrace and turning around him, just as I had when we'd danced. "Forgive me, but I can't, not yet."

"Yes, sweet, you can," he insisted. "We can together."

He caught me and pulled me close, my bottom snug against the front of his breeches. Even with all the layers of linen, silk, and wool between us, I could still feel the heat of those certain parts in such close proximity, yearning for connection as if there were no barriers between. With one arm like a band around my waist to keep me close, his other hand was free to dip beneath my fine linen kerchief to fondle and play with my breasts. I gasped, more with pleasure than with outrage, and I felt my traitorous body sway to his power, my breasts swelling beneath his clever touch and the sweet honey of desire gathering low in my belly. My battle now was as much with my own desires as with his, and only the sternest resolve made me break free again, this time to stand more at a distance.

"Forgive me, sir, please," I said breathlessly, for lustful desire had shortened my wind as much as his. "I am sure that it would be most pleasurable, and that you would be a most excellent tutor in the arts of love, but I—we—cannot yet, sir. It is what everyone in your Court expects of me, that I am only one more harlot imported to your Court for you to—to ravish for sport. And I won't be that harlot, sir. Your dear sister would not wish that for me, or for you."

"My sister has nothing to do with this, Louise," he said curtly, but still I heard the hesitation in his bold declaration.

"But she does, sir," I insisted, pressing home my point, "and neither of us can deny it. Her Highness wished better for me, sir. She wished for me to remain true to the honor of my ancient family, an honor that reflected on her as my mistress as well as myself. For me to put aside all her care and teaching and play the wanton with you while I still am dressed in mourning for her—"

"Then when, mademoiselle?" he demanded. "Damnation, when?"

I looked at him there before me in the moonlight, his face taut with frustration and denial, every muscle in his body tense. I knew because I felt much the same, miserable and unfulfilled and all a-quiver with half-roused longing. It was a dangerous gambit to play, twisting lovers' ways about to bind him more closely to me.

And to France: I must never forget that.

"When?" he asked again, more curtly. "Tell me, mademoiselle."

If I resisted him for too many nights, he could decide I was not worth the trouble, and send me back to France. If I denied him beyond his endurance, then he could take me by angry force, and no man would fault him for it. He was a large man, and strong, too, and I was but a lady. Most likely by his rights as king, Charles could ravish me now, here, in any manner he chose, and it would not be considered a rape. The sweet specter of Madame could protect me only so long.

"Soon, sir," I said, my voice trembling with emotion. "We'll both know when it is right."

He came and kissed me again. This time, however, he took care to kiss me without touching or embracing me in any way, so that only our lips bound us together. Two, it seemed, could play the same game, and he'd done this purposefully to prove it. I understood, and though it was torture, I kept my own hands to myself exactly as he had, my fingers knotted into tight fists at my sides; yet even that was sufficient to leave me feeling nigh sick with longing.

"I will wait, because I believe you are better," he said at last. "For you, Louise, I will wait."

Each week I wrote my dutiful letters to Louis's agents, and reported to them on my progress with the English king. I employed the code that had been given me, wherein each notable person was called by another name in case the letters were intercepted by the Dutch, at that time our most hated enemy. I didn't believe this was very likely. I gave my letters directly to Lord de Croissy, the French ambassador, who included them with his own diplomatic correspondence to be sent by a courier with an armed escort. The packets were weighted to sink, too, the way Madame's letters once had been, in the event the courier's boat was attacked whilst crossing the Channel. It all seemed a great deal of fuss for my little missives, and the even littler news they contained.

For that autumn, what truly did I have to write? I was accepted as a maid of honor to the queen, and shared lodgings with the other attendants at Whitehall Palace. I'd continued my acquaintance with certain prominent English ministers, like Lord Arlington and Sir Thomas Clifford, and broken with others, like Lord Buckingham. Most important, my friendship with His Majesty continued to grow, with him seeking my company twice a day and also often in the evening. The early hope that he would regard me as a connection to his sister had been fulfilled, and all remarked at the fondness and favor he showed to me.

I wrote nothing of being Charles's mistress, for there was nothing to write. I continued as much a virgin as when I had arrived, and though I was sorely and repeatedly tested by the king, I had remained steadfast. In return his attention to me had only increased, and to the dismay of both the duchess of Cleveland and Mrs. Gwyn, Charles now spent more time in my company than in theirs combined. This made for a pretty complement to my beauty, my grace, my conversation, and, to be sure, to the king's endless fascination with me as the one lady who dared refuse him.

There was, however, one peculiar aspect to this situation. Charles and I were among the very few in all of Whitehall (and doubtless far beyond those walls as well) who believed that I was not already his mistress. Oh, the usual share of lubricious jests was still made about my maidenhead, but without much conviction, and any protests I offered were met with winks and smirks. The handful of those who believed me were in their way far worse, damning me as cold-natured, calculating, and without passion.

One day in October, I'd bought a custard tart from a sweet-monger in the park. Though it had tasted well enough when I'd eaten it, I later supposed it had been too long in the sun and had spoiled, for later that afternoon I began to feel the first pangs of distress. I had been invited to dine in the evening at the French embassy along with several others of the Court. Just as the Palais-Royal under Madame had been a sanctuary and meeting place for all English gentlemen in Paris, so the embassy was to French visiting London, and I looked forward to seeing amicable faces such as the Comte de Grammont and Charles de Saint-Denis, Seigneur de Saint-Évremond, an elderly soldier turned author whom Madame had long ago befriended. Though I felt increasingly ill, I joined the other ladies in dressing and having my hair arranged, and rode with them in the carriage to the embassy.

But as soon as the first dish was brought to the table before me— a pickled sturgeon—I could no longer contain myself. Without asking for leave, I clasped my hand over my mouth and bolted from the table to find relief over a slops bucket left by servants in the hall. I was taken back to Whitehall and retreated weakly to my bed, and though

I retched throughout the night, by morning I was much improved, if empty to my very bowels. I entertained Charles, and went about my other duties as usual, and thought no more of my little misadventure, except to vow never to buy another sweet from a basket.

There is no place like a Court for swift-footed scandal, and no such thing as a little misadventure. Unbeknownst to me, word soon traveled of my illness. The following afternoon, I sat among the queen's ladies in her rooms while she rested, with each of us at our sundry occupations. To our surprise, the French ambassador and his wife were announced, and at once Lady de Croissy hurried to embrace me and kiss me, and congratulate me on my good fortune.

"I thank you for your wishes, madame," I said with bewilderment, "but if I have received good fortune, I should wish to know it."

The other ladies around me tittered knowingly behind their fans, while the ambassador's good wife had only smiled, her several chins quivering with happiness.

"You needn't pretend with us, mademoiselle," she said. "We all witnessed your indisposition last evening, and know perfectly well the joyful reason for it. My husband has already written to His Most Christian Majesty so he might share in the celebration. Now tell us, pray: have you a notion of the day of conception, so we might know when to expect the happy arrival of the royal infant?"

Such, then, were my days at the English Court in the last days of 1670: thwarted passion, idle foolishness, and ill-founded scandal. But in the new year, much in our world would change, enough to make me long for the times when the whispers of others were the most grave of my worries.

Chapter Sixteen

When I had sat at Madame's side and listened to her speak so glowingly of a treaty between France and England, I had seen this alliance through her eyes. I'd imagined a union that would mark a new respect and fellowship between the two most powerful Christian countries, and an opportunity for them to work side by side for common gain and glory. I thought the alliance would bring Frenchmen and English together in new fellowship and tolerance.

That I believed any of this sadly proves how much I trusted Madame, and how little I knew of the ways of great countries and even less of their people. It takes far more than a parchment, a seal, and the signatures of highborn ministers to change the beliefs of a nation. The hatred and distrust that the French and the English bore one another had lasted for so many generations and through so many centuries that this newest treaty was bound to meet with little support, nor did it.

The second, public treaty that had been so proudly negotiated by Lord Buckingham was finally signed with much fanfare four days before Christmas in 1670. Five lords put their names to it—Clifford, Arlington, Buckingham, Ashley, and Lauderdale—as did the king.

These lords were the most trusted members of the privy council, and it was a curious (some would say devious) coincidence that the first letters of their surnames spelled out the word "cabal." Lord Arlington himself once jovially explained to me the amusement of this, for while the word had come to mean a group of plotters, he claimed it originated from the ancient Latin word *cabbala*, or secret teaching. Surely there was much that was secret about this group, not the least of which was how many self-important gentlemen did contrive to keep their knowledge of the earlier treaty hidden from their unwitting peers. Not one broke his trust, and to this day, I believe it remains a secret still.

Except for the difficult clause regarding Charles's eventual conversion to the True Church, the second treaty was much the same as the one first negotiated at Dover Castle. The English and the French would unite their forces in a campaign against the Dutch. Louis wished to conquer as much of the Continent as he could, while Charles wanted the seas safe for English merchants and their ships. The English share of this venture would be fifty ships and six thousand soldiers, while the French were to contribute thirty ships and the rest of the necessary army. The English would oversee the naval encounters, and the French all operations on land. The arrangements were all tidy enough, and I thought again of boys dividing toy soldiers for a mock combat on the counterpane. The less organized realities of warfare would come all too soon.

But while Charles and Louis and their legions of ministers congratulated themselves on their new alliance (and even spared a few grateful thoughts for Madame, whose hard work and perseverance deserved far more credit than the rest of them), their bellicose optimism was not shared by the average Englishman. Two earlier wars had been waged against the Dutch during Charles's reign, and neither of them had brought rewards or glory. They had been costly in numbers of men and ships lost and money spent, and their memory was still uncomfortably fresh among those who would be expected to provide the soldiers, the sailors, and the money that the new treaty promised. While another such war was unwelcome, the notion that England now required the assistance of the French army to fight the Dutch was especially rankling.

Nor did most Englishmen trust the French as allies. The French were sly, conniving, superior, and confusing. They were difficult to understand, and ate peculiar foods. They were Romish, and prayed in Latin, and heeded the Pope. By some gross unfairness, they seemed vastly more wealthy, too, and when word crept into England of the great warships that Louis was having built, the countless cannons cast and munitions assembled and troops drilled and trained, it was impossible for the common Englishman in his alehouse or rum shop not to worry that all that French military power could too soon be directed toward England, treaty or no treaty.

It also seemed impossible for these same common Englishmen to look at the king who'd led them to this treaty and not see more French sympathy to him than they wished. He could not be blamed for being one-half French himself—that was his mother's misfortune—but the fact that Charles employed a French chef to oversee his kitchens, a French tailor to stitch his clothes, a French barber to tend his many wigs, and a French architect to oversee the renovations at Windsor Castle was widely known, and not appreciated. Why must their king drink French wines and dine on French-made dishes instead of sturdy English ale and roast beef? Why did he insist on following French tastes rather than those of his own people?

And why, when thoroughly English (and thoroughly common and vulgar, though no matter that) Mrs. Gwyn had just borne the king his latest bastard son, did he insist in dallying with a French-woman like me?

"You can see, Louise?" The queen leaned forward in her armchair, anxiously looking down past the other ladies sitting along the front of the playhouse box to find me. "So far you are! Are you sure?"

"Thank you, ma'am, I can see the stage well enough." I smiled halfheartedly at her, as much open complaint as I could dare. I couldn't whine or pout, or go against the accommodating persona I'd worked so hard to build with her. But even she'd noted it: my place was the worst among our group. From the luck of placing when the royal party had entered the playhouse, this last seat in the front row of the box had fallen to me. No one would notice me here, tucked back between one of the queen's dullest Portuguese attendants and a thick support column. "I am well enough where I am."

"Don't be so obliging, mademoiselle," Charles called from the queen's other side. "Come, take this chair by me."

Now this was better luck, I thought with satisfaction. I hesitated demurely, waiting while he unceremoniously sent the gentleman beside him to a different chair in the back of the box.

"Here you are, mademoiselle," Charles called again, patting the now-empty seat beside his. "Don't be shy about it. Unless you'd prefer the company of that wooden pillar beside you, eh?"

Of course after that, I'd no choice but to shift my place. Hiding my pleasure behind many apologies, I gathered my skirts closer to my legs and inched my way in front of the others to be more near to the king. He pulled the empty chair closer still to his own, and as soon as I sat, he patted my knee fondly.

"There," he said with satisfaction. "One never wants to miss a moment of Mr. Dryden's plays, and now you won't."

"Thank you, sir." I smiled, as I couldn't help but do whenever I was with him. This was where I should have been from the beginning, at his side, and where I was sure I belonged.

"You look lovely tonight, sweet," he said, studying me with approval. I had been in London for three months now, and while most of the Court had put aside their mourning for Madame, I still kept to somber grays and dark blues, albeit adorned with fashionable lace and ribbons, but subdued enough to subtly remind him of my connection to his sister. "I'm glad you like the pearls."

"Oh, sir, how could I not?" I said, touching my fingers to the heavy pearl drops that swung from my ears, his first gift to me and the first pearls I'd ever owned. I was glad he'd noticed, his gaze returning again and again to the pale column of my throat. I'd observed how greedy Lady Cleveland was, only acknowledging the presents he gave her as her due, and I'd learned from it. When Charles had given me the earrings, I'd wept with joy, refusing them at first as too valuable, and finally accepting them only if he'd put them in my ears for me: a pretty, gracious ceremony he'd much enjoyed, and one I hoped would soon garner me more such baubles as presents.

"I'm glad you wore the pearls," he said, as if sharing my thoughts. "They suit you. I've always thought pearls look best against fair skin."

"That they do, sir," I said, tipping my head coyly to one side to make them swing. "And what more beautiful way to show to others how kind and generous my dearest friend can be?"

He laughed, pleased, and touched a single finger first to one of the pearls, and then lightly along the side of my throat.

"Let them look their fill, my dear, let them look," he said, his eyes darkening with desire. "I'm the fortunate one to have you beside me."

I should note that this was all being acted out as if we were players, too, as we both knew perfectly well. In the time before the play began, the waiting audience usually turned away from the stage to ogle the grand folk in the royal box. Depending upon who had use of the seats, it could well be a better show than the one they'd paid to see.

Of course Charles was long accustomed to this constant scrutiny, while I was still learning. It felt odd to be recognized, to be remarked by name in shops or in the park, and sitting beside the king like this would only enhance my fame. Thus when I impulsively reached for his hand, I understood the gesture wasn't simply one of affection between us, but a declaration that the rest of London would see and note.

He understood, too, and raised our linked fingers to kiss my hand, there for all the world to see.

"I'm glad you're beside me, sweet," he said softly, the warmth of his eyes echoing his words. I'd come to love his eyes, how dark and deep they could be when he looked at me, and how when he smiled, the tiny lines would spread from the corners like the rays of the sun. "It's exactly where you belong."

He leaned forward and kissed me, his hand sliding beneath the swinging pearl to tangle in my artful curls. *That* was a declaration, especially sitting so near the queen. Now I know that we French have a reputation for romantic encounters, but at least at Court, discretion was the custom, and no one flaunted their intrigues. Even Louis, who had had at least as many mistresses as Charles, was never seen to exchange a single untoward embrace. The only reason we'd ever known he visited the apartments of Madame du Montespan was because it was announced as an item in his daily program. But Charles—Charles seemed to have no modesty at all. He kissed and embraced and fondled at will, without the least regard for who saw him. On warm days, he would even go to the bank of the Thames near the palace, remove every piece of his clothing, and swim in the river, naked for all of London to see and admire.

"My sweet Louise," he said when he was done kissing me, the endearment expressing much. Then he winked, and settled back comfortably in his seat to wait for the play to begin. Blushing with pleasure, I tried to do the same.

Though I'd seen many plays in Paris, I hadn't attended a playhouse until I came to London. There hadn't been any need to. All the best French playwrights, like Molière and Racine, were under royal patronage, and presented their latest works in full-staged productions first for the Court. Louis would never have ventured into a place as raucous as this one, the Theatre Royal in Drury Lane.

Only a few years old, the playhouse had been built in the manner of many of London's newer buildings: sturdy enough to withstand the rough usage imposed upon it by the city's impetuous citizens, yet with a gloss of gaudy gilding and scarlet paint to give it an air of tawdry gentility. Three tiers of boxes rose along the walls that encircled the stage, with the royal box in the first tier, and with the choicest sight of the players. The boxes above had wooden benches instead of chairs, with tickets costing commensurately less.

On the floor of the playhouse were more benches, and this space was justly called the pit. The audience who chose to sit there consisted of apprentices, bachelors, blades, and other ill-assorted men of the town, plus an unhealthy smattering of common drabs and more costly whores in black vizard masks, covering half their pox'd and patched faces while their whole jutting breasts were laid bare to their trade. The last low form of female to be found in the pit were the orange sellers, brash young women who wandered through the audience crying oranges and nuts and, only slightly less obviously, themselves as well.

If the play was slow or ill performed, this stew would often boil over, with brawls between the women and flashing swordplay among the gallants, or assignations so brazen that I was sure many couplings took place between the crowded benches. The players themselves were only slightly more elevated than those in the pit, as ready to hurl an oath and an orange back at a too-vocal critic as they were to deliver the sweet cadences of their lines. The tiring-rooms behind the painted sets were no better than bawdy houses, and every painted actress could be bought by any gentleman who had the price in his pocket. This was where Charles had first plucked up Mrs. Gwyn (one more thing that the fastidious Louis would never have lowered himself to do), and how heartily I wished Charles had left her there, too.

I didn't wonder that he loved the playhouse, though, and attended as often as he could. It was exciting and amusing and filled with wild company, and it asked nothing from him in return except that he enjoy himself. I suspect he also loved it for the same reason that I did: nothing shown on its stage was real, a blessed relief from the machinations of Whitehall.

But to my sorrowful regret, that lovely condition was about to change for me. The last songs and dances were finally done, and the audience quieted as much as it ever did. The play tonight was a new one, *The Conquest of Granada* by John Dryden, set against the struggles of the Christian Spaniards against the pagan Moors. The queen and the other ladies had spoken incessantly of this playwright, and his gift with dramatic history plays filled with love, betrayal, and honor. First, of course, would come the prologue, and I leaned forward in eager anticipation.

Instead of a bold Moor or Spanish maiden, however, the figure that came shuffling out to the center of the stage was Mrs. Gwyn, and inwardly I winced to see her. Her tiny figure was absurdly dressed in outsized men's clothing that dwarfed her: a ridiculous wide belt, a cropped jeweled doublet, a gruesome crucifix on a chain around her neck, and an enormous flopping cartwheel hat that she had to hold up from her face with both hands.

Beside me Charles roared with laughter, as did the entire rest of the house before she'd spoken a single line. The more she preened and pranced about, the greater response she drew. Clearly there was some inner, English jest that I didn't understand, and irritated beyond measure, I leaned closer to Charles.

"I beg you, sir, explain the jest to me, if you can," I asked impatiently, wanting to be included. "Where is the amusement?"

"It's Nell," he said, so overcome with his laughter that he could scarcely find the breath to speak. "She's dressed the same as Jamie Nokes from *The Cautious Coxcomb*. You remember, sweet, the play we saw at Dover."

"I didn't see it, sir." As much as I wished otherwise, I was beginning to understand the reasons for so much laughter around me. "Madame was unwell that night, and I stayed with her in her rooms."

"Yes, yes, I'm sorry to have forgotten," he said, his gaze still directed toward the actress's foolish antics. "Nokes played a worthless fop of a fellow named Arthur Addell, played him wickedly well, too. But it was his costuming that made us laugh aloud, made to ape those rascals that came with Minette's party."

"Now I recall, sir," I said, my uneasiness growing. "I heard the talk afterward."

What I'd heard had not been so amusing. The French gentlemen accompanying Madame had been dressed to honor the visit's significance, in the latest and most costly styles from Paris—as, for that matter, had I. But the English had deemed the modish Frenchmen no more than preening fops and peacocks, and when this play was presented as an entertainment, the lowest comic character had been dressed to ridicule the Frenchmen's dress. The French gentlemen had been so incensed by this mockery that it had taken all of Madame's persuasive gifts to keep them from withdrawing altogether from Dover.

Now Mrs. Gwyn was repeating the insult, even increasing it. The audience would indeed understand. The huge hat was meant to symbolize France's overweening ambition to devour all the rest of the Continent. The enormous cross represented the evils of the Catholic Church. The spangled doublet mocked French wealth and fashion, while the wide cinched belt proclaimed effeminate perversion, such as practiced by Monsieur and the Chevalier de Lorraine.

Finally, little Mrs. Gwyn herself represented plucky England, refusing to be swallowed whole by evil, overbearing France.

It was, in short, insufferable.

For any half-wit in the audience who still didn't comprehend, Mrs. Gwyn now smiled directly at Charles and bowed low. Then she spied me beside him. She screwed up her eyes, and squinted at me.

"Steady yourself, my dear," Charles warned, squeezing my hand to give me courage, even as he continued to laugh.

How was I to steady myself before such an insult? What I wished most to do was to rise and leave, to turn my back forever on this impudent rude creature. But I couldn't go without Charles's permission, and I knew better than to ask for it. All I could do was look away from the stage, and see instead the scores of faces turned up toward us, laughing, too, with the scorn and derision that Mrs. Gwyn had inspired.

Finally the laughter began to fade, forcing her at last to speak the prologue, some nonsensical piece that had nothing to do with the play that followed. But my pleasure in the play was spoiled and done, and later I could recall not so much of a single character's name from it. Afterward Charles and several of his gentlemen went to the tiring-rooms, ostensibly to congratulate Mr. Dryden and the players. I suspected he wished to see one impudent player in particular, and I left the playhouse with the queen and her ladies in her coach.

As soon as I was alone, I yanked the pearls from my ears, and raised my hand to hurl them at the wall, determined to show exactly how little I thought of Charles and his insolent actress.

Yet at the final instant, I stopped and slowly lowered my hand. The pearls were too valuable to treat like that. They weren't some simple, faithless trinket. Far from it. They represented my rising place in the king's affections and at his Court, and my success on behalf of my country. When I opened my fingers, I could see the imprints the earrings had pressed into my palm as I'd clutched them close, my flesh streaked red and white and my hand still quaking with emotion.

Hold tight, I thought, and leave a mark: as good advice as any. Carefully I wiped the pearls with my handkerchief and put them back into their plush-covered case. There'd be time enough to counter Mrs. Gwyn, time enough to keep the king for my own. And I'd be the one who held tight, and left my mark.

It wasn't until the following morning that Charles came to speak to me alone, pulling me aside in the hall outside the queen's presence chamber.

"I swear to you I did not know about the prologue last night, sweet," he said contritely. "Nelly likes her surprises."

I searched his face, wanting to believe him. I knew I must rein my temper, and instead let him see the wound he'd caused me. "I thought she'd left the stage, sir."

"It seems she could not keep away." The corners of his mouth twitched beneath his mustache. "You must admit it was rare sport."

"But it wasn't, sir!" I cried softly. "Not at all!"

"It was," he said firmly. "I've told you before, Louise. You must not be so tender over little things like this, else you'll never survive."

I raised my chin. I'd guessed he'd try this course with me, unfairly turning her error into becoming mine. For whatever reason, he insisted on making excuses for her and protecting her the way a well-meaning parent will for a spoiled child. But I'd prepared myself, and planned my defense, both for my own sake and for France. And in case I faltered, I'd worn the pearl earrings as reminders not to lose my purpose.

"I can ignore them when they laugh at me, sir," I said sorrowfully, "and when they mock France. It pains me, yes, but I can forgive their ignorance."

He looked relieved, as all men do when they think they've escaped a woman's wrath.

"That is wise of you," he said. "I told you, Nelly means nothing by it, nor did the audience."

Nothing, ha, I thought grimly, for I was certain the actress meant every word and gesture. Yet before Charles, I purposely kept such thoughts to myself, and with care composed my features to show only how troubled I was for him.

"I try to understand, sir, and to forgive," I said. "But when they laugh at you, oh, that I cannot bear, not at all!"

"My dear Louise," he said, all fond indulgence. He took my face in his hands, his palms warm against my cheeks. "Considering all I've survived until now, a little laughter will not kill me."

"But it's more than that, sir," I insisted. "I'm bringing you trouble. You saw how it was last night. You said I belonged at your side, but truly it would be far better for us both if I left now, and returned to France."

"Return to France?" he asked, clearly surprised. "Why would you wish to do that?"

"It's not that I wish it, sir." I slipped free of him and turned away, matching my actions to my words. "I'd never wish to leave you. But when you are kind to me, sir, your people don't understand, on account of my being French."

"Let them understand or not," he said, his hands at my waist, restlessly sliding them up and down. "I'd rather have your trouble."

"But at what cost, sir, what risk?" I turned back towards him, letting him see the tears in my eyes. "What if my presence puts the treaty in danger, and everything that you and Madame labored so hard to achieve? What if every time your people see me with you, they likewise only see what they fear most of France?"

"What if they do?" he asked. "What of it?"

"Because I will hurt you, sir," I said, letting the first tears trickle down my cheeks. "Because being with you, I hurt you, and harm you, and put your person at risk. And I'd never want to do that to you, sir, never."

"You won't," he said with a conviction that thrilled me. "I won't let them."

"Oh, sir, you are so brave!" I whispered. Much of my speech might have been calculated, but this part was real enough. He did seem extraordinarily brave to me, always confronting his unruly people, the same people who'd martyred his father. "Alas, I'm not as certain. I do not believe anyone would have noticed me with you at all until Mrs. Gwyn summoned their attention, and it—it frightened me, sir. I feared for you."

"I don't want you frightened," he said firmly. "You'll be safe, Louise. I'll see to that. You're far too important to me for it to be otherwise."

"But Mrs. Gwyn—"

"I'll speak to her," he said. "As droll as she was in the prologue, she shouldn't be using the stage to make light of our allies. Let her find sport in the Dutch, if she must."

"Oh, sir," I said with a sigh of content, "you are too kind to me."

"Not at all," he said, and kissed me, taking advantage of my gratitude to press me back against the paneled wall. I melted against him, kissing him in return, for I was not above taking a bit of advantage, either. Deftly he slipped his hand inside my bodice to fondle my breast, and I sighed restlessly, arching my back to offer the soft flesh to his caress. His fingers sought and tweaked my nipple, making it rise at once in proud salute, and making him groan, too.

"How much longer, Louise?" he asked, his whisper more a growl.

"Soon, sir," I breathed, and smiled over his shoulder. "Soon."

With his low-crowned hat in his hands, Lord de Croissy walked the length of the empty room, his footsteps echoing against the long row of bare windows. At last he came to stand before me, a spindle-shanked crow in his customary black.

"All this is yours, mademoiselle?" he asked again. "You are certain?"

"All," I said proudly, holding up the ring of keys to my new lodgings for him to see. "His Majesty brought me here himself yesterday to make certain the rooms would suit me."

"Oh, I am sure they do." The ambassador smiled, and granted me a small nod of approval. "You are to be congratulated, mademoiselle. His Majesty shows you very great favor indeed. Did he also grant you an allowance for refurbishing?"

"Whatever I wish is mine." I crossed the room to the window to look down on the privy garden below, the beds now green with the new shoots of spring. "Everything is to be charged to him."

Charles had indeed shown me great favor to grant such a large apartment for my own use. The rest of the Court was amazed, and could speak of nothing else. I'd this first chamber, and besides that a bedchamber, a privy chamber, a wardrobe, and a withdrawing chamber that could also serve for dining, all for my own use. There was even a small alcove, previously used for books, where I intended to set a prie-dieu and a shrine for private prayer and reflection.

The rooms were a considerable improvement over the crowded quarters I'd shared with the queen's other maids of honor. The only other unattached lady who'd received such impressive lodgings had been Lady Cleveland in her prime. I couldn't take possession yet, of course. First I meant to make a great many improvements to the rooms to agree to my taste, and transform them into the most beautiful in this shambling palace, so I could entertain Charles in a fashion that would truly befit a king. I knew he was anticipating a happy future for us, too, for my new rooms were situated conveniently close to his.

"His Majesty has done well for you, mademoiselle," the ambassador said, joining me at the window. "Am I to believe his persistence has been rewarded?"

I leaned closer to the glass, idly watching a small flock of brown sparrows swoop and dive over the gallery's roof. "That, monsieur, is between His Majesty and me."

"Forgive me, mademoiselle, but it is also the concern of His Most Christian Majesty," he said in his usual insistent manner, his voice quiet, reserved, but always expecting compliance. "Have you earned the privilege of these rooms? Have you accommodated the English king's desires as you were sent here to do, and secured a lasting place in his graces?"

I did not answer, for in these last months I'd grown exceptionally weary of the ambassador's meddling. I'd managed my affairs with Charles well enough thus far, and I'd no need of Lord de Croissy's endless suggestions. Weren't these new lodgings proof enough of my success, and the king's continuing interest in me?

The ambassador leaned closer, determined to make me listen to his advice. "His Majesty will not wait for you forever, mademoiselle. The world is full of women with greater beauty than yours, women who are happily willing to give themselves to him for far less than you demand."

Restlessly I tapped the ring of keys against the sill. "The king and I understand each other thoroughly, my lord," I said, terse in my own defense. "You may assure His Most Christian Majesty that I remain a most loyal daughter of France."

"If that were so, mademoiselle," he replied, his manner turning tart to match my own, "then you would have performed your duty to your country by now."

"Then what of the information I have sent to Paris?" I'd been proud of what I'd learned in my conversations with the king, and I'd believed that what I'd relayed had been useful to France as well. "What of the new ships being built in the Portsmouth yards, and their designs? What of the Duke of York entertaining the Dutch ambassador at St. James's Palace, but by the king's wish? Does none of that matter?"

"Yes, yes, yes," the ambassador said, sweeping his hand impatiently through the air. "Your information has been useful, but if information was all we wished from you, then we could easily have sent a gentleman in your place, and for less cost, too. You are here to seduce the English king, mademoiselle, and if you cannot oblige—"

"I will oblige, my lord," I said sharply. "If you'd wished me to present myself to the king like a mare to be covered for breeding, then I could have done so the day I arrived, and he would have been finished with me so swiftly that he'd not recall my name now. But if you wish me to seduce him, to become part of his life, to find a lasting place in this Court for the sake of France—that, my lord, takes time."

I frowned, restlessly slipping the ring of keys back and forth over my wrist like a bracelet. I'd explained my situation as well as I could, though not with perfect honesty. I was still young, and I still dreamed. I knew now I'd never replace the queen on the throne of England. That dream was done. Yet I dared to hope and to pray, too, that in time I might capture the wandering heart of Charles Stuart, the way he'd already done with mine.

But the ambassador only grumbled, unconvinced.

"Were you aware, mademoiselle, that Lord Buckingham has allied himself with Mrs. Gwyn again?" he said. "Have you heard that the two have resolved to work in union to depose you from the king's favor?"

"I have heard," I said with what I prayed was lofty disdain. I'd heard this rumor, yes, and likewise I'd heard how the two of them would shamelessly imitate both Charles and me before their friends. They mocked my accent and Charles's devotion to me, and called me "Squintabella." It had pained me, imagining their cruel satires, both for my sake and Charles's. But the only way to treat people as disrespectful as these was to ignore them, and that was what I'd done. "His Grace and Mrs. Gwyn are nothing to me."

"They should be," the ambassador cautioned. "You may have been granted these rooms, mademoiselle, but the king has given the actress a house in Pall Mall."

I'd already had myself driven by Mrs. Gwyn's new house to see it. It was handsome enough, I suppose, though only hers by lease. But I'd heard her entertainments were filled with riotous sport, music, and dance, combining her friends from the playhouse and every other walk of life with the most amusing people from the Court, and I suspected Charles went there more often than he admitted. Anxiously I glanced again about the empty space that would be my rooms. The sooner I had them ready and could begin my own form of entertainment, the better.

"Mrs. Gwyn is welcome to her house," I said, swallowing back my worries. "Why not, when she is too common to hold a place at Court or lodgings in the palace?"

"She is baseborn," agreed the ambassador, as if explaining the most obvious fact to a half-wit, "and undeserving of those favors, while you, mademoiselle, are a French lady of rank and entirely worthy, if you'd but bring yourself to fulfill your destiny."

I resented him lecturing me like this, and in defense my tongue turned tart.

"Why, thank you, my lord," I retorted. "How pleased I am to learn I am a lady! You know, I feared you'd forgotten."

He sighed, looking down his thin nose at me.

"Pray don't be cynical, mademoiselle," he cautioned. "It does not become you. Nor does this surfeit of pride. Recall instead that this vulgar wench maintains the greater hold on the English king, and all because she has given him one son, and let him fill her belly again with a second."

I looked at him sharply. "Mrs. Gwyn is with child again?"

"She is, mademoiselle," he said, "and without doubt the king is the father."

I looked down at the keys in my hand. When Charles had given these rooms to me, he'd held me close and whispered only the sweetest endearments to me, and promised I'd find nothing but happiness here. Yet now I learned he'd been with his Nelly, finding his own happiness with her in the house in Pall Mall.

"I did not intend to distress you, mademoiselle." The ambassador leaned closer, his voice full of urgency, not sympathy. "But you must listen to reason. His Majesty's desires are simple ones. He enjoys lying with young women, for they make him feel younger himself. He enjoys beautiful partners, for they flatter his pride. He sires bastards on his mistresses, for they prove his wife's barrenness is not the fault of his seed. The simple desires of a man, simply met. Good day, mademoiselle."

He bowed one final time, set his hat once again on his head, and closing the door, left me alone.

I stared from the window, no longer seeing the garden before me or the darting sparrows at their play.

Charles, Charles, my dear sir! Here I'd believed I was ahead of the race, and instead I'd fallen two paces behind.

Chapter Seventeen

WHITEHALL PALACE, LONDON
February 1671

*O*utwardly there is no finer life for a man than to be a king. He lives in a great palace and wants for nothing. His every whim and wish are instantly obeyed, and he is surrounded by friends, family, and courtiers who exist to sooth and flatter him. Ordained by God's wish, he has power and rank, and a secure place in the esteem of the world.

But life was not always as easy for the King of England. Accustomed as I was to how Louis had carefully ordered everything about him, I was astonished by how many conflicts, large and petty, swirled constantly around Charles. To be sure, some of these trials were of his own making, while others were far beyond the hand of any mortal man to change, no matter that he wears a crown. But all did test him, and often made the royal quarters of Whitehall a stormy place in which to be.

Most somber was the death of the duchess of York in March. The wife of Charles's brother, James, this poor lady was only thirty-three years of age, worn from endless pregnancies and stillbirths and finally consumed by a cancer of her breast. Like the queen, she had failed to give her husband a son, leaving only two young daughters, one being the Lady Anne, who had also served and mourned Madame.

In her final suffering, the duchess had turned her back on the Anglican Church and become a Roman Catholic, and the public outcry was harsh when her conversion became more widely known at her death. Worse still were the rumors that James had joined her in conversion. It was considered unlucky enough that the foreign-born queen was a Papist, but to have James, the only surviving male Stuart heir to the throne, made one as well was perceived as a dangerous sign by Protestant England.

To ease this furor, Charles immediately ordered a Protestant princess be found as a new wife and duchess for his widowed brother. James had chosen his first wife, an unsuitable commoner, without Charles's permission, and Charles was determined his brother would not err that way again. But James, whose grief was as embarrassingly short-lived as Monsieur's had been for Madame, insisted that his bride also be young and beautiful, and began his own negotiations with several Catholic princesses. To have his royal will challenged in this way much displeased Charles, as can be imagined, and the quarrels between the brothers were heated.

At the same time, a lesser but very public embarrassment was dealt the king by the duchess of Cleveland. Charles had not broken entirely with this lady and each day dutifully visited their five children at the great house he'd given her near St. James's Palace. She remained nominally one of his mistresses, and certainly received the income of a lady in favor. But in February she had begun a shamefully blatant intrigue with an officer ten years her junior. John Churchill was new returned from Tangier, with the burnished glow of a warrior to his handsome person, and though he was but twenty, the duchess had fair devoured him, parading him as her lover and making unlovely comparisons between his youthful prowess and that of the older king. Charles's patience and temper were sorely tested, and it seemed the final break between him and this lady must surely be near.

Nor was Mrs. Gwyn silent. As her belly swelled bigger and bigger with her latest bastard, her insolence seemed to grow as well. Now that Charles had set her in keeping in the Pall Mall house, she aimed next for a title such as Lady Cleveland had been granted. No matter that she'd been born in some low brothel. Now she greedily believed she should be ennobled, raised to at least a countess, and from what

I'd heard, she pestered and nagged poor Charles endlessly about it like the small mongrel bitch she was.

But most taxing of all to the king was his contentious relations with the English Parliament. The very notion of a Parliament was new to me, for in France there is no such corresponding body. His Most Christian Majesty ruled the country and in his supreme splendor and wisdom made every decision for France's welfare. But here in England, the king was forced to share his power with two groups. The House of Lords consisted of gentlemen of the greatest families in the land, at least by their rank worthy of advising the king. The House of Commons seemed sadly lacking in gentlemen of any variety; these rascals were chosen by election, voted to their place by the fancy of every common jack. Together these two Houses formed the Parliament, and no greater pack of scoundrels did ever exist to plague and confound a king. How Charles could bring himself to trust any of them was beyond me, for hadn't an earlier Parliament voted to execute his own father and remove Charles himself from his family's throne?

This latest crop of members had been called to London in February, and at once they set to challenging Charles's plans for a new war with the Dutch. Because Parliament controlled the country's treasury, Charles was forced to ask them for the funds for building the ships of war that he'd promised to Louis, and for raising and training the troops.

In turn this Parliament fussed and bothered like an old woman guarding her purse on market day, questioning the necessity of every last farthing and quarreling among themselves in their great House beside the river. They did not care about complying with the terms of the new treaty, nor that France had already begun her preparations for war, and at an imposing pace. Why should they, when they openly despised all things French? Nor did they care if they humiliated Charles by denying his requests. In fact they seemed to delight in trying to humble him, acting as if he didn't always put the welfare of England first in his thoughts, the way any good king should. Further, they began to question whether Charles should have the right to make treaties in the first place, or whether every last tom fool of them could do better.

Of course Charles had already begun to receive the monetary supplements from Louis as stipulated in the Secret Treaty. How exactly these made their way to him from France I never learned; I suppose through Monsieur Colbert or some other trusted minister. But Charles had considered those funds for his exclusive use, not to be spent on the navy or its ships. Nor, for obvious reasons, did he wish Parliament to know he'd accepted a golden gift from his cousin, or what he'd conceded in return.

Thus Charles followed Parliament's tedious arguments during that long and difficult spring, meeting often with his privy council as well as individual members of the two Houses. He even traveled to the House of Parliament himself to address them, hoping to sway them to the rightful path. Nothing worked. They remained stubborn and quarrelsome and thoroughly vexing.

Finally, in April, Charles decided he'd had enough or, rather, not enough. He prorogued Parliament, meaning he exercised his right to dissolve the session and sent the members back to their distant homes and estates, and as far as possible from the king in London. He was done with their contentious parsimony, but he was now forced to look for other means of funding his new ships. Notified by Lord de Croissy and by myself of these developments, Louis also began to make the most delicate of inquiries regarding whether England would be able to meet her promised contributions for the upcoming war. Swiftly Charles assured him he would, but I doubt even he had any notion of exactly how this would come to pass.

In short, it all made for a thoroughly displeasing time for Charles, who seemed to toil many hours on affairs of state and family with little to show for it. His time was occupied, and I did not see as much of him as I had when I'd first arrived in London last autumn.

Yet in a curious way, this all was to my advantage. With the advice of Lady de Croissy, I was able to find in London many skilled French carpenters, plaster workers, and painters who were eager to work for me to transform my new rooms at Whitehall into a glowing representation of French taste. I'd replaced the dark, old-fashioned paneling (surely there from the days of the last King Henry!) with white plaster trimmed in gold, and hung large looking glasses opposite the privy garden windows to make the room look double its size, and reflect all within in the most cunning fashion. I was exceptionally proud of these looking glasses, and it was only on account of my exceptional connections in Paris that I'd been able to have them sent to me. They were the product of the Royal Mirror Manufactory in the rue de Reuilly, the same company to produce the looking glass for Versailles, and their glittering clarity and size were far beyond any to be found in England, including the mean, dark glasses that Mrs. Gwyn had installed in her house. That they also served to reflect my own beauty over and over and display my person to best advantage was another benefit, and who, truly, could fault me for it?

What I wished most to achieve by my refurbishing, however, was to create a rare sanctuary within Whitehall for Charles. As I saw how tired and wearied he was made by his duties and the demands of others, I determined to make my rooms the one place where he could be at his ease. I'd leave the jugglers and the singing whores to Mrs. Gwyn's parlor. In my rooms, Charles could recline on the softest cushions while sipping the finest of wines. I acquired an excellent Parisian chef, who could concoct the most delectable of dishes to tempt Charles, and I made sure everything was served to him on the finest porcelain, silver, and crystal, all, of course, of French manufacture. Everything was designed to please him, without any compromise.

Most of all, I made sure that when he came to see me, I, too, was exactly to his taste. I took care to be exquisitely dressed and coiffed and perfumed, and always wore the jewels he'd given me. I spoke to him in French, not only because it was a softer, more gracious language to the ear than the grating harsh sounds of English, but also because, as Charles himself noted, French had been the native tongue of his mother, the late Dowager Queen, and thus bore the pleasantest associations for him.

But it was what I said to him—or more precisely, what I didn't—that mattered most. I never lectured him on politics, or made demands of him, or slandered others. I listened to all he said, and let him direct the conversation as it pleased him most. In my lodgings, he truly was KING, unchallenged, unrivaled, and absolute.

Was it any wonder, then, that he called on me as much as he possibly could? Or that he fell into the agreeable habit of coming to my rooms nearly every evening that spring, to the neglect of Mrs. Gwyn and her tawdry puppet shows and ale? Or that we would lie sprawled across my bed with the windows thrown open to the early-summer eve and his head pillowed upon my lap, sipping canary wine and listening to the nightingales calling to one another in St. James's Park?

Yet as sweet as all this was for us, the rough world outside my door was no more agreeable to me than it was to Charles. The expectations from all quarters that I bring my friendship with the king to its inevitable consummation were becoming more and more forceful. Not only did Lord de Croissy and his wife continue to press me on this point, but also Lord and Lady Arlington, whose wonder was so great that Her Ladyship once asked me directly if I preferred the Sapphic way of love, to have put off the king for so long.

That was certainly not true, as Charles himself could attest. As the spring had slipped into summer, I'd permitted him more and more small, delicious liberties with my person, withholding only the final capitulation of my weary maidenhead. But my virginity had become such a source of jeering discussion in London that even the French craftsmen I'd employed had made jests about it among themselves when they'd thought I'd not overhear. In fact, the entire small community of French people who resided in London had come to believe that I was somehow betraying France by not lying with the English king.

I'd heard this from many sources, yes, but I'd not realized quite how widely discussed I'd become until one day early in June, when Bette brought me a small package that had been delivered to my door. I recognized the mark at once as belonging to the Seigneur de Saint-Évremond, and I smiled with pleasurable anticipation. I was glad for the diversion. Charles had spent much of the summer at Windsor Castle with his cousin Prince Rupert and other gentlemen, fishing and riding, and because the queen remained at Whitehall, I did, too. A bit of scandal and innuendo from the seigneur was exactly what I needed after so much time in the exclusive, tedious company of the queen's ladies.

The seigneur was an older French gentleman, a dear friend of Madame's, and now banished by Louis over some misunderstanding or another. But France's loss was London's gain, for the seigneur had become a most amusing author, filtering his thoughts on politics, history, and famous personages through his libertine's glass into essays that he circulated among his closest circle. I was now happily one of them, and I eagerly opened the seal to read his latest words. By the various comments written in the margins, I guessed that the essay had already passed through the hands of several others, and likely more as well, for the seigneur commonly sent several copies of each work about among his friends for discussion. The sly title—"Problem in Imitation of the Spanish"—only hinted at the contents, but as soon as I began reading, I understood. The essay was contrived as a letter of advice to a lady, and though my name was not employed, a child could have guessed that the lady being advised was Louise de Keroualle.

My heart raced as my gaze flew across the page, reading as swiftly as I could. My careful virtue was ridiculed, my cautious steps toward Charles's bed denounced as empty, teasing torment. All of French-speaking London, people I'd trusted and regarded as my dear acquaintance, must be laughing at me because of this, and I felt sickened and exposed.

Yet the more I read, the more I realized that the witty advice meant to entertain contained more than a kernel of genuine wisdom that I might do well to consider.

> Perhaps, mademoiselle, it is vanity that makes you repulse what you most desire. Perhaps now you are vain enough to be pleased only with yourself and your honor; yet soon you will tire of this empty satisfaction, and you will need the riches of another's love if your life is to be

truly enjoyable. Otherwise your pride will make you return to France, mademoiselle, and France will toss you
into a convent to be forgotten, as has happened to so
many others before you. Even if you deliberately choose
this gloomy retreat, you must still be considered worthy
to enter it. How will a virgin do penance if she has done
nothing and loved no one?

The letters blurred through my tears. I hadn't thought of my
honor as a vanity. I'd wished to set myself above the Mrs. Gwyns of
the Court, to be better than they so that in turn I might better please
Charles. Yet what greater vanity is there than in believing that oneself is better than all others? What if I'd already sacrificed my only
chance at love by holding myself too high above the king? I was nearly
twenty-two, perilously old for innocence. What if I were left like the
virgins the seigneur described, left with nothing and no one, with not
even so much as a memory to repent?

I blinked back my tears to read the final words:

Even if there is scandal in loving without reserve, mademoiselle, it is the heavier hardship to go through life without love.

Without love, without love: the words echoed in my heart like the
tolling of the most solemn bell. I let the seigneur's letter drop from my
hands, and fled to my prie-dieu. I gathered up my rosary and knelt
before the little diptych of Our Lady. I bowed my head and closed my
eyes, and prayed for guidance. I prayed for Charles, and I prayed for
myself, my forgiveness, and my own miserable, selfish soul. I doubted
that this was the course that the seigneur could have predicted, but the
realization I did make was likely the same one he'd wished for me.

I do not know how long I stayed upon my knees. The evening sun
had faded from the sky, and behind me Bette had lit the candles. But
when finally I rose, I knew my heart and my purpose, just as I knew I
was never meant to live my life without love.

. . .

Eagerly I leaned forward from my seat, wishing to be the first in the carriage to spy the king. "Oh, my lady," I exclaimed, "how I wish we were at the beginning of the course, so we could see the race begin!"

Leaning back against the leather cushions, Lady Arlington smiled indulgently at my excitement. "Horse races are much like everything else, Louise. The finish accounts for far more than the beginning. No one recalls the start, but everyone knows the winner."

"But what if His Majesty has a poor showing at the start?" I asked anxiously. A score of dreadful possibilities filled my head. I could not quite believe that Charles himself would take his place among the other riders. I'd seen the earlier contests and the wild, thundering abandon of the horses and the men as they raced along the course. Though I knew Charles was a skilled horseman, he was also forty-one, and I feared for him among so many much younger and more reckless gentlemen. "What if his horse stumbles on the course, or he falls behind, or—"

"Or nothing." Her Ladyship laughed, her heavy-lidded eyes watching me with droll amusement. "His Majesty will not falter, Louise. You'll see. He's likely the best rider of the whole lot here today. Having you here to watch will only inspire him, I assure you."

"Very well, my lady." I sighed restlessly, my gaze intent on the distant crowd of horses and men where the race would start. This was the first time I'd been included in one of the parties here to Newmarket for the fall race meetings. Charles loved racing with a passion, and not only did he keep a large royal stable here for breeding, but he sponsored numerous races as well to encourage the sport, offering sterling plates and cups as prizes. Twice a year the little town swelled to accommodate all the courtiers who joined the king, plus all those others who simply followed the races. Every inn was full and every house let, and several years ago Charles himself had finally built himself a small palace directly in the center of town for his own use.

I wasn't staying in Newmarket, but for the past two weeks I had resided near Thetford, as a guest of the Arlingtons at their country seat of Euston Hall—a large, beautiful new house in the French style, and much more appropriate than raucous Newmarket for what was planned this night.

"You do look uneasy, Louise," Lady Arlington said. "Is it the race that worries you, or tonight?"

I looked up swiftly. "I've not changed my mind, my lady."

"I should hope not!" She laughed softly. "Even if you had, I don't think His Majesty would allow it now, not after the pretty dance you've led him for so long."

"I told you before, my lady," I said, more defensively than I'd intended, "it's what I wish. I wouldn't have accepted your invitation otherwise."

She smiled archly, and I blushed. We both knew the truth. If I'd the power to go back and reorder my life, I would not have confided my intentions to Lady Arlington, but simply welcomed Charles one night to my bed, and that would have been the end (and the beginning) of it.

But instead Lady Arlington had seized upon my deflowering as an event to be celebrated, even shared, and before I'd quite realized how it had happened, I found myself made the merry centerpiece of the autumn meetings. It was the only reason I'd been invited to Euston Hall, and everyone knew it, as if I were some sort of pagan sacrifice. All had been instantly arranged in such a manner that I could not refuse to accept, nor had I seen Charles alone here at Euston to ask if this was what he'd wished as well.

With gloomy certainty, I'd guessed that he did. He liked spectacle and sport and I knew he liked me, and combining the three together must have been irresistible to him. And, of course, he was king, and free to do whatever he pleased without consequence. Now my only choice would be either to weep and bleat like a lamb brought to slaughter, or to try to make the event my own as best I could. I'd always wished to be the center of the Court, and after this, there'd be no doubt that I would be.

"It's understandable for you to have misgivings, my dear," Her Ladyship said as if reading my thoughts. "Every maiden does. But the king is no ordinary man, nor will he be an ordinary lover. Surely you've found that to be true in part already, yes?"

I nodded, blushing furiously. Oh, how was I to survive this day and the night that would follow?

"You won't disappoint him, Louise," she said, and smiled slyly. "Nor will you, I believe, be disappointed by Old Rowley."

I frowned, not understanding. "Old Rowley, my lady?"

"Ha, I thought sure you would have heard that by now!" She rolled her eyes toward the heavens and laughed. "Old Rowley is the name of the largest and strongest of the king's stallions standing stud in his stables. They say he's sired hundreds of foals, yet never tires at his labors, and is always eager for more. It seems only natural that His Majesty be called after him in jest, doesn't it? Ah, look, the horses are off."

At once I turned back toward the course. The race was long, nearly four miles across the flat field, and I'd plenty of time to try to sort the dozen riders from one another. It didn't take long for them to begin to separate, with some fading and falling back while the stronger horses and riders pulled ahead. Soon the race was between only two, and now I could recognize the king as one of the leaders. Like all the riders, he wore a bright ribbon sash across his waistcoat, but I'd no trouble telling him apart. It wasn't just his height and size, but how he rode, with bold daring yet perfect ease, the way he did most everything, and in a manner that was thrilling to watch. With the finish in sight, he crouched low over his mount's neck, urging him onward.

Unable to keep still, I hopped from my seat and thrust my head and shoulders from the coach's window, adding my cheers of encouragement to the others from the great crowd gathered at the finish.

"Faster, sir, faster!" I shouted, my fists clenched with excitement. "Go on, sir, faster!"

I will not presume to claim my encouragement made the difference, but at the last instant the king's horse surged ahead of his rival and across the finish mark first. The crowd's cheers rose to a wordless roar as the drums rolled and the trumpets sounded to celebrate the race's end and the king's victory. One by one the others finished, too, and all the riders continued on to slow and cool their horses. Only the king and the next two riders returned to claim their shares of the crowd's acclaim, and it wasn't until then that I realized that the gentleman the king had beaten was his own son, the Duke of Monmouth, an admirable feat. Men and boys surged around them to offer their congratulations, while other ladies cheered from their coaches like ours, or from the covered pavilions on the nearby hill.

But Charles had already spotted Lady Arlington's coach and me with it, and as quickly as he could, he urged his weary horse toward us. To my eye, he had never looked more handsome: astride his noble mount like an ancient warrior, the silver spurs on his boots glinting in the autumn sun and the white sleeves of his shirt billowing about his arms and open at the throat. His close-fitting waistcoat displayed his lean yet manly chest to full advantage and his riding breeches performed the same service for his well-muscled thighs. His face glowed from his exertions and his victory, and I blush to recall exactly how virile and ripe with animal energy he did look. Not even the heroes of the romances I'd once read with Madame's ladies could ever rival such a picture, nor could those maidenly heroines experience the same sweet swell of pleasure I felt when he smiled at me. It was in that moment, too, that I realized that I loved him or, more properly, that I admitted it. I loved him; and that simple realization gave wings to my own desires, and put aside my worries over what would happen later that evening.

I loved the king, and he loved me. Were there ever more foolishly innocent words conceived in this world?

"Congratulations, sir!" I called happily. "I've never seen such a race!"

"It was all Jupiter's doing, not mine," he said, patting the neck of his mount as he smiled up at me. "That, and knowing I'd see you at the finish."

I grinned helplessly, too overwhelmed by his beauty and the affection I felt for him to speak. That remained for Lady Arlington to do, as she leaned from the other window of the coach.

"I trust you'll be joining us again this evening at Euston, sir?" she asked, as if there were any doubt. He and his brother, the duke, had ridden to Euston from Newmarket every night of the last week.

"Nothing would keep me from it, Lady Arlington," he said, yet though he addressed her, his gaze remained entirely on me. "I shall be honored."

"So shall we," she said, and looked at him coyly. "I only hope you're not so weary from your riding that you won't be strong company for us tonight."

I blushed again, fully understanding her meaning, and so did the king.

"Ah, my lady, you know better than to question my stamina," he said, chuckling. "I could be in the saddle from dawn to dusk, yet still be able to ride the night through."

Skillfully guiding the horse alongside the coach, he pulled the blue sash from around his chest and looped it over my head. I laughed, too, from the silly pleasure of it, and smoothed the silk ribbon over my shoulders and chest. The silk smelled of horse and leather and his own sweat, and I relished the intimacy of it.

"There's my token for the day, Louise," he said, his face close to mine, and filled with ardent desire. "I promise to pledge you another soon, eh?"

"Oh, yes, sir," I said breathlessly, leaning forward to kiss him warmly. When our lips parted, he grunted with male satisfaction, doubtless thinking of what (or who) lay before him at Euston.

"Until tonight, Louise," he whispered roughly. "Until you're mine."

He touched his hand to his breast over his heart, a tender salute I'd not expected, and smiled crookedly as if to remind me he was still my Charles. Then he nodded to Lady Arlington and steered his horse away and back to the others.

"My dear, my dear," Lady Arlington mused beside, "surely this day you must be the most fortunate lady in the kingdom. Old Rowley, indeed. I told you earlier, didn't I? In all things, it's the finish that matters most."

Indeed, I thought, as I stroked the ribbon sash lightly over my cheek and breathed his scent upon the silk. I watched him ride away and smiled happily.

Indeed.

"There you are now, Louise." Lady Arlington took me by the shoulders and began turning me around so I could see myself reflected in the glass. "Come now, miss. Don't wax shy with us."

The other ladies crowded close, eager to see my reaction to their ministrations. Some of them I recognized from Court, and others I didn't, but from their lavish dress and jewels, even here in the country, and the titled addresses that were tossed among them, I knew they were all great ladies, wed to gentlemen of wealth, power, and esteem. Yet to see their behavior now, in this bedchamber, I would have guessed them more familiar with the brothels in Drury Lane than the halls of Whitehall Palace. All had been drinking wine since we'd returned from the races, and most had crossed from drinking to drunkenness, their faces flushed and mottled beneath their paint, their laughter unseasonably loud, and their gestures exaggerated. I'd witnessed my share of gentlemen in this lamentable state at Court, but never so many ladies together, and it shocked me to see it now.

"Gaze upon yourself, Louise," Lady Arlington commanded, as full of wine as the others. "Behold the pretty face you bring to your groom!"

I looked, and gasped with dismay. The diversion that had been planned was a mock country wedding, with Charles and me to play the roles of the simple rural couple. We were to submit to the raillery of such a ceremony, and then at last be put to bed. It had sounded foolish and embarrassing to my natural modesty, but of little lasting harm, the sort of nonsensical prank that was endlessly popular among Charles's friends. Some of these in the past had gone horribly wrong when the leaders had included notorious rascals like Lord Buckingham and Lord Rochester, with the watch summoned and participants arrested, property destroyed, and common folk injured or even killed. By comparison, a mock wedding seemed tame, and besides, I was counting upon Charles as my "groom" to keep a measure of decorum to the sport.

At least I had until I saw myself in Lady Arlington's long dressing mirror.

Like any bride, my clothes had been carried away, and I'd been dressed instead in a white linen smock, with only my garters and stockings beneath, and my feet tucked into white silk slippers with high green heels. But unlike the sturdy linen smock that would have adorned a true village bride, these ladies had dressed me in one of finest cambric, with deep bandings of lace at the hems. As beautiful a garment as this was, it was also of so sheer a linen as to be nearly transparent, and as I stood before them all, I was as much as naked. All of my most secret charms were shamelessly revealed behind this slight haze of linen, my breasts full and rose-tipped, my waist small and my hips swelling in invitation, and the dark thatch of my maiden's hair a beckoning shadow at the top of my thighs.

Instinctively I moved to cover myself with my open hands, but Lady Arlington quickly pulled them aside. "No false modesty, now, else you'll disappoint the gentlemen."

I gasped again with dismay. "Oh, my lady, you cannot expect me to go before the gentlemen dressed in such a fashion!"

"Why ever not?" asked the Countess of Sunderland, a dear friend of Lady Arlington's. She swayed languidly and leered at me from the other side of the glass, a glass of golden canary in her hand. "When you appear among them, every last rogue will spring a cock stand in your honor. That's power, my dear, and be grateful you have it."

The others laughed as if this were the greatest wit imaginable, but I could only blush in misery.

"Oh, please, mademoiselle, do not *cry*," Lady Sunderland said with such droll disgust that the others laughed once again. "Everyone at Court already knows you could fill the very ocean with your tears once you begin."

That only made me flush deeper still and, worse, made me indeed wish to weep. It was bad enough to be mocked by the likes of Mrs. Gwyn, but I hadn't realized I'd been unwittingly entertaining the rest of the Court as well. Didn't they know that I cried because I could not help it, and not at will?

"I'll grant you a lock or two of hair, my dear," Lady Arlington said. They'd already unpinned and brushed my hair, letting the thick waves fall down my back, for this, too, was traditional for a bride. To help ease the untying of my virgin knot, there could be no bows or twists or braids anywhere on my person, and along with my unbound hair, all the little bows that trimmed the smock had been untied as well, the narrow ribbons kinked but hanging free. Lady Arlington drew two thick locks of my hair forward over my shoulders, twirled them round her fingers into curls, and carefully draped them over my breasts.

"There," she said, contented with her work. "A modicum of modesty entices the whole."

I could scarcely agree. If anything, the long dark curls seemed to enhance my shamelessness rather than cover it.

"Forgive me, my lady," I began again. "But I do not believe I can—"

"Ah, the bells!" exclaimed Lady Sunderland with gay abandon, raising her glass high over her head. "The bells are calling the bride below!"

I heard them, too, an irregular chorus of clattering handbells from downstairs, but near drowning them were the shouts of the gentlemen, clamoring for the bride (meaning me) to be brought out for their admiration. Before I could protest again, the ladies took my arms and swept me away, down the staircase and past the crowd of ogling gentlemen, most of them seeming as deep in their cups as their ladies. I recognized a good many of these gentlemen as well from Court, men whom it would now shame me to meet again in other circumstances, including the Dukes of Monmouth and York, and even the Marquis de Croissy. To my relief the ladies bore me swiftly past the gentlemen, perhaps from kindness, but more likely from not wishing their own husbands to admire or inspect me too closely. The ladies led me into the dining chamber and to my seat at the head of the table, and crowned me with a wreath of white flowers.

Before I sat, however, there were a few more impromptu fanfares, heralding the arrival in the room of the king, and as one we either bowed or curtsied, a perilous exercise for me, clad as I was. Yet I forgot my unhappiness when I saw Charles, entering the room to take his place at the table beside me. He, too, was dressed all in falsely virginal white, a modest presentation for a country bridegroom, and in the simplest of clothes: an open shirt without a neck cloth, a short doublet, and breeches, with a flowered crown much like my own. He looked at once at all I revealed, and was unabashed in his approval. He began to take me in his arms to kiss me, but Lady Arlington dared step between us.

"Not until after you are properly bedded, sir," she said archly, and guided us to separate chairs. The king laughed, and rolled his eyes heavenward to the roaring amusement of the other gentlemen. But still he'd noticed my distress as well as my near-nakedness, and once he had taken his seat beside me, he leaned his head close to mine.

"Don't let all this folly trouble you, sweet," he whispered fondly. "They mean to entertain themselves—that is all. Soon it will be done, and they'll leave us alone."

I smiled my gratitude, my eyes welling with tears. Soon, he'd promised. Soon it would be done, and they'd leave us alone. . . .

But the mock wedding feast seemed without end, with one lewd toast following another, and I vow an entire vineyard must have been drunk at that table. It took no effort at all for me to play the part of the quaking bride, and I was too sick with dread to eat any of the rich dishes set before me. Worst of all was realizing that, despite his kind solicitude toward me, Charles was reveling in every lubricious jest and toast to his manhood, and I truly began to fear what might happen next.

I learned soon enough.

He emptied his glass for the final time, and rose to his feet.

"Enough of your good wishes, my friends, and I thank you for them," he said to renewed laughter. "But the hour is late, and it's high time you offered honors to me and my delectable bride."

A band of fiddlers suddenly appeared—where had they been

waiting all the evening? I wondered—and to their playing, Charles led me up the stairs with all the others crowding after us. The best bedchamber in the house had been prepared for us, with the fire and candles lit, the brocaded curtains drawn around the bedstead and looped about the posts, the coverlet turned back, and extra pillows piled high at the head.

Once again Lady Arlington took possession of me, and with my other highborn handmaidens, soon divested me of my slippers and my flower crown, and helped me between the sheets. Throughout I kept my eyes downcast and struggled to keep from being ill; the only greater disgrace than this night would have been to have been forced to dive beneath the bed in search of the chamber pot before so many others. Every space in the chamber was taken, making a wall around the bed of grinning faces and gabbling tongues with the fiddlers' tunes sounding shrilly at an ever-quickening pace.

From the bawdy comments of the gentlemen, I knew that Charles was likewise being prepared for me, his doublet and breeches removed until only his shirt remained. Without raising my eyes, I knew when he joined me as the bedsprings creaked and sank beneath his weight. Before I could catch myself, I tipped down into the valley of the mattress against him, his bare thigh pressing against mine. I jerked away as if I'd been burned but Charles only laughed, and sought my hand, a small reassurance, but not enough.

"The bride's stocking!" called one of the gentlemen. "We must toss her stocking! Your Grace, you're a bachelor again. Make her show her leg and claim her stocking!"

I looked up just in time to find the Duke of York, his face flushed with excess, reaching to raise the coverlet from me, ready to pull the stocking from my leg. With visions of being hauled forcibly from the bed, I cried out softly, and at last Charles came to my rescue.

"Leave off, James," he said mildly, but with a warning to his words. "My bride is too shy and tender for the likes of you. Draw your own stocking, my dear, and give it to him for tossing."

The duke scowled. "Where's the sport in that, brother? We wish to judge the lady's leg."

"That's mine to judge, not yours." Charles smiled, the warning now so strong not even the thickheaded Duke could ignore it. "Louise, your stocking, if you please."

I reached beneath the sheets and swiftly peeled off my stockings to hand to the duke. His disappointment clear, he still went through the ritual of sitting on the foot of the bed and tossing the ball of my stocking back over his shoulder, where it landed on Charles's lap: a sure omen of another wedding before year's end, or so it would be if this were a true wedding to begin with.

"There you are, Your Grace, a fresh princess for you by Christmas!" called a gentleman from the back. "Wed her fast and fill her belly faster, eh?"

"Don't forget our own little bride," Lady Sunderland said, carrying a twin-handled posset cup in her hands that she handed first to me. "Drink up, mademoiselle, drink up. You'll need every drop to fortify you for your ride with Old Rowley!"

Bravely I held the posset cup to my lips and sipped with care. It was well I did, for the posset itself was so thick with sugar, beaten eggs, and sack—the white Spanish wine the English gentry so favored—that I felt its potency at once. Against more cheering, I pretended to drink, then passed the cup to Charles. Clearly he'd guessed my game but didn't give me away, and instead drank the rest down himself. With a flourish he returned the empty cup to Lady Sunderland; then he held his hands out to stop the applause, and the room fell eagerly quiet.

"Now that you've done your duty by me and my sweet bride, I must do mine by her," he said. "Leave us now, and you may count on a son in nine months' time."

A son, a child, another royal bastard by Old Rowley himself. Oh, Mother of God preserve me, I was not prepared for that so soon! I shivered and hugged my arms over my chest as they roared their approval, yet made no move to leave us.

"You don't mean to send us away, sir, do you?" called another gentleman. "We want to watch to make sure you fuck her proper."

"Aye, aye, sir!" shouted another. "It's not as if she's a true bride. She's only another whore, and a French one at that."

"No," said the king. "Leave us."

Three words, and yet that was sufficient to remind every last drunken lord that Charles was their master. Three words, and the crowd of ravening jackals turned as meek as lambs, stumbling over one another in their haste to back from the chamber and leave as he'd ordered. A solemn-faced manservant drew the bed's curtains shut around us, and from within I heard him close the bedchamber door and latch it shut.

Finally, miraculously, I was alone in bed with His Majesty the King of England.

Chapter Eighteen

There will be those who say that I had at last landed where I'd always wished most to be, in the king's bed with him happily beside me. These same folk will likewise shake their heads, and say sadly what a sinful world this must be for such a thing to come to pass in such a shameful manner, and with them I would, alas, concur. But there will also be those who heartily agree with whichever gentleman called me a French whore, and others who will denounce me as a cunning spy, and still more who will believe I was employed by His Holiness the Bishop of Rome himself to steal away the king's Anglican soul.

None was true. As I lay beside Charles in the best bed at Euston Hall, I was neither a whore, a spy, nor a missionary, nor even the village bride I'd so recently pretended to be. In truth I was but one thing, and that was a woman, a shy, uncertain woman of twenty-two years who desperately wanted to trust the man she loved.

Now I will grant that innocence is relative, and mine was worn and tattered indeed if compared to that imagined village bride. How could it be otherwise, considering all the wanton wickedness I'd seen at both royal Courts? But though I'd tenaciously preserved my maidenhead, I had also passed the last year dallying with the king, permitting him more and more familiar caresses and heated liberties until this moment had become inevitable, just as even the smallest river must in time join with the mighty sea.

"At last, Louise," he said softly, shifting to French to put me more at my ease, "here we are."

"Yes, sir," I whispered. I was trembling both from fear and excitement, and with great daring I reached for him first, sliding my hand along his arm to his shoulder. "Here I am, and here you are."

"And here, my sweet, are you." He leaned down to kiss me, shoving aside the insubstantial shift so he could freely explore my charms. "You're shivering. Are you cold?"

I shook my head against the pillow, breathless with longing after that single kiss. "How could I ever be cold with you, sir?"

He laughed, and eased his hand between my legs to stroke me there. I gasped, not from surprise, but delight, and shamelessly parted my legs farther to allow him more.

"Not cold at all," he said, pleased to find me already so ripe and welcoming. "I'd venture you found that foolishness more to your taste than you'd thought. Displaying yourself like that, knowing that every man in the room wanted to claim you as his own."

"But only you will, sir." It shocked me that he'd believe I'd been aroused by that humiliating false ceremony and not, as was the truth, simply by him. Yet such must have been the case with him, for when I reached to caress him in turn, I discovered his royal staff already standing tall as any truncheon.

That, it seemed, was all the encouragement he'd needed. Without another word, he moved to climb atop me, kissing me with a raw hunger that I answered as best I could. He was a large man, and I wasn't prepared for his weight upon me, or how forcibly strong he'd suddenly become. He pushed my thighs apart more wide and moved between them, his movements now spare and direct and driven entirely by his desire. Thus fairly poised for my ruin, I closed my eyes with dread. He stroked me again, easing me open, and I sighed with the sweetness of his touch. Then too soon that pleasing touch was replaced by his infinitely more demanding cock, and instead of pleasure, I felt as if I'd be torn asunder. I whimpered sadly, tugging against the sheets and striving to pull myself clear, but he was well past the time for retreat. With a few quick thrusts, he was buried deep within me, and the prize I'd withheld for so long was his.

"Open your eyes, Louise," he ordered. He was breathing as hard as a man who'd run a race uphill, his voice a rough rasp. "Don't hide yourself away. Look at me."

"Yes, sir," I whispered, forcing myself to obey. His face over mine was contorted as if in pain, and I feared I'd somehow wounded him as he had me. "Oh, sir, forgive me if I've—"

"There's nothing to forgive." Slowly he began to withdraw, only to plunge back in again with redoubled force. "Dear God, but your cunny's tight."

"Yes, sir," I whispered, feeling the first tears slide down my cheeks. "Yes, sir."

"Damnation, Louise, don't cry," he said gruffly. "It will be better, I promise you."

I did not see how that would be possible. Lady Arlington had sworn I'd not be disappointed, but disappointed I was, and painfully so. I felt ravaged and stretched beyond measure, without any pleasure left at all. Where was the joy of love that every poet promised? Where was the rapture that other ladies praised as they whispered behind their fans?

Then to my great surprise, he took me by the waist and rolled onto his back, bringing me with him. It was clumsily done, to be sure, yet somehow we remained joined. I was now astride him, my knees splayed wide on either side of his chest and my smock crumpled around my waist and stained with the crimson remnants of my tattered maidenhead. His rampant cock was now buried even deeper within me, yet the discomfort was mysteriously lessened.

"Now ride me," he ordered, breathing hard, his hands sliding along the inside of my thighs. "Go on. Ride until you find your pleasure."

I looked down at him uncertainly, my palms braced upon his chest and my tangled hair falling around us like another curtain. None of my well-learned graces were of use to me now. He reached up and hooked his fingers into the front of the smock, tearing the fine linen so that my breasts tumbled free.

"Go on, my pretty wanton," he ordered, fondling my breasts. "I'll not have it said I can't bring a virgin to spending."

With great care, I raised myself on my knees and along his cock, then slid back downward. It was not unpleasurable. I tried it again, and he groaned beneath me, rocking up to meet me in a most delicious fashion.

"Ah, there you are," he said, catching me by the hips to guide me to his rhythm as if we were again partners in a dance. "Ride me hard, lass, and do not stop."

That made sense to me, and now that I'd begun, I understood what was required of me. I thought of how I'd watched him ride so hard to win the race earlier that day, and how curious, yet exciting, it was to consider how now I was riding him in return. Before long I'd found confidence in my efforts, and as Charles had promised, pleasure soon replaced my first pain. I rode him and he drove me, the pair of us sweating and thrashing and crying out like two possessed, until at last I felt my cunny convulse with delight, and give up its maiden tribute to his plundering cock. I collapsed upon him, weary and sated, with his arm around my back.

"That was well done," he said, grinning proudly as he pulled a pillow beneath his head.

I laughed happily. "It was," I said. "I understand at last why this commerce is so much enjoyed."

" 'Commerce'?" he scoffed. "What nonsense is that? We're hardly a pair of Cornhill merchants bickering at the Exchange."

"It's what we did, sir," I said, laughing still. "That's what it's called at His Christian Majesty's Court, between Louis and his mistresses. Commerce."

"Commerce." Now he laughed, too, bumping me up and down as I lay across him. "My cousin is more daft than ever I suspected. Here in England, we're more plainspoken. We call it fucking."

I didn't laugh at that, but only smiled wistfully. I do not believe he noticed, which was well enough by me. Of course I'd heard that word before (many times this very night), and even employed it myself on occasion. I'd also come to understand its various shadings as a vulgar, common word, a word that a king might use, but also a Cheapside whore. My English was still not so wide as I could wish, but I knew another word that I'd have much preferred Charles had chosen to describe our actions that night. A simple word, yes, but to my sorrow, he never once did use it.

That word was "love."

I stayed at Euston Hall for the remainder of October, until the fall race meetings ended with the month. The weather was balmy and fair, the way the best autumn weather can be, and I felt as if our days that month were as golden as the trees around us.

Though Charles nominally kept his own lodgings in Newmarket, he spent most of his time in my company, and we'd soon evolved a satisfying schedule to our days. I would come with Lady Arlington or one of the other ladies in her coach to the racecourse to watch the afternoon program. Charles was always quick to find me, for even if he were not racing himself, he still would usually be on horseback, roaming among the crowd or riding back and forth between the start and finish. He treated Newmarket like another, smaller kingdom in a way that was quite charming to see, overseeing the welfare of every last nag and jockey, no matter how humble.

Often I would leave the coach and walk with Charles as he surveyed his racing domain. Other days I'd sit with the king in what was called his chair, a small private pavilion of fluttering striped cloth situated above the course, where we would watch the training gallops and drink canary. Unlike most gentlemen, he'd no fear of showing his affections before others, and thus, wherever we were, he lavished me with a thousand little endearments and kisses to match.

In the evenings he would always come to Euston Hall, which continued full to brimming over with guests. We would keep to the company through supper, but soon after, we'd repair upstairs to the same bedchamber we'd used that first night, now reserved for us alone. There he introduced me to every aspect of amorous amusement and satisfaction, as is often the way between a gentleman of experience and a novice lady. He proved to be a generous, inventive lover, as eager to learn what pleased me as to teach me what pleased him, and it gave him special delight to see me blossom and become more accomplished under his tutelage. Here in the country, he'd seemed altogether happier, merrier, even younger, the stern lines around his mouth softening and his smile without reserve. I liked to think I'd much to do with it.

But what pleased me the most was having his company to myself. Despite so many other courtiers visiting the county for the meetings, Charles and I were able to keep to ourselves as much as we wished. I'd no competition for his attention from ministers, ambassadors, or Parliament as I did in London, nor from any other of the beautiful women preening and pouting for his attention, like Lady Castlemaine, Mrs. Gwyn, and even the queen. For that month, I was his only lady, and I basked in the glory of his devotion, certain that this was only the beginning of a long and wondrous friendship.

On the last afternoon of our stay, Charles spent the whole day at Euston. We borrowed mounts from the Arlingtons' stables and rode out through the hall's parks and lands. The afternoon was cool and gray with the leaves gone from the trees and the first hint of coming frost in the air, a fitting day for farewells. In preparation for the winter, the gardeners had closed down the pipes to the park's fountains and wrapped the lead statues in dry leaves and rough cloth against the coming frosts. Now instead of cheery cupids clutching fat, spewing dolphins, we saw only dreary lumpen figures standing guard over the still ponds, like shrouded mourners for summer past.

We stopped by one of these ponds to water our horses, and Charles helped me down so I might stretch my legs as well. I wore a witty black beaver hat much like Charles's, and my scarlet riding habit, cut close to my body with flaring skirts, and laced with gold, offered the only cheery spot of color in the somber landscape.

"Summer's truly done now, sir," I said sadly, gazing over the empty fields. We were just within sight of the red brick hall, the famous twin domes on the north and south wings seeming to sit on the bare treetops like giant goose eggs in nests. "I wish we'd come out riding more often while we were here."

"So do I," he said, slipping his arm familiarly around my waist as we began to walk along the edge of the pond, leading our horses. "You ride well for a lady."

"Ha, that's weak praise from an old centaur like you," I scoffed, poking him lightly in the arm. "Well for a *lady*."

"I intended nothing weak about it," he said with mock indignation. "But to please you, I'll change it. You ride well."

I curtsied and grinned. "Thank you, sir. I learned from my father, who rode like the wind. I had to learn to keep up, or be left behind."

"You never speak of your father," he said, surprised. "Did he die when you were young?"

"Oh, no, sir, he lives still." I hadn't seen my family for several years now. I'd never told them my reasons for coming to England; they'd been disappointed enough in me without that. I could scarce imagine my proud father's reaction if he'd known the truth. "Guillaume de Penancoet, Comte de Keroualle, Seigneur de Kerboronné and de la Villeneuve. He lives with my mother and younger sister, in our old château near Brest."

"*Mirabile dictu,*" he said. "And here I've never thought of you as having a family."

"I didn't hatch from an egg, sir." I shrugged, absently kicking my skirts through the dry leaves and grass. It had always seemed to me that Charles had trouble enough with his own family without having to hear of mine as well; besides, once I'd left home, Madame and the others I'd met at Court had become more truly my family than the one I'd left behind.

"If you did," he teased, "it would have been the most beautiful egg imaginable, like a giant pearl lined with gold."

"Oh, sir, that is nonsense," I scolded, even as I delighted in his jests. It was a sign of how comfortable we'd become in each other's company that we could be foolish like this, as if he wasn't a king at all.

"No nonsense at all, when you are my rarest little bird," he said, kissing me lightly on my cheek. "What do you think he'd make of me, the old Comte de Keroualle?"

"My father?" I stopped walking, and unpinned my hat, rubbing my head where the pins had pulled in my hair. "My father is a stern old soldier, sir, and does not care for anyone he hasn't known for twenty years."

He laughed. "You're being exceptionally polite, Louise."

"I always am, sir." I swung my hat lightly in my hand. "My father sent me to Paris to find a husband, and he is not happy that I've yet to acquire one. Can you figure the rest, sir?"

"I can," he said softly, and from the thoughtful way he glanced at me, he'd likely filled in the details of my tale for himself, including his own awkward place in it. He took my hand and drew off my yellow glove, and kissed my fingers, watching me over my hand.

"I'd like to hear more, you know," he said. "Of your family, your home, your past. Of you."

"It's very ordinary, sir," I protested, and compared to his life, it was. "My family has lived in the same château for a hundred years, and my parents are content with that. My sister, Henriette-Mauricette, is eight years younger than I, and my brother, Sebastien, was three years older. He died two years ago, in the service of France."

"May your brother rest in God's arms," he said gravely, and with a sincerity that touched me. "I know what it is to lose a brother and a sister."

I tried to smile, and knew if I'd tried any harder, I'd cry. "I told you, sir," I said instead. "It's all ordinary enough."

"No, it's not," he said, "because it's your family, Louise, and to me there is nothing ordinary about you."

He pulled me tenderly against his chest, and I dropped my hat to the grass, slipping my arms around his waist to hold him close. He held me, lightly stroking my hair in a way that comforted us both.

"I've a notion, sweet," he said at last. "What if we keep riding now, and forget entirely about London tomorrow?"

"I'd like that, sir," I said, and I would. "I'd like that very much."

"So would I," he said, his voice tinged with melancholy. "I love

London, but I do not love all that will be waiting for me to tend to at Whitehall. We've had our merry time here, but alas, now it's back to my share of the world's woes."

I understood. All the troubles, large and small, that Charles had left behind in London would still be there when he returned, and by now likely doubled and joined with fresh cares as well. The coming war with the Dutch, England's lack of funds to pay for the preparations, his relations with Louis and France, and his brother's remarriage would each clamor for his attention, as would all the other more routine demands of ruling the country.

It pained me mightily to know I'd only added to his challenges. He'd already been criticized for having me, a Catholic Frenchwoman, among the queen's ladies, and faulted more for his open attentions to me. But once it became known (as it likely already was) that I was now his mistress, the attacks on us both would only grow.

"I am sorry, sir," I said, meaning everything. "I'm sorry."

He drew me close and smiled. "I am, too. But I'm sorriest that my time here with you is nearly done."

I felt a small catch in my heart at that. "But I'll return with you to Whitehall, sir," I said, pushing away far enough to gaze up into his face. "My lodgings will still be only a few steps from your rooms. Nothing need change for us."

"But it will, Louise," he said, his voice heavy with regret. "No matter how you or I might wish otherwise, it won't be the same. It can't be. Nothing in this life ever stays the same."

He kissed me then, a kiss more melancholy than passionate, while the dry leaves of last summer swirled around our feet.

The following day, Charles left Newmarket for London with his brother, his friends, and his attendants, doubtless a riotous group as they always were. My departure from Euston Hall was more sober, traveling as I did with Lady Arlington and her little daughter, Isabella, in their coach. For most of the journey to London, the two of them prattled on together in high-pitched singsong voices and dressed and undressed Isabella's three lady dolls. I was in no humor for child's play. Instead I drew the hood of my cloak up to shield my face and retreated to my corner of the seat, and there stared morosely from the window. The threatening gray skies of yesterday had yielded a chill and drizzling rain today, a perfect match for my dismal mood.

I had recently learned a new word of English, one that had caught my ear and my fancy. This word was "honeymoon," a pretty country expression for the halcyon days that followed a wedding, and the time when the first raptures of love between a new husband and wife will wax their fullest and most tender.

My mock wedding to Charles had been false from beginning to end, a cruel amusement that had pleased everyone, it seemed, but me. But the short weeks that had followed had been a true honeymoon for us, and I grieved to see them end.

I blew my breath against the window to make a tiny cloud upon the glass, and with my fingertip I traced a heart upon it.

Only hours before, Charles had warned me that nothing stayed the same in this life. To my sorrow, I'd learn soon enough how terribly true his words would be.

"You have done very well, mademoiselle." The Marquis de Croissy sat across from me, perched on the very edge of his chair like a crow ready poised for flight. He'd wasted no time calling on me once I'd returned to my Whitehall lodgings; I'd barely unpacked my trunks before he appeared.

"I reported all the affairs at Euston Hall to His Most Christian Majesty," he continued, "and he was exceptionally pleased by how you have attached yourself to the English king. He wishes me to commend you, mademoiselle, and congratulate you on your sacrifice for him, and for France."

I flushed, shamed to imagine Louis reading the ambassador's letter telling of how I had finally become Charles's mistress. Of course Louis would have been amused, even titillated—everyone else certainly was, whether they'd been among the party at Euston or simply heard of the events—and I cringed to think of my deflowering being discussed not only in London, but in Paris as well.

"Please tell His Most Christian Majesty that I am honored," I said, pouring myself more tea to mask my discomfort. "How many other Frenchwomen are offered royal congratulations for similar accomplishments?"

"Don't make light of this, mademoiselle," Lord de Croissy said sharply. "I assure you the king does not. Now that you have finally taken this first step, he is eager for you to proceed with your next responsibilities."

I looked up at him swiftly, the teapot still in my hand. "There is more, my lord?"

"Of course." He frowned, displeased with my surprise. "The seduction was only the beginning. Now that you have secured the king's confidence, we expect you to use it for the betterment of France. You are to encourage the king in his country's preparations for the war against the Dutch. You are to remind him of his promised conversion to our faith, and to urge him forward. Finally, you are to suggest that his brother, His Grace the Duke of York, wed a princess whose country is sympathetic to France. There will be letters coming to you shortly with more instruction in these matters, but the sooner you begin, the greater our profit."

"That is all, my lord?" With a righteous clatter, I set the teapot down on the table between us. "Why not ask me to sail a ship of war to conquer the Dutch myself? Would that satisfy His Most Christian Majesty? Or why not ask me to grow wings so that I might fly to the top of every English flagstaff in London and replace their colors with the French?"

He leaned forward over the table, his hands on the edge as if ready to leap across at me. "I speak in perfect seriousness, mademoiselle, and I would appreciate it if you would as well."

"But, my lord—"

"We all know the weaknesses of the English king," he said, "just as we now see how well you have exploited them. In the last month, you must surely have learned much of the king's habits and secrets, more than any of us could ever hope to know. We expect you to use this knowledge to the advantage of your country."

I looked down at my tea, unable to meet his eye. Yes, I'd learned much of Charles while at Euston, but I'd learned it because he'd trusted me not only as a partner in his bed, but as his friend. Now the ambassador expected me to twist that trust about and betray it for the sake of France. To be sure, it was no more than I'd promised Louis I'd do, but when I'd made that promise, I'd not realized what it would cost me to keep it. How could I, when I'd not loved Charles as I did now?

He sighed impatiently at my silence, and launched upon another course of persuasion. "You are a beautiful woman, mademoiselle. I need not advise you on the best ways to withhold or reward the king with the favors he most desires. These are skills that come naturally to a lady like yourself, and we'll trust you to use your advantages as you see fit."

"Thank you, my lord," I said softly, my head still bowed to hide my unease.

He tapped his fingers on the table from restlessness, or perhaps to draw my attention. "But I must urge haste, mademoiselle. The king is not known for his faithfulness. There is no knowing how long he will be infatuated with you."

I looked up at him with a small catch in my breath, Charles's own words echoing in my ears.

Nothing in this life ever stays the same. . . .

"What have you heard, my lord?" I demanded. "What has happened?"

The marquis smiled, clearly pleased he'd discovered the weakness in my own armor. "Nothing in that particular arena, mademoiselle," he said easily. "It would have taken a bold lady indeed to pry the king from your side this last month. But his friends have not been idle. There are many who already resent your power over him, and are doing their best to poison him against you."

"You mean Lord Buckingham."

He nodded. "His Grace is one such, yes. But there is another you would do wise to fear more, and that is Lord Rochester."

"Lord Rochester?" The earl wasn't like Lord Buckingham; there was only the slightest history between us. I tried to recall any offense I'd given him or reason for his disliking me, and could think of none. "He has no cause."

"He has two," Colbert said. "First, he is of the Anglican faith, and you are not. Second, he is a close acquaintance of Mrs. Gwyn, and you—you assuredly are not. He is also apparently a skilled satirist, and has made you a prime character in a scurrilous piece, a play of his composition entitled *Sodom*."

"*Sodom!*" I exclaimed with dismay. I'd heard enough of the wit popular among Charles's gentlemen to guess the nature of this satire. Scurrilous was likely too gentle a criticism. "Have you a copy in your possession, my lord? Does he dare use my given name in its pages?"

The marquis's expression was so grim, even for him, that I feared the worst.

"Thus far it exists only as a manuscript, surreptitiously passed among his lordship's friends," he said. "May it never be published more widely! But no, mademoiselle, your name is not sullied directly, though to those who have read it, the most sinful character, a maid of honor by design, is in fact and circumstance clearly drawn from your life."

"What name did he give her, then?" I asked, my voice trembling with anger. "I must know, my lord, so that if I am called this name by someone who wishes to insult me, I won't be trapped unknowingly."

"Oh, mademoiselle," he said, grimacing. "His Lordship has named the character Lady Clytoris."

I gasped, and shot to my feet. "That is not to be borne, my lord! I do not care if Lord Rochester is His Majesty's dear friend, or that his father saved His Majesty's life, or whatever other shabby defense he may offer. How dare His Majesty permit—"

"Mademoiselle, please, please, calm yourself!" the ambassador exclaimed, taking me by the shoulders and forcibly sitting me back down in my chair. "Please. His Majesty knows nothing of this satire, nothing at all, and if you are wise, you will not be the one who tells him of it."

For a long moment I wavered, then realized that, for once, the ambassador was right. I took a deep breath to calm myself, and steeled my determination.

"That is true, my lord," I admitted. "If I were to show it to him, I would be doing exactly as Lord Rochester desires. Far better for me to pretend as if the vile thing does not exist."

"Far better," he agreed. "For you it does not."

"No, it does not," I repeated firmly. So long as I had Charles by my side, I could ignore a legion of Rochesters and Gwyns. "His Majesty treats me with the regard of a lady, and no true lady would acknowledge the existence of such venomous slander."

"Not only a lady, mademoiselle, but a French lady." The ambassador smiled with approval, and finally rose to leave. "You'll do well with this matter, I am certain. This is the first time I have seen you willing to fight for what is yours by rights and talent, and that, too, is to be commended. I am pleased, mademoiselle. *We* are pleased. Only take care to measure your passions before you act, and you will succeed."

He paused as Bette gave him his cloak, and bowed his farewell to me. Yet at the door, he stopped again and came back, recalling one more bit of advice.

"Mademoiselle," he said, tapping his finger to his cheek, "one more question, I beg of you. I do not know how I forgot it until now. His Most Christian Majesty asked this specifically of me, and thus I must ask you."

"Yes, my lord?" I waited warily; after all the other indignities that had spilled out during his visit, his question could be anything.

He nodded, his thin lips pressed together as he chose his words with caution. "While we rejoice in your new position with the English king and the attraction he shows for you, your place could be even more secure if you could give him a child. You haven't employed any means to prohibit a possible conception while you have been with him, have you? Are you taking every opportunity for him to plant his seed vigorously within your womb so it may find fair purchase?"

I should have been shocked by the frankness of that question, and earlier this same year, I might well have fainted clear away. But now—now I was not. It was Charles's seed that he spoke of, Charles's seed within my own womb, and because I loved him, it seemed not shocking, but expected.

"I took no unnatural precautions nor used courtesan's tricks, my lord," I said softly. "It will be in God's hands to decide, not mine."

The ambassador's smile was wide with relief and rhapsodic admiration. "Ah, mademoiselle, you are both a true daughter of France, and of our Holy Church."

I nodded, and offered my cheek for him to kiss in blessing and farewell.

A daughter of France, a daughter of the Holy Church: but of the greatest importance to me was that I was Charles's to love.

I noticed the difference at Court immediately.

No matter where I went or what I did, everyone turned to look. I was worth the looking: the newest royal mistress. Some looked from curiosity, some from envy, some from scorn, some from amusement, some from lust, and some from bitter, blind hatred. I felt their stares upon me wherever I went, and heard their whispers. I'd a surprising stock of new friends who hoped to gain the king's favor through me, and I'd an even greater number of instant enemies, who wished for nothing but my downfall. Through it all I held my head as high as I could, acknowledging none of it, and striving to think of nothing beyond my own counsel. Charles himself advised me to pay none of it any heed, but then he was already so accustomed to comment and scrutiny that I believe he truly could ignore it.

Yet soon after we'd returned to London, I suffered two separate, scandalous insults that were impossible for me to do as he asked.

I had been away from my lodgings for most of the afternoon. The royal mantua maker had come to measure the queen for new gowns, and because Her Highness respected my taste over that of all others, she had insisted that I be at her side as the woman and her assistants presented their silks and other cloths for her consideration. By the time I was released, I'd had to rush to make ready for Charles's visit to me, and I was out of breath by the time I reached my rooms.

On the door was pinned a handwritten note, the words large and plain enough so that anyone passing along the hall (and many would, given my proximity to the king's chambers) would have been able to read them.

> *Within this place a bed's appointed*
> *For a French bitch and God's anointed.*

I tore it down at once, before Charles saw it, but I was far too late to stop the riotous amusement of all the others who'd read it first. No one claimed its authorship outright, but I soon heard that Lord Rochester and Mrs. Gwyn had boasted loudly of its wit, and they'd plenty of cronies to laugh with them.

But not all insults come from enemies. Soon after I'd ridden in Lady Arlington's coach from Euston, she appeared one night in an extravagant new necklace of diamonds. In my hearing, another lady complimented her upon the jewels, asking if the necklace had been a gift from His Lordship.

Lady Arlington had laughed, touching her fingers to the sparkling diamonds.

"As generous as my lord is to me, he'd never put ten thousand pounds around my neck," she said blithely. "This necklace is my reward from King Louis for playing the bawd for Old Rowley and his little French chit."

When I had been at the French Court, the sole person I'd trusted there had been Madame. Now, again, it was the same at this Court as well. The only one I trusted, my one true friend, was her brother and my Charles.

Chapter Nineteen

The coming war with Holland was much on Charles's mind that winter. It was strange to me how a gentleman of such a mild and pleasing humor could so crave the destruction and suffering of a war, but so it was with Charles. True, his public reasons were wise ones—to vanquish the Dutch supremacy at sea so as to forward England's merchant power in foreign waters, and thus make her stronger at home as well—but the private ones he confided to me seemed less so.

Though long past, he still resented England's defeat at Dutch hands in the two earlier wars of his reign, especially the vast and humiliating losses suffered by the English navy. He also seemed to harbor a peculiar contempt for the Dutch as a people, thinking them dull and thick, a dangerous presumption. He also believed that he could somehow make his young nephew (the son of his elder sister Mary) William of Orange into his pawn, and control Holland from within. Further, it pleased him to think of England not only as France's ally, but her equal, which, of course, it was not. How could it be, when he continued to accept gold from Louis, gold he very much needed?

I do not know if these ideas were Charles's own or the spawn of his ministers. Certainly they served the purposes of France, which I dutifully reported to the French ambassador. But his determination to conquer the Dutch had become an obsession with him, a troubling condition for one who should rule, rather than be ruled. He ignored the wishes of his people, who clearly did not want another war, and he proceeded with his plans as if he'd more gold in his treasury than Croesus himself, which he certainly did not.

To this end, he let himself be persuaded on a most hazardous course by Sir Thomas Clifford, one of his privy councilors. Without a Parliament in session to vote him the funds he still needed to pursue the war, Sir Thomas suggested the Stop of the Exchequer, which, simply put, meant that for one year the Crown ceased to make any payments on its outstanding debts. This did in fact give Charles a fresh source of funds, but in the process it also bankrupted a great many of the financial gentlemen who had shown their faith in him by loaning him large sums of money, and also ruined many lesser folk whose stocks had been lent to him.

It was a shortsighted move at best, and a cruel, unfortunate one at worst, and because Sir Thomas was also a Roman Catholic, this hated Stop was likewise damned as one more Papist plot to control England. All that Charles saw was the money he needed, and as a reward Sir Thomas was created Baron Clifford of Chudleigh.

Though I was as shocked by this as anyone, I said nothing. As a woman, it would never be my place to advise the king on his finances, and as his mistress, it would simply be foolish. My purpose was not to criticize, but to provide a pleasing haven for him from his troubles.

Besides, by the end of the year, I'd accounting troubles of my own. For whatever reason, I'd never been particularly regular with my courses, the way some women are, and the weeks since Euston had passed in such a pleasing blur because of Charles that I'd lost my reckoning. Now I sat with a calendar and tried to count the days, and balance them against the subtle changes I'd noticed in my body. My breasts seemed somehow fuller, my whole form rounder, and I was often so languid in the middle of the day that I returned to my bed. At first I'd dismissed these as due only to my loss of virginity, small differences to mark that I'd crossed into true womanhood.

But it was Charles who finally said what I'd not been able to.

He had come to me after his morning walk, as he often did. I'd given him his usual light repast, then taken him to my bed, as was also usual. Outside my windows, lazy snowflakes drifted into the court-yard of the privy garden, but I always took care with the fires in my rooms, and Charles and I were as snug and content as could be imag-ined. We had loved each other well—the brisk air of the park seemed always to invigorate him—and now we lay comfortably together in the warmth of my bed, still curled around one another.

"You have the most delicious breasts," he said, idly fondling mine to his obvious delight. "Exactly to my taste."

"As you are to me," I said, stretching indolently beneath his ca-ress. I'd gained flesh since I'd come to England, and Charles clearly enjoyed me more for it, rather than less. In this arena, I knew I clearly outdid my rivals: Mrs. Gwyn was small and puny, little more than an undersized girl, and Lady Cleveland worn and aged by hard use and childbearing.

"If I could, sir," I said, "I'd keep you here with me all the day long."

"If I could, I'd let you, Fubs," he said, using the charmingly silly nickname he'd minted for me on account of my babyish round cheeks. Lazily he rubbed his thumb over my rose-tipped nipple to rouse it. "You're far more diverting than another admiralty meeting."

"I should hope so," I said, and sighed with restless pleasure. "Venus or Mars, sir. It's your choice."

He groaned. "That's not a fair choice at all. You know it's my duty to attend. You're tempting me."

"Yes, I am," I confessed, laughing softly. "If you continue doing that, sir, then I'll insist upon you staying here at least another hour."

To prove my words, I pressed my bottom against his cock in sweet invitation, rubbing myself along his length in a fashion I knew he rel-ished. I could see us reflected in my Parisian mirrors, like the subjects of a secret painting, and I guessed he was looking, too. Why shouldn't we? I'd always liked seeing the contrast that our bodies made together, mine so pale and lushly rounded, while his was dark and lean and full of vitality, and I liked even more to watch how well we suited and served each other.

"My wicked mademoiselle," he said, grunting with appreciation, "who would believe you were the same shy innocent I first had at Arlington's place?"

I chuckled low. "It's all your doing, sir."

"I know that," he said, "and it pleases me that I've never shared you with any other man."

To my surprise, he rolled me over onto my back and leaned across me, his expression turning thoughtful. "How long has it been since that first night, Louise? Seven, eight weeks now?"

"I'd venture that's so, sir," I said, lightly tracing his mustache with my fingertip. "Seven weeks of bliss with you."

He turned my hand toward his lips, absently kissing the tips of my fingers while his gaze never left mine. "Seven weeks, then," he said gently. "In that time, you've yet to turn me away from your bed. How far gone are you, Fubs? Was it truly that first night?"

"Oh, sir." At once my eyes filled with tears, for now there was no more ignoring what I'd tried to deny. It was not that I didn't want his babe; in truth I could think of nothing finer than to bear the proof of my love for him. But this soon— Oh, I'd not wanted that. Mrs. Gwyn was ready to be delivered of her latest bastard offering most any day, and Lady Cleveland was with child again, too, though this one likely was credited not to Charles, but to her young officer, John Churchill. Yet still it all made me feel like one more breeding mare in the royal stables, a sad conviction for any lady in my condition.

"At least the first week, then." He smiled wryly. "I know at Euston we raised glasses to a son in nine months, but I gave it no real thought."

"You're not happy." I rolled away from him, curling myself into a tight ball as I wept, my tears bitter with chagrin.

"Oh, sweet," he said gruffly, putting his arms around my shuddering, woeful self. "Of course I am happy."

"You're—you're not," I sobbed, unconvinced. He'd already sired at least a dozen children, beginning with the Duke of Monmouth; what would he want with one more now? "You—you don't want another."

He placed his hand over my belly, still not betraying the tiny babe within, his fingers spreading wide as if to protect it already.

"I'll grant that I have my share," he said, "but this one will be special, because it will be yours. Yours, Louise, and mine. Ours."

"Ours," I whispered fiercely through my tears, and slipped my hand over his, over our child. "Ours."

I squeezed my eyes shut, my heart overflowing. This babe wouldn't be another careless by-blow. I'd make certain of that. This one would be special, and be loved above all the others. For how could any child born between Charles and me ever be otherwise?

The Christmas holidays passed, and New Year's Day and Twelfth Night as well. The early months of 1672 were unusually free of snow, which was fortunate for the furious pace of the preparations for the coming war. The exact date that Charles and Louis would decide to declare upon the Dutch was still anyone's guess, but given the pattern of most wars, early spring was most likely. There was a gloomy certainty to the whole affair that seemed to turn all Englishmen into pessimists, predicting grimly that the Dutch would once again triumph; it was all the same, whether whispered at Court or more publicly in streets and in shops. The war loomed on the country's horizon much like the darkest thundercloud on a summer's afternoon, and just like a storm, the lightning and the downpour would be upon us all too soon.

Yet still my life continued, as did everyone else's as well. At Charles's request, I sat for my first portrait early in the New Year. Like so many others members of the Court before me, I took my custom to the painting studio of Master Peter Lely, the king's principal painter in ordinary. Master Lely had become the most popular painter in London not just on account of his skill, which was considerable, but because he'd a rare gift for flattering ladies, depicting their most luscious qualities while softening any flaws, yet still keeping such a true likeness that all who saw his pictures marveled at it.

I'd admired the many examples of his work that hung on the walls of the palace, and I was eager to see what Master Lely would capture in my face. He in turn was delighted to have me sit for him, for painting the portraits of the king's mistresses was a lucrative commission. Not only did such public portraits bring more work to his studio, but he would also do an excellent business in making copies of the original painting, both in oils for wealthy collectors and in line engravings to be offered far more cheaply (but widely) by print sellers and other low vendors. It was much the fashion of gentlemen at that time to assemble collections of paintings of the greatest beauties of the day, and Master Peter was sure that, as the newest of Charles's mistresses, my visage would soon be much in demand.

I let him guide me in the choice of my pose and attire. We settled on having me sit in a pastoral landscape with a waterfall in the distance behind me, and in the guise of a shepherdess, though no true shepherdess would ever be lolling quite so indolently. I wore not a gown such as I'd choose for Court, but a rich silken version of undress, a loose-fitting red gown clasped together with jewels over my shift. It was clear that I wore no stays beneath, and clear, too, from how my breasts were freely offered for admiration that I was a mistress, rather than a wife or daughter.

My only requests to Master Lely were simple ones. I asked that he show my hair as I always dressed it, with clusters of curls on either side of my forehead (a style that, to my amusement, was now being much copied by other ladies), and that he not give me heavy-lidded eyes like Lady Cleveland's, as he did with so many of his portraits, but show mine as they truly were, almond-shaped and tending to tilt upward at the corners. He laughed, but was happy to oblige, and when the picture was done, Charles declared it one of Sir Peter's finest, though never so beautiful as the original.

Such a pretty compliment set me to blushing, but what made me happier still was how Charles ordered my picture hung at once in his bedchamber, where he'd see it as soon as he rose each morning. To do so, he likewise ordered an older portrait of Lady Cleveland shifted to another room entirely. As for Mrs. Gwyn, there were no portraits of her at all that I'd ever seen within the king's chambers.

And that, of course, pleased me very much indeed.

. . .

My swelling belly caused little remark at Whitehall. Such was the king's omnipotence, that it was assumed that any woman who lay with him would in time quicken with his child. That Mrs. Gwyn had given birth to her second bastard, another son, on Christmas Day was seen as only one more example. The only amusement came from the speed with which the royal seed had managed to impregnate me, an apparent record for the king. But given the other concerns around us, even that was soon forgotten.

Lord de Croissy was, naturally, overjoyed, as was His Most Christian Majesty. After seeing Lady Arlington's diamonds, I had expected to receive at least their equal from Louis, perhaps more. Instead he sent me his congratulations, and a gift of only a thousand gold livres. Though I thought this thoroughly ungenerous, even disrespectful, of him, I knew to protest would be the gravest folly, at least at this juncture of my life. Later, perhaps, when my position was stronger, I could make my displeasure more properly known. For the present, I simply accepted the gold and sent my thanks.

I was fortunate to suffer few discomforts with my pregnancy, and continued with my duties to the queen. To my surprise, she was not jealous of me, as I'd feared she'd be, but kind and solicitous for my welfare. Perhaps this was because, unlike Lady Cleveland, I had never grown too proud to cease being kind to the queen, or to show her the respect her royalty required. She in turn rewarded me with her favor, which in Whitehall I treasured greatly. She asked me daily how I fared, and whether I believed the child a boy or a girl, and all the other things natural for women to discuss if the child I was carrying was not her husband's. When my belly became too apparent to overlook in a so-called maid of honor, she tactfully elevated me to Lady of the Bedchamber in her household.

Charles, too, continued to be as ardently devoted as before, perhaps even more so. My changing body delighted him, doubtless because he himself was the reason for it. I knew how much it grieved him that the queen had never given him a rightful heir, and I suspected part of his pleasure in seeing me swell now was that it confirmed the fault was not his. Whether kings or not, all men do like to see the proof of their own virility, and as the weeks slipped by, I was the very image of glowing fecundity, my cheeks rosy, my belly high and round beneath my petticoats, and my breasts full and proud.

One afternoon in early March, I went walking in the park with the two young daughters of the Duke of York, the Lady Mary and the Lady Anne. It pleased His Grace that I speak to them in French, to improve their knowledge of the language. I had a fondness for the motherless princesses, and because I had known the Lady Anne in Paris when she, too, had been in Madame's household, it was an agreeable enough way to pass an afternoon. The elder princess, the Lady Mary, was by far the more appealing, a tall, spirited, beautiful girl who favored her Stuart blood, while the Lady Anne sadly continued to be plain and afflicted with rheumy eyes, though shyly eager to please. Bundled against the cold, we had planned to feed stale bread to the ducks that still gathered on the canal when one of the king's pages came running toward me.

"Mrs. Carwell, if you please," he said breathlessly, using the common name I'd come to be called by the English who could not manage my French one. "His Majesty wishes you to come at once."

Fearing the worst, I gave the two princesses over to their attendants and hurried after the page, who led me directly to the king's privy chamber. There I found Charles pacing back and forth in such a righteous fury that I nigh expected smoke to puff from beneath his wig.

"Where were you, Louise?" he demanded even before the page had left us alone. "I needed you, and you were not to be found."

"I was with the Lady Anne and the Lady Mary, sir," I said, still breathless from following the youthful page, and because we were alone, I dared to sit without his leave. From the papers scattered on the long table before his chair, I guessed he'd been attempting some sort of work, but the way his chair was shoved back and the pen tossed aside also told of how futile that attempt had been. "What has happened? What is—"

"How the devil do you manage de Croissy?" he demanded. "I know he sees you often enough. How have you not throttled the rascal by now?"

302   SUSAN HOLLOWAY SCOTT

"Has he been here to vex you, sir?"

" 'Vexing' does not begin to express what that arrogant, impertinent, officious— *Ah!*" He broke off in a wordless exclamation of furious disgust, and instead struck his palm so hard on the table that the ink bounced and splattered from its little well. Unlike most gentlemen, Charles seldom used strong oaths, and the fact that he was tempted now showed how very much the marquis must have angered him. He glanced at the spilled ink and nearly swore again, then looked at me.

"Come," he said, charging around the table to seize my hand. "You already have your cloak. Walk with me."

He marched me briskly down the halls, his expression so black that no one we passed dared greet him, only bowing or curtsying in fearful silence. As we left the palace, two of the king's guards fell in at a respectful distance behind us, yet still Charles did not speak, half dragging me across the walks and paths. I was not accustomed to such a pace of exercise—while he walked each morning, I was content to remain abed—and I was also four months with child, and finally I'd had enough.

"Please, sir, I beg you," I said, scarce finding the breath to speak. "I cannot continue like this."

He stopped abruptly, and looked down at me as if seeing me for the first time. At once his expression softened and shaded into remorse.

"Forgive me, Fubs," he said, and contritely led me to a nearby bench at the end of the canal. "Are you well? Should I send for anything, or—"

"I'm well enough, sir, now that we've come to roost." I glanced around us to make sure no one else was within hearing. The day was cool enough that there were few others in the park as it was, and the two guards were keeping others from venturing any closer. I smiled and laid my hand upon his sleeve by way of encouragement. "Now tell me, sir. How has Lord de Croissy vexed you this time?"

He sighed irritably. "It's the same as always. You know de Croissy. You know how he is. He grovels and pleads, and then dares to suggest the most preposterous, the most insinuating—"

"He wishes you to make good your profession of faith as was agreed at Dover," I said. "That was his request, wasn't it?"

"That is always his request," he answered crossly. "The rascal grabs hold to his notions like a terrier and will not let go. Today, however, he went too far. Today he not only invoked Minette's name, but my mother's as well, claiming that my conversion to their Church was a dying wish they had in common. De Croissy wasn't even in Paris when either of them died. He was here, plaguing me. How does he know their wishes for anything?"

I sighed. I knew exactly what he meant, for the ambassador's insistence was a trial to me as well, and on the same difficult subject. "Madame did speak to Her Majesty about it often, sir, often enough for Madame to mention it to me as well," I said carefully. "She said it was your mother's hope that, in time, you would choose to follow her lead."

He shook his head, not hiding his disgust. "It was always my mother's hope, Louise, from the moment each of her children was baptized as an Anglican. She succeeded with Madame, and she tried with my brother Henry, though he bravely stood fast against her battery of priests."

I looked down at my hand on his sleeve. It was still my duty to France to incline him toward conversion, even if my loyalty toward Charles felt stronger than that to Louis.

"What of you, sir?" I asked, striving to keep my voice light. "Do you mean to hold fast as well in spite of your promise to France?"

"I would rather face Louis a hundred times over than my mother once," he said wryly. "I'll tell you the same as I told de Croissy. Regardless of the state of my tattered old soul, this is not the time for me to make so momentous a decision for either me or England. The English Catholics are too few and too weak to bear the weight of it, nor would the majority of my people support it. In time, perhaps, in time, but not now."

"But what of your conversations with Father Patrick, sir?" I asked, naming the queen's confessor, an eloquent young priest whom Charles met on occasion to please his wife. "Has he done nothing to quell your doubts?"

"Please, Fubs," he said, covering my hand with his own. "I know you speak from concern for me, but it won't alter my mind. This is not the proper time for a Catholic to sit on the throne of England."

I nodded. As far as I was concerned, I'd done as I'd been instructed. As a Roman Catholic myself, I longed for Charles to join me in the True Church to ensure his soul of its rightful place in heaven, just as Madame had. How could I not? But I'd seen enough of England and the English to understand exactly how disastrous his conversion would be, likely costing him his crown, and possibly his life as well.

"But all is not lost for my Catholic friends," he continued, and finally he smiled. "I've a plan that will bring them great comfort, and will establish England as a land of Christian grace and tolerance. I cannot tell you the finer points of it just yet, sweet, but you'll learn of it soon enough."

"I've made plans of my own, sir, though surely not quite so grand as yours." I glanced at him sideways, shyly, from inside the hood of my cloak. I'd known my news for several days now, but I'd waited for the proper opportunity to tell it to Charles. "I have asked His Most Christian Majesty if I may become a citizen of England instead of France, and he has granted his permission."

Charles looked at me sharply. "You did that?"

"I did, sir," I said, blushing. "I judged it best for the sake of our child, and for me, and—and because I wished to share that with you."

Louis, of course, had seen my request in a different light. He believed that my naturalization in England was necessary to my position with Charles, a clever advantage for him, and that was what my carefully worded letter had suggested, too. But in truth I'd felt myself shifting away from France, and my pregnancy had only convinced me further. I meant to make sure that Charles ennobled our child as he had done with Lady Cleveland's, and I hoped for an English title and a respectable living for myself, too. It was ambitious, yes, but it also seemed only fair that I be recognized. The honors would come more readily if I were English. It all made perfect sense. My future, my fortune, and, most of all, my love lay here in England.

"You'd give up France for me?" Charles's smile slowly spread across his face. "I'm pleased, Fubs. No, more than pleased. I'm honored."

I leaned forward and kissed him, my hood bumping awkwardly against the brim of his hat in a way that made us both laugh, and pleased me even more than his compliment.

"Ah, look, another of my subjects come to pay homage," he said once we were untangled. He pointed down to a duck waddling across the grass from the canal toward us. The duck stopped, shook his tail, stretched his neck, and quacked up at us expectantly.

"You see how it is, Louise," Charles said mournfully. "Everyone wants something of me. Forgive me, friend, but I can't oblige you today. Leave your petition with the porter, and I'll see what can be done later."

"Here, sir, I wouldn't wish you to disappoint." I reached into my pocket for the little packet of crumbs I'd brought to feed the ducks with the princesses earlier. "Better to have a happy subject than one that's full of discontent."

He grinned. "Do you always have bread crumbs secured about your person?"

"I do when my king needs it," I said, laughing with him.

He took the crumbs from me and began tossing them to the duck, and before long a half dozen more hurried to claim their share, scuffling and quacking on the grass before us.

The ducks were happy, but I was happier still. I'd coaxed Charles from his ill humor, I'd proved my loyalty, and I'd made him smile. What more could I wish from a single afternoon?

"If it pleases you, sir, I've another thought," I said. "In the future, I'll invite Lord de Croissy to my rooms, and you can meet with him there instead. I'll remain quietly to one side, but I'll promise to intercede if he becomes too unbearable, and spare you the vexation."

"What an admirable suggestion, Fubs," Charles said. "Though I pity you, having to see more of de Croissy."

I smiled. "If it pleases you, sir, then I'm content."

Such an arrangement would also keep me knowledgeable of whatever the ambassador, and therefore Louis, said to Charles. It would help preserve my place between the two, but I was wise enough not to say that before Charles now. He'd no need of vexation from me, either.

He scattered the last of the crumbs before the ducks and sat back against the bench, his long legs stretched comfortably before him. He slipped his arm around my shoulders and I leaned against him, my head comfortably against his chest.

"You can calm me like no other, Louise," he said softly. "You bring me peace."

"If it pleases you, sir," I said again, "then I am content."

And at that moment, I was.

Within the week, I learned with the rest of England how Charles planned to make the country a place of "Christian grace and tolerance." It had always been one of Charles's most admirable ambitions. Having witnessed the strife and wickedness that came from religious intolerance during Cromwell's Puritan reign, Charles had always hoped that under his rule, religious differences would cease to be an excuse for conflict. He saw no reason why any man could not worship as suited his preference, so long as his faith brought no harm to his neighbor. Those who would most benefit were Catholics, and the various dissenting nonconformists, including Anabaptists and Quakers. These were but a tiny minority of England's population, with most following the Anglican Church, but it was a minority that had suffered greatly at the hands of the majority. This Charles meant to end.

He had tried to bring this about once before in 1662, soon after he'd returned to his throne, when he had tried to have Parliament agree to a declaration of tolerance. Parliament, being full of stubborn Anglicans, had refused.

Now Charles hoped to try again while Parliament was out of session. Reminding his people that, as king, he was in supreme control of ecclesiastical matters as well as secular ones, he issued the Declaration of Indulgence. Not only did this declaration grant to Catholics and nonconformists the right to worship as they pleased within their own homes, but also suspended all penal laws against them. It was a bold move, a noble move, and it had scarcely been made before the outcry rose against it.

As can be imagined, the declaration was seen less as a plea for tolerance than as a marked advantage for Catholics. At once rumor and bigotry overwhelmed any sensible discussion. It was believed the Pope would soon claim England as his own, with waves of invading priests and cardinals determined to forcibly convert every honest Anglican, and to burn his house and rape his women if he dared resist. Exactly how this was to happen, I could not fathom; fear and disgust can persuade even logical persons of the most absurd beliefs.

Once again the king's wisdom was questioned. Given that the disastrous Stop of the Exchequer was still fresh in people's minds, this new declaration did little to help his popularity with his people. Nor did it help that, soon after, Charles also issued a round of general honors. Nearly all of his closest counselors (those who formed the so-called Cabal) benefited: Lord Ashley was made Earl of Shaftesbury, Lord Arlington was granted an earldom and Lord Lauderdale a dukedom. Since these gentlemen were already known to be either Catholics or sympathetic to the faith, their elevation only added to the general hysteria.

As a Catholic myself, and especially a Catholic personally favored by the king, I immediately felt the fresh waves of hatred and attack. Clods of dirt and stones were thrown at my carriage if I dared to go out, and foul insults shouted at me. The same befell Lady Cleveland, who was likewise of the Romish faith. I feared for myself and my unborn child. Instead of benefiting Charles's Catholic friends, as he had hoped, the declaration served only to make us less the beneficiaries of a new freedom than the targets of intolerance.

Charles had said I brought him peace, and perhaps for that reason he kept to his ministers and other counselors for the rest of March, and I saw little of him. He was not in the humor for peace, not from me or anyone else.

On the sixth of April, he declared war on the Republic of the

Seven United Provinces. Finally—or rather again—the Dutch were England's enemy.

Was there ever a man at the start of a war who wasn't convinced that victory would be swift and easy?

Certainly that was the way with both Charles and Louis. Both kings were certain that the Dutch would prove no challenge at all to their combined might, and that between them they'd be merrily carving up the spoils by the middle of summer at the latest. Louis hoped to claim as his the various lands agreed upon in the Secret Treaty, while Charles anticipated putting several important foreign ports under an English flag, plus helping to plump his dwindling treasury with a few fat prizes plucked from the Dutch navy and shipping.

Certainly it would seem that the alliance between France and England had the overwhelming advantage, and they'd every reason for cheery optimism. Between the two countries, the French and English forces vastly outnumbered the Dutch in men, ships, and guns. Louis himself rode at the head of his army of more than one hundred twenty thousand men as they marched northward to invade Holland, his confidence so high that he'd brought along his own historian to document his glorious victory.

Not to be outdone, Charles made his first move even before his official declaration, sending the English fleet to intercept the Smyrna Fleet in the English Channel. Reputed to be the richest prize on the seas, the Smyrna Fleet was the annual convoy of Dutch merchantmen sailing from the Levant through the Mediterranean with an armed navy escort to protect them from Barbary pirates. They scarcely expected to be attacked by the English so close to their home port, but despite having surprise in their favor, the Dutch escorts beat back the English, who to Charles's humiliation captured only a handful of prizes.

Alas, this first engagement proved a sign of more misfortune to come. On the seventh of June, part of the English fleet was surprised by the Dutch at Southwold Bay, off the coast of East Anglia, and the battle that raged was enormously costly to both sides. Serving as commander, the Duke of York had two successive flagships destroyed and sunk beneath him, and despite the seeming advantage of the English, the Dutch were finally able to retreat into the fog without any clear victor decided.

Surely Louis's army—by repute the greatest since those of the ancient Caesars—would have better success against the tiny Dutch army. The French easily poured over the first two provinces of Gelderland and Utrecht, and Louis and Charles, believing the war was over, wished to begin negotiations for peace. But once again, the Dutch proved that surprise and cleverness can confound sheer might. Faced with invasion, the Dutch turned to their boyish leader (and Charles's nephew) twenty-one-year-old William of Orange, who ordered the famous network of dykes released and the Dutch Water Line flooded, creating an impossible barrier for the French army. Louis had no choice but to retreat, and plan a fresh attack in the winter, when the water would freeze and be crossable.

The English people could find little cheering in such woeful news, proving as it did that the Dutch were still their superiors. Many began urging Charles to sue for peace soon after the debacle at Southwold Bay. With so little support for the war or hope that it could be won, desertions ran high among the English soldiers and sailors, and officers complained about the flagging morale of those who remained.

Still Charles seemed unaffected both by his country's despair and his war's lack of glory. Instead he insisted that everything was well and good, and that victory lay just over the horizon. He wrote long letters of instruction to Lord Arlington, his emissary at the peace negotiations, listing terms and conditions when in truth England had yet to win anything. He made excuses for his brother's incompetence at Southwold Bay. He visited the fleet at the Nore in Chatham repeatedly, taking his Lord Chancellor, Lord Shaftesbury, and other advisers with him, as if on a summer pleasure junket. In early July, he even took Her Majesty and her attendants with him, as if a trip to the mouth of the Thames were a fit place for his queen.

And where, pray, was I amidst all this?

I was nearly nine months gone with Charles's child, my poor body so large and clumsy that I scarce left my bed. The palace was nearly empty, with everyone who'd somewhere else to go gone from London. I was left with only Bette and my other servants and a pair of midwives, who took turns watching over me in case my travails began early. My rooms seemed unbearably hot and close, and I was too large to find any comfort in food or drink. Without family or true friends about me, I felt abandoned and melancholy, and more than a little fearful of the coming birth. I wrote letters to my unborn child in the event that I died, I wept into my pillow, and I prayed, for myself, for my child, and for Charles.

My pains began before dawn on the twenty-sixth of July. Following the best advice for safe birthing, the windows to my rooms were sealed shut and roaring fires set in my hearths, no matter that it was the middle of summer. In addition to the midwives, I was attended by Mrs. Chiffinch, a cronish but venerable servant in the king's household. It was her responsibility to oversee and verify all royal births, and in Charles's service, she'd witnessed more than her share.

Because this was my first child, my pains were long and my labor so tedious that I feared I'd never be delivered from my suffering. Finally, as the sliver of a new moon was rising in the summer sky, my son was born, a large and lusty boy covered with muck and the blood of my suffering.

"Aye, that's His Majesty's get, no mistake," Mrs. Chiffinch proclaimed as the nursemaids washed my son—my son!—and wrapped him in his first swaddling. "Mark his size, and his hands, and the black hair. He's the king's, and I'll swear to it. I wish you much joy of him, mistress."

"Thank you," I said wearily as they finally put the babe in my arms. His tiny mouth opened like a bird's, and his head flopped awkwardly against my chest.

"He's hungry, mistress," explained one of the nursemaids. "Poor little mite. We'll give him over to the wet nurse soon as she arrives."

I'd planned to bind my breasts to stop my milk and let him be suckled by another, as was the custom for ladies. But when I gazed down at that tiny, toothless mouth, my eyes filled with tears and my heavy breasts ached with milk.

"I can't let him go hungry," I said, fumbling at the front of my gown. "I can't ever let him go without."

"Ah, that's a proper new mother speaking," the nurse said with approval. "Here, it won't hurt you, and 'twill do him more good than you know."

She helped me place the child at my breast, and at once he began to suckle, making tiny mewing noises of contentment, a contentment that matched my own. I was exhausted and torn, but I'd never been happier.

"What shall you call him, mistress?" asked the nurse. "Have you a name?"

"Charles," I said, the only name I'd ever considered. "His name is Charles."

Mrs. Chiffinch cackled. "'Course it's Charles," she said. "That's what they all name the first one. Yours is the fifth o' that name that His Majesty's sired, you know."

"But this is the first that he's sired with me," I said softly, and as I touched the dark, damp curls on our new son's head, I resolved my little Charles would always be that way: first among his peers, first at Court, but most of all, first in his father's affection.

And with me as his mother, how could it be otherwise?

Chapter Twenty

A lady's lying-in is usually the month following childbirth. The lady is permitted to remain abed the entire time, dressed prettily in a lace-trimmed smock with ribbons or a cap in her hair and, whilst recovering from her ordeal, receive the congratulations of her acquaintance. Special dishes and punches are served, and the lady receives gifts for her new child, as well as hears the gossip and news she may be missing during her time away from the greater world. At the end of lying-in, the lady is given churching, a special blessing by a priest in gratitude of her safe delivery, and is then welcomed back into her ordinary life.

But because my son was born at a time when my acquaintance were so scattered, I decided to let my lying-in continue beyond its traditional length, until the Court returned to the palace. No one would count the days, or leastways not to my face. It also gave me further time to recover my beauty, and for my little Charles to lose his wizened quality and plumpen, and become even more handsome. Of course to me he'd always been handsome, a true twig from his father's tree, but I also knew how cruel people could be about mocking a homely babe, and I didn't think I could bear that.

There was another reason for extending my lying-in. The priest who'd come for my counsel had sourly informed me that churching was reserved for women who were lawfully wedded, and refused my arguments that children of kings followed a different precedence. Impudent man, to dictate the laws of God! I'd rely on Lord de Croissy to persuade him of his error, or beseech Her Majesty's confessor once they returned to the palace. This might only be the first test for me and my son, but I'd not surrender meekly to it.

The greater challenge, however, was Charles. I'd sent word to him immediately after his son's birth. I expected him to rush to my side, to display the same joy over our new child as I did.

I was most sadly disappointed. Though the following day he wrote to congratulate me, he made no promises to return, or even offered so much as a hint of when he'd be back. I wept bitterly, wishing with all my heart that it were otherwise. Given the sorry state of the Dutch War, I knew he'd many good reasons for being kept from my side, but still his absence wounded me.

Yet when at last he did come, and held our son in his arms, I forgot all my unhappiness. Unlike many gentlemen, Charles was at ease with babes and children, and devoted a portion of his day in seeing his many offspring. Surely it was the cruelest irony that he'd sired none with his wife, but I found the sweetest pleasure in seeing him cradle the proof of our love in his arms, the babe's long white linen gown trailing over his dark sleeves.

"You've done well, Fubs," he said, I suspect as proud of himself as he was of me. Our son waved his tiny fists up in his father's face, tangling them in the long black curls of Charles's wig, and Charles laughed. "What a fine little lad!"

"Thank you, sir," I said, tears of rare happiness filling my eyes. "He favors and honors you, I think."

"That he does," he said. "Mrs. Chiffinch assured me he was mine."

"She did?" I asked, offended by that. "I was not aware there was any doubt in your mind, sir. You know you took my maidenhead at Euston, and I swear by all that's holy that I've been with no other man since you. Only you, sir. You shouldn't have needed anyone else to tell you that."

"Oh, I've never doubted you, sweet," he said easily, bending over to kiss me, and making our son squawk between us. "You alone have always been faithful to me."

"Then why did you—"

"Because it's the way of kings, Louise," he said. "And it's the way of all my ladies, too. Mrs. Chiffinch is a good old soul, and entirely reliable."

I didn't care for that mention of all his ladies, either. How was it with two quick sentences he'd managed to so thoroughly puncture my joy?

"You have called him Charles?" he said, still looking down at the babe.

"Yes, sir," I said. "There could be no other name for him but yours."

He chuckled as his son took his finger in his tiny grasp, seizing it as if he'd never let go. "True enough. Mark the strength he has already!"

"What of his other name, sir?" I'd hoped he would have told me by now, but he hadn't, so I'd no choice but to ask. His children by Lady Cleveland were all called Fitzroy, an appropriate surname with "roy" signifying the king, and "fitz" their illegitimacy. I expected something similar. There was not the least stigma to these illegitimate royal children; in fact earlier in the summer, the Arlingtons had wed their precious four-year-old daughter, Isabella, to the eight-year-old Duke of Grafton, son of Charles and Lady Cleveland. "What shall he be called?"

"Oh, Charles de Keroualle sounds well enough, doesn't it?" he said with terrible lack of concern. "More than enough for a brave tiny lad like this one."

"But—but it's not, sir," I said plaintively. "With my name alone, no one will realize that he's yours."

He laughed softly, still occupied with the babe in his arms. "Everyone will, Louise. Everyone does. And if they don't, they've only to look at the babe's face and see me writ large across it."

I wept, but he did not change his mind. I felt humiliated and disgraced, both for myself and our son, but Charles seemed to think

nothing of it. Though others pointed out to me that he'd not immediately recognized Lady Cleveland's children and that Mrs. Gwyn's still
had no other name than hers, I was not consoled. How could I be? I
was a lady, and my son deserved better treatment.

To his credit, Charles didn't neglect me in other ways. That autumn he bought me an emerald necklace and a new coach, lacquered
in a lovely shade of pale blue picked out in gold—the colors that Louis
himself preferred, to my amusement—and my income was raised to
include the upkeep of our son. I was now receiving £8,600 per annum
from the treasury, guaranteed to be paid for my life; an agreeable sum,
particularly since it was double what Charles granted Mrs. Gwyn and
£2,600 more than Lady Cleveland and all her brats received.

Now I know that I have been accused of being greedy and avaricious, a French woman taking so much English gold (which it wasn't:
for most of the moneys that came my way were from Louis's subsidies
to Charles) for my own. Perhaps it does appear that way when compared to the income of others. At this time, an English gentleman and
his family were said to live quite handsomely on £300 per annum,
while a common shopkeeper or tradesman kept his family on £50 or
even less.

But I wasn't a common shopkeeper or tradesman. My role in
life was to please His Majesty, and keep him as happy as was possible. I was always making improvements to my lodgings, striving
to maintain them as the most agreeable retreat for Charles in the
entire palace. I kept an excellent table, and my chef was the best in
London, perhaps in all England. Thanks to my connections, I'd the
best cellar, too, with an ample selection of French wines to be had.
Because of this, Charles often preferred to entertain foreign visitors
and diplomats in my rooms, and what had begun with him meeting
only Lord de Croissy there had soon grown to include the ambassadors of every other Court of any importance in Europe. He trusted
me that everything would be arranged to perfection for his guests,
and it was.

Further, I was extremely nice in my dress and appearance before Charles, always taking care that he saw me only in the finest

and most becoming of gowns and jewels, and with my hair well arranged. Though he himself dressed with exceptional plainness for a gentleman, let alone a king, he had a quick eye for ladies' finery, and it pleased him mightily to see me dressed in the newest fashions from Paris.

I was also still very much in the employ of His Most Christian Majesty. Louis was very pleased by the birth of my son, and pleased, too, by the influence I had within Whitehall. While my primary desire was to please Charles, I also strived to reflect well on France and, with a fine display of elegant taste, to show my pride in being French, as well.

As can be imagined, all this made for a costly undertaking, and the expenses of my household were very high. But long ago I'd also observed Louis's favorite mistresses, the Marquise du Montespan and the Marquise du la Vallière, and I'd learned from them. A king's affection can be fleeting, far more so than that of ordinary men. Though I loved Charles well and did my best to please him in all things, I wasn't so foolish to believe that in time another lady might not catch his eye and replace me in his favor, just as I had done with Lady Cleveland.

I remembered, too, the unpleasantness of impecuniousness, and the disgrace of being the poor lady among the rich, and I'd long ago resolved never to fall into that place again. I took care to set aside some of my income against my future, and whenever I heard of an annuity falling vacant—say, an excise tax on wines—I was not above begging prettily to Charles that it might be given to me.

As can be imagined, what I saw as supporting His Majesty and being providential for myself and my son was often not viewed in the same light by my enemies. Pamphlets, broadsides, and other low papers often printed virulent attacks on my person and, worse, on the king, too, for favoring me. Though I never sought to seek these out for myself, I'd enough enemies at Court that they were often left where I could not help but see them or, worse, read aloud purposely in my hearing and passed off as "wit." This was one such, unsigned, of course, as the slanders most often were:

While these brats and their mothers do live in such plenty,
The nation's impoverished, and the 'Chequer quite empty;
And though war was pretended when the money was lent,
More on whores, than on ships, or in war, hath been spent.

Not pleasing at all, any more than were the constant gibes by Mrs. Gwyn and her associates. To provoke me and gain the sympathies of the people, she'd styled herself the "Protestant Whore," to separate herself from me as the Catholic one. It was all very distasteful to me. I never thought of myself as a whore, but as a *maîtresse en titre*. I held my head high, and ignored their name-calling as beneath my notice.

Yet one other did call me a whore, too, and stung me to the heart. Soon after my son was born, some evil-minded persons saw fit to inform my father. Instead of rejoicing in the birth of his first grandchild, he damned me as a whore, and sent his curses to me as the final message between us. I'd not seen my family in some time, and his treatment wounded me deeply. Since the day I'd left our château years before, I'd believed I must rely upon myself and my wits for my future. With this last letter from my father, I realized now it was a certainty, and forever I put my girlhood behind me.

I sat for Master Lely again. My pose was similar to the first painting, with me sitting languidly in a dark landscape created from Master Lely's fancy. But instead of the foolishness of the lamb and shepherdess's crook, I was shown as myself, in pale blue undress. I held out my long hair, the richness of my dark locks always being a special pleasure to Charles, and I turned my head to one side the better to display my round cheeks and elegant eyes. My expression is beguiling, but also confident, for now I knew my place in the English Court and the world.

I was twenty-three, and not just a woman, but a lady of means, beloved by the King of England and the mother of his son.

It was, I thought, a good beginning.

As the fall of 1672 became winter, the news from Holland grew worse and worse. All hopes of a swift war were gone. It seemed preposterous that such a tiny country had managed to confound the two greatest powers in Europe, but it had, and their mortification was complete. To Charles's chagrin, his nephew William of Orange refused to listen to his overtures for peace with any seriousness, and as the months dragged onward, it became clear that he hoped to break the alliance between France and England, and make England once again a Dutch ally unified against the French.

This was, of course, not to France's favor, and thus not to mine, either. All that fall and winter, I listened to Charles's complaints, of the conniving of the Dutch and the weakness of Louis's army. This did not seem fair to me, for not once did Charles level any doubt against his faltering navy, but I tried to be as loyal to him as I could, even as again and again I gently steered him back toward Louis's way.

One evening in January he came to me late, after he'd met long with his privy council. I was dressed in a gown edged with sable and the best of my jewels, for that night the queen was giving a grand feast and a ball in honor of Twelfth Night. One look at Charles's expression, however, and I realized that we'd be late for Her Majesty's feast, if we arrived at all.

"Here, sir, sit," I urged him, leading him to the settee piled high with down-stuffed cushions and fur coverlets and sitting before the fire that snapped and crackled with dancing flames, as fine a place as any to spend a January evening. "I'll fetch you brandy, and you may tell me what has happened."

"There is nothing new, Louise," he said with a sigh of discouragement as he took the glass from me. "It's the same as always. That little rascal William has rejected the last terms presented by Arlington, and that's an end to it for the season. We'll all be forced to wait until spring to begin more attacks, and I haven't the funds. My pockets are as empty as a beggar's, Fubs, and it's all because of my wretched nephew."

I'd always thought both Charles and Louis had treated William too lightly, but I knew better than to speak that aloud.

"Perhaps he will come around to your view in time, sir." I came to stand behind him, rubbing his broad shoulders with my thumbs in a way that always helped to ease his worries. "He is still a young man."

"A young rogue, in my opinion," Charles declared, shifting his shoulders beneath my fingers like a large cat. "Do you recall dancing with him when he came to visit two years ago? I do: the sight of you was Caliban and Arial, though you were the only lady he'd deign to partner. Ah, Fubs, you do know how to do that!"

"I do remember the prince, sir," I said, and I did. Barely twenty, William had been short and dwarfish, with a large hook of a nose, without a hint of Stuart charm. I'd never decided why he'd danced with me, either, for the entire time he'd coughed and wheezed and complained about the English fires and the English air and English manners in general. "Who would have conceived he'd inspire so much confidence in his people?"

"It shows what fools his people are, if you ask me," Charles grumbled. "You know what they've taken to calling this: the *rampjaar*, the disaster year. Arlington told me that, yet still the Dutch will follow William. I've half a mind to wed my niece to him. That would bring him to heel, wouldn't it?"

"The Lady Mary, sir?" I said, unable to keep the dismay from my voice. The princess was eleven, and such an intelligent and willowy beauty that I hated to see her married off to this disagreeable little man. "Perhaps you should find a bride for her father first, sir."

"Oh, James," Charles said with a groan. "You're right. We do need to have that resolved, and soon."

"Yes, sir," I murmured. When the hunt for a suitable bride for His Grace had begun, I'd promoted a pair of French princesses, as Louis had desired me to, but as it became clear to me that this might be one too many French ladies at Whitehall and not advantageous to me, I'd let my support fade. The latest candidate seemed to be an Italian princess, Mary of Modena; she was of course a Roman Catholic, a benefit to Louis, but not French, which made her more agreeable to me. "What a pity William was not born a woman, so that James could wed her as the Protestant princess."

That made Charles laugh, as I'd hoped it would. "What an abominably ugly woman he would make! We'd have to put my brother in irons and drag him to the church to marry that one. But no matter. There's only one answer to my trials now. I must recall Parliament."

"Oh, sir, I am sorry," I said, understanding now his black mood when he'd entered. "Is there no help for it, then?"

"No help that I can see," he said bitterly. "I need money for my fleet, and the only way I can come by it is if Parliament votes it to me. And the only way they'll do that is if I recall them to Westminster."

"Do you truly believe they'll be so obliging?" I asked, recalling the furious disputes Charles had had with his Parliament in the past. "Will they vote you the funds for a fresh campaign?"

"They will," he said with ominous certainty, "because I've no other way to keep my obligations to my navy and my sailors, or to Louis, too. But they'll vote it to me. They will. They must."

The session of Parliament that met in February of 1673 could not have been less agreeable to Charles's demands. At once he presented his requests for funds to continue the war against the Dutch, and Parliament in turn demanded that he withdraw his much-hated Act of Intolerance from the previous year. Charles tried every possible way to convince them, but the feelings of his people ran far too strongly against the act, and in the end he'd no choice but to admit defeat and withdraw it. The decision left him humiliated and betrayed, and especially sorrowful that he'd been forced to disappoint the people he'd tried so hard to benefit. But in return, Parliament voted him £70,000 a month for the next three years to continue his war. There were many despairing evenings spent in my lodgings, where I did my best to calm him after this dreadful debacle, but worse was to come.

Feeling bold and fat with victory over the Act of Intolerance, Parliament decided to take matters even further, and passed the Test Act in the summer of 1673. This odious act required everyone who held office to take Holy Communion within the Anglican Church, and also framed a series of oaths and obligations that would effectively bar all Catholics from positions of importance. Catholic officers were forced to resign from the army and the navy, and Whitehall, too, was purged. Her Majesty was permitted to keep a certain number of her most trusted attendants; Lady Cleveland was asked to give up her place, but I, as Lady of the Bedchamber, was not, for the simple reason that I had always remained civil and respectful to the queen.

Charles made a sour jest that was often repeated: he'd insist on keeping his barber, a Catholic, claiming that he'd keep the man despite Parliament, for he was so well accustomed to his hand with a razor. His meaning was perfectly understood: if he bared his throat each morning to a Catholic hand, then why should the others around him who followed the True Church be considered any more dangerous?

But others who lost their posts were of far more consequence than his barber or we ladies. Before his hand was forced, the Duke of York reluctantly resigned his place as Lord High Admiral in June 1673, effectively announcing what the rest of the country had only feared: that he had in fact converted to Catholicism, and that now the heir to the English throne was as good as a puppet to Rome and the Pope. Lord Clifford, too, refused to take Anglican Communion or the oaths, and in September was ordered to resign as Lord Treasurer. He left the Court and retreated to the country, full of bitterness and rancor, and within the month, he'd looped his cravat over the rod of his bedstead and hanged himself.

The clamor for me to be sent away grew louder, but Charles ignored it, as did I. No matter what was said of me, I loved him too well not to remain at his side. Early that summer, he rewarded my loyalty, too, making me Baroness Petersfield, Countess of Fareham, and duchess of Portsmouth. I was, as can be imagined, both honored and delighted. How could I not be? I was only the second duchess in my own right in the country, and in England, as in France, duchies are generally held only by those of royal blood. Further, I'd gained in two years what it had taken Lady Cleveland ten to achieve, and the irksome Mrs. Gwyn, despite her constant lobbying and posturing, remained no more than that: Mrs. Gwyn.

I knew her disappointment and her bitterness, too, and I'd heard from Charles of how she nagged him incessantly for a title she didn't deserve. Therefore one September evening at Whitehall, when the ladies were gathered around tables playing cards and other games, I spotted Mrs. Gwyn prancing through the room with her usual outlandish freedom. She was dressed at gaudy expense, more fit for one of her roles on the stage than for a lady of the Court, and as she came near me, I couldn't help but comment.

"Why, Mrs. Gwyn, look at you," I said, languidly doing exactly that over the ivory blades of my fan. "From your dress, I'd wager you've grown rich."

The other ladies at my table tittered appreciatively. It was enough to make Mrs. Gwyn stop before me, her little feet spread wide and her hands at her waist, like some sort of diminutive mussels-monger or other fishwife ready for battle.

"Aye, I have grown rich, Y'Grace," she said, barely able to force my honorific from her mouth from jealousy, a most pleasing spectacle to me. "And I vow from the same pockets as you."

I smiled archly, and looked her up and down, taking in every last bit of her tawdry finery.

"Dressed as you are, Mrs. Gwyn," I said, "you're as fine as a queen."

"Quite right, Y'Grace," she replied tartly. "And you are whore enough to be a duchess."

As she flounced away, she might have believed she'd bettered me, and doubtless her creatures would tell her so. But to everyone about me who'd witnessed this little scene, it had been but one more sad example of her challenging her superiors, and wishing to be more than she'd been born to be.

My little Charles might still have no surname of his own, but he now had a duchess for a mother, and that was a fine and useful thing indeed. For now my title was limited to my life, and could not be passed to him, but in time I hoped Charles would correct that to favor our son. To celebrate, I held a huge ball for the Court beneath the autumn sky at Barn Elms, an open field near Richmond Hill. I laughed and danced with Charles, and by the winking light of the stars and moon, it was easy for us to forget all thoughts of war and prejudice.

Forget, yes, but not for long. The year was nearly done, and campaigns of 1673 were no more successful against the Dutch than those of the previous year, with all the news full of gloomy defeats and William's arrogance. Further, the Dutch had become more sly in their attacks, no longer relying only upon guns and ships. Instead Dutch gold began to find its way into the eager hands of the English Parliament and, worse still, into the pockets of Charles's privy council. Even as he remained in Holland as Charles's representative, Lord Arlington was said to embrace the Dutch cause and to be following William's bidding.

Another new form of attack came from Dutch printing presses. Though no one knew exactly how it was done, England was flooded with crudely printed pamphlets and ballads, pieces that slandered Charles and accused him of selling England to the Pope. My name and face were often mentioned, too, in the form of "Madame Carwell," and the vile taunts of Mrs. Gwyn and Lord Rochester were nothing compared to what was said of me now.

Yet as false as all this was, it fell into the same eager ears of those who'd supported the Test Act. Emboldened yet again, Parliament now claimed it was up to them to decide whom the Duke of York should marry, and they demanded the right to refuse any Catholic princess that the duke might suggest.

Unable to tolerate so much conflict at Westminster, Charles finally took the only course open to him, and prorogued Parliament again. The odious members dispersed to their homes, but the meanness of their spirits remained to hover over Charles and his Court.

I stood on the roof of the palace with Charles, bundled in furs against the cold bite of the November night. On balmier days, this was a favorite place of the Court, for from this lofty perch the entire city was spread before us, and the queen in particular enjoyed spending time here with her ladies. But on this night, Charles and I had the roof to ourselves, and as I pulled my fur tippet higher over my face, I could understand why.

"Mark the city, Fubs," he said, leaning over the stone rail. He'd insisted on coming up here from my rooms on impulse, and though I was warmly dressed, he hadn't even bothered to bring a hat. His long hair blew back over his shoulders, and the light of the lanterns at the windows below shone softly on his down-turned face. The Thames lay like a snake of silver, curling through the city in the dark, and the ragged clouds overhead hid the stars and most of the moon.

"No fireworks tonight, sir," I said, naming the most frequent reason for coming to the roof. "Though it would make for a pretty show against the clouds."

"There're fireworks of another kind," he said, pointing to the streets. "Bonfires."

I'd been so busily looking upward that I'd not noticed the fires in the streets below. Small patches of fire flickered here and there in the streets, usually at a crossing. At the nearer fires, it was possible to see the black silhouettes of figures dancing and sporting before them.

"You know what the fires are for, don't you?" he said. "That's how my people are displaying their displeasure over my brother's choice of a bride."

In the end, the duke had hastily pushed for Mary of Modena as his new wife, and though he had married her by proxy some weeks earlier, word of the marriage and her imminent arrival had only this day reached London. The princess was reputed to be very beautiful, which had favorably colored the duke's opinion of her, and very young, only fifteen, which had tickled his lubricious nature. She was also bringing a sizable dowry to the treasury, which had finally made her acceptable to Charles. I knew that much of that dower had been contributed by Louis, who wanted very much for the heir to the English throne to wed a Catholic. I knew, but I hadn't confided that knowledge to Charles, deciding in the end it would be better for all if I pretended ignorance. The money was welcome, no matter whence it had come.

"When I wed the queen," he said sadly, "there were bonfires, too, but those were more cheery. These are of a different type entirely."

I tucked my hand into the crook of his arm. "How do you know, sir?"

"I don't, not from here," he admitted. "But I've been told that most of these fires tonight will include straw effigies either of the Pope or my brother. There may even be a few of me before the night is done, if there's enough drink to conceive a likeness."

"Oh, sir," I said, now looking down at the fires with a far different impression. "I am sorry, sir."

"'Tis not your doing, sweet," he said heavily, "nor need you apologize for it. I only hope that by the time the lady arrives in London, their interest will have gone off in some other direction, and she'll not be plagued with sights such as these. The sight of my brother rampant on his wedding night will be horrifying enough, eh?"

I laughed, as he'd expected me to, but we both knew the jest fell flat. How could it not? Charles could claim they were burning him or the Pope in effigy, but the straw figures could just as well be representing me. How much longer could he afford to keep me? How much longer should I stay, with my presence risking harm to him and his reign?

I'd no answers. Instead I rested my head against Charles's shoulder, and whispered a silent prayer, for peace, for tolerance, and for us.

Chapter Twenty-one

"I'm impressed, Your Grace," Lord Danby said, walking slowly through my rooms as if to appraise the value of every last tapestry and candlestick within. "I'd heard much of the magnificence of your lodgings, but none of that comes near to their true glory."

"Thank you, Lord Danby," I said, my smile as warm as I could make it for this chilly man. The Earl of Danby's face was white as new snow, his lips thin and tight, his cheeks pinched: clearly a visage made for parsimony, and fit, too, to belong to Charles's new Lord Treasurer. Though he'd promised Charles to guide him toward a more stable treasury, Lord Danby also seemed determined to use his influence to lead England away from France. I'd soon enough recognized his ambition, just as he had doubtless recognized my own. In the past, I would have done my best to avoid such a man. Now, more secure in my place and more confident in myself, I believed it better to confront him before he became troublesome.

"I am glad you came to me, my lord," I said, gracefully offering him an armchair before the fire. "I'm honored that you found the time."

"Only a fool refuses a summons from you, Your Grace," he said. "How many rooms do you have in these lodgings?"

I widened my eyes disingenuously. The answer was forty, after my last expansion, not that I'd tell him. "Why, I've not counted, my lord. I rely on His Majesty's generosity in such things."

He grunted. "Then I must inform you that His Majesty's generosity is about to become less so. For the sake of the country's welfare, it is imperative that he retrench and cut his expenses. If he follows my advice, he should soon see an increase in revenues that will benefit us all."

"So he has told me, my lord," I said. "Yet if I dare to be honest, we both know that the king's treasury has many parts, and while most contain funds voted to him by Parliament, there are other, more private sources that should remain unaffected by this 'retrenchment.'"

"The subsidies," he said, fair spitting the word from his obvious loathing of those sums. "Of course you would know of Louis's little offerings, Your Grace. You're French."

"I am," I agreed. "And you do not like the French."

"No, Your Grace, I do not," he said bluntly. "I would as soon have England as it was meant to be: an Anglican country without Papists or Frenchmen."

"But His Majesty doesn't quite agree with you, does he?" I said, keeping my voice purposefully soft to counter his own vehemence. "While he is willing for the stability your retrenchment promises— even eager for it!—he will not give up all things French in return to please you."

His small, tight mouth grew tighter still. "Meaning yourself, Your Grace."

I smiled. "Because I please His Majesty, my lord, he chooses to please me."

"And if I do not choose to please you, Your Grace?" he demanded. "What manner of punishment are you determined to inflict?"

I clucked my tongue in dismay. "Oh, I would not call it 'punishment,' my lord. That is far too harsh. But I can incline the king toward you, or I . . . cannot. To be sure, I do not dictate to him, for he is the king. La, I would never be so bold as to even pretend that!"

"Never," he said sourly. "What is the price of all this pleasing, Your Grace?"

"That I be spared your retrenchment," I said simply. "That when I have a small request of you, that it be paid as before, from that certain part of the treasury."

"I will do nothing to forward the French."

"I will not ask it of you," I said. I wouldn't, either, for his hatred was too deep for him ever to be trusted with anything related to France. But that sat well enough with me. Where the treasury was concerned, I was far more concerned with my own welfare.

He nodded brusquely, all the agreement I'd receive, but all I needed, too. "Have you any requests outstanding, Your Grace?"

"Have I?" I repeated, musing, though of course I had. "There is a certain pair of diamond earrings that Lady Northumberland is offering for sale—earrings that would greatly please His Majesty to see hanging from my ears. I believe Her Ladyship is asking three thousand pounds for them."

"Three thousand pounds," he repeated, as if he'd never heard of diamonds worth that sum. "Very well, Your Grace. It will be done."

"Thank you," I murmured. "You are too kind."

"Kindness has very little to do with it, Your Grace," he said curtly, "as we both know."

"Then I am pleased that we have achieved this understanding between us," I said, rising and offering him my hand by way of dismissal.

He bowed over my fingers, as brief a bob as could be managed. "It's always pleasing with you, isn't it, Your Grace?"

"Yes, my lord," I said, and smiled. "It always is."

That same February, in 1674, Charles finally made peace with William of Orange, and signed the Treaty of Westminster. This treaty was filled with the usual meaningless back and forth of all treaties, of distant ports exchanged and certain policies reversed or enforced. But for England its primary meaning was not only the end of a costly war that few had wanted, but also the end of France as an ally, while Louis continued doggedly to attempt to win on land against William. Parliament, being Parliament, took full credit for this, and viewed the treaty as another victory for an Anglican England.

Later that spring came a proclamation ordering all priests and

Jesuits to leave England, an order pushed through by Parliament that sadly displeased Charles. With the end of the war and its financial drains, Lord Danby's plans for a more stable economy were already plumping the treasury, and his favor and power were likewise increasing. Now, more than ever, a gentleman's success in Parliament depended on the deepness of his hatred toward France, as Lord Danby's success proved.

There were a good many folk at Court who wondered how I continued to prosper beneath the new treasurer while both Mrs. Gwyn and Lady Cleveland howled about how he'd cut their incomes and refused their requests. I told them nothing. Lord Danby and I had our "understanding," and it was clear that he'd chosen me over the others. Much to my amusement, whispers rippled through the Court that I must have taken Lord Danby as my lover, for what other reason could there be for his obvious favor? It was so preposterous that I told it to Charles, who laughed, too, and teased me about fancying a man without any blood.

But I'd another triumph, too. That black-clad crow who'd plagued me for so long, Lord de Croissy, was at last recalled for his ineptitude and irritating manner (as I could have long ago informed His Most Christian Majesty he should have been), and replaced by the Marquis de Ruvigny as the new French ambassador to the Court of St. James. Where Lord de Croissy had often crept perilously close to nagging, Lord de Ruvigny was forthright and direct, and the English did love him for it. Most important to me, however, he recognized at once my significance and my usefulness to both Charles and Louis, and respected me accordingly, which Colbert had never done.

Even if Lord de Ruvigny's personal qualities had not recommended him to me, he brought a favor from Louis that certainly did, one that I'd coveted for many years. As pleased as I'd been to be made an English duchess, it was the French title of *duchesse* that I'd longed for even more, the right to have a taboret of my own and to sit in the presence of the Queen of France. It would mean that I was the equal of Madame de la Vallière, *maîtresse en titre* who'd been raised on account of her service to the French king. How sweet it would be to know that I'd triumphed over those who'd ignored me when I'd been in Madame's household, the gentlemen too superior to dance with me, the ladies too fine to know my name!

What de Ruvigny brought me was the deed of gift for the estates of Aubigny and La Verrerie, the two châteaus, and the duchy that went with it. To my giddy delight, in France I was now Madame la duchesse du Aubigny; more important, it was an estate to be inherited by my son and to mark him as a gentleman in France. At least I could offer him that much.

It grieved me greatly that Charles had still not formally acknowledged our son's paternity. My lovely babe was nearly a year old, and it was shameful that he'd nothing but his baptismal name. Charles had offered no answer when I asked, no reason when I pleaded. Surely it wasn't a lack of affection for our child. I wept from tenderness when I saw how he delighted in our son, holding and toying with him each day with a fondness rare in any father, let alone a royal one. All I could do now was to trust to time, and to Charles.

"You make a fair country lass, Fubsy," Charles said, smiling with happy approval as we rode side by side through the Great Park at Windsor. We'd come up from London with the rest of the Court at the end of May to spend the summer months here in the country at Windsor Castle, far from the dust and heat of London. "The fairest of the fair."

"I'm no such creature, sir," I retorted, laughing with him. "How can I be a country lass if I cannot ride out with you in the midday sun from fear of burning red as a strawberry?"

"I said you were a *fair* country lass, and that you are." He was not so far from a handsome country lad himself, with only a waistcoat instead of a doublet or coat, and the sleeves of his shirt rolled back over his forearms. "The fairest of the fair, with skin whiter than new cream. Is that more to your liking?"

"It's more the truth, sir," I said, tipping my head beneath the wide brim of my straw hat. That braided straw was my single concession to the country, for the hat itself was crowned with my usual white plumes and blue silk ribbons. But even though my pale skin meant I must limit my rides with Charles to dusk, I still relished them above all things.

Now we were making our way slowly back toward the castle, walking our horses at a pace more suited for conversation than any real progress. The early June evening was drowsy-warm and the sky gray with that rare soft moment between day and night, and the first mists from the river already clung to the bottom of the castle's ancient walls. The first stars had begun to show and the new moon to rise, and the birds in the trees below the castle were sounding their good-night chatter, as if sharing the last ripe gossip of their avian day.

"The castle's handsome tonight, isn't it?" Charles asked like any other proud landlord. "I'm glad I had the gardeners pull down those scrub trees and that brush around the bottom of the towers. This way you can see those glorious old stones for what they are."

What they were was unappealing to me, rough and worn, but I knew better than to criticize Windsor Castle to Charles. Windsor was his darling, his favorite of the many palaces he possessed, and the one he lavished endless attention and expense upon. To the rest of us, it was a drafty, ancient fortification, but to Charles it was a magical place, and deserving of the legions of architects, carpenters, plasterers, and painters he routinely turned loose in the name of "improvements."

"You've done a great many things that I can see, sir," I said loyally. "Some large, some small, but all to the benefit of the property."

"It's fortunate I'll have the whole summer now to continue," he said, and from his thoughtful expression, I knew he was already envisioning the next trees to be planted or pulled up, new staircases added and floors redone. "Four months is not much time."

"Four months is a splendid amount of time, sir," I assured him. "You've never brought the Court here for so long before. It will do you much good to be away from London."

"It will," he said, his thoughts still on the castle. "Tell me, Fubs. Does Windsor come close to what my cousin does at his place at Versailles?"

"Oh, sir," I protested diplomatically, "it has been many years since I've been to Versailles."

"No, no, pray be honest," he insisted. "Don't you judge Signor Verrio's new paintings in the presence chamber to be every bit as fine as anything Louis can muster?"

I smiled fondly. Windsor was greatly improved, yes, but it would never compare to the glorious splendor of Versailles. But like every other gentleman, the more Charles begged for honesty, the less of it he truly wished to hear; and like every other lady who loved her gentleman, I would tell him exactly what he wanted.

"Windsor is magnificent, sir," I declared. "Even Louis would be impressed."

He grinned with happy pride. "I thought as much. You do approve of your own rooms?"

"How could I not be more than content, sir?" Indeed, how couldn't I? Mrs. Gwyn had been given the lease to some sort of low house in the town of Windsor, but I was the one who had a suite of rooms furnished to my own taste in the castle, there as part of the royal apartments. "Truly you are generosity itself."

"Only the best for you, my dear life." He drew off his hat and leaned across the space between our horses to kiss me, both with affection and desire. Though we'd just celebrated his forty-fourth birthday, he was as vigorous as ever, and after he'd kissed me, his gaze lingered over my throat and breasts with growing interest. "Your skin *is* most wondrous fair, Fubs. I never tire of it."

I smiled wickedly, my lips ripe and inviting from his kiss. "If it pleases you so, sir, then catch me, and I'll show you far more."

I kicked my heels to urge my mount onward, and laughed merrily as he chased me. Of course he caught me. Of course I'd wished it. Of course we both were pleased, and pleasured.

I doubted I could ever be happier than I was that day, my life any more splendid or my love more perfect.

I was only twenty-five, and not half so wise as I believed. But happiness is too often followed by sorrow, and gilded splendor can turn to humbling ashes in an instant. And as for love— Ah, love can prove the most fragile of all.

It was raining the morning I discovered the first sores.

Restless, I'd slipped from my bed early, before Bette had brought my breakfast. Never one to lie abed past dawn, Charles had long ago left me. I'd heard the rain all the night long and it rained still, drumming hard against the castle walls. Because the wind had blown from the west, I'd been able to keep my bedchamber windows open, for besides the heaviness of summer rain the air itself was heavy and poisonous. All had made for a poor night for rest, and I yawned as I stood before the nearest window to stare across the sodden lawns and dripping trees. August was nearly done, and with it our time here at Windsor. There'd be no picnics or other merry pleasures today, I thought, and idly rubbed my hands together.

And winced. They hurt, my hands, a pain that stung in the way a scalding or a blister did. I turned my palms open and held them to the rainy light, and found a peppering of spots the color of worn copper. Some spots had already opened into sores, their surface glistening where I'd rubbed them together.

With a frightened little cry, I ran to my dressing table and bent before the glass, frantically turning my face from side to side to spy out any hint of other such spots. Was that a tiny one, there, scarce more than a freckle at the corner of my mouth? Swiftly I twisted about to turn the sole of my bare foot toward the window's light. I saw more spots, more sores, my pale skin now marked with the most shameful of banners.

"Good day, Your Grace," Bette said with her customary cheer, my tray in her arms. "Why are you from your bed on a morn such as this? Back beneath the sheets, now, and I'll fetch you your chocolate properly."

Fearful she'd see my distress or the reason for it, I hurried to do as she'd bid, slipping swiftly into the bed with the sheets drawn high. With the tray resting against her hip, she smoothed the coverlet and set the tray upon it, the same way she did it every morning. She poured my first cup of chocolate and passed it to me, the tiny silver spoon balanced flat over the top. But the shock of my discovery had set my hands to trembling, and as soon as she'd put the cup in my fingers I let it slip, spilling chocolate over my fingers and onto the pale green silk coverlet in foaming brown rivulets.

"Forgive my clumsiness, Your Grace. Forgive me!" she exclaimed, as if it had truly been her fault. At once she took my hand to wipe it clean with the hem of her apron, and as she did, she gasped.

"Your poor hand!" she cried. "Oh, Your Grace, what has happened?"

I pulled my hand away, cradling it close to my chest as at last I began to weep.

"Is it from all that riding about, Your Grace?" asked Bette with coaxing concern. "Come now, let me see it. There's plenty of salves that will cure that. I'll venture it's from wearing your gloves too tight while you held the reins in this hot weather."

I shook my head and held my palms out for her to see. There was no use in hiding the sores from her. She'd see them soon enough, as would the rest of the Court.

Her eyes widened with shock, then filled with such acute sympathy that I almost could not bear it. She knew what she saw, as did I. How could it be otherwise, when we'd both been so long at Courts and among profligate courtiers and highborn libertines?

"I'll send for His Majesty's physicians directly, Your Grace," she said gently. "And for His Majesty, too."

"At his pleasure, Bette," I whispered wearily through my tears. "Only at his pleasure."

Of all the humiliations I'd suffered in my life, surely this was the worst. To have my bedchamber invaded by long-faced medical gentlemen, there to inspect and handle my most private parts and make the most indelicate of inquiries into my habits, was beyond shaming. Having

Charles there beside me with his hand upon my shoulder only made my mortification infinitely worse.

Now there are those who will scoff at the notion of a woman who lives such a life as mine having any scrap of shame or conscience, but I assure you that I remained at heart a modest lady, especially when compared to the flagrantly lewd conduct of my rivals. I've always believed it was part of my attraction for Charles, that I reserved my wanton pleasures for only him. Likewise I'd sadly known he'd not shown me the same fidelity, nor was it in his constitution to do so to any woman. It had little to do with love. There was simply a part of his being that craved the variety that no single mortal woman could ever supply. I knew of the whorehouse frolics organized by Lord Buckingham and the parade of nameless low women escorted up the back stairs to the royal bedchamber as surely as I knew of Mrs. Gwyn and Lady Cleveland. But I'd never suspected I'd be so publicly confronted with Charles's faithlessness, or so painfully.

"*Morbus Gallicus* is a most pernicious disease, Your Majesty," explained Sir Henry Scarborough, Charles's chief physician, in the most baleful tones.

"Here, now," Charles warned. "I'll ask you not to lay blame on the French for this."

Sir Henry bowed, but pointedly did not apologize to me. Did he think I was too stupid to understand his Latin, or that he'd just described my affliction as the French pox?

"Forgive me, Your Majesty," he said, bowing like any other practiced courtier. "For clarity, I shall employ the simple vulgar name of the pox instead. The sores must be left uncovered to help drain the pus, and thus draw the foulest of the humors from the body. While the wells of Bath and Tunbridge are chosen by many for this purpose—Tunbridge's chalybeate springs are said to be particularly salubrious—I myself prefer a more aggressive course of hot mercury baths, enemas, and vapors."

I pressed the sodden ball of my handkerchief to my eyes. Of course I'd heard of the pain and unpleasantness of the mercury treatments, and I was not eager to experience them for myself. But more important than any mere discomfort, I worried about the time it would cause me to be apart from the king.

Sir Henry, however, was not yet done. "Regardless of the treatment, Your Majesty, Her Grace must limit her diet, her exertions, and her contact with others while the disease is in this period of activity. Naturally, she must be denied intimate congress of any sort with you until the cure has been effected and the rash has completely subsided."

Was Charles aware that at that exact moment he withdrew his hand from my shoulder? Or did that count as intimate congress, too, even if he'd not so much as touched my skin?

"His Majesty's health is our constant concern, Your Grace," intoned another royal physician, Sir Edmund Cox. "His Majesty's life and health must come before all else. Surely you must agree with us, Your Grace."

Sir Henry nodded vigorously. "For the same reasons, Your Majesty, we must also deny Her Grace any further contact with your son."

"His Majesty's son?" I asked, my voice rising into a wail of bewilderment. "But he is my son as well. I am forbidden the company of my own child, my babe?"

"Gentlemen," Charles said quickly, "if you would please leave us."

Immediately the physicians bowed and backed from the room, likely as glad to be done with me as I was with them.

Careful not to show him my blighted palms, I twisted in my chair to look up at Charles, standing behind me. "Charles is my babe, sir, my little angel. How can they forbid a mother her own son?"

"It's for the boy's own sake, Louise," he said with a heartiness we both knew was completely false. "Not for long, either. Only until you're better. These fellows may seem like a pack of rascals, I know, but they're the best there is to be found at their trade. You can stay here at Windsor for as long as your cure takes. I'll make sure you'll want for nothing, and they'll have you back to rights by Christmas."

"Christmas, sir!" I cried plaintively, too distraught to bother with my handkerchief now. "But that's months and months! My babe is only two, sir. He'll not understand where his mama has gone."

I'd never seen Charles look less at ease as he stood there clasping and unclasping his hands behind his back, as if by force forbidding himself to touch me.

"I tell you, sweet, it's for his own good, and yours as well," he said finally. "He won't forget you. Children never do, not their mothers. Besides, the cures aren't half so bad as they sound. I've survived them several times, and I'm none the worse for it."

"But, sir," I said, those two words saying all that I couldn't: that he was a man full of strength, while I was a woman, and not. What would become of my beauty? Would my skin ever be perfect enough again to delight him, or my body capable of bringing him the pleasure he'd so often enjoyed? What would I have left if that was gone? What would I be to him?

"You'll see," he promised. "You'll dance with me at Christmas and outshine every last one of them."

Everyone. Oh, I'd not wanted to consider that. I'd so many enemies at Court. There were those who hated me for being French or a Catholic, and more who envied me Charles's devotion and the fortunes that had come with it. They'd all be rejoicing now, delighting in my fall, predicting how disfigured I'd become, jostling among themselves like so many jackals to replace me. It didn't matter that on any given day of the year, likely half of Charles's Court shared this same affliction to some degree (the most obvious at present being Mrs. Gwyn's supporter, Lord Rochester). Now it was the duchess of Portsmouth. Now it was *me.*

"They'll know," I said. "All of them. They'll *know.*"

Not even Charles could deny that. "Yes, they will. Not even I can do anything about that."

"Oh, sir," I said, my voice breaking just as did my heart, "but worst of all is being kept from you."

"I'm sorry, Fubs," he said gruffly. "It should never have happened to you. Not you. I'm sorry."

Yet he could not take me into his arms the way we both wished, or embrace me to prove he meant what he said. We both felt lost without it. Already I felt myself drifting away, like a little skiff that had lost her sturdy anchor. Truly my future was an unknown ocean: the forbidding, empty world of my life without Charles at its core.

"My dearest sir," I whispered through my tears. "Why is it I am ordered from you, but you were never ordered to keep from me?"

His dark eyes filled with more sorrow and regret than I'd ever seen there before. I wouldn't have dared ask such a question if I'd not been so consumed with despair, and even so I didn't truly expect him to reply. He didn't need to. The answer hung there unspoken in the humid air of that rainy day, and we both knew it. Because he was king, he was denied nothing. Because I was only—*only!*—his mistress and his love, I was obliged to grant him whatever he wanted.

"I am sorry, Fubs. Truly." He tried to smile at me, and couldn't. "I'm sorry."

Then he turned on his heel, and fled.

The next day, Charles sent a different royal doctor to me, a gentleman named Dr. Crimp, who was kindness itself. He promised to treat me there at Windsor in complete privacy and as much comfort as was possible, and to do his best to restore me in perfect health to Charles by year's end.

Two days later, the rest of the Court returned to London without me, and I humbly put myself in the care of Dr. Crimp. I took the hot baths and vapors of mercury that he prescribed, feeling quite like a *fricassée de la Keroualle*. I drank no wine, and took only the food that was prepared for me. I slept, and I prayed, too enervated by the rigors of the treatment to do much else.

But I did write endless letters to Charles, of course, to assure him of my unconditional love and devotion. He in turn wrote to me twice a day and often more, letters that were full of affection and concern and news of our son, which was very gladdening to me and my poor aching heart.

I wrote to Lord Danby as well, so that he would know how often the king wrote to me, that I'd not (yet) fallen from his favor, and was thereby still deserving of our "understanding." I wrote to the Marquis du Ruvigny, and even to His Most Christian Majesty himself, reassuring them also of the king's attentions. I had worked too hard to achieve my place at Court to lose it now.

But despite my efforts, my situation was too delicious to be ignored by the tattlers and scandalmongers. The duchess of Portsmouth poxed! Who among my enemies could resist that? Removed though I was at Windsor, I still heard enough to make me cringe. I'd caught the pox not from His Majesty, but from one of my legions of lovers or, more titillating, from my confessor. I'd been blinded, or gone mad, or even died. Even in France I was discussed, to Charles's detriment as much as my own: while the King of France was busily winning new provinces to add to his glorious kingdom (for he still continued to war with the Dutch), Charles was ridiculed for having won only the pox, which he in turn had gallantly passed on to me.

To ease my distress, Charles sent me delicacies from the royal gardens and greenhouses, as well as two trinkets of a more lasting sort: a pearl necklace valued at £4,000, and a rare diamond, set into a ring, valued at £6,000. I was sweetly touched, and recognized them for what they were, part of his seemingly endless apology (and not, as the wicked tongues would whisper, my farewell gifts).

I did not quite return to Court by Christmas 1674, but I was in the Banqueting Hall to dance on Charles's arm for the queen's ball on Twelfth Night. I was thinner than I'd been, more delicate, but my beauty was again without blemish, and because I wore the new diamond necklace that Charles had given me, no one would dare take notice of any infinitesimal flaw. For every courtier who welcomed me back, there was doubtless a score who cursed my return.

But I didn't care. I was once again where I belonged, on the arm and in the bed of the King of England.

Chapter Twenty-two

When I returned to Court, most everything seemed to be as it always had. Charles was with me as much as he could be, and truly it did seem that my absence had made his heart grow fonder, as the old poem claimed. I returned, thankfully, as if I'd never been away.

The one thing that was much changed was my son, Charles. Four months to a small child is as much as a decade to a person grown, and in the time I'd been away, I vow he'd grown at least two more inches in height, and learned to chatter entirely in English.

I was devastated that I'd missed so much of his life, and upset all the more when at our reunion, he hurried not toward me, but away, forgetting who I was. I crouched down at his level on the nursery floor and wept, heartbroken.

Yet in a few moments he came slowly toward me, as unable as his father to remain unmoved by the sight of my tears. As he drew closer I smiled and coaxed him in French. At that he smiled, too, so sudden and wide he showed his darling dimples, and all trouble between us was forgotten. His hair had grown much thicker, with glossy black curls that were the very image of his father's at the same age; when I saw old portraits, the resemblance between the two was astonishing. He'd become less a babe and more a small gentleman, and I marveled at the change, as every mother does.

Yet even as I held my handsome lad, I wondered how the same

time that had so changed him could truly have left me untouched. I'd turned twenty-six while at Windsor, and while my cheeks remained as babyishly plump as my own dear child's, I lived in a Court that most prized the green beauty of fifteen-year-old girls. I remained nearly twenty years younger than Charles, and always would be, but was that enough to hold his love? He'd told me again and again how glad he was to have me returned, and yet in my heart lay shameful doubt: not of Charles, but myself.

Did he love me still for my beauty, or did his devotion spring only from guilt for having given me the pox? Did I truly remain his "own dear life," as he fashioned me, or was the phrase only a habit ingrained by use?

It did not help that Lord Rochester had written a particularly virulent little poem about me at this time called "Portsmouth's Looking Glass." Just as he'd done with the couplet he'd once pinned to the door of my lodgings, copies of this new slander had been well circulated among the Court and the city's coffeehouses before he'd finally had a confederate audaciously tuck a copy into one of the largest mirrors in my reception chamber.

> Methinks I see you, newly risen
> From your embroider'd Bed and pissing,
> With studied mien and much grimace
> Present yourself before your glass,
> To varnish and smooth o'er those graces,
> You rub'd off in your Night Embraces.

Charles was furious, and banished Rochester from Court and off into the country for his sordid unkindness. Another thing that did not change, I thought, yet somehow I wasn't as wounded as I once would have been. Perhaps I truly was growing old and weary, in my spirit if not my face. I couldn't deny that the pox had changed me. I saw more the fragility of my life, and less its boundless possibility. Yet Court is a poor place for doubts of any sort, and I knew the moment I began to falter, a rival would rise to seize my place.

Instead I draped myself with the brightest of my diamonds, composed my face into perfect serenity, and once again sailed forth, ready for battle.

"Go look in my coat," Charles said, pushing himself up a little higher against the pillows. "There's a little something for you in my pocket."

"For me, sir?" I asked, rubbing my naked thigh against his in languorous invitation. We'd already shared one encounter this night, and at forty-four, Charles had reached the age for gentlemen that once was sufficient. But I also knew he'd prefer to believe that this was from choice rather than possibility, and thus I always took care to be as wantonly available as ever. "If it pleases you, sir, I'll look for it later."

"I think you should look now," he said with cheerful anticipation, for he loved to give me things as much as I loved receiving them. He linked his hands behind his head to make himself more comfortable. "Besides, I like to watch your ass when you walk across the room."

"You can do that anytime, sir," I said, laughing. Obediently I slid from the bed, slipped my feet into my black silk mules, and crossed the room to where he'd tossed his coat. I made a show of it, knowing he was watching, letting the high red heels of my slippers slap lightly on my feet and the long strand of pearls (for another thing he liked was for me to wear my jewels to bed) swing back and forth across my bare breasts. He was a large man and his coat was even larger, and it was no quick task to search through his pockets—which, of course, was exactly his intention.

"It's not a box," he said by way of a hint. "It's folded."

"Folded, sir?" I asked, playing the game, but at once my heart began to beat faster. Folded meant paper, and there was only one paper I desired. At last I found what he'd hidden, the folds blunted by the heavy parchment, and I held it in my hands as if it were a far greater treasure than any jewel—which, if my guess were right, it was.

"Is it, sir?" I asked, not yet daring to open the page and read it for myself. "Is it?"

"It is, indeed," he declared. "Go on, read it for yourself."

With fingers all a-tremble with excitement, I hurried to the nearest candlestick and tipped toward the light the patent (for so it was) for my son's ennoblement, and I read aloud the titles he'd been granted. "'For Charles Lennox'—oh, sir, I do like that name!—'Baron Settrington, Earl of March, Duke of Richmond.' Oh, sir! However shall I thank you?"

"I expect you'll find a way." He grinned and patted the bed beside him. "But the boy deserves it, and so do you."

At once I'd recognized the spite behind this particular title. Frances Stuart had been the single lady at Court to spurn Charles's advances in favor of marrying the Duke of Richmond. When this gentleman had tragically drowned soon after, leaving no heir and Frances childless, his dukedomes had reverted to the Crown for disposal. That Charles now granted them to my son was doubtless intentional, a warning for whoever might cross the royal will. Not that I would let Frances's sorrow spoil my own joy.

I hopped back into the bed, still clutching the precious patent, and showered him with so many kisses that he began to laugh.

"There now, don't smother me!" he said, laughing still, though it was clear he was thoroughly enjoying my attentions. At last he held me still, there against his chest, and to my surprise his expression grew solemn, yet fair overflowing with tenderness.

"I mean it, Fubs," he said softly. "You deserve whatever I give you, for all you have given and done for me, in every way. I cannot begin to tell you how much I missed you when you were away from me, or how much I regretted the circumstances."

"It's done, sir," I said, lightly pressing my fingers to his lips to silence him. "Far better to look ahead than behind."

He took my fingers, kissing each tip in succession as he held my hand. "Only if I know you'll be here with me."

"So long as you wish it of me, sir," I whispered. "I will stay."

"My dearest life," he said, drawing my face close to his. "Then that will be forever."

We kissed, a kiss of such rare devotion that I wish I could have preserved it to keep with me always. Instead it ended, as all kisses must; this time the blame lay with the stiff parchment of the patent letter held in my hand between us, and poking him in his ribs.

"Here now, take care of that," he said as I quickly sat back on my heels. "I know you've felt I neglected our son, but I hope you'll mark I didn't even make him wait until his third birthday for the honors. I've raised Barbara's last boy, Henry, today as well, and he's eleven."

Instantly I was alert to any hint of favoritism, of Lady Cleveland's boy receiving more than my Charles. "What will he be, sir?"

"Henry Fitzroy, Duke of Northumberland," he said, reaching out to pull me back with him under the coverlet. "But mind you, none of it's legal until both you and Barbara have the patents signed and sealed by Danby. Within the next fortnight or so will likely be soon enough."

But I knew better than to wait so long, not where the future of my son was concerned. The last thing I wished was for Lady Cleveland to have her son's patent sealed before mine, and thus ever after my Dukes of Richmond bound by precedence to follow after her Dukes of Northumberland. As soon as Charles left my bed for his own that night, I immediately dressed and had myself driven to Lord Danby's house. It was well past midnight, but as I'd guessed, Danby was still awake and working at his desk in a flannel cap and a gray wool dressing gown over his shirt and breeches: another gentleman who seldom slept.

"Is all well at the palace, Your Grace?" he asked with alarm as soon as I was shown in by a sleepy-eyed footman.

"Perfectly fine," I said, holding out my precious patent. "But I knew you were leaving for Bristol at dawn to visit your wife's family, and I'd no wish to leave this until you returned."

He took the patent, and laughed. "Meaning you'd no wish to let Her Grace the duchess of Cleveland possibly surpass you."

I smiled, content in my triumph, though I did rather wish I could see Lady Cleveland's face when she learned my son would forever have precedence of rank over hers. "I'm a good mother, Danby. No one will say otherwise of me."

"No one would dare, Your Grace." He solemnized the patent with his signature as first minister, and prepared the wax for the privy seal.

I looked at that wax as it melted, and considered how much its glossy red seal would bring to my son's life. My son, His Grace, Lord Richmond. I'd have to practice saying it without the awe I now felt.

The patent also meant that because my son was now recognized as Charles Lennox, gentleman, without the bastardy of being merely Charles de Keroualle, my duchy in France could now be his as well. That blotch of molten wax, now being impressed with the great seal of England, had made my son three times a duke in the space of a few seconds: a considerable inheritance of honors for a gentleman not yet three years in age!

"Thank you," I said softly as I took the signed and sealed patent from Danby's hands. "I'll leave you to prepare for your journey tomorrow."

He made a wry, unhappy face. His wife was widely known as a bullying shrew, and I could imagine well enough why he'd not anticipate a visit with her family.

"A word or two before you take your leave, Your Grace, if you please," he said. "Perhaps it's wise we speak here before I go from London."

He gestured for me to sit, and intrigued, I did. My midnight conversations were seldom of politics.

"You have heard that the Duke of York has given his interest more fully to Buckingham and Arlington?" he asked. "The two have been observed much at St. James's, and now are boasting of their new alliance."

"Alliance, ha," I scoffed, more with disgust than anything else. Even in a political world that thrived on selfish opportunism, Buckingham, Shaftesbury, and Arlington stood above all others, or perhaps crawled lower. Like sunflowers in the sun, each turned his face toward whichever cause or party seemed at that instant the one with the greatest potential for personal gain and profit. Most currently they seemed determined on any course that ran counter to Danby's.

Through this untidy sea Danby had in turn continued his best to steer the government toward an Anglican England and Crown, financial stability, and dissolving ties with Catholic France while strengthening them with the Protestant Dutch. He labored hard within Parliament, hoping to persuade them to vote funds to the king that would be sufficient to free him from the constant, binding need of supplementary payments from France—supplements that he told me he despised as much as if they'd been pulled from his own pockets.

With goals for France so contrary to Danby's own, why, then, was I now sitting beside his desk? Because I knew what the others did not: that very much against his personal will, Danby had been obliged by Charles to conduct the most secret negotiations to continue relations with France, and retain the French subsidies with them. And, of course, it was my task (as assigned by both Charles and by de Ruvigny and Louis) to offer the necessary encouragement to see that he did.

La, I did enjoy the privileges of my power!

"I would not worry over any alliance with the Duke of York," I continued. "While brave and bluff to a fault, he is not the best-liked gentleman in the kingdom."

Danby's nod was more of a bow, likely more concession to my rank than to my wisdom; like most other men, he found it difficult to heed advice from a woman. "I have heard that they will introduce a motion to Parliament for my impeachment, Your Grace."

I raised a single brow with surprise. "Pray, on what possible grounds?"

He sighed. "I do not know. But if they are determined to be rid of me, they will find reason."

"Don't worry overmuch, my lord." I rose, tucking the patent into my muff. "His Majesty is loyal to those who are loyal to him. They wish to be rid of me as well, yet still I remain."

He bowed me toward the door, his dressing gown flapping around his spindly legs like a lady's petticoats.

"Forgive me for speaking plainly, Your Grace," he said sourly, "but I should venture your place with the king is a good deal more secure than mine could ever be."

I smiled, and answered nothing. In all games of chance, the most useful cards are the ones that are kept unknown.

Soon after, in the summer of 1675, a bill calling for Danby's im-

peachment was in fact introduced in Parliament, on preposterous
charges worth nothing. With little support, the bill withered and
died, as was right, yet still the members continued to buzz and sting
at one another like angry wasps, and not even Charles's appearance
one night was able to calm them in their differences. When the bickering became too great by the beginning of autumn, Charles simply
prorogued the session yet again, and left it that way, uncalled and unwanted and far away from London.

It all made perfect sense to him, and to me, though not at all to
the angry nameless scribes who haunted the coffeehouses. The most
popular ballad of the season, called "The Royal-Buss; or, The Proro-
gation," might have lacked Lord Rochester's artfulness, but none of
his venom.

> *Then Portsm—th, the incestuous Punk,*
> *Made our most gracious Sov'reign drunk.*
> *And drunk she made him give that Buss*
> *That all the Kingdoms bound to curse,*
> *And so red-hot with Wine and Whore,*
> *He kick't the Commons out the door.*

I ignored it, as I did all the others. And as soon as the Court returned from its now-annual summer at Windsor, the meetings to negotiate another secret treaty between France and England began in
earnest in the most private of my rooms. Just as Madame had done
before me, I made everything as easy for the gentlemen as I could.

For my efforts, Louis sent me a letter of thanks written in his own
hand. With it came the gift of a pair of earrings set with diamonds
and rubies from the best goldsmith in Paris. Their value, over £18,000,
made them the most sizable single gift sent by France to England that
year. I was enchanted; Louis anticipated my tastes in jewels so well.

As 1675 came to its end, I believed myself truly not only recovered, but returned. Abbé Prignani's long-ago fortune for me had in
fact come true. I was prized by two kings, a duchess in my own right,
and mother to a duke. I was in fact in such a proud fettle that I dared

to jest to Charles (and only Charles) that I was like a phoenix born again, though rising ready not from ashes, but from a tub of mercury vapors. He laughed, as I knew he would, and it seemed I'd finally put my doubts behind me.

Until, that is, the arrival of Hortense de Mancini.

Dutifully I stood in the gallery of St. James's Palace, with the thirteen-year-old Lady Mary on one side of me and Charles and his brother James, the Duke of York, on the other. The day was gray, with flurries of snow drifting into the courtyard, and biting with the deep-winter cold of January. His Grace's young and very pregnant wife, Mary Beatrice, had invited me to remain with her in their quarters beside the fire, but I'd judged it better to come out with the others.

I'd good reason, too. The duchesse de Mancini, Her Grace's cousin and the Yorks' current guest at St. James's, was presenting a demonstration of her dueling skills. The duchesse's opponent—or rather, her partner, for this duel was only pretend—was her African man-servant, Mustapha. Mustapha looked painfully cold, his golden hoops quivering beneath the woolen scarf he'd wrapped beneath his bright yellow turban.

But I guessed the duchesse herself was never cold. She was older than I, taller than I, and far less pretty than I, with a full mouth and many teeth, flashing dark eyes, and masses of black hair that she made no effort to control, letting them flow as wild as Medusa's locks. She bore a strong resemblance to the ancient ladies shown on antique coins, with a strong nose and stronger brow.

But I wasn't sure what she resembled that day in the courtyard. Dressed in gentlemen's clothes, even to boots and breeches, she shamelessly moved like a gentleman, her gestures bold as she tested her sword, laughing and swearing in a mixture of French, Italian, and English. As uninformed of dueling as I was, I quickly saw that her efforts were not near so expert as she'd boasted, but hacking slashes that only such a raging virago would claim.

Yet as I stood there in my long blue cloak and my usual pearls, my hands tucked inside my oversized sable muff, my feet near frozen in yellow satin slippers with the high red heels that marked my nobility—dressed like that, I felt like a tiny doll, precious and exquisite but carved of wood. The feeling only doubled when I saw the looks of undisguised admiration on the faces of Charles and James, and grew again when she came striding toward me, offering me the hilt of her sword.

"Here you are, Louise," she said, for she'd already presumed familiarity based on our French duchies. "Have a try against me, or Mustapha, if you'd prefer."

Horrified by such a suggestion, I looked to Mustapha, who bowed and beckoned me to join him.

"Thank you, madame, no," I said politely, my hands clasped tight with dismay within my muff. "Dueling is not to my taste."

Beside me I heard Charles turn his smothered laugh into a cough. I thought several unkind things about him.

"Then what is to your taste, Louise?" Hortense demanded. She loomed over me, steam rising from her doublet after her exertions. The "Roman Eagle," that was what her admirers called her, and I could well understand it. "How do you amuse yourself? Do you hunt? Hawk? Swim in the river?"

"I game, madame. I play loo," I said, the only thing that came to my mind, and of course she seized upon it.

"Very well, then, Louise," she said, clapping me on the back as she passed me by. "I'll play you at loo, and I'll teach you every cheat known on the Continent, so you'll win every night. York, I've a thirst that will only be tamed by more of that excellent canary from dinner."

Then striding off she went, down the gallery with James and Mustapha trotting happily after her. At least Charles didn't, remaining with the Lady Mary and me, though I didn't dare meet his gaze from fear of what I'd say.

"She's a bold jade," declared Lady Mary soundly, and I could have kissed her.

But Charles—Charles thought differently. "She's no jade," he said as he stared after her brazen departing figure. "She's magnificent."

And I knew my time of peace was done.

Over the next weeks, I learned as much as I could of the duchesse de Mazarin, striving to better fight this new rival. I learned that her husband was mad, enough excuse to take lovers wherever she pleased. I learned that in fact she had once nearly been betrothed to Charles when he'd been a prince without a kingdom in exile. And I learned soon, sadly, that those early flames of desire between Charles and the duchesse might burn still between them.

By the end of January, I was certain he was visiting the duchesse's bed, for he was visiting mine far less. Now she was the one always at Charles's side, daring him to join her in every wild escapade with a ferocious energy that drew Charles constantly to her.

How could I compete with a creature like this? She wasn't like my other rivals; she wasn't like any other lady. The more I tried to display the qualities that had once beguiled Charles—my grace, my soft voice, my voluptuously feminine body, my fashionable dress—the more stiff and formal I became in comparison. The splendid welcoming haven I'd always offered to Charles had become boring and dull, and was of little interest to him now. I, who had always chosen to ignore my rivals, now in turn was the one ignored. It was not a pleasing place to be.

I'd a brief respite in February, when the new treaty was finally completed and I'd again become indispensable to Charles. Signed in my rooms, this treaty was even more secret than the one signed long ago at Dover. Charles was delighted. It was not just the money (he'd receive £100,000 in exchange for his cooperation regarding the Dutch) or renewing Louis's favor; I do believe he enjoyed acting on his own for the good of his country, without having to justify every step to a critical Parliament.

"You please me better than all my ministers combined, Fubs," Charles had said as we'd dined together in my bedchamber after the signing. "No one suits me better than you. How could I swim in these rough waters without you to keep me afloat?"

Yet the next morning he was back with Hortense.

Speculation grew that she'd soon replace me as the favorite mistress. Some claimed she already had. In the summer, when Charles offered her lodgings in the palace, in the old rooms once held by Lady Cleveland, the tongues wagged even faster.

One evening Mrs. Gwyn trailed through the Court clad in deepest black mourning. When asked who she grieved for, she wept and wailed in mockery of me, and when pressed further, her answer made me wish to cry in earnest.

"Who do I mourn?" she replied. "Why, I'm showing my respect t' the duchess o' Portsmouth herself, who is newly dead to the king and the Court."

Through de Ruvigny, Louis expressed his deep concern. He'd invested much trust and money in me. Didn't I realize that the Dutch would feel their position strengthened if they believed my influence over Charles was fading? Why didn't I fight harder?

Yet how could I fight when there was no true battle? In his ever-charming way, Charles had never attempted to sever our ties, nor could I claim the indignation of a jealous wife. Mistresses exist to offer comfort, not strife, and besides, screaming rages and hurled porcelain had never been my manner. All I could do was continue as I had. I was beautiful, gracious, and obliging, smiling blithely before the Court while I wept alone in my bed. And each night before I slept, I'd added a new prayer: that for the sake of her soul, Hortense would be shown the depth of her sinful neglect of her marriage, and return dutifully to her husband in Rome as soon as she possibly could.

The rest of the world continued as well. Louis pursued his relentless war with the Dutch, finally realizing a series of great victories that had proved devastating to the United Provinces. Feelings against the French ran so strong now that I never dared go about London on my own, from fear that my coach would be attacked.

I heard Mrs. Gwyn herself tell (and tell, and tell, and tell) how she'd been stopped by such a mob who'd mistaken her carriage for mine. Angrily they'd held her horses and cursed her as a foul French slut. But being no better than the lowest-bred mongrel herself, she knew exactly how to address such a crowd. She leaned from the carriage's window as if she were back upon her stage, tossed her mop of ginger curls, and called out in her dreadful screeching voice.

"Pray, good people, be civil," she'd cried, her hands held high for peace. "As you can see, I am the *Protestant* whore!"

For that, they'd cheered her, and hurried her on her way with a brace of roaring apprentices as escort. It made for an amusing tale for her, I suppose; I found it only chilling, knowing I'd never have escaped so lightly.

Thus matters went through the summer of 1677, when my prayers were answered, though not perhaps in a way that was best for Hortense's eternal soul. His Royal Highness the Prince of Monaco appeared in London in June. He was handsome and dashing and young, and his seduction of the duchesse took less time than it takes me now to write it. Perhaps Charles would have indulged Hortense and looked aside if she'd been discreet, but that was not her nature. She conducted her intrigue with the prince exactly as she'd dueled: boldly and badly. Disgusted and unwilling to play the fool, Charles curtly withdrew his support. Hortense shrugged with unconcern, and swiftly decamped after the prince. As easily as that, Charles was once again mine.

"I'm glad that you're here, sir," I said softly, soon after as we lay together in my bed like the finest of old times. "I've missed you."

"I've missed you, too, Fubs," he said with a contented sigh, settling his arms more comfortably around my waist. "For a great many reasons, but most of all, I think, I missed the peace you bring me."

"Indeed, sir," I said, glad the dark hid my smile. "I should imagine you did."

"What was that, Louise?" he asked, teasing. "Did I hear a hint of a reproach?"

"It was an observation, sir, not a reproach," I said firmly. "If you wish to be flayed for your sins, then I can recommend my confessor."

He laughed. "Likely I deserve that," he said. "I behaved like an ass over that woman."

"No, sir," I said, laughing with him. "You behaved like a man."

"Well, then, a foolish excuse for a man." He pulled me up to kiss me, a splendid sort of apology. "But I've a great question to put to you, Louise, one of monumental importance. I'm considering shaving away my mustache."

"You are!" I exclaimed, astonished.

"I am," he said, lightly stroking his fingers over his upper lip as he considered the mustache's fate. "Do you think I should?"

"Why do you wish to do so, sir?" I asked, curious. "Is it because Louis wears one as well?"

"Not exactly," he said. "I rather thought I might look younger without it."

"Oh, sir," I said, oddly touched. "Have your barber shave away the mustache if that pleases you, but you needn't do so to look younger. No one would judge you to be old, sir. You're in your prime."

"I'm forty-seven, Fubs," he said mournfully. "That is old by anyone's book."

"Not mine, sir," I said. "You'll always be young to me."

"My own dear life," he said softly. "Then pray oblige me, and prove it."

As cynical as I might have become by the necessities of my life, I still cherished a romantic notion or two. One of them was that a marriage was doubly blessed when the persons to be wed were in love.

Sadly, in November 1677, I was witness to a grievous example to the contrary, the wedding of the Lady Mary to William of Orange. While this match had much to recommend it from an English point of view—the eldest Protestant princess wed to a Protestant prince, and nary a French Catholic about it—Louis did not wish it, for obvious reasons, and I was likewise against it, but for sentimental ones. I watched the willowy, beautiful girl sob through the ceremony, her heart broken at the sight of her dispassionate, ugly groom, and I wept in sympathy with her. Worse still was how William carried her back to Holland immediately afterward, like more plunder of his unending wars.

Louis was so angry with Charles that he immediately stopped all payments between them, but Charles thought the whole affair a masterful stroke of diplomacy. So did Danby. Parliament and London rejoiced, and the ill-suited couple was honored with gun salutes and bonfires in the streets. Three days later, the celebrations were halted by the birth of a son to James and Mary Beatrice, a son whom James was determined to raise as a Catholic heir to the throne.

The Protestant celebrations needn't have stopped. Within the month, the poor little babe had died of smallpox, following so many other unfortunate royal children to his grave.

No one was in much of a humor for the merriment of the Christmas season as 1677 drew to its end. But every royal Court is expected to maintain a certain degree of celebration, ceremony, and excess, and ours was no different.

Thus one evening in early December, I sat at my dressing table and prepared to attend a supper and a ball that the queen was giving that evening to mark the beginning of Advent. My hair had already been dressed and I'd likewise rubbed my cheeks rosy with Spanish paper and lined my eyes with henna, and added one tiny black patch in the shape of a star just above the corner of my mouth.

"Here are the two pairs of earrings for your choosing, Your Grace," Bette said, a leather case in each hand. Such a pleasing decision to be made between different settings of diamonds and pearls, and I smiled as I began to turn toward the cases in Bette's hands. But as I did, my view of Bette and my dressing table seemed to skew wildly to one side, so wildly that I grabbed at the edge of the table to catch myself from falling with it.

"Your Grace!" Bette exclaimed, seizing me by the arm. "Is something amiss, Your Grace? Are you unwell?"

What was unwell was her voice, far away and echoing, as if she weren't standing directly before me. I tried to open my lips to tell her so, but the words seemed stuck in my throat and refused to dislodge as I felt myself slip from the bench and gently, gently to the floor, my silk skirts *shush*ing in a whisper around me.

I heard nothing more after that.

It was only because others told me that I know I was ill for the next five weeks, delirious with fever one day and sunk deep into unconsciousness the next. With gratifying haste, Charles had rushed to my bedside, and had himself overseen the physicians who tended me with bleeding and purges. They declared it was a "distemperous fever" that ravaged me until my very life was in despair, and the physicians gave way to priests.

All that I knew for myself was that when I finally awoke, Charles's face was the first that I saw. As weak and poorly as I was, I smiled.

"Fubs," he said, and I vow I saw tears in his eyes, "you're awake."

"Yes, sir," I whispered, my voice raspy from disuse.

"Hush now, and save yourself," he said. "You're not clear of danger yet."

"You're here, sir," I said. "I shall be fine."

He tried to smile. "I refused to let you go, you know. I even prayed for you."

"As an Anglican, sir, or a Catholic?"

He paused too long, taking that moment to glance thoughtfully at the Catholic crucifix that had been hung over my bed to protect me in my illness.

"I prayed," he said finally, "in the manner that would, God willing, keep you here in this life with me. And as you still are, my prayers were answered."

I understood. "Thank you, sir," I said. "Thank you."

And as 1678 began, the new French ambassador, Paul Barrillion (a man more like a bookkeeper's clerk than a diplomat), could write to Louis that the duchess of Portsmouth had never been more greatly beloved by the king, nor more firmly in his favor. Considering what would befall us all that year, I was never more blessed by his affection.

Chapter Twenty-three

Great events, both good and ill, often rise from the most humble of roots. So it was with the great nightmare that darkened the autumn of 1678: an insignificant event lay at its beginning, so slight that Charles forgot to mention it to me until late that night.

"A most curious thing happened to me this morning in the park," he said as we sat together to share a glass of sillery.

I'd kept the windows thrown open to welcome the evening air from the river, for this had been another hot day, so hot that Charles had decided to shift us all back to Windsor the day after tomorrow to escape it. "I've only now remembered it, else I would have told you earlier."

"What manner of curious thing, sir?" I asked idly, for it was too warm to be anything else. "Did a giant sea serpent slither from the duck pond across the lawn to menace you?"

He smiled, but briskly, more intent on his own tale than my jests. "I'm serious, Louise. The hour was very early, as you know is my habit, and the mists still hung low on the grass. I'd scarce entered the park when this fellow came charging up to me."

At once I sat upright, turning to face him. "You weren't alone, sir, were you? You'd waited for your guardsmen to follow?"

"Well, no," he admitted. "I was eager to be off, and the guardsmen can be slow old sticks."

"Old sticks!" I exclaimed. "They're supposed to be keeping you safe. What if this fellow had intended you harm?"

"That's the curious part of it, Fubs," he said. "He wasn't entirely unknown to me. His name is Kirkby, a chemical scientist, but what he was so determined to tell me had nothing to do with science. He warned me of a plot to kill me, that I might even be attacked if I continued through the park."

"Yet you went on, sir?" Fear swept over me, and blindly I reached for his hand. "You put yourself at risk because you'd no wish to be slowed by guards?"

"I did." He linked his fingers into mine to reassure me. "I did, because of whom he blamed. The Jesuits."

"Jesuits, sir?" More trouble for Roman Catholics and the French, I thought with dismay. "That makes no sense."

"It made no sense to me, either." He smiled wryly. "Every Jesuit I've known has seemed most intelligent, and no man with any sense would prefer my brother as king instead of me. I thought no more of it. But later today Kirkby returned, coming to Court this time with a vicar named Israel Tonge, who claimed to have uncovered the entire wretched plot."

"What did he say, sir? Who did he fault?"

"To be honest, sweet, I'd no patience for his ramblings," he said with a sigh. "I sent him off to see Danby. He'll sort it out, if anyone can. What matters most is that I'm still here."

Charles's safety did matter the most, especially to me. Two days later, we left for Windsor on a river that shimmered with the heat, and I doubt he gave more than a passing thought to either Kirkby or Tonge.

But Danby did. Wrapped in the confident knowledge that he was only preserving the welfare of the king, he listened eagerly to Tonge's tale. Surely there was no other minister who so hated the French, or so believed in the superiority of Anglicans over Catholics (as I knew myself all too well), and surely, too, there could have been none more receptive to the despicable hatred behind this plot.

The details, as Tonge explained them, were ludicrous. Under

the command of Louis, the Jesuits and the English Catholics would murder Charles, then form a rebellious army to keep James from the throne and throw England into the disorder of another civil war. Finally, the French armies would invade, and Louis would claim England as another province of France.

Yet Danby's bigotry let him believe this rubbish to the point that brought the matter to the council for further investigation, and Tonge produced his source: a former Anglican converted to Catholicism who claimed to have infiltrated the deepest of Jesuit circles. This man was called Titus Oates, and no more dangerous nor evil prevaricator has ever raised his despicable, piggish head to destroy the lives of others.

Under oath before the council, Oates did not waste time and, among many others, implicated two Catholic servants close to the royal family: Edward Coleman, secretary to the Duke of York, and Sir George Wakeman, Queen Catherine's own personal physician. While Coleman was accused of corresponding with Louis, Dr. Wakeman, a most honorable gentleman, was charged with using his medical knowledge for a plan to poison the king.

Of course Danby informed Charles, who was outraged, but refused to believe that the accusations would be taken seriously. Still, we were a somber party when we returned to London at the end of September. This testimony, combined with the coming session of Parliament, did not bode for a pretty, easy autumn.

But days before the new session was to begin, the magistrate who'd been hearing Oates's slanderous deposition was found murdered by the side of an empty road. This sad news struck perilously close to me: I'd known Sir Edmund Berry Godfrey myself, a good and honest man who'd never deserved such a death. Charles hoped that the new session of Parliament would see the irrational folly of the plot, but after Sir Edmund's body had been found, the only talk was of how the Jesuits were bent on murdering every English Protestant. All London was on edge, and gentlemen went about their business armed, and ladies tucked pistols in their muffs. Coleman's correspondence had been confiscated, and based on his letters, five Catholic lords, aged and revered gentlemen, had been sent to the Tower.

Waiting to turn the hysteria to his gain was Lord Shaftesbury, now relentlessly pursuing an entirely Protestant course. He had continued to link himself to Charles's illegitimate son Lord Monmouth, and to embrace Monmouth's claim as the Protestant heir to his father's throne, doubtless for his own gain. For the first time, Shaftesbury attacked the Catholic Duke of York, demanding that he be barred from the privy council, and supporting a new bill that would disallow Catholics entirely from Parliament.

Worse was to come. In his next round of accusations, Oates dared to implicate the queen herself, claiming that she had been heard plotting with Dr. Wakeman to poison the king on account of his many infidelities to her over the years of their marriage.

That was too much, even for Charles, who at last ordered Oates imprisoned. The Commons demanded he be released, and in turn accused Charles of obstructing the truth and protecting the Catholics in Whitehall. Charles refused to give way; he was still king, and Catherine his queen, and he would stand fast to defend her. Cleverly he had the investigator ask Oates to describe the room in the palace where he'd overheard the queen, and the liar showed exactly how ignorant he was of her quarters, let alone of any wrongdoing by that good lady.

Yet still Oates continued to invent fresh accusations, and still the world listened as if he spoke the truth. The madness continued in Parliament, but at least for now the queen was safe.

Coleman, the Duke of York's indiscreet secretary, was condemned by the judges without a trial. On the first of December, he was executed as befit a traitor: before a howling, vengeful crowd, he was cut open alive, his bowels torn out and burned under his eyes.

I appealed to the French ambassador, Barrillion, and with his assistance hurriedly arranged for passports for all of my French servants who wished to return to France. I had long been in the habit of sending money to my business agents in Paris against the distant time I would one day return. Now I sent far more, as well as some of my jewels, fearing that the distant day might come sooner than I'd expected.

Parliament voted to restrict all Catholics in the royal households and those employed within the palace. Even Charles had to beg special exemption for Father Huddleston, the elderly Benedictine who had helped him escape Cromwell's men after the Battle of Worcester, and who now served as one of the Queen's chaplains.

On a gray December afternoon, the queen called her ladies and other attendants to her presence chamber. All of us wept, including Catherine, and none of us hid our tears. While some of us were English, some Portuguese like the queen herself, and I the only Frenchwoman, we were each of us Catholics, bound together by our faith and the celebration of Mass each day in the queen's chapel. Now our small circle was to be broken apart forever by the will of the Anglican gentlemen at Westminster.

"A sad day, my dear sisters, a sad day," Catherine said, her hands clasped tightly at her waist. "You all know the will of Parliament. I'm only permitted ten Catholic ladies in this household, including myself, and the rest will be sent from Court. Only ten! Now I must submit a list of names of these ten to be spared. My name must needs be first on the list. I must ask you to draw lots to see who stays with me, and who must go, and may the Blessed Mother guide each of your hands."

Solemnly the youngest maid of honor carried a basket from lady to lady so that each might draw a folded slip of paper with their fate written within. She stopped and curtsied before me, her tear-streaked face bent over the basket. Poor poppet, I thought sadly, though perhaps it would be far better for her if her career at Court ended now, before she found her way to some lord's bed.

I reached my hand into the basket to take my lot.

"You needn't draw, Lady Portsmouth," the queen said softly. "I have already decided you will be one who will remain with me."

Stunned, I swiftly looked her way. "Are you certain, ma'am?"

"You have always been kind to me, Lady Portsmouth. Now I can be kind to you." Her uneven smile was gentle and full of sorrow. "His Majesty will save me, yes, and I will save you for him."

.   .   .

"It was Catherine's idea entirely, Louise, not mine," Charles said when I told him later, much later, that night.

These days he met constantly with Danby and other ministers and members from both Houses, and personally interrogated Oates and the other, lesser witnesses for inconsistencies to prove their fabrications false. Not that it mattered. I'd only to look at Charles's face to see that.

"When the queen learned she had to submit that infernal list to Parliament," he continued, "yours was the first name she wished to mark down. She has always liked you, you know. You are the only one who has always shown respect to her person and rank."

"She likes me well enough, yes," I said softly. "But I believe she did it because she loves you more."

"She is an extraordinarily kind and good woman, Fubs," he said wearily, "which is why I hate to see her so harried and abused. She is my wife and my queen, and their queen as well, if only those jackals would cease their ravening long enough to remember it."

"Here, sir, here, make yourself at ease," I urged, slipping another cushion behind his shoulders as he sat before the fire. I guessed he'd gone for a last walk to try to put his thoughts at rest, for he still wore his boots and his gloves. At least now I knew he wouldn't venture out unattended; even he realized the danger.

"They have arrested three more of her servants," he said, staring into the fire. "They're supposed to be accomplices of Wakefield's, led by him in the plot to poison me. What can Shaftesbury hope to gain from all this, save a place for himself in the brightest flames of hell?"

" 'Little Sincerity,' indeed," I said, bitterly using the old nickname that Charles had once coined to describe both Shaftesbury's small stature and how little he was to be trusted. "He wants to bring down Danby."

"He does, but I won't let him. Danby's too useful to me for that." He sipped his wine, his thoughts turned inward. "Did you know your French ambassador deigned to see me today?"

"Monsieur Barrillion's not been avoiding you, sir," I protested in defense of the Frenchman. I crouched down at Charles's feet, my dressing gown crumpling around me in a pile of quilted silk, as one by one, I pulled off his boots. "He knows you have much else that is more pressing to occupy you."

He grunted with animal pleasure as I rubbed the soles of his stocking'd feet with my thumbs, the way I knew he liked.

"You needn't cover for Louis, sweet," he said. "My dear cousin hasn't paid me a ha'penny since William wed my niece last year. He's as spiteful as an old bitch in heat."

"I've written him that you intended no harm to France by the Lady Mary's wedding, sir." By the fire's light the lines on his face were carved deep, and with concern I could see how much these last weeks had affected him. "I've told him that you were forced to do it to please your Protestant subjects."

"Oh, I'm sure you have, Fubs," he said. "You do as well as you can between your two masters. Except this one has precious little to offer you by way of reward. Do you know I'm so poor at present that I may have to call back some of my foreign ambassadors? What poor sort of king is that?"

"Not poor, sir, but most excellent," I said firmly. "You are a king who loves his people like a father does his children, despite their sins and flaws."

"Oh, yes, and a fine lot of spoiled, willful children they are, too," he said, turning cynical. "The way they are now, they won't be content until I've gone Spanish, and begin ordering bonfires of heretics on Tower Hill. Barrillion also told me you were considering returning to Paris."

I looked up sharply, taken by surprise. "He told you that?"

"Is it true?"

With a sigh, I sat back on my heels. His question was asked in precisely the same voice he'd been employing all along, but then he had always been most adept at hiding his true thoughts and fears.

"There are times, sir, that I believe you would fare better without me," I said softly. "That, for many reasons, I am both a curse and a bane to you."

"Are you leaving me, Fubs?" he asked, barely more than a whisper. "You, too?"

"No, sir," I said, and at that moment I knew I never would. "Nothing could make me part from you."

I took his hand and drew off his glove, meaning to kiss his hand by way of demonstrating both my love and my tender fealty. But instead I gasped, and understood at once why he'd taken to wearing gloves even when he'd addressed Parliament: he'd bitten his nails to the quick, the ends raw and painful to see.

"I haven't done it since I was a boy," he said, shamefully closing his fingers into his palm to hide them. "Don't tell anyone, mind?"

"Never, sir," I said, kissing him. "Never."

In the end, it wasn't Shaftesbury who brought down Danby, but Lady Cleveland. If what happened next had been part of one of Mrs. Gwyn's merry plays, I would have laughed as heartily as anyone, for surely the events were sufficiently foolish for that. But because they ruined the public careers of two different gentlemen, it was hard to see the humor.

With a stunning lack of common sense, Ralph Montagu, the English ambassador to the Court of France (and my onetime savior when I'd been abandoned by Buckingham), had dared to seduce Lady Cleveland's wedded daughter, Anne, Countess of Sussex. Granted, the girl was not known for her virtue any more than her mother had been, but Lady Cleveland was furious, and only partly because she, too, had traipsed through Montagu's bed. She demanded that Charles act, and with a father's indignation, he did, removing Montagu from his post.

But Montagu placed the blame for his disgrace squarely, if wrongly, on Danby's narrow shoulders, and resolved to see him removed for office just as he had been. Montagu produced letters written by Danby to Louis, and read them aloud in the House of Commons. No matter that the letters had been written at Charles's request, or that Montagu neglected to inform the House of this little fact. At once

Danby was impeached, on charges that ranged from him being a Papist sympathizer and friends with Louis, to having been party to the same nonexistent plot to murder the king.

To stop the trial, Charles did the one thing in his power: he finally dissolved Parliament at the very end of 1678, calling for the first new election in eighteen years. It was a desperate move, intended not just to save Danby's reputation and possibly his life, but also to prevent the inevitable revelations about Charles's true relations with Louis that could, given Shaftesbury's intensity, bring down the very crown from Charles's head.

Disgruntled, Montagu turned his attention to defaming me to anyone who would listen. He claimed knowledge of my life at the French Court, including debaucheries I'd never experienced and lovers I'd never had. Irritating, yes, but as nothing compared to everything else.

Because by that time the new session of Parliament was seated in March 1679, with a new set of members in the House of Commons who were even more hostile toward Charles and his French sympathies, and also more firmly in Shaftesbury's grasp. It was abundantly clear to us all that Shaftesbury and this party of his had set their sights on far larger game than me, or the pitiful group of Catholic servants they'd persecuted until now. Even Danby was swiftly dispensed: soon after meeting, the Commons had him arrested and sent to the Tower, while Charles was reluctantly compelled to accept his resignation.

No, Shaftesbury's desire now was lofty indeed: he wanted Charles to remove his Catholic brother, the Duke of York, from the succession, and instead name as his heir his illegitimate Protestant son, the Duke of Monmouth.

As soon as this became known, Charles sent his brother off on a prolonged stay in the Netherlands, ostensibly to visit his daughter Mary. Monmouth was also sent far from harm's way, into Scotland. Clearly Charles had no intention of giving in and was preparing for a hard battle with this Parliament, the most difficult of his long reign.

Yet as I listened to the rising voices of dissent in London, all

I could wonder was if, at last, Charles had joined in a fight he could not win.

When Parliament opened in March 1679, Charles addressed them, and told them in no uncertain terms that he would not change the descent of the Crown through the rightful line.

Soon after, Shaftesbury's whispering liars grew even bolder. Because of them, the first rumors began circulating that I'd bewitched the king into declaring our son heir to the Crown, with the preposterous goal of eventually handing all of England over to Louis and the French.

In April, the Exclusion Bill—that is, a bill demanding that the Catholic Duke of York be excluded from the succession by reason of his faith—was introduced into the House of Commons, and carried on its first reading.

Also in April, Titus Oates soundly declared that Jesuits had caused both the deaths of James I and Charles I, and that the Duke of York had himself set the Great Fire of 1666. He was widely believed.

I continued to hear Mass each day in the queen's chapel, and wondered how something that brought me such comfort could bring only murderous discord to Anglicans.

In May, the Exclusion Bill received its second reading, and was carried by an even greater majority. Only one more reading was necessary before the bill was passed to the House of Lords. But before this could happen, Charles prorogued the session.

In June, six more Jesuits were charged with plotting to assassinate the king, and executed without trials. And in Westminster, Shaftesbury and several other lords and members of the House appeared before the Court of King's Bench to proclaim the dangers of Popery to England. He asked for the Duke of York's indictment, and then demanded that I be denounced as a "public scandal" and charged accordingly.

But there was more. A printed pamphlet was mysteriously distributed in the House, with none claiming its authorship, but everyone reading it, and embracing it entirely. *The Articles of High Treason, & Other High Crimes & Misdemeanors Against the duchess of Portsmouth* listed twenty-two separate charges against me, from seeking to foment rebellion, to promoting Popery, to lying with the king "having had foul and contagious distempers, to the manifest danger and hazard of the king's person" (a most cruel allusion to the pox he had given to me), and finally, that I had tried to poison him. To my horror, the House seemed to accept this vile document as truth, and at once members began to demand my trial for treason, murder, and any number of other charges, while the kindest ones suggested I merely be banished back to France.

Terrified, I ran to Charles as soon as I heard.

"What will they do to me, sir?" I asked, sobbing. My English had improved over time, but I was frightened near to death of defending myself under oath before a tribunal of too-clever Englishmen bent on my destruction. "They will sentence me to the Tower, sir, and carry me away from you forever. They will sentence me to death!"

"There now, Fubs, they'll do no such thing," he said, taking me into his arms. "It will never come to that. I won't allow it."

Once released, my tears spilled over without stop. He held me closely against his chest, his hand cradling my head as if I were a child, and whispered nonsense to me until I stopped trembling. With him to protect me, I felt safe. But for how long? I wondered. How long?

Two weeks afterward, in early July, against the advice of his ministers, he dissolved Parliament. The outcry among the members was immediate and angry. Charles replied mildly that he was weary, and wished to fish in peace, and took the Court to Windsor. Perhaps he'd sensed something the rest of us had missed, a change in the air that, finally, might let common sense prevail, for later that month came word from London that the queen's physician, Dr. Wakefield, had been acquitted of all the charges against him. But while Charles found joy in this news, more trouble came from an entirely different source.

On a day in late August, he played a vigorous game of tennis in the hot sun, and then went down to the river's edge to cool himself, lolling and laughing with his gentlemen as was his habit. That evening, he was struck with a violent ague, trembling and shaking as a high fever seized him. At once he was bled, to no avail, and as he passed in and out of consciousness and delirium, his doctors began to despair of his recovery. At once the question of the succession seemed horribly relevant, and the ministers and other great men who crowded his bedchamber decided at last to summon the Duke of York from Brussels.

All I cared for was not the king, but for my Charles. Though I begged and pleaded to be admitted to his side, I was kept from his chamber, and left to weep with fearful anxiety in the hall as I waited for news. Yet as ill as he was, it was Charles himself who prescribed his own cure, a newly discovered remedy that he'd heard of from one of his scientific gentlemen. Called Jesuit's bark, his physicians resisted its use, for how could anything named for the Jesuits be of use to an Anglican king? Charles insisted, and despite its name, the remedy brought about an immediate improvement in his condition and saved him from certain death. Finally, with the danger passed, I was permitted into his room and left alone with him in tearful reunion.

"There now, Fubs, save your tears for when I truly die," he said with what I considered inordinate jollity, considering how dire his condition had been only days before. His face looked thinner and he still was pale beneath the gray stubble of his unshaven beard, but otherwise he seemed no worse for his ordeal as he sat up in his bed to greet me. "It was the Jesuit's bark that saved me, and don't think for a moment that I missed the sweet irony of that."

He laughed, and tried to kiss me, but I pushed him aside.

"Hush, sir. Don't," I scolded. "You should be thanking God for your delivery rather than making jests about the Jesuit fathers."

"I'm not jesting, sweet," he protested. "I'm perfectly serious. I owe my life to the Jesuits, and that's enough to make any man pause and think."

I frowned. "Of what, sir?"

His face grew serious. "What if God meant that as a sign for me, Fubs?" he said, lowering his voice to a confidential level meant only for my ears. "What if having the work of those holy gentlemen save my body was intended to point my soul in a similar direction?"

My eyes widened, for I'd never heard him speak so openly of conversion.

"Oh, sir," I whispered, "you know it was always Madame's dearest wish that you return to the True Church."

"I know it was," he said, his expression so thoughtful I could not mistake his meaning. "But not now. Not yet. Not if I wish to keep peace in my country, in any event."

"No, sir," I said softly, in perfect agreement. I knew his wishes; I'd not forget them. "No."

"Don't look so solemn," he said softly, and reached out to lay his hand over mine. "No matter what foolishness Monmouth attempts, I will stop him, like a good father should. No matter what Shaftesbury and the others try, I will prevail, and do what is right for England, not for them. That is how it's always been, and how it always will be. And most of all for you, dear Fubs, remember that I always protect those I love. Always."

Chapter Twenty-four

*I*t was a night as any other at Whitehall: how strange it seems now to say that, and yet at once how sadly true.

After a supper with the queen, Charles had come to my rooms, as was usual for him. I greeted him warmly, bidding him sit on the settee beside me, before the fire. I'd been his mistress for thirteen years, a prodigious time for any lady in my position, because I'd long ago learned what pleased him best. I brought him the wine he liked in the evenings, and poured it for him myself, the way I always did. I'd arranged for a young French boy to sing love songs to us, his golden curls and dulcet voice giving him the air of an angel, and sweetly melancholy, too. There were perhaps twenty others there in my rooms that night, playing for high stakes at basset, with a mound of gold pieces piled in the middle. This, I suppose, might have been the single mark of sinful behavior on that night, being a Sunday; but then those who played had likely sinned in so many other, more grievous ways during their lives, that no one gave it much thought.

The two greatest sinners were not far from Charles and me: Lady Cleveland and Lady Mazarin, each back from their wanderings and by fate come as guests to my rooms that night. Lady Cleveland had turned blowsy, her once-remarkable beauty long gone and her figure so large now that she fair overflowed her armchair, but she still possessed a bawdy charm that made Charles laugh. Lady Mazarin was more somber, her once-brazen cheer swallowed up by too much drink and sor-rowful reflection, but Charles welcomed her presence, too. While both of these ladies had been my rivals in past years, I could now afford to be generous to them. The king's heart was mine, as mine was his, and no one who saw us together would ever doubt it.

When at last he decided to retire, I walked with him from my rooms to his, his gentlemen keeping a discreet distance. We paused at his doorway, as we'd done so many times before, and I slipped my arms around his waist to bid him good night.

"My dear life," he said. "My only Fubs, what would I be without you, eh?"

He kissed me, and I kissed him, and afterward I held him close, my cheek pressed against the wool of his coat so I could hear the steady beat of his heart. I do not know why I lingered like that, or why, when at last I separated from him, I reached up to lay my hand against his cheek.

"Good night, dear sir," I said, my eyes filling with tears. "Rest well, my love."

"Why tears for a good night?" he asked, teasing me gently. "I vow you've shed enough tears over me to water any forest."

I shook my head. "Oh, sir, you know how I am," I said, wiping my eyes. "I cannot help myself, and never have."

"I wouldn't wish you otherwise, Louise." He kissed me again, on my forehead. Then he opened the door to his chamber and a scurry of welcoming dogs, and I returned to my rooms and my other guests.

And that was all.

It was the thumping on my door that roused me, the frantic gentle-man's voice that could only mean ill tidings. By the time Bette brought him to my bedchamber, I was already nearly dressed.

"The king is taken gravely ill," the man said, his face ghostly by the light of the candlestick. "You must come at once."

Without waiting for him to guide me, I ran ahead to Charles's bedchamber, knowing the way perfectly well. Already a ring of gentlemen and physicians was gathered around him, and already I could tell the worst. The king lay still, far too still for him, his face pale and sweating and his gaze fixed on the canopy overhead.

At once I crouched beside his bed, and was rewarded with a flicker of recognition. Then I was hurried aside by the doctors, intent on doing what doctors do.

Over the next days and nights, I saw the king be given a score of different medicines and treatments, some that seemed so painful that I could not believe he could withstand them. Fourteen doctors tended him, yet not one had any real notion of what to do. The king's head was shaved, and he was bled repeatedly, once even from his jugular vein as a final measure of desperation.

Nothing helped. Though there were times when he'd rally enough to give us hope, I knew in my heart he was leaving us. Desperate to remain in his dear company as long as I could, I performed every service a wife could, chafing his hands and offering whispers of comfort, and though I wept freely, no one now would fault me for it. The queen was so distraught that when she would appear, she needed to be carried from the room, to be bled herself to ease her hysteria. Most touching of all was my old rival Mrs. Gwyn: for from being ever a commoner, she was forbidden to enter the deathbed chamber, and kept by guards outside the king's room. Instead she was left to crouch in the hall, sobbing at the same door that would never open for her.

As a duchess, I stayed with the king, believing it my rightful place, until at last his royal family was assembled and brought to say farewell. I stepped back, and through my tears watched as he gave a final blessing to our son, Richmond, now a sturdy young gentleman of twelve years, his last and dearest son. Richmond bent to kiss his father's cheek, and then turned toward me, his handsome face contorted with suffering. With his tears streaming, he bowed to me with a courtliness that painfully reminded me of his father, offered me his arm, and led me from the room. Young as he was, he understood why it was his duty to do so, and I did as well. No matter how I grieved for Charles, he remained the king, and I did not belong amidst the final royal farewells.

Yet throughout I noticed Charles had steadfastly refused to be given his last rites as an Anglican, claiming that it was too soon or that he was not ready. I remembered back to another such terrible scene, the death of his sister, Henriette, my dear Madame, and I recalled the comfort she'd found in the final ceremonies of the Catholic Church. Could it be that at last Charles wished it, too? I remembered what he'd told me at Windsor, when he'd been so ill with the fever, and how he'd believed that God had been directing him toward the True Church by saving him through Jesuit's bark. Now that the end was undeniably near, could he truly have decided to preserve his soul in the rightful way?

I crept back to his chamber, determined to do this final duty. Only the Duke of York remained by his brother's side, and I beckoned for him to join me out of Charles's hearing.

"Lady Portsmouth," he said through his own tears when he saw me. "You've returned."

"Please, Your Grace, I must beg your indulgence," I said. "It is my belief that His Majesty wishes to die in our faith. I beseech you, if you can, ask him. Ask him now!"

He looked at me sharply. "You are sure of this?"

I nodded, and he returned to his brother's bedside, speaking to him in an earnest whisper I could not hear. It pained me that I could not ask so tender a question of Charles myself, but I knew the awful significance of it, and I knew, too, that as a Frenchwoman, my motives would be questioned. For Charles's sake, it was his brother and heir who must ask, and when I heard Charles's voice, stronger than it had been in days, make the final reply—"With all my heart"—I knew I'd followed both my duty and my love.

With a startling efficiency, the one English priest in Whitehall was produced, an elderly gentleman who had known Charles when he was still a wandering prince. Charles greeted Father Huddleston with a cry of joy, and as the old priest murmured the words of conversion, followed by the last rites, I sank to my knees at the foot of the bed and prayed with him, as did the duke. Finally Father Huddleston placed his crucifix into Charles's hands and wrapped a rosary around them to hold it steady, and said the final prayers for his salvation. With that it was done, and I rose unsteadily to my feet. Charles's eyes were closed, not in pain, but at rest, and I'd never seen such peace on his face. Long ago he'd told me that I, above all others, brought him peace. Now, at last, I truly had.

"Farewell, my love," I whispered. "Farewell, my dearest friend."

I kissed him one last time, his lips already chill beneath mine, and retreated to my rooms. I'd no place as death finally claimed him: that belonged to his wife, his brother, his children. I was no more than his mistress, and a French one at that.

But in the end, I'd gained all I could wish. I'd saved his soul for all eternity, and I'd won his heart for my own.

And how could ever I wish for more?

Author's Note

Louise de Keroualle may have been the most hated woman in seventeenth-century England. Every pamphlet, ballad, and article from her time blasts her as avaricious, conniving, and deceitful, and she was publicly denounced from pulpits and Parliament alike. She was a Roman Catholic and French, never a good combination to most Englishmen, and she also was quite openly on the payroll of Louis XIV even as she shared Charles II's bed. Perhaps Lady Sunderland (not exactly an impartial witness) best sums up the general feeling toward Louise by declaring "so damned a jade as this would sell us without hesitation for fifty guineas."

Yet despite this, Charles clearly loved her. She represented French sophistication and elegance, and a quiet calm in the midst of his raucous Court. Unlike his other mistresses, she was entirely faithful to him, and he was her only lover. While others bemoaned her quick tears and stiff formality, he focused on her soft, accented voice, speaking gently to him much as his French mother once had done. Over and over he defended and protected her, even as she became a growing political liability and his friends and ministers begged him to send her packing. He granted her more honors and more gifts than all of his other mistresses combined, and the dukedom of Lennox and Richmond that he created for their son remains today one of the royal line, and one of the wealthiest in Britain. Louise was the mistress who tended Charles on his deathbed, the one Charles recommended most specifically to his brother James's care, and the one who, quite possibly, made sure that he died a Roman Catholic.

"I have always loved her," Charles said among his last words, "and

I die loving her." From a man who had loved so widely, surely that declaration must have brought Louise considerable comfort.

Charles died in his fifty-fifth year, most likely of the effects of chronic kidney disease, though no one now knows for certain. Those fourteen doctors crowded into his bedchamber likely did more to hasten his death than ease it. Fittingly for the king known as the "Merrie Monarch," he was buried on Valentine's Day, 1685. By order of the Lord Chamberlain, the duchess of Portsmouth, the duchess of Cleveland, and Nell Gwyn were permitted to wear black mourning in Charles's honor, but were not allowed to put their households into full mourning: the fine distinction between sleeping with royalty and being married to it. Meanwhile, the entire country plunged into heartfelt mourning. Despite the many crises of his reign, Charles had remained immensely popular with his people, and was much lamented when he died.

Perhaps part of their sorrow was knowing who their next king would be. James II swiftly used up every bit of goodwill that his much-loved brother had left behind with a reign that was marked by dictatorial ill management, egotism, and a determined effort to force England to share his Catholicism. Charles had predicted that James, due to his "turbulent and excessive nature," would not last four years on the throne. That was almost exactly how long it took before the English people had had enough of James and, in the bloodless Glorious Revolution of 1688, sent him into exile in favor of the Protestant couple of William of Orange and James's elder daughter, Mary.

James's rule was also blackened by his ruthless treatment of Charles's feckless illegitimate son, James, Duke of Monmouth. Under an Anglican banner, Monmouth led a poorly organized rebellion against his uncle in 1686. James crushed the rebellion and its lower-class supporters with all the force of the English army, and after ignoring his nephew's pleas for mercy, insisted on his execution.

Louise was devastated by Charles's death. Not only had she lost the one love of her life, but also the center of her world. Overnight, she ceased to be important. James quickly made it clear that her days as a political power and a royal favorite were finished, and that she'd have no place in the diplomacy of his Court. She was only thirty-three when Charles died and still exceptionally beautiful, but in many ways her life was done. She left England in 1685 with her thirteen-year-old son, Lord Richmond, her jewels, several pensions, and a small fortune in gold that had been left her by Charles. It took several ships to carry all the possessions she'd acquired to fill those forty rooms in Whitehall Palace, and the English people were heartily glad to wave her farewell.

Louise lived the rest of her life in France, falling in and out of favor with Louis XIV and losing great amounts of her fortune to gaming. She never married, and the taboret of a *duchesse* that she'd so coveted brought her little happiness. The French nobility that she'd longed to impress had no use for her, and she had few friends. Finally she retreated to the estates at Aubigny that were part of her duchy, and dedicated herself to good works and prayer. Shortly before her death, she was introduced to Voltaire, who marveled at her still-impressive beauty. She died in 1734 at the considerable age of eighty-five, having survived Charles by fifty years.

Charles Lennox, Duke of Richmond, spent his childhood torn between the wishes of his two exceptional parents. He was a favorite among Charles's numerous sons, and delighted his royal father by riding in his first race at Newmarket at the tender age of eleven. Louise, on the other hand, tried hard to mold him into a model French gentleman with beautiful manners, which was not nearly as much fun. Richmond was raised a Protestant, as were all of the king's children, though Louise made sure he converted to Catholicism after the two of them returned to France. Louise hoped the young duke would find favor at the French Court, but he preferred England, and as soon as William of Orange had displaced his uncle James, Richmond swiftly returned to London. He once again became an Anglican, wed an English beauty, and took his seat in the House of Lords. He liked to gamble, drink, and ride, and despite his enormous wealth, he found it difficult to keep within his income. Having sired three children, including the son necessary to continue his title, he died before his mother in 1723.

The fortunes of the rest of Louise's acquaintances were mixed. Charles's long-suffering queen, Catherine of Braganza, had earned the respect and regard of the English, and continued to live in England as a venerable Dowager Queen until 1692, before finally returning to Portugal, where she died in 1705. Nell Gwyn suffered a paralyzing stroke soon after Charles's death, and died deeply in debt in 1687 at only thirty-seven. Her close friend and Louise's gadfly, John Wilmot, Earl of Rochester, fared even worse, succumbing at thirty-three in 1680 to the effects of chronic alcoholism and syphilis. By comparison, George Villiers, Duke of Buckingham, lived far longer than his self-indulgent life should have merited, dying in the country in 1687 at fifty-nine.

After more than three hundred years, it's very hard to find traces of Louise as the woman Charles must have adored. Much of her problem is that while she had allies at the English Court, she had almost no friends beyond Charles, and none who defended her for posterity. The same propaganda that worked so hard to defame her during her life has continued successfully long afterward. Some of the vilest invented slanders have been repeated and reprinted so many times that casual historians now often present them as fact, even if other, more trustworthy evidence refutes it. Where Louise is concerned, the malevolent spirit of Titus Oates never quite died.

I've tried to separate at least a few grains of truth from all the scandalous chaff, and discover the woman behind the great villainess of too many tears. Wherever the hard facts of history are tantalizingly vague, I tried to keep to Louise's spirit as much as possible, and the occasional liberty I've been forced to take in telling her story was made with the best of intentions. As I've often said before, I'm a novelist, not a historian. But in the end, I dare to hope that Charles himself would be pleased with what I've written of the woman he loved so dearly.

Susan Holloway Scott
January 2009

The French Mistress

A NOVEL OF
THE DUCHESS OF PORTSMOUTH AND KING CHARLES II

SUSAN HOLLOWAY SCOTT

QUESTIONS
FOR DISCUSSION

1. The title of this book, *The French Mistress,* can describe not only how the English viewed Louise de Keroualle, but also as the way she described herself as well. Which do you think is more apt?

2. Charles II was crowned only after a prolonged exile following his father's beheading and the English Civil War. He was determined to create a Court that was more relaxed and informal than his father's had been, yet often found his authority challenged during his reign. His cousin Louis XIV also had a difficult childhood for a royal prince, and he, too, was exiled from Paris by the enemies of his family during the Fronde. Yet Louis reacted to his past by insisting on a rigidly ritualized Court that he could completely control and manipulate. Which model do you feel worked better? As a courtier, which would you prefer?

3. Louise saw no shame in her position as a royal mistress. Do you think this was because of the material wealth she amassed, the power she acquired, her ability to help her native France, or simply because of the love she felt for Charles?

4. Louise had the opportunity to observe several arranged royal couples firsthand: Madame and Monsieur; Louis and Therese; Charles and Catherine; James and Mary Beatrice; William and Mary. Do you think this influenced her decision to become Charles's mistress rather than pursue a marriage of her own?

5. Charles's mistresses were constantly faulted for their greed, and Louise was regarded as the most avaricious of them all. Do you think she was in fact greedy, or merely making the most of a brief and unpredictable opportunity to provide for herself and her son?

6. Anti-Catholic prejudice and persecution reached hysterical levels during Charles's reign. How do you think this compares to religious intolerance in the world today?

7. Although Louise was undeniably a beautiful and desirable woman, she chose to emphasize her talents as a hostess and as an exemplar of elegant taste to help her maintain a lasting relationship with Charles. Do you agree with her decision? Do you think she would have held Charles's interest if she had relied simply on her beauty?

8. Louise made virtually no friends in England beyond Charles. Do you agree with her opinion that she was surrounded by enemies, and could trust no one but herself, or the opinions of others at the English Court: that she was chilly and aloof and too self-centered for friendship?

9. Treatment and understanding of syphilis were rudimentary in the seventeenth century. Given Charles's wide-ranging habits and Louise's monogamy, it's safe to say that he infected her. Yet she was the one was "punished" by being isolated from him and her son during the time the disease was being treated. Do you think this double standard was fair? Would it have been different if Charles hadn't been king? Do you think Louise expected it?

10. Louise was a favorite target both of Court satire as exemplified by the Earl of Rochester and of the more common ballads and

pamphlets that circulated through coffeehouses and taverns. How do you think today's tabloid-style journalism would treat Louise? Do you think she would be followed more for her political role, her sexual relationship with the king, or as a stylish trendsetter?

11. While Louis treated Louise as an agent of the French, Charles chose to regard her more as a facilitator, a special kind of diplomat that he felt he could trust. How would you regard her role: as a spy or a savvy diplomat?

12. Although Charles had many women in his life, he was surprisingly careful with his endearments. His pet names for Louise were "Fubs"—an abbreviation of fubsy, a seventeenth-century synonym for chubby—and "My Dear Life." He used both in conversation and throughout his letters to her. What do you think these nicknames reveal about their relationship?

13. Late in the book, Louise sees one of the queen's maids of honor who is facing dismissal on account of her faith: "Poor poppet, I thought sadly, though perhaps it would be far better for her if her career at Court ended now, before she found her way to some lord's bed." Do you think Louise truly believed this? Do you think if she had her life to do over that she would have made a choice other than coming to Court?

Photo by Brenda Carpenter Photography

Susan Holloway Scott is the author of more than forty historical novels. A graduate of Brown University, she lives with her family in Pennsylvania. Visit her Web site at www.susanhollowayscott.com.

"No dry dust of history here, but a vivid portrait of an intriguing woman with all her flaws and strengths. Rich in period details, the novel also has all the ingredients necessary for a compelling read: conflict, suspense, intrigue, and the romance between Sarah and John Churchill, one of history's great love stories."

—Susan Carroll, author of *Twilight of a Queen*

*L*ondon, 1673. With her family ruined by war, penniless thirteen-year-old Sarah Jennings is overjoyed to be chosen as a maid of honor at the bawdy Restoration Court of Charles II. She soon wins the trust of Lady Anne of York, a lonely princess who becomes one of her staunchest allies. And though Sarah's beauty stirs the desires of the jaded aristocrats, she wants a grander future for herself than that of a pampered mistress. Only one man possesses ambition and passions that match her own: John Churchill, a dashing young military hero. He would ask for her hand—and win her heart for a lifetime. . . .

Brimming with the intrigue and sensuality of one of history's most decadent courts, *duchess* brings to vivid life the story of an unforgettable woman who determined her own destiny—outspoken, outrageous, but most of all true to herself.

Royal Harlot

A NOVEL OF THE COUNTESS OF CASTLEMAINE AND KING CHARLES II

"Among this novel's many strengths are Scott's impressive depiction of time and place, her evocation of the Restoration-era mind-set, the exuberance of the period, and her sure, succinct presentation of complex historical events. The reader can well believe that this is a memoir penned by a woman who—in reality—was clearly too busy living to ever write one!"   —*The Historical Novels Review*

London, 1660. Ready to throw off a generation of Puritan rule, all England rejoices when Charles Stuart returns to reclaim the throne. Among those welcoming him is young Barbara Villiers Palmer, a breathtaking Royalist beauty whose sensuality and clever wit instantly captivate the handsome, jaded king.

Though each is promised to another, Barbara soon becomes Charles's mistress and closest friend, and the uncrowned queen of his bawdy Restoration Court. Rewarded with titles, land, and jewels, she is the most envied and desired woman in England—and the most powerful.

But the role of royal mistress is a precarious one, and Barbara's enemies and rivals are everywhere in the palace. Now even kings can lose their heads to treason, and swirling political intrigue brings new threats and danger—until not even Charles is safe.

In this world where love is no more than a game, and power the ultimate aphrodisiac, only one woman holds the key to it all: Barbara, Countess of Castlemaine, duchess of Cleveland, and the royal harlot.

The King's Favorite

A NOVEL OF NELL GWYN AND KING CHARLES II

"This is a wild joyride through Restoration England, with Nell firmly gripping the reins. Susan Holloway Scott is so intuitive with period language and so involved in the psyches of her characters, that you are at all times *there* with them, seeing what they're seeing, feeling what they're feeling—and always, *always* rooting for the petite whirlwind of a heroine."   —Robin Maxwell, author of *Signora da Vinci*

Nell Gwyn was never a lady, nor did she pretend to be one. The daughter of a Royalist soldier, she is taken to London by her widowed mother to work in a bawdy house. At fourteen, she becomes the mistress of a wealthy merchant, who introduces her to the world of the theater. Blessed with impudent wit and saucy good looks, she swiftly rises from an orange seller to a leading lady, and she is still in her teens when she catches the eye of King Charles II. She trades the stage for Whitehall Palace and the glorious role of a royal mistress.

Yet even as she delights the king, she must learn to negotiate the cutthroat Court, where intrigue and lust for power rule the hearts of all around her. Beneath her charm and lightheartedness, Nell has her own ambition: to become no less than the king's favorite.